D1316548

DARKWOLFE

A Medieval Romance
Book Five in the de Wolfe Pack Series

By Kathryn Le Veque

© Copyright 2017 by Kathryn Le Veque Novels, Inc. DBA Dragonblade Publishing, Inc. Print Edition

Text by Kathryn Le Veque
Cover by Kim Killion

Reproduction of any kind except where it pertains to short quotes in relation to advertising or promotion is strictly prohibited.

All Rights Reserved.

The characters and events portrayed in this book are fictitious. Any similarity to real persons, living or dead, is purely coincidental and not intended by the author.

KATHRYN LE VEQUE NOVELS

Medieval Romance:

The de Russe Legacy:
The White Lord of Wellesbourne
The Dark One: Dark Knight
Beast
Lord of War: Black Angel
The Iron Knight

The de Lohr Dynasty:
While Angels Slept (Lords of East Anglia)
Rise of the Defender
Steelheart
Spectre of the Sword
Archangel
Unending Love
Shadowmoor
Silversword

Great Lords of le Bec:
Great Protector
To the Lady Born (House of de Royans)
Lord of Winter (Lords of de Royans)

Lords of Eire:
The Darkland (Master Knights of Connaught)
Black Sword
Echoes of Ancient Dreams (time travel)

De Wolfe Pack Series:
The Wolfe
Serpent
Scorpion (Saxon Lords of Hage – Also related to The Questing)
The Lion of the North
Walls of Babylon

Dark Destroyer
Nighthawk
Warwolfe
ShadowWolfe
DarkWolfe

Ancient Kings of Anglecynn:
The Whispering Night
Netherworld

Battle Lords of de Velt:
The Dark Lord
Devil's Dominion

Reign of the House of de Winter:
Lespada
Swords and Shields (also related to The Questing, While Angels Slept)

De Reyne Domination:
Guardian of Darkness
The Fallen One (part of Dragonblade Series)
With Dreams Only of You

Unrelated characters or family groups:
The Gorgon (Also related to Lords of Thunder)
The Warrior Poet (St. John and de Gare)
Tender is the Knight (House of d'Vant)
Lord of Light
The Questing (related to The Dark Lord, Scorpion)
The Legend (House of Summerlin)

The Dragonblade Series: (Great Marcher Lords of de Lara)
Dragonblade
Island of Glass (House of St. Hever)

The Savage Curtain (Lords of Pembury)
The Fallen One (De Reyne Domination)
Fragments of Grace (House of St. Hever)
Lord of the Shadows
Queen of Lost Stars (House of St. Hever)

Lords of Thunder: The de Shera Brotherhood Trilogy
The Thunder Lord
The Thunder Warrior
The Thunder Knight

The Great Knights of de Moray:
Shield of Kronos

Highland Warriors of Munro:
The Red Lion
Deep Into Darkness

The House of Ashbourne:
Upon a Midnight Dream

The House of D'Aurilliac:
Valiant Chaos

The House of De Nerra:
The Falls of Erith
Vestiges of Valor

The House of De Dere:
Of Love and Legend

Time Travel Romance: (Saxon Lords of Hage)
The Crusader
Kingdom Come

Contemporary Romance:

Kathlyn Trent/Marcus Burton Series:
Valley of the Shadow
The Eden Factor
Canyon of the Sphinx

The American Heroes Series:
The Lucius Robe
Fires of Autumn
Evenshade
Sea of Dreams
Purgatory

Other Contemporary Romance:
Lady of Heaven
Darkling, I Listen
In the Dreaming Hour

Sons of Poseidon:
The Immortal Sea

Multi-author Collections/Anthologies:
Sirens of the Northern Seas (Viking romance)

Note: All Kathryn's novels are designed to be read as stand-alones, although many have cross-over characters or cross-over family groups. Novels that are grouped together have related characters or family groups.

Series are clearly marked. All series contain the same characters or family groups except the American Heroes Series, which is an anthology with unrelated characters.

There is NO particular chronological order for any of the novels because they can all be read as stand-alones, even the series.

For more information, find it in **A Reader's Guide to the Medieval World of Le Veque.**

TABLE OF CONTENTS

AUTHOR'S NOTES

Finally, the last of the older sons of William and Jordan has his story!

Much as Scott in *ShadowWolfe* went through an evolution, so does his twin, Troy. If this is your first de Wolfe Pack novel, then know this book is a stand-alone just like all of them, but after you read this one, make sure to read *ShadowWolfe*, *Nighthawk*, and *The Wolfe* to get a feel for these powerful English knights. The older sons of William and Jordan are Scott, Troy, and Patrick – Scott and Troy are twins and Patrick is not quite two years younger than the twins, so they are a trio of very powerful, very closely-knit brothers and it has been an absolute pleasure to tell their stories.

What's cool about this particular story is that we get a glimpse at James de Wolfe, the fourth brother, who ends up dying in Wales about ten years after this book is set. Although I would love to do a story for James, I can't bring myself to do it, knowing that the man dies young. I can't give him a wonderful story and a happily ever after only to know that he is destined to lose it all in Wales, but this is a nice glimpse into the man he is. He's very much his mother's son, gentle and kind. There's even a scene in the book where he discusses the future, not knowing of course that he won't be around to see it. It's sort of heartbreaking. I'm starting to wish I hadn't killed him off so young! Boo me! But never say never – you just never know what will happen in the world of de Wolfe Pack...

On to more pleasant things. A few old friends make an appearance in this book – William de Wolfe, Paris de Norville, Kieran Hage, Michael de Bocage, and a few others you will recognize. You will also get to meet Sable de Moray de Shera, who married Cassius de Shera at the very end of *The Thunder Knight*. If you've read the Lords of Thunder series, then you know that Cassius is Maximus de Shera's bastard son, a handsome and noble lad with a speech impediment who marries Sable de Moray, Bose de Moray's (THE GORGON) daughter. Sable is not only the daughter of Bose and Summer, but she's the granddaughter of Garret and Lyssa from *SHIELD OF KRONOS*. She has her grandmother's beauty and her mother's sweetness. Lastly, you'll catch a glimpse of Brodie de Reyne, the grandson of Creed and Carrington de Reyne (GUARDIAN OF DARKNESS). Brodie is a prime candidate for his own story at some point.

Something that's noteworthy – cotton is mentioned in this novel, briefly. At this point in the High Middle Ages, cotton was around but not widely used. It was thought to have been brought back with the Crusaders returning from the Holy Land. In fact, it seemed as if no one really knew where cotton came from because it wasn't grown in England during the period when this book is set. A writer in 1350 commented that cotton was grown in India by plants that had tiny lambs at the end of its branches, so cotton was from animals that were "plant-borne". Weird.

And what can I say about Troy and Rhoswyn, our hero and heroine? Only that I think you're going to love them both. Troy is quick to temper, but he has his mother's gentle streak in him, making it an odd combination. He's aggressive, but oh-so-patient with Rhoswyn, whose life is in upheaval since meeting him. She's a fierce lass but she also has the capacity for understanding and compassion. It was a joy to get to know her and I think she's more than worthy for a wife of de Wolfe.

Read and enjoy!

Hugs,
Kathryn

THE NEXT GENERATION WOLFE PACK

(Issue = children)

Scott (Wife #1 Lady Athena de Norville, has issue. Wife #2, Lady Avrielle Huntley du Rennic, has issue.)

Troy (Wife #1 Lady Helene de Norville, has issue. Wife #2 Lady Rhoswyn Kerr, has issue.)

Patrick (married to Lady Brighton de Favereux, has issue)

James – Killed in Wales June 1282 (married to Lady Rose Hage, has issue)

Katheryn (James' twin) Married Sir Alec Hage, has issue

Evelyn (married to Sir Hector de Norville, has issue)

Baby de Wolfe – died same day. Christened Madeleine.

Edward (married to Lady Cassiopeia de Norville, has issue)

Thomas

Penelope (married to Bhrodi de Shera, hereditary King of Anglesey and Earl of Coventry, has issue)

Kieran and Jemma Scott Hage

Mary Alys (adopted) married, has issue

Baby Hage, died same day. Christened Bridget.

Alec (married to Lady Katheryn de Wolfe, has issue)

Christian (died Holy Land 1269 A.D.) no issue

Moira (married to Sir Apollo de Norville, has issue)

Kevin (married to Lady Annavieve de Ferrers, has issue)

Rose (widow of Sir James de Wolfe, has issue)

Nathaniel

Paris and Caladora Scott de Norville

Hector (married to Lady Evelyn de Wolfe, has issue)

Apollo (married to Lady Moira Hage, has issue)

Helene (married to Sir Troy de Wolfe, has issue)

Athena (married to Sir Scott de Wolfe, has issue)

Adonis

Cassiopeia (married to Sir Edward de Wolfe, has issue)

The Darkest Wolfe

From the Chronicles of Brother Audric, 13th c.

Discovered in Jedburgh Abbey's archive

Original text:

Whyth th blud uf Saracyns, hs vane,

Premier uf th Wolfe.

Ayes uf gilt, hare uf night,

A hart uf stel.

He is bekum Legynd.

Translation:

With the blood of Saracens in his veins,

The boldest border Wolfe.

Eyes of gold, hair of black,

And a heart of steel.

He is become legend.

PROLOGUE

April, 1270 A.D.
Castle Questing, Northumberland

S HE WAS COLD to the touch.

She was also wet, wrapped in a blanket with the twins, who were also cold and wet to the touch. But it was more than the coldness and the dampness of their flesh; it was also the color. Gray, like the color of stone. There was an odd quality to it as well. It wasn't the flesh he knew. It wasn't the warmth of Helene as he knew it, and the faces of his children weren't the lively and smiling faces he recognized.

Acacia was the older twin by several minutes. Her face was pressed into her mother's torso and he couldn't see it, but Arista – his blond, vivacious Arista – was lying next to her sister, her sightless eyes half-lidded, staring up at the ceiling. As he stood there staring at them, his father reached down and closed the little girl's eyelids.

"I am so sorry, my son," William de Wolfe whispered hoarsely, tears trickling from his one good eye. The other eye, patched, was something he'd lost years ago. "It was an accident. A terrible, terrible accident…"

His handsome face was lined with the fatigue of sorrow, something Troy had never before seen on his father. At least, not like this. Perhaps that, more than anything else, disturbed him because it conveyed to him the hopelessness and grief of the situation almost more than anything else could. If his father was in tears, and the man was the strongest man he knew, then surely the situation was as horrible as Troy's disbelieving eyes were telling him.

Dead.

They were all dead.

An odd buzzing filled Troy's head. It made the room swim. When he looked at the bodies of his wife and two younger children, his stomach started to lurch. Behind him, on the floor and lying on wet blankets, were the wife and two younger children of his twin brother, Scott. He'd seen the three of them when he'd first entered the stale, warm solar. In fact, he'd seen them before he ever saw his own family. Scott's wife was lying on her side as if she were sleeping, her children lying right next to her as if they, too, were sleeping. But they were all wet, much as his wife and children were. They were all wet because not three hours earlier, they'd all drowned.

Troy's knees buckled.

"God," he groaned, gripping the nearest chair as if it could support his substantial weight. Hands were holding him steady, the hands of his parents, but he didn't notice. All he could see was the lifelessness before him. "*Nay*... it cannot be. Tell me this is not true."

William had a tight grip on his faltering son. "It *is* true," he said, his voice hoarse as his emotions got the better of him. "It was purely by accident, Troy. No one is to blame."

Troy still couldn't grasp the situation, not entirely. "*What* happened?"

He spoke harshly and William glanced at his weeping wife before continuing. This was such a horrific moment for all of them, the death of children and grandchildren, and it was only by God's good grace that William was able to keep his composure. He'd been the first to see the bodies of his daughters-in-law and grandchildren when they'd been brought back by their escort of soldiers, men who were weeping even as they told him the appalling story of what had happened.

As William listened in horror, he noticed that all of the soldiers were soaking wet to varied degrees. They'd all tried to jump in to save the women and children after the bridge collapsed and the carriage was washed down the rain-swollen creek, but their efforts had been futile.

Now, the dead had been returned home.

Therefore, William was prepared for Troy's question, a father demanding the reasons for the precious lives of his family that had been suddenly ended. The husband who was now a widower. William could hear the anguish in Troy's tone and it cut him to the bone.

"Your wife and her sister were traveling this morning to see Patrick and Bridey's new son," he said, trying to remain calm. "They have been planning it for weeks. You know this, Troy. That is why your wife came to stay with us last week and brought the children, so she could travel with her sister to see your brother's newest son."

Troy wasn't getting the answer he wanted; his big body tensed. "I know," he rumbled. "Stop telling me what I already know. Tell me what I *don't* know, Papa."

William sighed faintly, feeling his son's pain through his words, through his tone. It was only growing worse. "They wanted to take the enclosed carriage because of the children and the cold weather, so I permitted it," he said. "Scott was here this morning before they departed and he assigned a contingent of soldiers to go with them, so they were well protected."

Troy was staring at the gray face of his dead wife, his hands quivering violently where they held on to the chair. "Scott?" he repeated. "Where is he? Did he go with them? Oh... my sweet God, Papa, tell me that Scott did not meet the same fate."

William shook his head. "Nay, he did not," he said quickly. "He is fine. I sent him on business to Northwood Castle this morning after the women left because I needed him to relay counsel to the commanders of Northwood. He was there the entire time."

Troy didn't know if he felt better or worse about that. His brother was safe, his wife was dead... he was being torn into a thousand pieces of pain, in all directions. "Then he does not know?"

"Not yet," William said quietly. "I have sent for him. Troy, we did all we could to protect the women as they went on their journey, but there are things we could not have known. All of the rain we have had this spring has made the creeks and rivers very swollen, but that was not a concern where it should have been because…"

He trailed off, hardly able to continue, and Troy jerked his head in his father's direction as the man stumbled over his explanation.

"Because *what?*" Troy demanded. "Tell me!"

William sighed again, struggling with his composure. "The soldiers who escorted Athena and Helene to Berwick said that when they reached the River Till, it was very swollen and they were uncomfortable with the bridge crossing. It seemed to them that the strong flow of water had weakened the bridge. When they told the ladies their concerns, their warning was not heeded."

Troy stared at him as the realization began to settle. Now, the pieces of the puzzle were coming together. "And they went over the bridge."

"They did."

The tremble in Troy's hands grew worse. His eyes widened as he understood, clearly, what had happened.

"Nay," he hissed. "*Nay!* Helene would have listened. She would have heeded such advice. But Athena would have discounted the soldiers because the woman does not listen to anyone, not even to Scott. It was *her!* She did this!"

William held up his hands, hastening to calm his son before the situation went from bad to worse. "You will not blame her," he said firmly. "By all accounts, both the women insisted on proceeding, so you will not blame Athena solely. It was everyone's fault but no one's fault. Surely they did not know this would happen."

Troy didn't seem to be listening. "Athena did this! She killed them all!"

William grabbed the man by the shoulders, trying to shake some sense into him before he went mad with grief. "Casting blame does not bring them back!" he implored. "Would you truly curse the dead,

Troy?"

Troy was nearly incoherent with rage. "That bitch," he snarled. "My children are dead because of her! My wife is dead because of her!"

"It is God's will, Troy," William said steadily. "You must believe that what happened is…"

Troy cut him off savagely. "There *is* no God," he barked. "God would not have allowed small children to drown while their mother watched and could do nothing to help them. He would not have taken innocent lives so cruelly. Nay, Papa, speak not to me of God. He had nothing to do with this. This *is* Athena's fault!"

William could see that his words weren't getting through and he was genuinely afraid; afraid of what Troy would do because the man was quick to rage and even quicker to act upon it. He didn't have the calm that most of William's sons had. Troy was aggressive and deadly, the first man into battle and the last man to leave. It was a fearsome de Wolfe quality but, in this case, it would do him no good. The man was raging at a dead woman, blaming her for his misery. William was expecting Troy's brother at any moment and he didn't want Troy to attack his brother in a fit of insanity. Therefore, he did the only thing he could – he forced Troy to face the object of his rage.

Yanking the man up by the arm, which was no mean feat considering Troy's size, he dragged the man towards the lifeless body of Scott's wife. When Troy dug his heels in to stop his father's momentum, William grabbed him by the hair and pulled him, hauling him the last few feet until Troy was looking down at Athena and her children. William got a hand in behind Troy's head and shoved it down, closer to the bodies so he could truly see who he was angry with.

"There!" William boomed. "There she is! Tell her of your anger, Troy. Tell her how you blame her for the deaths of Helene and the girls. Go on – tell her how stubborn and foolish she is. *Tell her you hate her!*"

Troy found himself looking into his sister-in-law's frozen face. He hadn't taken a good look at her when he'd entered the solar but now that he was, he could see that she didn't look as if she were sleeping at all. Her eyes were half-open, the blue orbs dull in death. But the first thing he noticed was the fact that her features seemed to be frozen in a permanent expression of terror. Her mouth was slightly open, the ends downturned, and when Troy managed to look at her arms, stretched over the children, he could see that her nails were broken and dark with blood, as if something or someone had shredded them. Troy had seen that kind of thing before; it occurred to him why.

My God, he thought, *she tried to claw her way out of the cab. She tried to free them!*

His anger turned to shock, and shock to grief. He suddenly fell to his knees beside Athena, putting his hand on her cold head, feeling the sobs coming forth. Or maybe not sobs; something was trying to bubble up from his chest but he wasn't sure what it was. An explosion of agony the likes of which he'd never experienced before. Biting off a groan, he bent down and kissed her on her wet, dirty head.

Lurching to his feet, he yanked himself away from his father's grip and staggered over to his wife and children. His mother was still standing beside them, weeping quietly, but he ignored the woman. In fact, he ignored everything but those three figures lying at his feet. Falling to his knees beside them, he reached down and gathered Helene into his arms, pulling her against his chest and burying his face in her neck.

Troy thought he might cry but, in truth, what he felt went too deep for tears. It cut through him like a knife, eviscerating him, carving him clean of everything he had ever felt or ever possibly could feel. He felt as if all of his insides had just been sucked out and there was nothing left but a hollow shell. That hollow shell was now holding what was left of the woman he loved.

He may have been living, but his soul was dead.

So, he held her and rocked her, unable to do anything else. Time passed, but he was unaware of it. He was locked in his own little world, yet somewhere in the midst of it, Troy heard someone enter the solar to tell William that Scott had arrived. William went to deliver the terrible news to his other son while his wife, the shattered mother and grandmother, remained with Troy. In fact, Troy could feel his mother's warm and gentle hands on his shoulder but, still, he couldn't acknowledge her. He couldn't acknowledge anything but the agony that now filled his hollow insides.

He rocked and he rocked. Helene's body felt like so much dead weight. She'd always been so warm and sensual and weightless in his arms that this was completely unnatural. All of it, so unnatural and, at some point, it occurred to him that he couldn't breathe. He tried, but he couldn't seem to inhale. Something about that dead weight in his arms wouldn't allow him to breathe and as the room began to spin, he released Helene and stood up, thinking that he had to leave. He had to get out of that room. Maybe when he wasn't looking at the vestiges of the life he once knew could he breathe again.

Blindly, he ran from the solar with his mother behind him, calling softly to him, but he wasn't listening. He was heading for the open entry door and the bailey beyond. Once outside, the light seemed to blind him. He couldn't seem to breathe any better. He caught a glimpse of his brother, Scott, as his father stood next to him. He could hear weeping sounds but he wasn't sure who they were coming from; it seemed that everyone was weeping. He thought, perhaps, it was his mother.

He never realized that the sounds were coming from him.

A few feet away from the keep entry, he came to a halt and tumbled onto his knees. Whatever had been bubbling up inside of him came out in a rush, and he vomited all over the mud of the bailey, gagging and choking until nothing more would come. But even still, he hunched over and continued to heave.

It was all he could do to stay conscious.

Men were moving around him, speaking softly, and he heard his father call out to his brother repeatedly but he didn't know why. He didn't care why. All he knew was that he'd lost his life today, drained from him by the three bodies back in the solar.

For the rest of the day, Troy remained on his knees in the mud, surrounded by his own vomit, and refusing to move. He simply sat there and stared out into space, unable to move or think, unable to deal with his grief. Somewhere in the madness, his younger brothers, Edward and Thomas, came to stand silent vigil over him. He remained there all night and so did his brothers. But when the morning finally dawned, so did Troy's understanding of what his future would now be.

Without a wife, without his younger children. It was his cross to bear.

That morning, Troy de Wolfe's world became a dark and hopeless place.

The darkest Wolfe of all.

CHAPTER ONE

Year of Our Lord 1272
September
Twelve miles southwest of Castle Questing (over the Scots border)

*W*HOOSH!

A very large rock had sailed too close to his head and Troy immediately retaliated, managing to uppercut the Scotsman who'd tried to take his head off with a long dagger he'd pulled from a sheath concealed on his hip. It went straight into the Scotsman's neck, his preferred target, and the man fell heavily into the grassy sod. Blood gushed onto the sweet Scottish earth.

But Troy didn't stop there; he was a man of action and little rest, and once his opponent was down, he went after any man he didn't personally recognize as being English. There was much at stake in this battle, not the least of which was some peace along the Marches where his outpost, Kale Castle, was front and center during these turbulent times. It was an outpost of Castle Questing, his father's seat, and the first line of defense against the Scots in this area. It was a small but strategic tower castle that sat between Questing and Wolfe's Lair, his father's major outpost in the area. The de Wolfe holdings protected perhaps one of the most volatile stretches of the Scottish Marches.

In fact, that was what this particular skirmish was all about – subduing a particularly bad section of the border that was in rugged and mountainous land. A band of marauding Scots, an amalgamation of a few clans including Murray, Douglas, and Gordon, had been using a pele tower about twelve miles southwest of Castle Questing as a base from which to launch their raids. As far as his father had been able to determine, these *reivers* were not sanctioned by the clans they represented, but they were doing a great deal of damage and William wanted it stopped.

William's order to his armies had been to capture this base, called Monteviot Tower, and hold it for the English. He was tired of losing men and material to these raiders, so he wanted to end it once and for all. He had, therefore, called upon a rather large army to purge Monteviot of her marauders, so men from the castles of Northwood, Kale, Wark, Berwick, Questing, and Wolfe's Lair had moved on the isolated tower at dawn on a crisp autumn morning.

The Scots, taken by surprise, had been ill equipped to handle nearly two thousand English soldiers. So as the day neared the nooning hour, there were just a few pockets of holdouts, including the tower itself, where about forty Scots were holed up, keeping the English at bay.

But that wasn't going to last. While the younger knights secured the big bailey of Monteviot, the older and more wily – or sneaky – knights were planning the incursion into the tower. Even as Troy concentrated on purging the Scots from a big stone outbuilding that also seemed to be the stable, he could still see his father, his Uncle Paris, his Uncle Kieran, and his Uncle Michael at the base of the tower determining the best course of action to penetrate it.

It was an auspicious gathering. These men were legendary knights along the border... *William de Wolfe... Paris de Norville... Kieran Hage... Michael de Bocage...* names that meant something on the Marches because they were the names of the men who had survived decades of skirmishes. They'd fought together for over forty years and even though they were well into their advanced years, it didn't much slow them down. They still rode with their armies and they still participated in combat, although Troy and his brothers, Patrick and

James, tried to keep their father out of heavy fighting while Paris' older sons, Hector and Apollo, attempted to do the same with their father.

Kieran had his own sons, Alec and Kevin, who tried to keep their mighty father from getting hurt, which resulted in him being grievously offended sometimes. Even Michael, quite possibly the tallest man on the borders, had three equally tall sons who tried to ease their father's load. But he, too, was insulted that they would even make the attempt.

Old knights who didn't want to be reminded of the younger, stronger generation.

Troy was the oldest of all the next-generation knights and, by virtue of his age and skill, was always the man in charge of the siege. Therefore, it was Troy who eventually put the older warriors on planning the breach of the tower. As he and Tobias de Bocage, Michael's eldest son, cleared out the stone outbuilding, Troy could see the elder knights congregating at the base of the tower in conference as they looked up the very tall, rectangular keep with small windows.

The apertures on the second level were barred with iron, making penetration impossible, but the levels above that – and there were at least two – had small windows for ventilation and light. It was a typical tower house, built for protection more than comfort. There was, however, a roof where the Scots were gathering and throwing projectiles down on the knights. That was where most of the resistance was coming from.

Troy had been watching that standoff, intermittently, for the last hour. Fortunately, the older knights knew to stay out of the way. At some point, the Scots ran out of ammunition and began to throw things from inside the tower – broken bed frames, pots, stools – anything they could get their hands on. That's how Troy and the others knew the end was near. Once the Scots started doing that, there was nothing left to fight with or to fight for. They would soon be starved out if their situation didn't change.

Then, it became a waiting game.

With Tobias and a few other knights handling the final purging of the outbuildings, Troy finally broke away and made his way over to the older knights as they congregated below the tower. He flipped up his visor, gazing up at the gray-stoned structure just as the others were.

"Well?" he said, shielding his eyes from the bright sun overhead. "I have finished my task. The outbuildings are clear. Why haven't you rushed the tower yet?"

William glanced at his son; big, muscular, and terrifying when he wanted to be, William was particularly proud of Troy. He had such an easy command presence and was much-loved by the men, mostly because they knew that Troy would fight or die for any one of them without question. A noble heart inspired great loyalty, and that was what Troy had – a heart that was as true as the day was long. But he was also easy to anger, could make rash decisions, would punch a man for looking the wrong way at him, and argumentative. Therefore, William knew the question out of his mouth wasn't a jest in any way; knowing Troy, the man was serious.

"We were just discussing the tactics," he said evenly. Then, he pointed at Paris, standing next to him. "Paris wants to burn them out."

Troy glanced at Paris, who was also the father of his deceased wife. Paris de Norville was the commander of Northwood Castle, a tall, blond, arrogant but deeply compassionate man whom Troy had known his entire life. He looked at Paris as a second father. But Paris always thought he knew best, and he liked to question everyone's decisions, which irked Troy terribly. Even now, he could see an expression on Paris' face that suggested he didn't approve of the current command opinion.

"If you burn it out, you will also have an outpost that no one will be able to use," Troy pointed out. "It would give the *reivers* no haven to hide in."

"And it would give me an outpost that was nothing more than a burned-out shell."

"Then what do you want to do?"

William pursed his lips in annoyance, in full disdain of Paris. "Determine a better way to remove the men inside. I am *not* burning it up."

He sounded final. Troy sighed pensively as he looked up at the tower again, noticing that Paris and Kieran were now moving closer as if to inspect the tower personally. "I would not do that if I were you," Troy warned them.

Kieran and Paris knew better, but they also suffered from an abundance of confidence brought on by years of experience.

"They cannot drop anything else on us," Kieran said; a massive mountain of a man, he was still the strongest man Troy knew in spite of his advancing years and bad heart. He was also quite calm and gentle, a great contrast to his fiery Scottish wife. "There is nothing left unless they want to start demolishing the building itself to find material to throw from the windows."

Troy didn't share the man's opinion. He looked at his father. "It will take one heavy stone to crash on Uncle Kieran's head and then we will have a grave problem on our hands."

William knew that, but he was siding with Paris and Kieran. He'd seen enough of these sieges to know.

"The Scots would not dare chip away at the stone and weaken the building," he said, moving away from his son and towards his comrades. He called out to them. "What are you looking at?"

As Paris and Kieran began to point something out to William, and the older men did exactly what they pleased in spite of the warnings, Troy noticed that his brothers, Patrick and James, had made their way over. He glanced at his brothers as they came to stand on either side of him.

"There is a contingent of Scots bottled in the keep," he said as Patrick and James approached. "Father is determining the best course of action as we speak."

Both brothers looked up to the very tall tower. "Burn them out," Patrick said. "What is he waiting for?"

Troy looked to his brother. Patrick was less than two years younger than he was, an enormous man with black hair and blue eyes, a brilliant knight who was the commander of Berwick Castle. It was a great responsibility but Patrick, known by the childhood nickname of "Atty", was the perfect commander. Skilled and extremely powerful, he was also wise and fair, and Troy adored him. He also respected his opinion. Before he could speak, however, more knights came to join them.

"What are they waiting for?" Kevin Hage demanded. A very big and powerful knight like his father, he was also young and with that youth came enthusiasm for destruction. "All we need do is lob flaming projectiles onto the roof platform and start a blaze that will chase them out."

Next to Kevin, Case and Corbin de Bocage, also very young men with a thirst for devastation, nodded eagerly. They were like wild bulls sometimes, and Troy held up a hand to ease their fiery blood.

"The wise elders are working on the problem, gentle knights," he said evenly. "This is the task that has been assigned to them. Let them work through it."

Although the more seasoned knights were willing to do that, the younger knights were very impatient. They liked fighting the enemy and the thought of thirty Scots hiding out in the tower was exciting to them. They wanted them out so they could defeat them, hand-to-hand. Nothing fed their bloodlust more than killing Scots.

"Ridiculous," Kevin said, pushing past Troy and his brothers. "I will make them come out."

Case and Corbin followed him, but Troy stood back with Patrick and James, watching and waiting. Undoubtedly, the three were going to do something foolish, something their fathers and the older knights wouldn't tolerate. It was always great fun to see the arrogant younger knights get their ears boxed. Fighting off a smile, Troy folded his big arms across his chest and watched the situation play out.

"I will bet you two marks of silver that Kieran throws a punch at his son," Patrick muttered.

Troy reached out, shaking his brother's hand. "Agreed."

"I want in on this," James said from Patrick's other side. Big, blond, and somewhat gentle, James was one of the kindest and most understanding men Troy had ever met. The man came across as quiet and reserved, but that was far from the truth – a fire raged somewhere in the man, a fire that saw him explode in the heat of battle. There was no one fiercer in a fight. "I will match your four silver marks with four of my own. Winner take all."

Troy agreed. "What is your bet?"

"That Father moves against them before Kieran or Michael does."

"Bloodied or no?"

"Bloodied, of course."

"Broken nose?"

"I will bet against that."

Troy and Patrick thought that was a fair bet. "Agreed," Troy said. "Let us see how well we know our father and the others."

With that, the three de Wolfe brothers stood back, watching with satisfaction as Kevin, Case, and Corbin pushed past the elder knights and headed straight to the tower. As the older knights looked on with some shock, the three younger knights came to within a few feet of the tower wall. It was close enough to have something dumped on them, or worse. It was far too close for comfort. But they didn't seem to care, filled with a sense of self-importance as they were.

"We have killed your men and stolen your horses!" Kevin bellowed up for all to hear. "If you do not surrender immediately, then you are bigger fools than I could ever imagine. Come out of there at once!"

There wasn't much of a response. Irritated, and perhaps embarrassed in the slightest that the Scots didn't immediately surrender, Kevin looked at Case, who took up the cry.

"Fools!" he roared. "You are defeated! Open the door this instant and throw yourselves upon our mercy!"

Case planted his hands on his hips, waiting expectantly for the door of the tower to open and the Scots to come out with their heads hanging in defeat. What he received, instead, were several naked arses hanging over the side of the roof in defiant response, just enough to thoroughly irritate him and Kevin. While the elder knights stood well back and watched the spectacle, and Troy and his brothers stood even further back and tried not to burst out laughing, Corbin de Bocage took over the negotiations. He was certain he would succeed where the other two had failed.

"I see you are showing us your brains," he shouted up to them. "Certainly, men like you keep your brains in your arses! Do you know what I am going to do when I get into that tower? I am going to kick your brains in! And then I shall thrust my sword into your gullets and take great delight in watching you drown in your own blood! Well? What have you to say to that?"

The reply wasn't long in coming. Great buckets of piss were suddenly poured off the roof, right down onto the three English knights who had been lobbing insults and threats. Kevin managed to dodge most of it, but Case and Corbin were covered in it.

Roaring with fury, the de Bocage brothers ripped off their tunics and pulled off their helms, covered in piss and absolutely furious for it. They were jumping up and down, shaking their fists at the Scots even as they dodged more streams of piss. As most of the English laughed uproariously, Michael went to his smelly, humiliated sons and pulled them away, making them go to the well and wash off, while William and Paris and Kieran laughed until they wept. In fact, they were wiping away the tears when Troy, Patrick, and James came up to them.

"You had better do something quickly before Case and Corbin and Kevin scale those walls out of pure anger and get themselves killed," Troy said to his snorting father. "The next time, we might not be laughing."

William couldn't seem to stop chortling. "You are correct, I am certain," he said, "but I have been waiting many a battle to see those three have their comeuppance. Mayhap, they will not be so eager to rush things from now on."

"That is doubtful."

William sobered. "Probably," he said, taking a deep breath to regain his composure. "But, God, it was worth it to see that."

William's satisfaction made Troy smile, glancing to his brothers, who started chuckling again. Soon, all of them were laughing again, but that quickly ended when William suddenly turned for the tower and called up to the Scots.

"You had every right to curb my enthusiastic men," he shouted. "In fact, I applaud you for it. My name is William de Wolfe and I ask to speak to your commander."

The mere mention of the man's name had the Scots buzzing. Everyone could hear it, but Troy and Patrick didn't think that had been such a good move on their father's part. The Scot who killed William de Wolfe would be a hero to his people. With that in mind, Troy and his brothers rushed up to their father, essentially boxing the man in so that if anyone with an arrow decided to take aim, they would be the targets.

William knew what his sons were doing and he wasn't thrilled that they'd made themselves human shields. He tried to move but no one would let him. When he tried to push Patrick out of the way, Patrick pushed back. Resigned, William called up to the Scots once more.

"Bring me your commander," he said again.

More buzzing and grumbling from the Scots. They could see that there was some shuffling going on; men moving about on the roof and more than one head popped from the windows on the top floor. As the English grew increasingly impatient, a shaggy, gray head appeared on the roof, looking down upon them.

"De Wolfe?" the man said in a heavy Scottish brogue. "I canna see well, but I can see the mark on yer face. 'Tis the Wolfe in the flesh."

He meant the eyepatch. Every man on the border knew that William de Wolfe sported an eye patch over a missing left eye. It was part of his mystique, part of his power. It was a mark that earned respect.

"Aye," William replied steadily. "May I have your name?"

"Barden."

William realized that his sons were moving him back, away from the tower, and he struggled not to trip on his feet – and theirs – as they pushed him back. He knew they were doing it for his own safety but it was still annoying. It made him look weak. Frustrated, he dug in his heels.

"Barden," William said, coming to a halt and refusing to move any further from the tower. "Who is your clan?"

The Scotsman didn't answer immediately. "Me own," he finally said, to the titters of his men. "But I was born a Gordon."

"And they sent you here?"

"No one sends me anywhere."

"Then you have been raiding my lands for your own benefit."

A pause. "I have been takin' what I need."

It seemed to confirm to William and the others that these men were not sanctioned by their clans. Knowing he was dealing with rogue Scots, men who cared not for honor or, more than likely, reason, William proceeded carefully.

"Barden, we are at a crossroads," he said. "My men have invaded your bailey and captured your tower. Your men are either subdued or dead. That only leaves the tower at this point, and we shall take it eventually. We can, therefore, do one of two things; you can surrender and I promise you and your men shall not be harmed, or I will order my men to begin bombarding the roof with flaming oil. You cannot combat it and it will eventually burn everyone in the tower. You know this. I will, therefore, give you the choice of how you wish to proceed."

Barden was seriously contemplating what he'd been told. De Wolfe was giving him the choice of what should be done, which saved his pride in a sense. Barden understood that, but he also understood that either choice would end in his surrender. He turned back to his men and snippets of angry conversation could be heard. It was several moments before he replied.

"We'll not yield tae ye," he said, "and most of this tower is made of stone. If ye must burn us down, then get on with it."

That brought a bit of information William hadn't known – most of this tower is made of stone. He could mean the walls and the stairs, but what of the floors? They could be wood or stone, or a combination of both. William wanted the tower intact, but maybe he could burn enough of it – whatever would burn – to smoke them out.

"Then you would die with your men rather than surrender and go free?" William asked. "I do not intend to take you prisoner but, in order to go free, you must surrender your weapons and leave. I'll not have bands of armed Scots roaming these lands."

Barden seemed to grow angry. "These are *our* lands, Sassenach," he said. "Ye're in our country and ye have no right tae be. If ye want a surrender, it 'twill not be from us. Ye'll have tae kill us first."

William was coming to see that there was no way around it. He had suspected this would be their answer and he was prepared. He was about to reply when an arrow suddenly sailed out of the tower, from the roof area, and hit James on the upper arm, penetrating his mail. It wasn't a bad strike, but bad enough. The message was clear. When William saw the arrow protruding out of his son's arm, it was all he needed to give the command for the archers to launch.

He would waste no more time.

Men began scrambling to fulfill his command and, soon enough, the sky was full of flaming arrows, hitting the stone walls of the tower but also hitting the roof, igniting both men and wood. William had brought two smaller trebuchets with him, war machines that had managed to burn a great deal of the interior of the bailey. And now those same engines were hurling flaming bombs of oil that, when smashing on the roof of the tower house, sent flames flying everywhere.

Very quickly, the siege turned into a raging inferno as the tower house began to burn. Screams could be heard from inside the stone structure as the English eased up on their bombardment. The flames were doing more than they ever could at this point. Troy stood with his father, watching heavy black smoke rise up into the afternoon sky and listening to the cries of the men inside. He shook his head sadly.

"Rather than surrender, they will die," he said. "I cannot fathom that kind of zealous behavior."

William watched the smoke pour from the windows. "Put men on chopping through the door," he said. "Open it. At least if there are men who wish to escape, they can do so. It could be quite possible that they are being prevented from escaping."

Troy looked at his father. "Opening that door could increase the flames," he said. "Are you sure that is what you want to do?"

William cocked a dark eyebrow. "It does not matter," he said. "Whether the flames grow stronger or weaker, they are burning inside. It is an ugly death. Mayhap if we cut down the entry door, some will be saved."

Troy moved away from his father, grabbing Patrick and Tobias and telling them what his father had ordered. Very quickly, there were two very big men with axes chopping through the heavy oak and iron entry door to the tower, making holes in it, enough for terrible black smoke to escape. They could hear the Scots on the other side, coughing and crying out in fear but then cursing the English who were trying to break through. Troy, who was standing right behind the big soldiers who were doing the axing, began to shout at the men inside.

"Save yourselves!" he yelled, coughing as the smoke poured into his face. "Get out of there!"

More cursing, more chopping, until a portion of the door broke down and half-unconscious Scots began to push through the opening, one at a time. The knights standing at the entry, and there were several of them, began to pull the men out and away from the fire, which was gaining intensity. Only ten or so Scots made it out, leaving the rest to die in the inferno that burned long into the night. The smell of smoke and human flesh hung heavy on the air for days after that.

It was a smell not many of them would soon forget.

Monteviot Tower, or what was left of it, now belonged to William de Wolfe. As dawn broke over the following day, it was the green and black de Wolfe banners that flew proudly from the walls. But true to his word, William allowed those men who had escaped the tower to flee without taking them prisoner.

Flee they did, and word of de Wolfe's victory spread very quickly in Southern Scotland. In particular, it spread to the clans who had an uneasy peace with de Wolfe. Fearful of rousing the man's anger, no one sent any men to counter him. De Wolfe's anger could bring tens of thousands of English, and no one wanted that.

But no one wanted him with another base in Scotland, either.

For a lesser branch of the Clan Kerr, it was a particular issue because Monteviot Tower was on their land. It was an issue they needed to deal with. Their lands bordered de Wolfe lands all along the border from Coldstream to Carter Bar. They already had to tolerate Wolfe's Lair in their lands, mighty English bastion that it was, but now there was a second fortress for de Wolfe to gain a foothold.

Keith Kerr of Clan Kerr, chief of a smaller offshoot of the clan, was the one who mostly had to deal with de Wolfe. Known as Red Keith, he knew he couldn't shake de Wolfe. It was better not to try. But he also didn't like de Wolfe becoming greedy and taking a disputed outpost.

Therefore, he would have to deal with de Wolfe in a way the man would understand.

He would have to bargain with his very blood.

CHAPTER TWO

Sibbald's Hold
Home of Red Keith Kerr
Thirteen miles west of Monteviot Tower

"PA, HOW CAN ye ignore what the Wolfe is doin'? Are ye blind to him, then?"

A very angry young woman dressed in hose and layers of tunics stood in the low-ceilinged hall of her father's home, smoke gathering near her head from the hearth that was spitting sparks and gray ribbons into the darkened room. But the man she spoke to, sitting near the fire in his long tunic and coat of heavy, dirty wool, gazed back at her with some displeasure.

"De Wolfe was cleanin' out the rebels from Monteviot Tower," he muttered. "Those same men have been raidin' his lands. We expected he would do this, so it is of no great surprise."

The woman let her hand slap against her thigh in frustration. "So ye let the *Sassenach* remain? Now Monteviot becomes his holdin'?"

It was sunset over the land and, deep in the heart of the clan of the Red Keith Kerr, Keith Kerr eyed his passionate, strong, big-mouthed daughter with increasing disapproval. It wasn't that anything she said was wrong in any fashion; the great Wolfe of the Border had, indeed, launched a siege on Scot lands and, technically, on one of his holdings.

Monteviot Tower belonged to Keith but he didn't have enough men to hold it, so *reivers* had confiscated the property and had been using it for their base to launch raids into English lands. Most of those lands belonged to de Wolfe, so Keith had been expecting, at some point, that de Wolfe would come after Monteviot. The exchange for purging the *reivers* was that now de Wolfe had another holding in Kerr lands.

But there wasn't much he could do about it.

"Lass," Keith growled, perturbed that she was calling him out in front of his men, "ye know the situation. Ye know that I dunna have the men tae hold Monteviot much less take it back from de Wolfe. If ye can bring me a thousand Scots, I may be able tae reclaim the property, but for now... I canna do it by force."

"Ye mean ye willna."

"I mean I *canna*."

Rhoswyn Whitton Kerr faced off against her father, feeling an abundance of shame and frustration. He didn't seem willing to fight the English off of his very land and, to Rhoswyn, that was a sign of weakness.

She'd never known her father to be weak before.

And his excuse... that he didn't have enough men to do it. Her father was chief of a smaller clan, an offshoot of the larger Clan Kerr that held most of the lands in this area. Why, all her father had to do was to call upon his cousin, the Kerr of Clan Kerr, and he could have those thousand men he needed to chase off de Wolfe. Never mind that her father and his cousin were at odds, and had been ever since her father had married her mother those years ago. His cousin had wanted the woman for himself and it had been the cause of an estrangement between them. But that was old history as far as Rhoswyn was concerned.

Couldn't bygones be bygones?

"Ye could if ye wanted tae," she pointed out. "But ye willna ask the Kerr for his help. It is a silly grudge ye hold against him and..."

"*Silly?*"

"Aye," Rhoswyn pointed a long finger at him. "It has gone on for nearly twenty years now, since before me birth. It is time tae make amends, Pa. It is time tae pull together tae fight de Wolfe from our lands."

Keith sighed heavily. It was his own fault that his daughter was the way she was. He'd only had one child – Rhoswyn – and for a man who had badly wanted a son, the girl bore the brunt of that longing. He'd raised her like a son, teaching her to fight, to track, to hunt, and any number of things that men did. She could drink most men under the table and she had been known to fight on occasion. It was something her mother, God rest her soul, had tried to balance out by teaching her daughter what she considered the finer points of being a lady – sewing, singing, and learning to both speak and read in three languages. Rhoswyn was a fine student, and very intelligent, but her natural personality had her thriving on the things her father taught her more than the ones her mother insisted upon. The result was a warrior all men feared, a woman who was as tough and strong as most men.

And she knew it.

But Rhoswyn was also a woman of exquisite beauty. Her hair was long and thick and straight, hanging to mid-waist, in a shade of auburn that looked like the shimmering color of leaves when they changed in the autumn. It was all shades of burnished reds and golds. She had the face of angels, her mother had said, and big brown eyes with a fringe of dusky lashes. With a dusting of freckles across her nose, she looked like a fine porcelain statue and incapable of anything other than softness and love.

That was what most men thought before she drove a sword into their bellies.

Aye, Rhoswyn was both his exquisite creation and his disaster. Finding a husband for her had been impossible because no Scotsman in his right mind wanted a wife who could best him in a fight. And it was that thought alone that caused Keith a good deal of sleepless nights until he'd heard that de Wolfe had taken over Monteviot Tower.

Then, an idea had struck him.

Keith knew he couldn't beat de Wolfe in a fight. A show of force wouldn't do. But perhaps an alliance of sorts would. If he couldn't run the man off his lands, then he really had no choice but to join with him. If he could only trick de Wolfe... that is, *convince* de Wolfe into accepting Rhoswyn as a wife for one of his men, or better, one of his sons, then he wouldn't have to worry about de Wolfe on his lands at all. Rhoswyn would be married into the man's family and, therefore, they would all be considered family. It might even make his snobbish cousin, the Kerr, respect him just a little. An alliance with de Wolfe would make him more powerful in his cousin's eyes.

But, in truth, an alliance like that wouldn't be for respect. It would be for survival. It was far better to be at de Wolfe's side than in his path.

Of course, Rhoswyn didn't know any of this, nor would she until the time was right. Until then, Keith had to keep his scheme to himself. He couldn't even tell his men, because he knew it would get back to his daughter. Nay, he had to bide his time on this one. He had to make peace with de Wolfe because he didn't have the numbers to stand against him.

Rhoswyn *was* that peace.

"I am not sure we can," Keith said after a moment. "Lass, ye know old angers die hard. The Kerr has never forgiven me for takin' yer mother away from him and whenever he looks at ye, he sees her. Ye remind him of what he lost."

"Then ye willna even try?" Rhoswyn asked, exasperated.

Keith held up a quieting hand. "It seems tae me that de Wolfe isna a threat," he said. "He's held Wolfe's Lair for more than twenty years and the only threat he's ever had, aside from an occasional Scots raid, is attack from the English. Ye were just a wee lass at the time but nigh ten years ago, Carlisle marched on de Wolfe and laid siege tae the Lair."

Rhoswyn had heard of that battle, many years ago. It had something to do with Simon de Montfort at the time, and the fact that de Wolfe supported Henry, but she didn't care about foolish English feuds. They were a ridiculous lot, anyway.

"I remember bein' told," she said impatiently, "and I dunna care. All I care about is gettin' the man off our lands. If ye willna make amends with the Kerr, then what *will* ye do?"

There she was again, challenging his authority in all matters. Keith glanced to the men around him; his younger brother, Fergus, and Fergus' sons Artis and Dunsmore. Fergus was even more of the passive type – the man didn't like confrontation – while his sons were much more like Rhoswyn. The younger generation had the fire of ambition in them and the fuel of inexperience to feed it.

"I will do what needs tae be done, Daughter," he finally said, with a firm tone that told her she'd better still her tongue. "Trust that, in all things, I will do what is best for us all."

Rhoswyn heard the warning tone but she'd never been one to back away. "And what *is* that, Pa?"

Keith eyed the woman. He knew she wasn't going to leave this alone unless he gave her a satisfactory answer. Rather than let her continue to publicly humiliate him, he stood up, straight into the haze of smoke that was hanging around the room. His eyes stung. But his gaze was sharp on his daughter.

"With me," he said.

He was motioning to Rhoswyn and she immediately went to him, following him out of the hall and into the bailey beyond.

It was a small bailey, crowded with men and animals, and smelling like a barnyard. Sibbald's Hold was a small but highly fortified tower that had been built about sixty years before by a man named Sibbald Kerr. As Keith's father, he'd passed the fortress to his son and it became Keith's permanent home after his falling out with his cousin. It was comprised of a tower attached to a hall that used two of the exterior walls of the fortress as part of the structure.

Everything was packed in so tightly into the bailey that there was little room for anything more than what they already had, including people. Keith turned to his daughter when he sensed they had a nominal amount of privacy.

"I'll not have ye questionin' every move I make," he said, his tone low. "I have tae do what's best for our people. If I charge de Wolfe, he will destroy us. Do ye not understand that?"

Rhoswyn did, deep down, but it wasn't in her nature to relent. "But Pa," she said. "If ye dunna challenge him, then mayhap the next time, he'll come for Sibbald. What will ye do then? If ye let him gain more of a foothold than he has, then he'll walk over us before we know it."

Keith cocked a dark eyebrow. "Then what would ye have me do?"

Rhoswyn blinked in surprise; he didn't usually ask her opinion. Even so, she was ready with it. "If ye send tae the Kerr…"

Keith cut her off. "I will *not* send word tae me cousin," he said flatly. "He wouldna come, anyway. Ye can put that thought out of yer mind. Tell me again what ye would do."

Truth be told, Rhoswyn didn't have much of a backup plan. "What of yer allies?" she asked. "If ye send word, they will help ye."

Keith shook his head. "'Tis a fool ye are, lass," he said. "Do ye really believe the Elliot and the Armstrong would send men tae purge de Wolfe from a tiny outpost? And risk the wrath of all of the English lairds along the border? Nay, lass, they wouldna. Tae fight de Wolfe, we must be smarter than he is. And wolves are smart animals."

Rhoswyn knew what he said about their allies was true; they wouldn't risk angering de Wolfe because the man could very well take it out on them. But she hated feeling so alone and so helpless.

"How would ye be smarter than him, then?" she asked.

Keith held up a finger as if a grand thought had occurred to him. "By attackin' the English the only way we can."

"And do what?"

There was a glimmer in Keith's dark eyes. "We can pick away at them," he said. "I could send men every week tae pick at the outpost, tae steal their horses or their cattle, tae make their lives miserable. I may not be able tae bring a massive army tae their door, but I can make their lives uneasy. Now, by all accounts, de Wolfe is a reasonable man. He's not given tae fits of fury or madness. Mayhap, I will invite de Wolfe tae

Sibbald and discuss a truce. If he doesna agree, then we will pick at his men like vermin. There willna be many of us, but enough tae give them no peace."

Rhoswyn was shaking her head, even as he spoke. "That willna matter tae them," she said. "With their numbers, we would simply be flies buzzin' around their heads. It would be annoyin' and nothin' more. They may even swat at the flies and kill one or two. Do we want tae risk our men like that?"

She had a point. Keith crossed his arms thoughtfully. "Ye have another idea, then?"

Rhoswyn thought on the situation seriously. Her only plan had been to send for allies, but clearly that wasn't the answer. She had to come up with something else, something to hit the English where it would do the most damage.

Something to damage that fragile male ego. An idea took hold.

"The English have considerable pride, Pa," she said after a moment. "I dunna suppose they could turn down a challenge, could they?"

He looked at her strangely. "What *kind* of challenge?"

She gazed at her father intently. "Would they accept a challenge that had yer best warrior against their best warrior?" she asked. "The winner would name the terms, and when I won, I would tell them they had tae leave Monteviot."

Keith's brow furrowed. "*Yer* terms?"

She nodded eagerly, thinking she was on to something brilliant. "Aye," she said. "We could go tae Monteviot and challenge them, but I wouldna reveal meself until the battle. Once the English warrior sees I am a woman, he has tae fight me. It would shame him if he dinna."

Keith scratched his chin thoughtfully. In truth, it wasn't a bad scheme. Perhaps, he could coerce and insult the English enough that they would take on a single-combat challenge, winner take all. It would most certainly be a matter of pride. The only negative point to that entire plan was the fact that Rhoswyn was determined to be the warrior facing the English. Although his daughter was good – very good – he wasn't sure he wanted to pit her against an English knight.

Still, she had an excellent point – not revealing her identity until it was too late. The English knight would have no choice but to go through with it simply to save his pride, woman or no. Or... he could surrender because fighting a woman would be beneath him.

One way, Keith might lose a daughter. The other way... he'd gain back his outpost and keep his child intact.

It was a difficult choice to make.

"And what happens if ye lose?" he asked quietly. "What then? They could name their terms, too."

Rhoswyn wasn't one to entertain defeat in any case, but she had to be realistic. "What is the worst they could do?" she asked. "Demand we go home? Demand we leave Monteviot Tower to them and never return?"

Keith was much older and much more experienced. He knew that a counter-demand could be much more serious than she was making it out to be.

"They could demand *ye*," he said. "Or, they could demand we turn over Sibbald."

Rhoswyn thrust her chin up. "Then we would be without honor because they couldna have me *or* Sibbald. We would run for home and hope they would not catch us."

She was serious; Keith could see it. In his opinion, she wasn't being reasonable. Still, in her suggestion, he could see that she was more than willing to sacrifice herself and that was the mark of a noble warrior. He appreciated that.

After a moment, he sighed and put his arm around Rhoswyn's shoulders, giving her a squeeze. For just a moment, she was his little girl again and she hugged her father, tightly. But it was only for a moment; she quickly released him, embarrassed to show any emotion.

"Ye understand that I must do what I feel best," Keith said to her, fingering a tendril of her hair. "In spite of what ye think of me, de Wolfe's incursion *will* be answered. I willna cower from him. The man is on me land and I must let him know that *I* know."

Rhoswyn nodded. "I know."

"But I'm not sure I'm a-wantin' ye tae fight their best warrior for the prize of Monteviot Tower."

"There is no one better *than* me. Ye know that."

Keith snorted softly. "There are a few, lass."

"But they willna have the advantage I have – of being a woman."

"That is true."

"Then we will go on the morrow?"

He lifted an eyebrow. "Now?"

She nodded firmly. "Why should we wait? The sooner we go, the sooner they leave."

Hesitantly, he nodded, and the plan was set. As much as Keith didn't want to entertain the possibility, the more he thought on it, the more sense it was starting to make. Having his daughter challenge the English, winner take all, and then revealing her sex when they accepted the challenge. Those foolish English knights with their sense of chivalry might very well lay down their weapons rather than fight a woman. In fact, he was willing to bet that would be the case.

He was about to stake Rhoswyn's life on it.

As Keith glanced at his tall, proud daughter, he began to think of the terms they would relay once she triumphed over the arrogant English. Not a few minutes earlier, he was thinking on offering her to de Wolfe to create an alliance. He still thought it was a good idea. And if the winner was the one to set the terms of victory, Keith had a different idea of terms set forth than his daughter did. His terms wouldn't be that the English should clear out and leave Monteviot Tower.

His terms would be that the loser marry his daughter. He'd have his alliance, his daughter would have a husband, and all would be well in the world – even if her husband *was* English.

Rhoswyn's plan to challenge the English was looking better and better.

CHAPTER THREE

Monteviot Tower

THE GREAT HALL of Monteviot smelled like smoke and burned flesh, but they were all so exhausted and hungry that no one seemed to care. Three days after the burning of the tower, the restoration of the grounds was already underway.

The bodies of the dead Scots had been piled outside of the walls of Monteviot and, at William's request, Troy had sent to Jedburgh Abbey for a canon to come and pray over the departed souls. They waited two days for the holy man to come but at the end of the second day, the stench of the dead was so bad that Troy ordered the funeral pyre lit.

Of course, it was appropriate that the canon should come just as the sky filled with black, greasy smoke from the burning bodies and the wiry man with his skull suitably shaved to denote his piety arrived on an old palfrey and promptly launched himself from the horse to berate the English who were disposing of the bodies.

Hector de Norville, Paris' eldest son, had been the first to receive the holy tongue lashing because he happened to be standing closest to the priest when he arrived. But Hector was much like his father in that he didn't take most things too seriously; he knew his duty, he knew what was best, and he simply brushed the priest off when the man tried to tell him that burning the dead without a priest's blessing was condemning the souls to Purgatory.

As Hector walked away, Troy watched from his position across the pyre. The frustrated priest seemed to be scolding any English knight he came in contact with but the knights were all following Hector's example and either ignoring the priest or walking away.

As the priest came close to a tantrum as the flames of the dead burned brightly, Troy made his way over to the man who was now trying to berate the soldiers who were piling up the bodies. With the knights gone, the soldiers were the next targets, but the soldiers looked at the priest as if they had no care for his ranting. They continued their duty of stripping the dead and then throwing them onto the pile. They had their orders and no one, not even a Scottish priest with a heavy accent, was going to stop them.

"You," Troy said as he walked up behind the frantic priest. "Are you from Jedburgh?"

The man whirled around, his eyes widening at the sight of the very big, very dark knight. "I am," he said, breathless. "Ye sent for me. Now I am here and I find ye burnin' the bodies of the dead?"

Troy held up a hand to calm the man. "We had no choice," he said. "Some of them were burned already because they had been caught in the fire that burned out the tower. For the rest of them… it was starting to smell very badly around here. We had to do something."

The priest threw up his hands. "Then bury them!"

Troy eyed the man before kicking at the ground. "In this?" he said, pointing. "Look at it; there is more rock than soil here. We could never dig through this. Or did you have in mind that we should take them in a caravan to Jedburgh so that you and your fellow priests could properly bury them?"

That seemed to bring some pause to the priest. His gaze lingered on Troy before looking to the ground, seeing what the knight had meant. It was extremely rocky ground, meaning it would have been very difficult to dig out a mass grave. Soil such as this was nearly impossible to cut through. Unhappy, the priest sighed.

"Then why did ye send for me?" he asked. "Ye've already burned the men. Ye've already done what needed tae be done."

"I sent for you to pray for these men," Troy said. "It was not by my choice, I assure you. My father requested it. All of these men are thieves and murderers, so prayer will not do them any good. Their paths were set in life and they are set in death. But my father requested that a priest pray for them just the same. It is a merciful gesture, I suppose."

The priest scratched his head, fingers digging into thin hair that stood up like straw in places. He seemed to be calming after his initial flare up.

"Then yer father is a pious man," he said, eyeing the big knight. "Who are ye?"

"Troy de Wolfe. My father is William de Wolfe."

That brought a reaction from the priest. "The Wolfe of the Border?"

"Aye."

Now, the priest wasn't quite so irate. In fact, he seemed to be more interested in his surroundings. "A de Wolfe battle in Scotland?" he asked. "What goes on here, then? What happened?"

Troy looked up at the burned-out tower, at his general surroundings as the sky darkened into night overhead. The stars were starting to come out.

"This place was a haven for *reivers*," he said. "We have eliminated the threat. My father is taking over command of this outpost and it will become English property. In fact, this tower is located between my father's seat of Castle Questing and his major outpost of Wolfe's Lair. Have you heard of the Lair?"

"I have."

"Now we shall have two outposts on the Scottish side of the border."

The priest was looking around, growing more subdued by the minute as he realized what had taken place and what it meant for the area in general; the Scots weren't policing this part of the border very well so now the English were. And, knowing de Wolfe, he would not relinquish the property without a major fight, which no one in this area could give him.

The English were here to stay.

"I'd heard of some raids out here," the priest admitted. "These are Kerr lands. Did ye know that?"

Troy nodded. "I did. So does my father. But the raids were not on Kerr lands; they were on de Wolfe lands."

The priest looked at him. "But these lands belong tae Red Keith Kerr," he said. "Does he know ye're here?"

Troy shrugged. "Does it matter? He did nothing to control the *reivers* on his land so we had to take care of the problem. If he has issue with us being in his lands, then let him come forth and discuss it."

The priest sighed heavily. "I'm sure he will."

Troy knew that. He'd been fighting the Scots a long time and he knew of Red Keith and his band of Lowlanders. Troy had never had much action with the man, for he tended to keep to himself, but those incidents that Troy had heard of where Red Keith had been involved gave the man a legendary temper and men who were quite zealous. If Troy believed what he'd been told, then Red Keith had some fearsome warriors.

But it occurred to Troy as he pondered the reputation of Red Keith Kerr that this priest would possibly know the lands and the clans better than he did. It was true that William was quite knowledgeable about those who bordered his lands, and Troy was also very knowledgeable by virtue of the time he'd spent on the Marches, but this priest might know things they wouldn't, including intimate details of Red Keith Kerr. An interest in what the priest might know had him behaving a bit more friendly towards the man.

"You did not tell me your name," he said.

The priest glanced at him. "Audric."

Troy looked at the man a moment, trying to gauge how to proceed. "Thank you for answering the summons to come and pray over the bodies of your dead countrymen," he said, "but I am sure you could use some rest before you do. Come inside and meet my father. Let us discuss how to keep peace now that we've purged the *reivers* from Kerr land. I am sure my father would appreciate any advice you might have."

He began to lead the priest towards the bailey. Audric sensed a change in demeanor with Troy but he didn't say anything. He, too, was trying to get a sense of these English, and of what had occurred here beyond the purging of *reivers*.

Audric wondered if that was all there was, considering de Wolfe had at least two properties in the area that were a day's ride or less away. Wolfe's Lair was well-known in these parts, even to the clergy of Jedburgh and Kelso to the northeast, and Kale Water was known to house fanatic English who were fearsome fighters. Now, he had Monteviot Tower. Perhaps if Audric could find out what de Wolfe's intentions really were, he could tell his superiors and even Scots lairds in the area who would want to know. These men *were* English, after all, and any peace with them was tenuous at best.

Aye... perhaps he should find out all he could. Let his visit here mean something other than saying prayers for those who didn't need them now, anyway.

Let him find out what was *really* going on, for what affected the border affected the rest of Scotland as well.

⁊

WHILE THE VAST majority of the fortified tower smelled of smoke and burned bodies, the great hall had remained oddly untouched. It smelled of dogs and of smoke and of unwashed men, but it didn't have the rank smell of burned flesh that the rest of the fortress seemed to have. Therefore, the meal that night could be eaten in relative comfort, and eat the English did.

It was the end of the third day after the conquest of Monteviot Tower and the English were relaxing somewhat. The cleanup was nearly over as far as the dead were concerned and some of the knights had begun what would be the restoration of the tower. Burned wood was hauled out and anything salvageable was set aside.

From Michael and his sons, who were to be deeply involved in the assessment and salvage of the tower, Troy had learned that the second and third levels were nearly undamaged. Those levels were the laird's hall, which was a smaller hall, and then two bedchambers above it. A narrow spiral staircase built into the thickness of the wall had also been completely spared.

The majority of the damage had come from the roof collapsing into the fourth floor, and then burning men and anything else it could use for fuel. Most deaths had come from smoke inhalation rather than actually burning, although they did have their share of the burned bodies. Michael seemed to think that skilled craftsman could easily repair the roof and William vowed to send some of his craftsmen from Castle Questing to help with the repairs. In truth, the tower had been built mostly of stone, as Barden had said, and the structure itself had mostly survived.

As William had hoped, he still had a tower.

As evening fell and the night turned dark and crisp, the smell of roasting meat mingled with all the other smells of the tower, making for a rather pungent experience. A cow had been slaughtered and the men were greatly anticipating the meal. With the majority of the army in the enclosed bailey, with the repaired gates now sealed for the night, the knights and senior soldiers had found their way into the hall.

With the short, skinny priest at his side, Troy made his way into the rather crowded hall, full of men drinking and tearing their way through the beef that was being pulled straight off the roasting spit in the bailey. Somewhere off in a corner, a soldier had produced a mandolin, and songs of love and victory filtered through the smoky air.

There was a table near the open-pit hearth in the center of the hall and Troy could see his father and most of the other knights sitting there. He led the priest towards the table, catching his father's attention as he drew close.

"The priest from Jedburgh has arrived, Papa," he said, indicating the short man in the dirty brown robes. "This is Father Audric."

Audric found himself under intense scrutiny as most of the table within earshot turned to look at him. In particular, at least three of the younger English knights were looking at him with extreme suspicion and he met their gaze, rather warily, wondering if they were going to rush him then and there. Hatred for the Scots burned deep in these young English warriors. Fortunately, Troy grasped him by the arm before any trouble could start and pulled him away from the unfriendly faces and over to a seat the end of the bench while he went around the table to sit with his father.

Audric sat down and someone put a wooden cup in front of him. There was a pitcher of liquid within arm's reach and he timidly picked it up, pouring what turned out to be the dregs of the wine into his cup. It was cloudy and full of sediment, but he drank it anyway, thirsty. From across the table, William was the first to speak.

"You are from Jedburgh?" he asked.

Audric nodded. "Aye, m'lord."

"We sent for you two days ago. What took so long?"

Audric sensed a rebuke in that question. He looked around at the table of men; he'd never seen such a collection in his entire life. They were big; some of them were even huge. Scarred, battle-worn, bruised and even a few that had bloodied hands or a nick to the face. Even so, they were the victors and that victory radiated from them like a stench. Sassenach men who had come to fight the righteous fight, to rid the land of a threat but, in that action, Audric could still sense conquest. It was in their blood, the English against the Scots, something that was seared into their souls from one generation to the next.

But in that understanding, Audric knew one thing – that he couldn't show any fear. The English were intimidating and, truth be told, he'd never been this close to English knights before. Therefore, he answered William firmly.

"It took a day tae reach Jedburgh with yer message," he said. "I came as soon as I could, as soon as the abbot gave permission. I am tae bless the dead and report back on the situation."

It wasn't quite the truth, but it sounded reasonable enough. He figured if he said he needed to report on the situation, then the English would know that he was expected back and not try to move against him. Kill him, even. It might keep the young bucks at bay. But he could see that William was unimpressed.

"The situation is that we cleared Monteviot Tower of a band of *reivers* who were doing a good deal of damage to my lands," William said, his tone a bit testy. "I realize that it is the job of a priest to save souls, to save the souls of the good as well as the wicked, but it is my job to protect my land and my people. I did what needed to be done."

The younger knights banged their cups against the old, worn table, loudly agreeing with William's statement with a bit of bloodlust in their eyes. Audric looked down the table to see those younger knights again, eyeing him with hostility as if daring him to contradict the great Wolfe.

"No one is disputin' yer need tae protect yer lands, m'lord," he said. "Yer lands border these lands."

"They do."

"Surely ye have alliances with yer Kerr neighbors?"

William scratched his stubbled cheek thoughtfully. "My wife is from Clan Scott," he said. "I have an alliance with Clan Scott but Clan Kerr is known to be their rivals. I have never had any trouble with them, however, so you could say that there is a tentative peace. They know me, I know them, and we simply stay out of each other's way."

Someone shoved a cracked trencher full of beef and bread in front of Audric. Gravy spilled from the broken side and onto the table, trickling onto his robes, but he didn't notice. He was more interested in shoving meat into his mouth.

"As I told yer son, this castle and these lands belong tae Red Keith Kerr," he said, "but I would assume ye already know that."

William nodded. "There are two minor Kerr clans along this stretch of the border. I assumed this property was Red Keith's because his lands are concentrated in this area."

Audric continued to speak and chew, bits of food flying from his mouth. "Do ye know him, then?"

William held up his cup for Patrick to pour him more wine. "I have met him twice," he said. "Once when there was a convergence of the border clans a few years ago and another time when I was traveling to Wolfe's Lair. Both times, the man hardly said more than two words to me."

Audric swallowed the food in his mouth. "That may change now that ye have another outpost on his lands."

"I have two. Kale Water and now Monteviot. Troy is in command of Kale Water and he might know more about him than I do."

Seated down the table from his father between James and Patrick, Troy was heavily into his meal. When he heard his name, and his father's statement, he simply shook his head.

"He keeps to himself," he said. "His home of Sibbald's Hold is barely five miles from Kale, but I have seen the man about as much as you have. He does not venture from Sibbald's and he has very few men. I heard tale that he is not welcome within Clan Kerr, so I suppose that explains why he keeps to himself."

He was looking at Audric, expecting that the man would elaborate if he knew anything. The priest saw the expression and also noticed that William was looking at him as well. He could see that they were anticipating that he should add something more to the conversation. Audric cleared his throat and shoved bread into his mouth.

"I can only tell ye what I've heard," he said. "Jedburgh is in Kerr lands and they are great patrons of the church. Ralph Kerr is The Kerr, the clan chief, and a great man he is. Keith is his cousin, and I've heard tale that Ralph banished Keith because he stole the man's woman. That is all I can tell ye other than Red Keith is called that for his temper, not for the color of his hair. The man may keep tae himself, but he is nothin' tae be trifled with. I have a feelin' ye'll soon find that out."

Troy glanced at his father, but William didn't seem too concerned about it. Without much more to say on the matter, Troy returned to his food. Audric did the same, hoping his interrogation was over for the moment. Still, there was information he wanted, and he waded carefully into that part of the conversation.

"Whether or not Red Keith actually shows his face, it 'tis the truth that ye know how tae deal with Scots," he said to William. "But if Keith wants his holdin' back, will ye give it tae him? These are his lands, after all."

William took a long drink of his wine as he pondered his answer. "Troy says that the man has very few men," he said. "That is why *reivers* were able to take over Monteviot in the first place. Therefore, in answer to your question, I will not give it back to him, not unless he can prove to me that he can keep it out of the hands of the outlaws."

Audric thought that might be the answer. In truth, it made sense because, clearly, Keith Kerr was unable to police his own property. Still, another de Wolfe holding in Kerr lands would not go over well with the bulk of the clan. That could be trouble. As he pondered that possibility, Troy spoke to his father.

"I brought almost five hundred men from Kale," he said. "I can leave two hundred of them here if you will leave another one hundred. That should be enough manpower for whoever you put in command."

William was looking at his wine cup. "I thought to put you in command."

Troy stopped chewing. "Me?" he said. Then, he shook his head. "You need me at Kale. The clans are going to be up in arms over the capture of Monteviot and you will need me at Kale to support Wolfe's Lair. But you can put me in command of the Lair, Papa. You probably should."

William didn't say anything for a moment. "That is your brother's post," he said quietly.

Troy's features tensed. "And Scott has not been at the Lair in over two years," he said. There was no patience in his tone. "He is off to the south with Edward somewhere."

"Even so, it still belongs to him."

"When are you going to realize that he is not coming back?"

It was an extremely sore subject with both William and Troy. On that terrible April day two years ago when both Scott and Troy had lost their wives and younger children, each men had handled the grief very differently. Scott had run off and left everything behind, family included, leaving Troy to soldier on and endure grief no man should have to endure. Scott's reaction was to shut down while Troy's had been to live the agony every day and resent his brother for being too cowardly to face it.

Now, they were on that terrible subject and the men around the table, including Paris, quieted their conversation when the forbidden topic came up. As the father of the women who had drowned, and the grandfather of the children that were lost, Paris was especially sensitive to this manner of conversation. He knew how volatile it could be.

"He will be back," William said calmly. "He is simply dealing with his grief differently than you."

"He ran like a weakling."

"You will not say such things about your brother, Troy."

Troy slammed his cup on the table, splashing wine onto James. "Are we going to bring up this subject again?" he snarled. "By all means, let us do that. Wolfe's Lair was Scott's outpost because he is the eldest. By ten bloody minutes, he is your eldest son. Wake up, Papa; Scott has run off. He does not want anything more to do with you or me or the Lair, and now you have a massive outpost that is without a de Wolfe as a commander because you feel that Scott is going to come walking back into our lives someday. I am telling you that he is not, and you let that massive outpost sit there with Kieran to command it while you stick me at a smaller outpost as if it is a consolation in prize for your second-born son. As if I am not a good enough commander to helm the Lair. Oh, hell... do what you want. I am finished speaking to you about this. I am sick of the favoritism you show Scott, as if the rest of us do not matter."

With that, he shoved away from the table, storming out of the hall, leaving the table sitting in awkward silence. Seated beside his father,

Patrick stood up and put a hand on William's shoulder.

"I will go and speak to him," he said quietly. "I can calm him."

William shook his head. "Let him go," he said. "We have had this conversation too many times. He is correct. He does not understand."

Patrick was gazing down at his father. After a moment, he sighed heavily. "Nor do I, Papa," he said. "There is no reason why he should not have command of the Lair. He is more capable than any of us when it comes to command."

William looked up at his son with pain in his eye. "And I have not given Troy all of my confidence?"

Patrick shook his head. "Not when it comes to that."

He moved away from the table, following Troy's path from the hall. As William watched his biggest son head out, James, too, stood up and followed Patrick. Both of them heading out to comfort Troy. William turned to look at Paris, across the table from him.

"Well?" he asked. "Do you think that, too?"

Paris was William's oldest and dearest friend. They had seen so much in life together, the bonds of which were stronger than blood. Paris was careful in his reply, knowing that whatever he said, William would take to heart.

"I think you spend so much time praying for Scott's return that you neglect the sons that have not left you," he said quietly. "I have told you this, William. Scott has made his choice; he has chosen to leave and begin his life again elsewhere. Although I do not blame you for hoping he will return someday, you must not let yourself be consumed by it. It is Scott's ghost that stands between you and Troy and the rest of your sons, and you are very clear about that. It is painful for Troy to accept."

William didn't want to hear the truth but, in hindsight, he knew Paris was correct. He spent a good deal of time anticipating Scott's return, his prodigal son, and that included having a temporary commander at Wolfe's Lair. Kieran was his second in command at Castle Questing but ever since Scott's departure, Kieran had been in command of Wolfe's Lair. Kieran was there because William couldn't bear to give the command to another because, in his mind, that would be admitting that Scott was never to return. Therefore, there was truth to what Paris and Patrick and Troy had said – William was holding the Lair for Scott's return. Perhaps it *was* time for him to accept that Scott wasn't coming back.

But he couldn't give up on a father's hope.

"Let us get past the settlement of Monteviot and then I will reconsider the situation with the Lair," William said reluctantly. "The truth is that I do want Troy here because he is the best man for the job, especially if Clan Kerr is unhappy with the fact that we are now in possession of this property. Troy has a relationship with the clan in that they know him and he knows them; if anyone can negotiate a truce, it is Troy."

Paris lifted his eyebrows at him. "Then mayhap you should tell him that, William. Let the man know you appreciate him."

William nodded faintly, feeling very badly that his own turmoil with Scott's grief was clouding his relationship with Troy. "Of course I appreciate him," he said quietly. "I draw my strength from him. Had he left as well, I am not sure I could have dealt with the pain."

Paris looked to his right, seeing his own sons sitting there. They weren't paying attention to the conversation with the older knight, or even Troy's outburst. Hector and Apollo were in conversation with Kevin and Tobias, sitting across the table from them. They were laughing about something, as they often did. Further down the table were Kieran and Michael, old knights and the best of friends, lost to their own conversation while Case and Corbin, Michael's two younger sons, were arm wrestling at the end of the table while some of the soldiers took bets.

Paris loved moments like this. He found such satisfaction in seeing his friends with sons of their own, all strong and intelligent young men, the future generation. There was a great deal of pride there. There were other sons, of course – Alec Hage had remained at Berwick with Adonis, Paris' youngest son, while Patrick and Kevin heeded the call to battle. William had two younger sons, Thomas and Edward, and Kieran had his youngest son, Nathaniel, who was fostering at Northwood and hadn't come on the battle march. So many young men, all of them ready and willing to continue the fight of their forefathers.

But there was one missing and it was a hole that all of them felt.

Paris understood William's lament over Scott. Paris lamented the man's loss, too, but he knew as William did that all men grieve in their own way. They could only hope that Scott would come to his senses at some point and return to the fold. Even with all of the young men, arm wrestling or laughing or eating, it was clear that someone was missing.

And Paris knew that no one felt that loss more than Troy.

Before he could reply to William, however, there was shouting down at the end of the table. Evidently bored with the arm wrestling, Case and Corbin had confiscated the mandolin from the soldier who had been wandering around, singing songs. Case managed to acquire the instrument but Apollo saw it and made a grab for it, yanking it from Case's grip. When Case tried to take it back, the older and bigger knight shoved him back by the chest.

"Easy, lad," Apollo said. He was very much like his father, suave and rather full of himself. With his bright red hair and stunning blue eyes, he was quite handsome. He was also an excellent performer. He began to strum the mandolin for all to hear. "Let me give the men some decent entertainment, de Bocage."

Case was outraged. "I can entertain better than you!"

Apollo grinned slyly. "You cannot carry a tune," he said. "Let me show you how it is done."

As Case scowled, grossly offended, Apollo played a few chords and began to sing.

There once was a lady fair;
With silver bells in her hair.
I knew her to have,
A luscious kiss... it drove me mad!

But she denied me… and I was so terribly sad.

He was singing quite dramatically and, at this point, the soldiers around them were listening and cheering him on. They all knew the song and when the chorus came around, they all began to sing at the top of their lungs.

Lily, my girl,
Your flower, I will unfurl
With my cock and a bit of good luck!
Your kiss divine;
I'll make you mine,
And keep you a-bed for a fuck!

It was a bawdy song, one that had the half-drunk men laughing and cheering. When Apollo started the second verse, which was as lewd as the first, half the room was singing along with him. Paris grinned at his son, who reminded him so much of himself. Apollo was never shy about anything and the men loved him for it.

As Paris turned around to collect his cup, he caught William's expression. The man was staring into the dregs of his cup as if his mind were a thousand miles away and Paris' good mood faded. It was hard to show joy when William was so worried about Scott and Troy. It was a terrible burden for a father. It was true that Paris had lost two daughters when Scott and Troy lost their wives, but somehow with their deaths, he was able to reconcile them. They were with God and they were at peace. But with William… one son was lost and the other in turmoil.

There was no peace for his sons.

"Go talk to him, William," Paris said softly. "Atty and James can only comfort him so far. He needs to hear from you."

William glanced up at him. "And tell him what?"

"Tell him that once things are settled here, you will be giving him command of the Lair. It is time."

William gazed at Paris for a moment before simply nodding his head. But there was huge and heavy sorrow in that gesture, something that stabbed at Paris' heart. There was such finality to it. Without another word, William set his cup aside and stood up, leaving the table and heading from the hall to find his sons. Paris watched him go, his gaze inevitably falling on Audric, who was still sitting at the end of the table, shoving food into his mouth.

But as Paris looked at the priest, his eyes narrowed. It occurred to him that the priest had heard everything that was said, including the discord between William and his sons. When Audric happened to look up from his food and make eye contact with Paris, the older knight took on a menacing expression.

"You heard none of that conversation," he hissed. "Do you understand me?"

Audric quickly took on a look of both surprise and fear. "Hear what, m'lord?" he asked. "I heard nothin'."

Paris scooted down the bench, grabbing the priest by the shoulder. It was a biting grip. "And that is the story you will adhere to," he rumbled. "If I hear that you have been spreading rumors about unrest in the House of de Wolfe, I will cut out your tongue."

Audric was trying not to cower. "I told ye, I dinna hear anythin'."

Paris' eyes narrowed dramatically. "Swear it?"

"I do."

Paris released the man but he didn't take his eyes off him. Audric spent the rest of the evening being glared at in a fashion that made him want to run from the hall screaming. It was only pure hunger that made him remain and finish his meal but, after that, he was fairly certain he would brave the dark night simply to make it home to avoid the big knight's poison stare.

Truth be told, he'd lied. He had, indeed, heard the entire conversation and that told him a great deal about what was happening in the House of de Wolfe, the exact information he'd been hoping to glean. It may be risking his life to repeat it, but his superiors would hear about it.

A weakened House of de Wolfe might very well mean strength for the clan who wanted their property back.

CB

OUT IN THE darkened baily of Monteviot, William could see his sons lingering near the main gate.

They weren't hard to miss; three of the biggest men in the whole of England, and probably Scotland, too. Troy with his impossibly broad shoulders, Patrick with his sheer height and breadth, and James for his soaring height as well. It wasn't as if William was a short man; he was a few inches over six feet, but his sons had either met that height or, in the cases of Patrick and James, had exceeded it. His boys had never been difficult to pick out in a crowd.

His sons. Men he loved deeply, each for their own special gifts. William felt so guilty that he'd let his longing for Scott overshadow his relationship with them, mostly Troy. Paris had been right; they'd all been right. William knew that but he didn't know how to overcome it. For the sake of his relationship with his remaining sons, however, he knew that he had to.

As William approached the group, James caught sight of him. Tall, blond, gentle James. Held up a hand to his father in greeting but in the same movement, told his brothers that their father was on the approach because they all turned to look at him. William smiled weakly as he came into the group.

"I came to tell you that Adonis has the men worked up into a frenzy with his songs," he said to break the ice. "James, he will need you. No one can sing like you can."

James grinned at his father. "It does not work well when I sing with Apollo," he said. "He tries to shout over me and eventually we come to blows."

William began to laugh. "Not always," he said. "I have heard the two of you do excellent duets."

James swished a hand at him, a dismissive gesture. "Only when he feels like sharing the attention," he said. "More often than not, Apollo wants to have all of the attention. I will not fight him for it."

It was very true. William had to concede the point. "He is too much like his father," he said. "You know how your Uncle Paris can be. If all eyes are not upon him, then he is not happy."

"Then it must have made for an interesting experience working side by side with him since you were both young," Patrick said. "It is a wonder you did not beat him to a bloody pulp at times."

William lifted his eyebrows. "Who is to say that I did not?" he said. Then, he shrugged his big shoulders. "But beneath all of that pomp and bluster, Paris is the best man I know. He would do anything for those he loves and he is wise beyond measure. Do not tell him I said that."

The men shook their head. "Never," Patrick said. Then, he sobered, glancing at his brothers as he spoke. "Talk of Uncle Paris aside, Papa, we were just discussing our departure from Monteviot. I will be returning to Berwick on the morrow and James must return to Wark. Have you decided what you are going to do about the staffing at Monteviot?"

William nodded, looking straight at Troy. "There is no one I would trust more than Troy to man the tower at the moment," he said. "Troy, the reason I asked you to remain here for a time is not to punish you, lad. It is because I do not believe there is anyone more capable. You know this area and you know the Kerr. If anyone can keep peace here, it is you."

Troy was looking at his father with a rather guarded gaze. He sighed heavily. "If that is your wish, I will remain. But what about Kale?"

William cocked his head thoughtfully. "Your knights are in charge of Kale at the moment," he said. "Brodie de Reyne and Cassius de Shera have the command and I am sure they are doing an excellent job. They will be able to manage things until you return."

Troy had calmed after his outburst in the hall, feeling guilty that he'd yelled at his father but still feeling snubbed in the face of his brother's absence. Still, he knew his father was only doing as he felt best. Troy knew his father didn't think him incapable of commanding the Lair; it was simply that he held out hope Scott would return. Aye, Troy understood that even though it didn't make the situation any more bearable. He still felt overlooked and underappreciated.

"If we are to have trouble with the Kerr at Monteviot, then I want Brodie and Cassius here with me," he said. "Send Apollo or Tobias to command Kale until we are sure the Kerr will not try to dig us out."

William nodded, thinking on the shifting of knights to keep his holdings protected. "If that is your wish, then send for them," he said. "I will go speak with Tobias right now. I am not sure Patrick wants to part with Apollo."

Patrick, brought into the conversation, lifted his big shoulders. "I would prefer not to because we must remember that if the Kerr are unsettled, it may spread on the border. We may all end up defending our posts against angry clans."

William mulled over that thought. "It is a distinct possibility. Therefore, pulling Tobias from Northwood may be a smarter move. Uncle Paris has many knights who serve him there, so pulling one knight out of the group will not diminish his strength."

"Agreed," said Patrick.

William looked to James at that point. "And you?" he asked. "If the clans go to war along the border because of this, you are prepared to defend your post, are you not?"

James nodded. "I mostly deal with the Gordon and I have an excellent relationship with them," he said. "I do not expect any trouble, not even if the Kerr go to war."

Troy shook his head. "You are so amiable, no one would go to battle against you," he said. "You've charmed the Gordon to the point that they look at you as a brother. In fact, if the Kerr went to war against de Wolfe, I am certain the Gordon would protect you. We should all learn a lesson in diplomacy from you, James."

James smiled at his brother, reaching out to grasp the man affectionately on the shoulder. "That is because a man can gain his wants better with honey than with a blade," he said. "I am not fond of confrontation, as you well know. Sometimes you must give a little in order to receive, and as the new commander of Monteviot, you would do well to remember that."

Troy frowned. "There is nothing I can give other than my sword to a Scot's belly," he said. "But something just occurred to me."

"What?" James asked."

Troy looked around the bailey, torn up by the battle. "Rule Water Castle is called Wolfe's Lair, Kale Water Castle is called Wolfe's Den, Wark Castle is called Wolfe's Eye, and Atty's castle at Berwick is called Wolfe's Teeth. I wonder what name the Scots will give to Monteviot now that it belongs to the House of de Wolfe?"

William simply shook his head, a smile playing on his lips, as James answered. "Remember when our brother, Thomas, spoke of naming his future command the Wolfe's Arse?" he asked. "Mayhap this is the one. It is in the arse-end of Scotland, after all. Mayhap it is Monteviot who will shite upon the enemy as the Wolfe's Arse."

The four of them chuckled, but it was William who spoke. "Nay," he said. "This place is not the hindquarters of a beast. In fact, it will cement us deep into this border land, creating a trio of castles that will ward off any Scots' incursion. If it must be known as something, I'd prefer to call it the Wolfe's Shield. The last line of defense between England and the Scots."

It was appropriate. Monteviot Tower became Wolfe's Shield and as Troy looked around, he wasn't so opposed to remaining. It would be a volatile place until things settled down, and he was a knight. He needed to be where the action was. More and more, he was becoming resigned to his father stationing him there. Perhaps it wouldn't be so bad, after all.

"The Shield it is," he said quietly. "Papa, if you wish to discuss the organization of the outpost, then I am ready. I am assuming most everyone will be leaving, along with Atty, on the morrow?"

William nodded. "There is no longer any reason for the armies to remain and they are anxious to return, I am sure," he said. "However, you mentioned leaving two hundred men from Kale here and asked me to leave one hundred from Questing. I will be happy to do that. And you will call forth de Reyne and de Shera from Kale to come to Monteviot?"

"I shall."

"Then we can do no more. It will be crowded here, however. Do you have enough supplies?"

Troy shrugged. "I can take all you can send me. I shall have Brodie and Cassius bring provisions with them, but anything you can send me from Questing would be a blessing. You can also send me those men you promised to repair the tower. I would like to repair it as soon as possible."

It seemed there wasn't much more to say about the fortification of Monteviot, so James and Patrick excused themselves, returning to the hall so that William and Troy could iron out the smaller details. It was also a chance for them to mend any hurt feelings from their earlier tussle. Once James and Patrick were out of earshot, William spoke to Troy.

"When Monteviot is settled, I will send Edward here," he said, speaking of his twenty-two-year-old son, his third youngest child in fact, who served at Wolfe's Lair along with Kieran. When Kieran brought the army to Monteviot, he'd left Edward in command of the mighty Lair. "Edward has learned a great deal serving with Kieran and I believe he will be ready for command."

Troy agreed; Edward was level-headed and steady, like the rest of them, in spite of his youth. "It will be a good first command for him," he said. "I have every confidence that he will do well here."

William nodded; he was looking at his feet as if considering other issues, other things. "When Edward comes to Monteviot, I will pull Kieran out of Wolfe's Lair," he said after a moment. "I find that I need him with me at Questing. I am getting old, Troy. I do not wish to bear the burden of my empire alone and Kieran is a great help to me."

Troy looked at him. "That will leave the Lair without a command-er."

William shook his head, lifting it to look at him. "It will not," he said softly. "I will put you in command of it."

Troy stared at him a moment; there was disbelief and wariness in his eyes. "What about Scott?" he asked. "We just had this discussion. You said that it is Scott's command."

William's features washed with sadness. "You are correct," he said. "He has been gone these two years. Mayhap, he is never coming back. I should not wait for him so. He has made his choice but I suppose I simply do not wish to acknowledge it and removing him as commander of the Lair... in doing so, I am admitting my son is never coming home. That is the same as him being dead, Troy. I do not wish for your brother to be dead."

Troy felt his father's agony like a stab to the gut. Now, he felt so terribly guilty for being angry about what he perceived as a slight against him. Deep down, he supposed he always knew that his father loved him as equally as his brother, but the past two years had seen tumult for them all. They had all lived through so much emotion, making it difficult to remain steady over such matters. He sighed heavily.

"I am sorry I became angry with you, Papa," he said. "I do not want Scott to be dead, either. He is my brother, the person I know best in this world. When he left, I lost a part of me. I had lost my wife; I did not need to lose my brother, too."

William put a hand on his arm. "I know," he murmured. "It has been so very hard on you. Scott ran to escape and you remained to take the brunt of it. I cannot tell you how much I admire your strength in all things, Troy. You are stronger than I could ever be in such matters."

Troy looked at his father, the man he loved most. He had been the most patient, loving, and gracious father a man could have ever hoped for and Troy considered himself extremely blessed. His anger towards William dissolved away until all that was left were the remnants of guilt for having become so angry in the first place.

"I am not strong," he said. "I simply did what needed to be done. Running from grief does not make it go away."

William shook his head. "It does not, but it was easier for Scott to do what he did. You must not judge him for it. We all do what we need in order to survive, and he did what he needed to do. I still believe he will return. I cannot stomach the alternative."

Troy wasn't going to contradict him. Whether or not he believed that his brother would return someday was inconsequential; it was what his father believed that mattered. He wouldn't destroy the man's hope. He put his arm around his father's neck and pulled him close.

"For your sake, I hope he does," he whispered, giving him a hug. "And forgive me for being angry about it, but I am angry with him for leaving. I have been ever since that terrible day, but that is my cross to bear."

William understood. He cupped his son's face and kissed his cheek before releasing him. "Then I pray you find peace with it someday," he said. "Scott did not leave because he did not love you, Troy. His leaving had nothing to do with you."

They hadn't spoken so openly and calmly about the subject in a very long time and Troy simply shrugged. "He left me behind to bear this burden of grief alone," he said. "Mayhap, he did not think on it that way, but that was the end result. He left me alone."

William suspected that was what Troy felt. When a twin departed, leaving the other twin, it was literally as if the man had lost half of himself. It had always been Scott and Troy, since birth, the two of them always together as if they were shadows of one another. The loss of one's shadow was a difficult thing to reconcile. He patted his son on the cheek.

"You are not alone, lad," he assured him. "You are never alone. You have me and Atty and James and Edward and Thomas. You even have your mother. How you think you could be alone with that brood, I will never know."

There was a gleam of mirth in his eye as he spoke and Troy smiled weakly. "It does become crowded at times," he admitted.

William moved softly and took him by the arm, pulling him back towards the hall. "That is true, but I would not have it any other way," he said. "Now, come inside and finish your meal. Enjoy this night before everyone leaves and you really are alone. You deserve this night, Troy. It belongs to you."

Troy let his father drag him back into the hall without much resistance. Truth be told, he was looking forward to more of that bitter wine and, perhaps, losing himself in a few hours of much-needed sleep. But for tonight, Monteviot was secure and, for a few brief and blissful hours, Troy would find peace. Peace was essential because one never knew what the morrow would bring.

That rang doubly true at Monteviot Tower, in the heart of enemy territory.

CHAPTER FOUR

I T WAS A cold, blustery dawn when they set out from Sibbald's Hold, heading southwest to the isolated outpost known as Monteviot.

Autumn was descending with full force, for the cold winds were blowing and the leaves on the trees were scattering. Soon, the weather would give way to the snows of winter that would cover the mountains and vales through March. Winters could be long this far north, and even as the party from Sibbald's rode south, following the rocky vale that would lead them to the border lands where they would head due east to Monteviot, they could see that the farmers were already up and tending to their fields and herds.

They, too, felt the change in seasons and it was imperative to make preparations for the coming winter. Late crops of barley and oats were in the fields, the majority of the fields having been harvested in August. But there would be a late harvest on some of them, as late as November or early December, or before the snow came in earnest.

Keith may have had a small fortress on the moors, but he was smart about what that fortress produced to keep them fed. A small village was established around Sibbald's and there were also many farms in the surrounding area that Keith supported. He would pay for seed and the farmers would grow the crops, giving Keith about three-quarters of the yield. There were also farmers who raised the shaggy cows so prevalent to the area for meat and milk, and more sheep herders than they could count. The Lowlands of Scotland were rich, agriculturally, and Keith benefitted from that. It had made him rather wealthy, or at least wealthy enough to sustain what he had.

Fortunately, Rhoswyn had followed in her father's footsteps with her financial savvy. She understood what it took to keep men fed and she was often in on business decisions but, beyond that, she knew nothing more about running a house or hold. Sibbald's had a host of female servants that knew how to run a fortress, from stuffing mattresses to washing clothing to cooking sides of sheep. Rhoswyn had never bothered with such things. Her focus had been on the things her father had taught her.

Things regarding men and war. Even now, she was thinking ahead to the confrontation with de Wolfe. Astride her big black beast of a horse, Rhoswyn wore what she usually wore to battle, and she had seen a few. This felt like a battle. She had seen skirmishes with her father; not many, but enough that she had fought against men and she had killed against them, too. It had never been easy for her to kill, but there had been times when it had been necessary. She certainly wasn't afraid to lift a dagger.

While her kinsmen wore the long tunics and braies, heavy cloaks against the cold wind, Rhoswyn wore leather hose because they were warmer and softer than the woolen braies. They also provided some protection against a sharp blade. Over that, she wore a heavy tunic of yellow – the fighting tunic, the men called it – dyed with expensive saffron her father had purchased. Still, over that, she wore a padded tunic and then a mail coat that her father, long ago, had stolen off of a dead Sassenach soldier during one of the battles at the border.

Along with that mail coat came a beautiful weapon and a helm, all of which now belonged to Rhoswyn. The helm had a metal strip down the center of it to protect her nose and, with her hair braided and shoved up into the helm, it was difficult to see that she was a woman. In fact, no one would know unless they heard her speak or got a close look at her. Considering she was about to challenge de Wolfe's best warrior, she didn't want them to know a woman was part of the challenge until it was too late.

Until their honor was at stake.

And she was eager for that moment. Rhoswyn could see her father riding at the head of the group, astride a horse that was starting to grow its winter coat. She knew he was uncomfortable, venturing out of Sibbald's as he was, because Keith usually stayed to himself unless forced to ride out. Their clan had a few run-ins with a smaller branch of Clan Elliot over the years, and Keith had risen to the call, but he didn't like to do it. He liked to stay to Sibbald, drinking his wine or playing games with his men. In spite of Keith's temper, and it could be fierce, he really did prefer to live in peace. That meant the trip to Monteviot was a duty, not a want.

Rhoswyn understood that.

Looking around, she could see her father's men riding with them. There were about fifty of them, men who had been with Keith or with Keith's father. Some of them were quite old, but they were fearsome and trusted. They remembered the old days when the Kerr was in nearly every battle on this section of the border, and there were some who liked to relive those days. She could feel their determination, their hatred against the Sassenach invasion. Because of it, Rhoswyn was glad she had convinced her father to confront de Wolfe. Otherwise, he could have very well lost the respect of his men.

To a Scotsman, that would have been a fate worse than death.

In silence, they rode as the horizon in the east turned shades of pink and purple, brightening gradually to reveal a sky with darkened clouds off towards the north. A storm was approaching but it didn't deter their path. They would continue on to Monteviot which, at this pace, they would see in a couple of hours.

The anticipation was building.

There was a creek in the center of the vale they were traveling in, with muddied ground and thick, green grass that the horses slogged through. The hills were gentle but rather tall; still, they could be crossed with some effort. It wasn't difficult. The morning progressed and the party from Sibbald passed over a series of hills and into another vale. This vale, however, dumped out into the south end of the valley that contained Monteviot and they weren't halfway across the vale when they began to smell smoke.

But not just any smoke; it was putrid and ghastly, hanging heavily on the land. The grass and the hills were full of it. Rhoswyn spurred her horse up next to her father.

"What is that terrible smell?" she asked, pinching her nose.

Keith's expression didn't register the trepidation he was now feeling. "That's the smell of burned flesh," he said quietly. "They must have burned the bodies of the dead."

Rhoswyn looked at her father in horror. "Ye know this for certain?"

Keith nodded slowly; there wasn't a doubt on his face. As Rhoswyn tried to reconcile herself to the smell of burning bodies and the horror it provoked, her uncle and cousins rode forward to join in the conversation.

"Och," Fergus growled. "I dunna like this already. If they're burnin' men, then they could do anything. Mayhap we'd better think about this for a moment, Keith. We dunna want tae go chargin' in if the Sassenach are burnin' men."

Keith reined his horse to a halt, turning to look at his brother. Fergus didn't like any manner of confrontation, a trait that some men would call cowardly. But the truth was that Fergus simply didn't have the fire in him that most Scotsmen did. Therefore, a comment like that was to be expected from him. It was his fear of conflict talking.

"Then what are ye thinkin' of, Fergus?" he asked his brother. "I'll not go back. Ye know I willna."

Fergus shook his head, shaggy and red. "Nay; not go back," he said. "But were ye proposin' that we simply ride intae their midst?"

"Do ye have a better idea?"

Fergus nodded. "I do," he said, turning to point at the men behind them who had now come to a halt. "Dunna show him yer numbers. Ye take Rhoswyn with ye since she's determined tae fight, but leave the rest of us on the hill. Let them look tae the hill, see yer men, and wonder if there are a thousand more they canna see."

It was actually good advice. Keith hadn't thought much of showing all of the men he had to the English; he was simply going to confront them and issue the challenge. Perhaps not the most cunning tactic, but an honest one. But now that they were smelling burned man-flesh, he was rethinking his approach. Fergus was right; if they were burning men, then perhaps they wouldn't think twice about burning him and his men. And his daughter. He'd never heard of brutal de Wolfe tactics but there was always a first time.

Perhaps it was better to be cautious.

"As ye say," he said after a moment. "Take the men with ye. Rhosie and I will see tae the English."

"And issue the challenge?"

"That's why we've come."

Fergus gazed at him a moment. "Are ye sure that's what ye want tae do?" he asked quietly. "I never agreed with this plan from the start, Keith. Rhosie is an excellent warrior, but…"

"She's the best."

"She is, but she's a woman. In combat with an English knight? She'll be lucky if she survives."

"She'll survive. Dunna doubt her."

Fergus sighed heavily. "But if this plan doesna work, ye'll be sacrificin' yer daughter."

Fergus' cautious attitude was starting to wear on Keith; he didn't have time for it. "And if I do nothin' at all, I'll be sacrificin' me honor," he hissed. "We discussed this last night. I have no army I can turn tae, at least not one that will answer the call against de Wolfe. What we do, we must depend on ourselves for it, and if we can convince de Wolfe tae pledge one knight in a battle where the victor sets the terms, then I have tae do it."

"Ye feel so strongly about it?"

"I do."

There was nothing more Fergus could say. When he'd first heard of the plan last night, he'd tried to talk his brother out of such a thing but Keith wouldn't be swayed, convinced that Rhoswyn's plan of wagering the entire outcome of Monteviot on one challenge was the chance they needed to take. That his brother would take the advice of his daughter over anyone else was something that greatly disturbed Fergus, but he couldn't fight against it. His attitude was one of extreme caution, whereas Keith didn't share that same perspective. They'd never seen eye to eye on conflict or confrontation. But Fergus could have never imagined that his brother saw a greater hope in Rhoswyn's victory, the hope of a marriage and alliance with de Wolfe. Perhaps if Fergus had known, then he might have understood Keith's resolve.

But he wouldn't have agreed with him.

Still, the fact remained that he knew nothing. No one did. They all thought Keith had gone mad, but it could not be helped. So Fergus simply shook his head and turned away, motioning for the men to follow him to the crest of the hill that overlooked Monteviot. He thought his brother was a bleeding idiot, but that could not be helped.

Keith was determined.

As Fergus and the men began to trudge up the rocky hill overlooking the vale of Monteviot, Keith watched his brother for a moment before turning to his daughter astride her big, black horse. She looked like a warrior, in fact; long-legged, wearing mail that concealed her womanly figure, she did, indeed, look like a warrior and, for a moment, Keith saw the son he'd always wanted.

It was just the flash of a vision, one that quickly faded. Then he felt guilty for it. *But, no…* he thought. It was his daughter he was preparing to pit against an English knight of de Wolfe's choosing, or so he hoped. If de Wolfe wouldn't let the outcome of Monteviot be decided in one-on-one combat, then there was nothing more Keith could do but leave his outpost in the hands of the English and his daughter would remain unmarried. There was no other alternative, so it was a moment like this that tested a man's true bravery.

Or… a woman's.

CB

"TROY!" PATRICK HISSED. "Scots approaching!"

The entire bailey was full of men preparing to depart, men spilling out of the gates and into the area outside of the walls as five separate armies were organizing to return home. The army from Berwick was spilling into the clearing outside of the gates and it was from the outside that Patrick had just come, running to find his brother, who was near the burned-out tower with his father and a few other men. But those hissed words from Patrick brought all conversation to a standstill.

"Scots?" Troy repeated; he was a little hungover from all of the wine he'd had the night before, now struggling to overcome both a headache and a muddled mind. "Damnation, then get your army back inside and close the gates!"

Patrick nodded his head. "I have already given the command," he said. "Most of them are outside the gates, including the wagons, so we are moving as fast as we can. Fortunately, there are only two Scots that I can see."

Troy abruptly turned for the gates. "You know as well as I do that it is the ones you *cannot* see that you must worry about."

"Which is why I am moving them back inside."

Patrick took off after his brother then, as did William, Paris, Kieran, Michael, and a very hungover Apollo. All of them moving swiftly for the gates where the Berwick men were starting to shuffle around nervously, trying to move back into the bailey of Monteviot. The knights pushed through the ranks to get a clear line of sight on the incoming Scots.

A day that had started off relatively quiet was quickly becoming wrought with apprehension as two Scots were sighted. The knights stood in front of the crowd of soldiers at the gate, watching the approach of the Scots. But not everyone was looking at the pair;

William, too, felt that there were probably more than just the two Scots, so he sent men to the walls to watch for more clansmen. Perhaps this was a ruse, perhaps not, but the closer the pair approached, the more nervous the English became.

Enemies in an enemy land.

As activity went on behind him with his father and the other knights moving men about, Troy watched the pair come closer and it occurred to him that he wasn't wearing most of his protection. He hadn't put it on yet because he'd spent the morning with his father in the hall and then assessing the burned-out tower. He wasn't expecting to go into combat. But it further occurred to him that his father wasn't wearing any protection, either. William was planning on departing later that morning for the five-hour trip back to Questing and, like Troy, simply hadn't fully dressed. Troy turned to his father, standing a few feet away and watching the men populate on the walls.

"Papa, mayhap you should return to the hall and put on your protection," he said quietly. "If the Scots are planning an attack, I do not want you to be caught out here without any protection."

William looked at him. "The same could be said for you," he said. "You are as vulnerable as I."

"Aye, but the difference is that my name is not William de Wolfe," Troy pointed out. "We have discussed this time and time again. You would make a national hero out of the Scot who managed to kill you, not to mention the fact that Mother would murder me with her bare hands if I allowed anything to happen to you." He turned slightly, putting a hand on his father and trying to force him back into the fortress. "Please, Papa, go back inside."

William's attention had turned from the wall to the Scots, who were now quite close. "You shame me, lad," he muttered. "Do not act as if I cannot take care of myself."

"That is not my intent. I simply do not want you to get hurt."

William didn't say another word. He knew that, but he was tired of his sons trying to protect him all of the time as if he were an old man who needed protecting. It was bad enough on the day they'd burned out Monteviot's tower, and now they sought to protect him from a pair of Scots riders. He loved his sons, but they acted like old women sometimes.

As Troy watched, his father stepped forward, away from him, and held out a hand to the Scots who were, by now, about fifteen feet away. One was dressed like a soldier while the other one was simply clad in woolens and braies.

"Stop," William said forcefully. "Announce yourselves."

The man in the woolens and braies answered. "I will be askin' ye the same thing, Sassenach," he said. "Ye're in me land. What are ye doin' here?"

William studied the man; he had an excellent memory and it seemed to him as if he'd seen the man before. With the light of the rising sun coming over the hills, he had a fairly good view of the man with the thick auburn hair and bushy red beard. *Ye're in me land.* It suddenly occurred to William where he'd seen the man before.

"You are Keith Kerr," he finally said.

Spurred by the fact that the English knight recognized him, Keith peered closer, his features lined with confusion. But only momentarily; realization dawned. It was the eye patch that gave it away. Everyone knew there was only one English warrior on the border with an eye patch like that.

"De Wolfe," he finally hissed. "I'd heard tale it was ye who confiscated Monteviot but I had tae see it with me own eyes."

In his periphery, William could see that Troy was now standing beside him but he didn't look at his son. He was focused on the elusive Red Keith Kerr. In truth, he wasn't entirely surprised to see the man. They were on his lands, after all, and he'd dutifully come to see why the English had landed. He wondered if Keith would be surprised, in turn, to hear the truth.

"Then word traveled to you quickly," William said. "We have only been here a few days."

Keith's gaze lingered on William before moving to Troy. Then, he looked at all of the Englishmen behind him, knights of the highest caliber, and more English soldiers than Keith had seen in a very long time, all cramming back into the bailey of Monteviot. It occurred to him that he'd been right; there was no way he could have summoned enough men to take back Monteviot, not even had he sent to his cousin. He hadn't expected a force of this size. He gestured to the hundreds of men behind William.

"Why did ye bring so many men?" he asked. "Did ye expect so much resistance from a small outpost?"

William turned to look at all of the men behind him before answering. "I had to clear out the *reivers* who had been using Monteviot as a base to launch raids into my lands," he said frankly. "Surely this is no surprise to you. You had to know that Monteviot was infested by *reivers*."

Keith was feeling defensive as William pointed out something he already knew, very well. There was a message in his mild rebuke – *you have failed to police your own lands and now I must do it for you!*

"What men do on me lands is me own business," Keith said. "And who says they were *reivers*?"

William could feel a stab of impatience; so the man was going to deny such a thing? "Because they have been raiding my lands and my men followed them back to Monteviot," he said. "It is true that whatever happens on your land is your own business, but when the men from Monteviot ride into my lands and steal from my people, it becomes *my* business. Two weeks ago, they rode deep into England and burned a small village, killing a priest and burning out a church. You know as well as I do that I could not remain idle after that. Since you were allowing outlaws to live on your lands and did not do anything about it, I had to."

Keith knew that all of this was true – every last word of it. But the way de Wolfe put it, it made it sound like Keith was a weakling and a fool, incapable of monitoring his own lands. While it was true he didn't have enough men to supervise his lands, he was far from being a weakling. If nothing else, he was an opportunist, and what he saw before him with de Wolfe was an opportunity like none other. De Wolfe had come and now Keith wanted something. He dismounted his horse, taking several steps in William's direction.

"So ye've appointed yerself judge and jury for not only yer lands, but mine," he said. "I dunna fault ye for protectin' yer people, but now ye're in *my* lands. What do ye intend tae do with Monteviot now that ye've purged her of the men ye call outlaws?"

Oddly enough, it almost sounded like a civil question, as if Keith was genuinely curious and not simply outraged that the English had come. William hoped that meant they could keep the rest of the conversation polite, but considering what he was about to say, he doubted it.

"It belongs to me now," he said. "I will not have it becoming a haven for *reivers* again."

"I did not give ye permission tae stay."

"That is of no consequence. Why did you let the outlaws settle here in the first place?"

The truth behind that was, of course, that Keith couldn't have kept them out if he'd wanted to. But he wouldn't admit it. Instead, he grinned, a most unnerving gesture.

"No one has proven tae me that they were *reivers*," he said. "Bring forth these men so that I may see them."

"I cannot."

"Because they're dead?"

"Most of them. Those that did not die in the siege ran off. I did not take them prisoner."

Keith sniffed the air. "Did ye burn them, de Wolfe?"

William shook his head. "The tower burned, but what you smell is a funeral pyre. We had a priest come from Jedburgh to bless the dead."

Keith's eyebrows lifted; it was difficult to know if it was a condescending expression or one of respect. "A pious Sassenach, are ye?"

William took it as a condescending one. His impatience was growing. "Is that why you came here today?" he asked. "To find out if I am pious? Somehow, I do not think that is why you are here. State your business, Kerr. I have work to do."

Keith's smile faded. So much for pleasantries with de Wolfe; the time had come for the purpose behind his visit and there was no use in stalling. Looking over his shoulder, Keith caught sight of the hill to the south, seeing the small figures of his brother and nephews and the majority of his men on the crest. It made the hill look rather crowded, which would work to his advantage. He pointed.

"See me men up there?" he asked before turning to face William. "That is only a small portion of them. There are a thousand of us behind that hill, waiting tae charge Monteviot, but I dunna believe ye want another battle so soon after havin' suffered through one. Yer men are tired and some are even injured. I dunna think ye want another battle, not now."

William and Troy could see the figures on the distant hill and, in truth, they had no reason to believe there weren't a thousand Scots behind the hill just as Keith said. The Scots rarely made their numbers known, instead choosing to travel – and fight – in stealth. As William considered that possibility in silence, Troy began silently cursing himself because the gates were still open and half of Patrick's army was standing outside of the walls. That made them very vulnerable should the Scots decide to come down from the hill and make a run at them.

But Troy didn't give a hint of what he was thinking. In his estimation, Red Keith Kerr had the advantage already and he didn't want to give the man any more ammunition. He had to get the army back in the fortress and the gates closed, or this could go badly for all of them. Now, it was his turn to take over the negotiations.

"What do you want, Kerr?" Troy asked in a tone that didn't hint at what he was thinking. "Be plain."

Keith's attention turned to the big, dark knight standing next to William. He could see the resemblance.

"And yer name, knight?" he asked.

Troy didn't hesitate. "I am Troy de Wolfe, commander of Kale Water Castle," he said. "Even if you do not know my face, you should know my name."

Keith's eyebrows lifted. "Kale Water Castle," he said, sounding surprised. "Ye're in Kerr lands, laddie."

"That may be, but it is a de Wolfe holding. And there is peace with the Kerr neighbors."

Keith's jaw ticked. Now, he realized that he not only had William in front of him, but William's son as well. Two de Wolfes; two powerful Sassenach border lords. Kale Water Castle was in Ralph's lands and it was Ralph who permitted the House of de Wolfe to maintain their castles there. Perhaps it was out of a greater fear of stirring a hornet's nest to try and remove them but, in any case, de Wolfe was there to stay.

But Keith wasn't so fearful. He could be quite courageous when he wanted to be, when something mattered. In truth, he didn't have as much to lose as Ralph did. But in this case, he clearly had what de Wolfe wanted. Or, at least, what de Wolfe wanted to keep secure. It was here where he would make his final stand.

"Ye say there is peace, yet ye come tae take me property," he said. "If ye want tae keep it, then ye'll have tae fight for it."

Troy suspected it would come to this but he, too, held his ground. "If you have come for a fight, then get on with it."

Keith looked at Troy, at William, and at the host of men standing behind him, men who were in various stages of dress. Most had returned to the bailey, but the gates were still open and some were still standing there, watching and waiting. Some had mail and protection on, but some didn't. It was clear they weren't prepared for a battle and Keith used that to his advantage.

"Look at yer men," he said, pointing. "And look at yerselves. Are ye ready for a fight? Or did I catch ye unaware?"

"We are ready for whatever you have in mind."

It was a confident answer, one that Keith believed implicitly. But *he* wasn't ready for what they thought he had in mind. He turned to look at his men on the crest behind them.

"If we can settle this without riskin' our men, would ye be willing?"

That wasn't an offer Troy had been expecting and he was momentarily confused. "What do you mean?" he asked.

Keith shrugged his shoulders, a casual gesture, as if he really wasn't concerned about the English giving him a fight. "I dunna believe ye want tae risk yer men against me thousand," he said. "Yer men have seen a big battle. I can see it in them; they're weary and they want tae go home. *I* want them tae go home. But I have brought a thousand Scots who have come to push ye off me land, so I can fight ye if I have tae. But I have a solution that is much easier and much cleaner than a big battle for this worthless piece of rock."

Troy wasn't sure what that could be. In fact, that kind of proposition didn't make much sense to him. He'd never heard of a Scotsman so willing to bargain peacefully rather than bring forth pikes and swords against the English. He looked at his father before answering.

"What solution?" he asked.

Keith took a step towards him, fixing him in the eye. "Me best warrior against yer best warrior," he said. "Only two men fight, not thousands, and the winner shall name the terms of surrender."

It was not an unheard of proposal, but Troy was frankly surprised. He looked at his father, who looked at him in return. Immediately, he could see that his father was inclined to agree with the proposal but Troy was still puzzled by it all. He glanced at Keith.

"Man against man?" he clarified.

Keith nodded shortly. "Warrior against warrior."

"And the winner names the terms?"

"Aye."

Troy cocked a dark eyebrow. "And when we name the terms, you swear to abide by them?"

The corners of Keith's mouth twitched. "Aye," he said. "As long as ye swear ye'll abide by the terms I set should me warrior win."

It seemed like a sound enough proposition. In fact, Troy was rather pleased by it; surely he could lick whatever warrior Kerr brought forth. In fact, this seemed like the easiest way out of this situation.

"A moment, please," he said to Keith. "Let me discuss this before we proceed."

Keith simply moved away, strolling back over to his horse and the other warrior, still mounted. Troy grasped his father by the arm and turned the man around, motioning to his brothers and the other knights in the same movement. The English came together in a big huddle as Keith stood back by his horses.

"He wants to pit his best warrior against our best warrior to decide the fate of Monteviot," Troy explained quickly to the host of curious faces gazing back at him. "Whoever wins will dictate the terms of surrender. I must say, I was not expecting that."

Neither were some of the others. At least, the younger knights weren't. They were looking at each other with some surprise as the older knights discussed the situation.

"If he is sincere, then that is the perfect solution," Paris whispered to William. "Pit Atty or Troy against his warrior. They can destroy anything on two legs."

"Do not forget about Kevin," Kieran pointed out. "Or even Tobias. We have many fine warriors here that could easily take on a Scotsman and win."

William held up a hand before this turned into a debate on who was the greatest warrior among them. "There is no question on that," he said. "And, truly, pitting one man against another will save many lives, quite possibly including my own sons. If this is what Keith truly wants, then I am inclined to agree. It would be much simpler and cleaner to have a one-on-one battle."

Michael, standing next to Kieran, shook his head. "S-Something is not right about this," he said in his deep, rumbling tone. The man rarely spoke because he had a stammer in his speech, but when he did speak, it was for a distinct purpose. "Why would he pledge s-such a thing if he has a thousand S-Scots waiting to fight us?"

William lifted his eyebrows. "That has occurred to me," he admitted. "It is possible he does not have the numbers he says he has but, then again, it is like a Scots not to reveal his numbers. We cannot assume that he is not telling the truth and if we can get our armies home with no loss of life, I am willing to take that chance."

It made sense and the group was of the same mindset. If they could avoid a battle, then they would. But questions lingered.

"But what if we l-lose?" Michael asked. "He names the terms and you l-lose Monteviot, William. What about that?"

William pondered that possibility. "If I lose Monteviot, then I will make it clear to Kerr that my eye will be on it. Any more *reiver* activity and I will not hesitate to purge it again."

It was a reasonable statement. With nothing more to say and with the questions satisfactorily answered, the group of knights seemed to all agree that accepting Keith's proposal was the thing to do. All except for one last question.

"Then *who* will f-fight his warrior?" Michael asked what they were all thinking.

William knew that the decision was up to him and it wasn't one he took lightly. He looked at the faces around him; Paris and Apollo, looking at him both apprehensively and hopefully, in that order. Paris didn't want to fight, Apollo did. Then there was Patrick and James, trying not to appear too willing to lift a sword. They wanted the honor. Kieran and Kevin came next, both of them looking as if they very much wanted to do battle against the Scots, before coming to Michael, Tobias, Case, and Corbin. Michael didn't appear too eager, but his sons did.

And then there was Troy. Standing next to his father, he, too, was waiting for William's word. William sighed heavily when he realized there was only one choice he could make.

"This is to be Troy's outpost until we settle on a permanent commander," he said reluctantly. "It is my sense that Troy should be the one to accept the challenge. He is the one who needs to earn Red Keith's respect, after all."

Troy was the only one pleased to hear his father's decision. Everyone else was disappointed to varying degrees, but it was Patrick who spoke.

"That is a wise decision, Papa," he said. "You are correct; if Troy is to know any peace, then he has to earn their respect. But know this; if he falls, I will step into the battle in his stead."

"And I shall step in if Patrick falters," James said firmly.

William held up his hand to stop the declarations of bravery. "That defeats the purpose of single combat," he said. "While I am sure Troy appreciates your bravery, there will be no second and third warriors to take his place. Although I will not let him become terribly injured, should he be unable to continue, then the Kerr wins the fight. Is that understood?"

The thought of losing a fight to a Scots didn't sit well with the English knights, but they reluctantly agreed. They understood the rules of engagement, but there wasn't one man who wasn't willing to step in and ignore those rules. William looked most pointedly at Patrick and James, who weren't happy about complying, before looking to Kevin, who would be the one to charge off regardless of what he'd agreed to. William even pointed at him.

"Give me your oath, Kevin," he said.

Kevin frowned unhappily until his father elbowed him in the ribs. Only then did he answer. "Very well," he said. "You have it."

William wasn't sure if he believed the man, but he had the courtesy not to dispute him, at least not openly. With that matter settled more or less, there was still more on William's mind. He looked to Troy.

"Go and don your protection," he instructed. As his son turned and headed back into the enclosure of Monteviot, William looked to Patrick. "Get all of your army back into the gates and make sure the gates are secured. I expect Troy to be the victor in this and I would not be surprised if Keith went back on his word and launched his army at us. Make sure Monteviot is as prepared for an assault as it can be. Paris, you and Patrick will be in command for now. My focus will be on Troy until this combat is over."

The group broke up and began to move swiftly, as William turned his attention back to Keith. The man was still standing near his horse and was seemingly interested in what was going on with the English. The knights were yelling commands, moving the men who lingered outside the gates back into the bailey. William approached him cautiously.

"We accept your challenge," he said. "Your best warrior against my best warrior. Although I have many warriors that are excellent, I have selected my son, Troy. He will be in command of Monteviot for the near future so you should know what kind of man he is. He will fight your warrior and he will win."

Keith couldn't say that he was all that glad to hear it. Troy de Wolfe was an enormous man, and if William de Wolfe was selecting him to fight above all of the other magnificent knights he had at his disposal, then it meant that Troy was the best of the best. The thought of Rhoswyn going against such a beast of a man unsettled him greatly, but he couldn't turn back now.

"Very well," Keith said, confidence in his voice that he did not feel. "Bring him forth. Let us get on with it."

William's gaze lingered on him and Keith was afraid that the man might have heard his hesitation. But Keith kept his expression neutral and William finally turned away, heading for the gates where everyone was cramming back into the fortress. When he was out of earshot, Keith turned to Rhoswyn.

"Did ye hear that?" he asked quietly. "Ye have tae fight the big man that was standin' next tae de Wolfe. That is his son, Troy."

Rhoswyn had, indeed, seen the man. In fact, she had seen and heard everything that was said in spite of being several feet back from where the conversation was taking place. But she wasn't intimidated in the least. Such was her level of confidence in not only her abilities, but in the pride of an English knight. She'd been planning her assault since last night and she knew exactly what she was going to do. Her plan was going to work.

She had no doubt.

"Have no fear, Pa," she said quietly. "He will fold when the time is right."

"And if he doesna?"

Rhoswyn's gaze was on the English as they were herded back into the keep. "Then I will fight him."

Keith sighed sharply. "He is twice yer size and twice yer strength, lass. Dunna be foolish."

Rhoswyn's focus moved to her father. She could see how worried he was. Perhaps there was something wrong with her in that she was not worried in the least, but she truly didn't believe there was anything to be concerned over. To entertain otherwise would cause her to doubt herself, and doubt could be deadly.

She wasn't in the habit of doubting her abilities.

"There are other ways tae win a fight than brute strength," she said. "De Wolfe canna outsmart me. I *will* win."

She sounded very confident and Keith didn't want to damage that confidence. But the truth was that he was frightened for her; frightened that the de Wolfe son would simply look at a female warrior as another Scot, another target, and he would take his hatred out on her.

Soon enough, they would find out.

Keith realized that he was very much dreading that moment.

CHAPTER FIVE

THE CLOUDS FROM the north that had been visible at dawn, black and angry, had moved south and were now gathering overhead as Troy stood out in front of the closed gates of Monteviot, securing a glove as his father stood next to him. Thunder rolled and big splashes of rain came down now and again, spattering in the dirt at their feet. Along with that thunder came the pangs of apprehension and anticipation.

The air was full of it.

"I will not give you any final advice for this because you do not need it," William said quietly. "But know that if you are disabled in any way, I have archers on the walls. They will take out your opponent before he can land a death blow."

Troy tugged at the leather strap, tightening his left gauntlet just a bit. "And then what?"

"Then we must face Red Keith and his thousand men."

Troy looked at his father, lifting an eyebrow at the irony of that statement. "You are in Scotland, after all," he said. "They do not want us here."

"That is their misfortune."

Troy grinned as he finished with the strap. "Have no fear," he said. "I will not be disabled. And this should not take long."

That was arrogant Troy talking. Fortunately, he was rarely wrong and William didn't expect this to be one of those occurrences. But he wasn't taking any chances; he had the archers positioned but he also had something else up his sleeve. Help from the heavens, as it were. As he stood with his son, Audric emerged from the closed gates and headed in their direction. When Troy glanced up and saw the priest, he frowned.

"What does he want?" he demanded.

William cleared his throat softly. "I sent for him."

"Why?"

"To say a prayer."

Troy rolled his eyes, grossly unhappy and impatient, as Audric came to stand next to him. Then he proceeded to ignore the priest by fussing with his other glove. William cocked an eyebrow at his disrespectful son as he addressed Audric.

"I realize that you are a Scots priest, but you are a man of God over all, so your prayers should be good for English as well as for Scots," he said. "I would be grateful if you could bless my son before this event."

Before Audric could speak, Troy held out a hand. "I do not need prayers from a Scots," he declared. "Besides, he could curse me. Do you really think the man is going to give me his blessing?"

William frowned. "If I thought he was going to curse you, do *you* really think I would ask him to say a prayer?"

Troy gave his father a long look. "You have become very pious in your old age, Papa. I do not need a witch cursing me in Gaelic. You could say a prayer over me and it will do just as well."

William sighed heavily at his foolish son. "I say a prayer over you every day," he said. "Prayer for strength not to throttle you."

Troy thought that was rather funny. He turned away from the priest and his father, snorting, as he finished with his glove. He eyed Keith and the warrior the man had brought with him, a warrior still astride a rather handsome black horse. Finished fussing with the glove, he collected his shield, propped on the ground against some rocks.

"Well?" he boomed to Keith. "Let us get on with this."

William and Audric looked to Keith, who immediately turned to the warrior beside him. As they watched, the warrior slid off the horse and removed a *targe*, or round wooden shield, from the back of the beast. The warrior moved gracefully, long-legged and bogged down with tunics and mail that was not Scottish-borne. He was not big by any means, certainly not as muscular or bulky as the English knights, which was surprising considering that Scots could be bred for size. Some of the biggest warriors William had ever seen were Scottish.

Of all the warriors to choose, Keith had chosen a lithe man of little bulk, but heavily dressed and protected. The helm on his head was decidedly English, of an older style, and the broadsword, from what he could see, was not Scottish, either. It was English, too. William was starting to wonder if the warrior wasn't English-trained as well. It was all quite curious.

Little did he know that a curious situation was about to take a shocking turn.

Ↄ

ACROSS THE CLEARING, Rhoswyn was fully aware that the English were inspecting her.

She could feel their eyes upon her, touching her like unseen fingers, probing curiously. Her skin was crawling because of it. She'd truthfully never been this close to the English before. She had the advantage of watching her father interact with de Wolfe and his son, and when the son had emerged dressed in full battle protection, massive and weighty stuff that fit his big body perfectly. In truth, she'd taken a good look at the man when her father had been speaking to him and, as far as the English went, he was quite handsome.

He was darker, though – his hair was like coal, his skin tanned. He didn't look as if he belonged in a land of pale-skinned people. From what she could see of him, he had dark, serious brows and a square jaw covered with the beginnings of a beard. But it was the shape of him that had initially caught her attention – big neck, broad shoulders, massive

76

arms and chest, and a trim torso. She could see it quite clearly in what he'd been wearing before – a simple tunic and breeches – but now that he was covered in mail and protection, his size was mammoth. It hardly seemed real that a man that size could actually exist.

And this was the man she was to fight.

"Rhosie," her father spoke, capturing her attention. He even reached out to grasp her arm, preventing her from moving any closer to de Wolfe. "Tell me what ye intend tae do."

Rhoswyn had been so focused on the English knight that the sound of her father's voice startled her.

"Lift me weapon and then reveal meself," she said quietly. "And then I relay the terms."

Keith didn't want her dictating anything; that would be his moment to ensure the security and future of his clan and he didn't want her overeagerness to ruin that. "Nay, lass," he said firmly. "I'm still yer pa. Ye will let me dictate terms."

"But…!"

"Nay," he cut her off. "'Twould look weak for a woman tae do it. 'Tis the clan chief who will make the terms for their surrender. Do ye understand me?"

Rhoswyn did. She wasn't happy about it, but she understood. In truth, if she were to do it, the English might not even take her seriously so it would be best for the humiliating terms to come from her father. No one would dispute a dictum coming from Red Keith Kerr.

"As ye say," she said reluctantly.

"Promise me ye'll not speak a word of terms, lass. Promise me."

"I promise."

"I'll speak the terms and ye'll not contradict or question me, either. Ye'll not say a word. Swear this tae me."

"I told ye I would."

Keith nodded, hoping she meant to hold to that vow. If she didn't, it could ruin everything. But he patted her on the shoulder in a show of confidence in what she was about to do.

"Good," he said. "Then get on with it."

Rhoswyn gave her father a brief nod before turning her full focus to the English knight about twenty feet away from her. Was she nervous? Perhaps a little. But she was also quite determined. Now, it was time for her to shine.

It was going to be a short fight.

Taking a deep breath, Rhoswyn lifted her sword and began to stalk the English knight. But he saw her coming, immediately, and went into a defensive position. As they faced off, an odd stillness settled as men began shuffling around to get a better position to watch the fight. In the bailey of Monteviot, soldiers were even taking bets on how long it would take Troy de Wolfe to defeat the Scotsman. They had men on the walls, watching the unfolding battle, preparing to give them a report.

Everyone was waiting with great anticipation, wondering just how much blood would be spilled and by whom. Even Patrick and James watched from the open gate with some apprehension, watching their older brother square off and prepare to charge. They could see his body coil. But the Scotsman was being crafty; he was hanging back, waiting for Troy to make the first move. It was smart of him, and Troy didn't disappoint. He charged forward but the Scotsman quickly lowered his sword in a clear gesture of submission or surrender. Puzzled, Troy came to a halt.

And what happened next was something men would speak of for years to come.

As Troy came to a halt, the Scotsman suddenly pulled off his helm. Or, more correctly, *her* helm. Braided hair, long and mussed, spilled out of the helm as she faced Troy without any fear. In fact, she marched up on him, getting in his face and making sure he understood it was a woman that he was preparing to fight.

But it was a distraction tactic and it worked. Troy was surprised enough that Rhoswyn was able to get the immediate advantage. As his face twisted with astonishment, and perhaps even outrage, she was close enough to lift a knee and ram it right into his groin.

Troy was wearing mail chausses, or mail trousers to protect his legs and groin area, but because the uniform of a knight was made so the men could easily ride their horses, the manhood of a knight was perhaps the least protected. He wore a split tunic, and a split mail coat, so once she lifted a knee into his groin, as hard as she could, she made contact and Troy staggered.

The element of surprise was his undoing.

It was a good hit. Startled by the move, and facing debilitating pain, Troy moved to lift his sword but Rhoswyn smashed her wooden shield right into his chest, sending him off balance. Another strike to the face and he ended up on his back. Rhoswyn pounced. In no time at all, she had a small dagger pressed into the side of his face.

The fight was over before it ever began.

"Dunna move, Sassenach," she said in her deep, silky voice. "Surrender or I'll drive me dirk through yer face."

Troy could hardly believe it. He looked at the woman; God help him, he never saw this coming. Not even in his wildest dreams did he see it coming. But here he was, flat on his back, with a dirk tip poking him in the left cheek. Gazing up at the woman, he had no doubt she meant her threat. Scots women were rough and barbaric; he'd seen enough of what they could do in the aftermath of a battle to know just how brutal they were. He could easily see this woman cutting up the dead for the gold they wore or the rings they had on their fingers. She had that look.

And he knew he was sunk.

Slowly, he took a breath, settling down to think through the situation. He had two options at that moment; he could throw her off of him and brutalize her, but he wasn't in the habit of brutalizing women. Not even Scots. Or, he could capitulate. And he knew that if he did anything other than surrender, it would be viewed as dishonorable. But, damnation, he was angry now. So very angry.

He knew he'd lost, and with it went Monteviot.

"So Red Keith lets a woman do his fighting, does he?" he rumbled.

"I should be surprised but I suppose I am not. Only a coward and a weakling would dress a woman as a warrior and then hide behind her trickery. It is the only way he could win the battle."

The woman's features rippled with rage. "I can fight ye, English," she hissed. "I dunna hide behind trickery."

"You used dishonorable tactics to get me into this position."

Her eyes narrowed. "*Ye* froze. 'Tis yer own stupidity that caused ye tae lose. Now, do ye surrender or must I use me dirk on ye?"

Troy eyed her. In spite of his anger, he could see that she was, in truth, quite lovely. Why, in God's name, he should be considering her comely appearance at this moment was beyond him. All he knew was that the woman was quite pretty with her auburn hair and big brown eyes. He'd never seen a Scot that was so lovely other than his own mother and aunts and cousins.

But this lass… she was quite astonishing.

"If you feel the need to use then dirk, then I cannot stop you," he said. "But know this; it may go through my cheek and it may injure me, but before you can do any serious damage, I will have my arm around your neck and snap it. If I must defend myself against you, then I will defend myself to the death. Do you understand what will happen now?"

To her credit, the woman didn't cower. She looked as if she were considering her options. "I understand," she said, "but do ye? Since I have won our battle, 'tis I who will tell ye what will happen now – and ye will surrender to it."

"I will not surrender to someone who tricked me."

"I dinna trick ye," she said again, calmly. "And either way, ye're on yer back. What will yer men say if ye try tae fight me once I've put ye tae the ground?"

Quick as a flash, Troy brought up a hand and smacked her in the side of the head, knocking her off him and onto the dirt. He flipped over and threw himself on top of her, pinning her as the dirk in her hand went flying. But the woman would not be easily pinned; she was a fighter. She got a hand free and poked a long finger into Troy's left eye, causing the man to falter.

In spite of his stinging eye, Troy still held her tightly, at least tightly enough that she couldn't get away from him completely. When she balled a fist and tried to club him, he simply grabbed her by the hair. She didn't scream even though he held it very tightly, effectively subduing her. Blinking his poked eye to clear his vision, Troy rose to his knees with his left hand wrapped up in his opponent's hair.

"Stop," he commanded softly. "You are only hurting yourself."

Grunting unhappily, she still tried to pull away from him. "Let me go," she demanded. "I won. I beat ye fairly!"

As Troy tried to clear his vision, he could see a shadow approach and he looked up to see his father. William's expression was grim.

"Let her go," he said quietly. "Go on, Troy, release her."

Troy wasn't so sure. "If I do, she will collect that dirk and try to ram it into me."

William sighed heavily. "She will not," he said. "The fight is over and she is the victor. Release her."

Frustrated that his father was declaring the wench the winner, truth though it might be, Troy held on to the woman's hair just a bit longer – and even gave it a tug – before letting her go. He separated himself from her quickly and put distance between them, anticipating that she would collect her dirk and come after him as he said she would. He gave her a wide berth as he spoke to his father.

"It was not a fair fight and you know it," he said. "She deliberately tricked me."

William could see that Troy wasn't merely angry; he was humiliated. William understood completely but it didn't change facts.

"She used her sex to her advantage," William said evenly. "She wanted to throw you off-balance and it worked; it was you who faltered. She used the element of surprise and you fell for it."

Troy couldn't believe what he was hearing. But the truth was that his father was right; he knew it, they all knew it. Now, he was angry at himself more than anything. That split-second of surprise when she revealed herself had cost him. As he growled and stomped his feet, turning his back on his father and the woman, Keith came up to the group.

"She is me best warrior," he said, looking at the distraught knight and William, who simply seemed resigned to the situation. "The lass can fight, have no doubt. But she is also very smart; when she knows she is facing a greater opponent, she uses her brain. That is what she did today. It wasna meant tae shame ye. It was meant tae win."

Troy didn't say a word; he couldn't. He just stood there with his hands on his hips, his back turned to them. Faced with a very unexpected surrender, William answered for his speechless son.

"What are your terms?" he asked.

Keith had been waiting for this moment. What he'd hoped for had actually come about and he was nearly beside himself with glee, but he dare not show it. The English were accepting the outcome and it wouldn't do any good to gloat. Muttering to the woman, Keith sent her away, and she headed over to pick up her dirk before returning to her horse. Keith watched her go, making sure she couldn't hear him, before turning to William.

"I will only discuss the terms with ye, de Wolfe," he said. "Send yer son away."

William didn't even have to tell Troy; the man simply threw up his hands and stomped off to his brothers, who were ready to console him. William simply stood there, unsure what to say. He had to accept the terms graciously. There wasn't anything else he could do.

"Now," Keith said when it was just him and William. "Ye've agreed tae accept any terms I give ye."

"Within reason."

"What does that mean?"

"It means I will not give you any of my properties, save Monteviot, and it means that I will accept a surrender within reason."

Keith cocked his head. "Those werena the terms I was goin' tae give."

William looked at him, curiously. "I am assuming you want Monteviot returned to you."

Keith shook his head. "Nay," he said. "I want somethin' more."

"What more do you want?"

Keith was thoughtful. "An alliance."

That perked William up somewhat; he wasn't expecting that. "I am always willing to ally with a neighbor," he said. "Are those the terms that you are setting?"

"In a way," Keith said. "Yer son, Troy – is he a good man?"

"One of the finest you will ever know."

"Does he have a wife?"

William hesitated. "His wife died two years ago."

"He's not remarried?"

"Nay."

"Is he yer eldest?"

"I have twin sons that are my eldest. He is one of the pair."

Keith turned to glance at the lady warrior, over by the horses. "That is me daughter," he said to William. "I have no sons, ye see, so I raised her as one. Rhoswyn can fight and do anythin' a man can do. She's strong and intelligent and loyal. But the prospects for a husband are dismal, de Wolfe. There's no man in me clan worthy of the lass and she'd make a fine wife tae a strong and honorable man. Ye ask me what me terms are? Me terms are for yer son to marry me daughter. As a man of honor, ye canna refuse."

William stared at him. "A *marriage*?" he repeated. "Those are your terms?"

"An alliance through a marriage."

William was genuinely speechless. This wasn't something he had expected in the least. He turned to look at Troy, who was standing over by his brothers, as his mind raced with the possibilities – although a marital alliance hadn't crossed his mind, the more he thought on it, the more he thought a marriage for Troy might be a good idea. The man had been alone these past two years and it simply wasn't right for him to be so lonely. He'd even admitted it the night before; *alone.*

He felt alone.

But, on the other hand, William wasn't sure he wanted to saddle Troy with a Scots bride who had tried to kill him. That would be worse than being alone. His attention returned to Keith.

"I am honored by your proposal, but I am not sure it is feasible," he said. "Your daughter and my son just fought each other. There is bound to be a great deal of animosity between them. That would be a terrible way to start a marriage. I would rather give you back Monteviot."

Keith shook his head. "Keep Monteviot," he said. "I dunna have the men tae spare, which is why the *reivers* were able tae take her. Ye were correct, de Wolfe; I canna control Monteviot. It would be better in yer hands. But if ye want the outpost, ye have tae take me daughter, too. She's a good lass; she'll not be any trouble. And I'll not let ye refuse me. We'll feast here tonight and our children will come tae know one another."

William pointed to the area where Troy and Rhoswyn had battled. "They have already come to know each other, and not in a good way," he said with some irony.

Keith brushed it off. "Time will heal the sting of their first meetin'," he said, sounding confident. "Will ye agree tae me terms, de Wolfe? Will ye make an honorable bargain as ye said ye would?"

William knew he had little choice. He'd already said that he would agree to any terms set forth, and here they were. Not exactly the terms he'd been expecting or even hoping for, but they were here nonetheless. Any refusal and he would be without honor, as Keith said. Besides... there was a large part of him, buried deep, that wanted to see Troy married. His son needed a chance for happiness again or if not happiness, then at least contentment. And marrying him to Red Keith's daughter would secure an alliance all along the border, one he very badly needed.

Perhaps this wasn't the best of terms... but it was a term that made sense. Heavily, he sighed.

"Aye," he finally said. "I will agree to them."

"The sooner the better. I will send tae Jedburgh for a priest."

"No need. There is already a priest in my ranks."

Keith was pleased to hear that. "Then we can have the mass said for them before the night is through," he said. "I willna give ye a chance tae go back on yer agreement."

"I am not in the habit of going back on my agreements. My son, on the other hand…"

He trailed off and Keith grinned. He could see how hard this was for de Wolfe, concerned for his son's reaction to all of this. In truth, Keith was concerned for Rhoswyn's reaction but it didn't deter him. It was for a greater good and she would have to understand that.

"Then the marriage is today," he said. "'Tis a great day, de Wolfe. A day we will long remember."

William wasn't sure how great the day was, but it was certainly one they would remember. "That remains to be seen," he muttered.

As William walked away, Keith was forced to wipe the grin off his face. He had everything he wanted and he could not have planned this moment better. But, much like William, now he had to explain to Rhoswyn the course that the terms of surrender had taken. A great alliance had been agreed to and he wasn't going to let her ruin it, any of it. Much as de Wolfe had to agree to the terms to remain honorable, Rhoswyn would have to realize that her honor was at stake, too. Her father had made a bargain that she couldn't back out of.

Those weren't the terms that Rhoswyn had been expecting. Not strangely, she didn't see it that way.

CHAPTER SIX

KEITH HAD WAITED until he'd pulled his men off of the rise overlooking Monteviot and hustled them out of view of the English in a grove of pine trees before telling Rhoswyn of his bargain.

He wanted to do it in front of everyone because she was less apt to argue or fight him if there was an audience. Rhoswyn could be bold with an untamed tongue, but she did have some tact and decorum. That was her mother's influence. Keith hoped that she had enough sense not to contest him on the bargain he'd struck with the English but, in hindsight, that had been too much to hope for.

When he announced the terms of surrender for the English, the fight was on.

"A marriage?" Rhoswyn repeated when her father's words settled. "A *marriage*?"

Keith faced her firmly; he knew that was the only tactic to take. "Aye."

"With me?"

Keith nodded. "It is the best possible solution," he said evenly. "We know that we canna remove de Wolfe from Monteviot. He has it and he'll keep it. The man has castles all along the border, all the way tae Berwick, so marryin' intae his family is the best solution. It'll make the man our ally and it will put ye in a place of importance in the House of de Wolfe, lass. Do ye not understand the honor?"

Rhoswyn stared at him, her face turning red with rage and embarrassment as she realized what her father had done. Now, it occurred to her why he'd been so insistent that he dictate the terms of surrender. He'd made her promise not to say a word and she hadn't. Now, she knew why. God help her, she knew why her father had behaved as he had. He'd had plans she didn't know anything about, plans involving her. When that understanding settled, it was all she could do not to run at the man and punch him in the throat.

She'd been a fool!

"These were yer terms all along," she said hoarsely. There was much emotion involved. "Ye made me promise not tae speak terms upon me victory and this is why. Ye had this planned all along."

Keith knew that his men were in support of the marriage to the English. It was the way treaties were conducted and there was nothing unusual about it. Except in this case, it involved a woman who was not quiet or obedient. It involved a woman who could fight with the best of them and being submissive wasn't something she was good at. But these were terms her father had dictated and Keith had no intention of allowing Rhoswyn to deny him on this. He had to take charge before she did.

"And if I had, what is it tae ye?" he said, knowing his only hope was to be more of a bully than she was. "Ye're not in command, Daughter. *I* am. I must do what is best for me clan and if that means an alliance with the English, so be it. If that means ye must be sacrificed for the greater good, then I am willin' tae do it. Whatever made ye think ye had a say in yer future, Rhoswyn? Ye dinna from the day ye were born. Yer future has always been in me hands and now ye know what that future will be. Ye'll be an ambassador of peace for yer people. That is a great callin' for any woman."

He made it sound so noble when, in truth, it was anything but noble. *Sacrifice*, he'd said. She was to be the sacrifice to the English so they wouldn't overrun Kerr lands. At least, that's how she saw it. Rhoswyn simply couldn't believe this was her father's true intention. It had never occurred to her that he would do this and along with her anger and revulsion, she felt the distinct pangs of betrayal.

"Ye care about the clan more than me," she hissed. "That ye'd give me over tae the English... that ye'd been plannin' it all along... why dinna ye tell me what ye planned tae do? Did I not have a right tae know?"

Keith lifted his eyebrows. "Would it have made a difference? Would it have made ye lose the battle? Let the English win? Tell me, lass – would ye have done anythin' differently?"

Of course she wouldn't have. Her pride wouldn't have let her. "So ye betrayed me tae the English," she said, realizing that she felt very much like weeping. "How could ye do this tae me, Pa? I thought ye loved me!"

"I do, lass."

She threw up her hands, a frustrated gesture. "Ye loved me so much that ye bartered me like a prized mare!" she declared. Then, she pointed a finger at him. "Ye had no right tae do it without me consent."

Now, she was challenging his authority in front of his men and Keith wouldn't have it. Rhoswyn could only push him so far before he felt the need to push back. In this case, he had to push back – and push hard – because she was challenging him in front of his men. If he couldn't control his own daughter, then his men would cease to have any respect for him. He already ran a fine line with that and he had for years. Therefore, he did what he had to do – he marched up on her and scowled into her red, angry face.

"When did ye ever think I had tae listen tae me own daughter?" he growled. "Ye have no say in anythin', Rhoswyn. Ye do what I tell ye tae do, when I tell ye tae do it. I dunna need yer consent for anythin' I do. We need this alliance with de Wolfe and ye know it. Ye'll be marryin' his eldest son. Do ye know what that means? It means when de Wolfe dies, ye'll be the wife tae the head of the family. Are ye so stupid and stubborn that ye dunna see what an honor that is?"

Rhoswyn's face was turning positively scarlet. "I dunna care what an honor it is!"

Keith was animated as he spoke. "Ye have tae marry sometime and I canna promise that I'll find a man willin' tae marry a woman who can best him in a fight, so this is the best option ye have. Or do ye intend tae become an old maid and let yer cousins and their heirs take what rightfully belongs tae me? It will be them that takes me place as the chief when I die because ye know as well as I do that a woman canna become chief. At least if ye marry de Wolfe's son, there's a chance that ye'll bear a son tae carry on me bloodlines, a lad I can be proud of!"

Rhoswyn was so angry that she was shaking. "An English-born son," she said through clenched teeth. "Is that what ye want? A *Sassenach* grandson?"

Keith's jaw ticked. "'Tis better than seein' me blood die off," he said. "Since yer mother couldna provide me with a son, I expect ye tae do what she dinna."

Gazing at her father, Rhoswyn suddenly saw, for the first time in her life, how disappointed her father was that she'd been born a girl. He'd never expressed that to her before, not ever, and she'd grown up thinking he'd been wildly proud of her. He'd raised her as a son and she'd excelled at everything he'd taught her. But he couldn't teach her to be a man; that was the one thing she would never truly be able to do. Take over the clan and be the son he'd always wanted. It was like a slap in the face to realize that.

But Rhoswyn wasn't going to give up without a fight.

Without another word, she turned on her heel and ran for her horse. Before Keith realized that she was trying to escape, she managed to mount the beast and take off at a dead run. Only then did Keith and his men swing into action. Keith didn't want her injured, but he instructed his men to capture her at all costs and bring her back. She had a wedding to attend and if she had to do it bound in ropes, then that was her choice.

Keith wasn't about to let this opportunity slip away.

It was close to sunset when Fergus and his sons managed to capture

Rhoswyn, who had stopped by a stream to relieve herself. It was quite a fight, with Fergus coming away with a black eye and his son, Artis, with loose teeth, but three men against one woman eventually wore Rhoswyn down, but not completely. They were still forced to bind her.

Even when they reached Monteviot, keeping her bound was the only way she would not run again.

It made for a rather interesting evening.

ೞ

"THIS IS THE best we can do," James said. "With most of this place stripped of anything useful, this is going to be a less than desirable marital bed."

James stood with Patrick and Apollo on the third floor of the tower, in the one of the two big chambers that had survived the fire due to stone walls and stone floors. Although it smelled heavily of smoke, it essentially hadn't been scorched. But heavier even than the smell of smoke was the prevailing mood in the chamber.

Gloom and apprehension were in the air.

While William, Paris, and Kieran remained with Troy, trying to help the man accept a marriage that he was literally being forced into, James and Patrick had slipped away at William's instruction to prepare a chamber for the new bride and groom to spend their wedding night in. Being that there were no female servants at Monteviot, there was little choice but for the knights to try and accomplish domestic duties.

But it was a difficult task.

The *reivers* had destroyed nearly all of the furniture in the tower, but they'd left the mattresses intact. Also, there was a big wardrobe on this level that they oddly hadn't broken up for projectiles or firewood, although the contents of it had long been emptied. The men had virtually nothing to work with, but they managed to find a crumpled-up mattress that they re-stuffed with old hay found in one of the outbuildings. Bedrolls and cloaks made up the bedding. It wasn't much, but it was all they had. Patrick even started a fire in the tiny hearth.

"This is a piss-poor way to start a marriage," he grunted as James finished with the mattress. "God's Bones, I feel sorry for Troy."

"Do not tell him that," James said firmly. "He does not need to hear it. There is nothing he can do about this so do not make him feel any worse."

Patrick waved him off. "I would not tell him that, of course. But the man has my sympathies. First to be publicly humiliated by the woman and then forced to marry her. She couldn't have stripped him more of his manhood had she cut off his ballocks."

"But imagine how a woman like that would be in bed," Apollo said. He was trying to fix one of the doors on the wardrobe and when Patrick and James looked at him, he lifted his eyebrows. "We know she is a fighter. She is not afraid to put a man in the position of submission. Imagine how aggressive a woman like that would be in bed."

Patrick cocked a dark eyebrow. "Troy has already been forced to submit to her twice – once in battle and once for the marriage offer. Now he will not even be able to dominate her in the bedchamber?"

Apollo gave him a rather lascivious expression but Patrick couldn't agree with him, nor could James. In fact, James sighed heavily as he finished dragging the mattress against the wall next to the hearth.

"If I thought I could get away with it, I would help him to escape," he said. "But Papa would have my head. 'Tis too bad that we cannot swap Troy out for another groom. Mayhap one of the soldiers. Do you think Red Keith would notice?"

Patrick grinned in spite of himself. "I think Red Keith had his eye on Troy the moment the man engaged his daughter. In hindsight, it could have been his plan all along. Did he truly plan on letting his daughter go to battle against a de Wolfe knight? I cannot imagine he truly believed she could win."

James looked at his handiwork on the bed. It wasn't wonderful, but it was all he could do. "I did not get a good look at her," he said, "but she moved with confidence. She certainly attacked Troy with confidence. She knew if she did not take the man down at the very first, the battle would be over. That speaks of a cunning woman."

"Or a ruthless one."

James moved away from the bed, heading over to the fire that Patrick was blowing to life. "God help him," he muttered. "I hope he does not kill her before the night is out. That will bring the Kerr in droves to the border and we will not be able to stop them."

"He knows that," Patrick muttered.

"Does he?"

Patrick stood up from the hearth, wiping his hands off on his breeches. "I am sure Papa is having that conversation with him even now."

James looked at his brother, wondering if, indeed, their father was having such a conversation with Troy at the moment. For certain, the last time they saw Troy, the man was fit to be tied. Rage didn't quite cover it. As James and Patrick debated on the mood between their brother and their father at the moment, Apollo came away from the wardrobe.

"Mayhap we had better go to the hall and see if we can be of service," he said. "If not to tie Troy up so he can't run away, to at least keep the peace. If Troy becomes angry enough, there is no telling what he might do."

Patrick simply stood there, gazing into his fledgling fire. "He has been known to destroy things when he is angry," he said quietly. "He is a man who allows his emotions to feed his strength. In fact, the first battle we faced after the death of Helene and Athena, I clearly remember Troy ripping a man's head clean from his body. You were there, James. You saw it."

James had. He thought back to that terrible skirmish about a month after the tragic deaths, a battle that had been a big misunderstanding. A lass from Clan Hume had run off with an English soldier and The Hume had believed Wark Castle to be the destination. James, in command of Wark, knew nothing of the lass or of the disappearance, but found himself in a very nasty fight with a band of rabid Scotsmen.

Berwick, Northwood, and Questing had ridden to their aid, including Troy, but he hadn't been ready for that battle. Every pain, every anguish he'd been feeling since his wife's death had manifested itself in brute strength and barbaric actions. As far as the others knew, he'd never used his sword once in that battle. Everything he did, he'd done with his bare hands, and it had been a bloodbath. That was the capability of Troy's anger and they all knew it.

It wasn't something they wanted to see again.

"I did, indeed, see it," James said after a moment's reflection. "But that was a different time, Atty. Helene had just died and he'd not yet come to grips with it."

Patrick was still staring into the fire, watching the flames lick against the old wood. Thoughts of Troy, of that day, and of Helene filled his brain. There was a long pause before he spoke again.

"It was my fault, you know," he whispered. "All of this is my fault."

James knew what he meant. He sighed heavily. "Atty, nay…"

"They were coming to see my son," Patrick insisted. "Had they not been coming to Berwick, none…"

James cut him off, slapping a gentle hand on Patrick's chest to get his attention, to pull him away from a guilt that had consumed him since that day. He rarely spoke of it, but the family knew his feelings. He had been tortured since that day, no matter what anyone said to him. Even Troy had spoken to him about it but a brother's absolution hadn't alleviated that guilt.

That burden had been Patrick's alone to bear.

"It was *not* your fault," he said firmly. "Troy has never blamed you. It was a tragic accident and nothing more."

Patrick's jaw ticked faintly. "Mayhap," he said. "But I cannot tear myself away from that guilt. I feel as if all of this… I am responsible for it. I am responsible for Troy's pain and Scott's departure."

"That is not true."

"Because of me, our family is fractured. True or not, that is the guilt I live with. The evidence is there."

James patted him on the chest. "I cannot say that I would not feel the same way from your perspective but, someday, you must come to terms with the fact that you did nothing to cause any of this," he said. "Things like this… they happen, Atty. Women die and men die. It is the way of life. But I would like to think that in the grand scheme of things, a death serves a higher purpose. Mayhap we do not understand what the purpose is when it happens but, in time, we will see the light. We will see that everything in life happens as it should."

Patrick looked at his brother; James was two years younger than he was, a fine and noble man with a good heart. When the entire world was upended, James could always be looked upon for comfort and calm guidance. He had their mother's gentleness and her uncanny wisdom. That was simply his gift.

"And you think Helene's death has a higher purpose to Troy?" Patrick asked. "I am sure he does not see that."

James nodded. "Mayhap not now but, in time, he will," he said with quiet resolve. "Mayhap he was meant to marry the Scots lass to forge a larger bond with the Scots. Mayhap their son will be the greatest knight who has ever lived, a man who brings peace to the borders. Who knows? Only time will tell. I only hope I am around to see it."

Patrick smiled weakly. "You will be," he said. "And then remind me of this conversation when we are old. Let us look back on lives well-lived and see if everything really does happen for a reason."

James smiled in return. "I can promise you that it does," he said. Then, he looked around the chamber, seeing the pitifulness of it. It certainly didn't look like the chamber of a newly married couple, but that couldn't be helped. His smile faded. "But for now, I do not suppose there is anything more we can do here. Let us take Apollo's suggestion and retreat to the hall."

With great reluctance, the three of them headed back down to the hall where the future of Troy de Wolfe – and an alliance with Clan Kerr – were being forged in blood.

Troy's…

CHAPTER SEVEN

"**I** WILL *NOT* do it."

William had been listening to those same five words since Troy's humiliating defeat that morning. It was nearing sunset as he and Paris and Kieran tried to ply Troy with enough wine to make the man more malleable and receptive to the idea that he was to have a new wife. Not just any wife; the woman who had defeated him in full view of his men.

A woman who had humiliated him.

Perhaps that was part of the problem. Troy was being forced to marry a woman who, for a split-second in battle, had been smarter than him. The shame of it was more than he could bear. In fact, the shame was so bad that Patrick sent his army back to Berwick without him, instead choosing to remain behind to comfort his embarrassed brother. James, too, had sent the bulk of his men back to Wark while he, too, remained at Troy's side.

The brothers were sympathetic; perhaps *too* sympathetic. That was why William had sent them away to prepare a bedchamber for the soon-to-be-married couple. He didn't want Troy feeding off of the sympathy from Patrick and James, so it was important that he separate the brothers. William had made a bargain and Troy was expected to fulfill it, no matter how supportive Patrick and James were.

"Troy, I understand your reluctance, but we have been over this,"

William said patiently. "The terms of your defeat were set forth and marriage was the term. You were specifically requested. It is important to the peace of this entire stretch of border and you will comply, like it or not."

In a corner of the big great hall, Troy was literally backed against the stone. He sat with his back to the corner while his father and brothers tried to talk sense into him. At the table behind them sat Paris and Kieran and Michael and the rest of them, because no one was leaving while Troy was in such turmoil. More than that, they wanted to witness the wedding to the warrior lady who had kneed Troy in the groin and then pushed him to the ground. There was great morbid curiosity in their presence.

Troy knew that. He, too, would have had some morbid curiosity about the situation, if only it wasn't happening to him. At the moment, he was beside himself with frustration and angst. He didn't want to marry and he certainly didn't want to marry a woman who had humiliated him in front of his men. But his father had made the bargain and he couldn't refuse.

And he hated the very thought of it.

As Troy raged and the English formed a sympathetic cushion around him, Audric had been watching the entire happenstance with great interest. He would have quite a tale to tell when he returned to Jedburgh; Red Keith Kerr had come forth to confront de Wolfe for taking Monteviot and had cleverly had his daughter fight an English knight, the outcome of which would decide the fate of Monteviot.

But it wasn't Monteviot that Keith had been interested in; it had been an alliance and a marriage for his daughter, who would now marry into inarguably the most powerful English family on the border. It had been a brilliant move by Keith and Audric had to admit that he was impressed. He was also vastly glad to see that the House of de Wolfe would be allied with the Clan Kerr.

If they could get the bride and groom together long enough to conduct the ceremony.

William had already asked Audric to remain and perform the mass. The best they could do was have it take place at the entrance to the hall instead of the entrance to the church, but there were over a thousand men still at Monteviot to witness the merger of the two houses. Audric was more than willing to conduct the wedding mass and as the day went on, he waited patiently, drinking and eating anything anyone would put in front of him. As evening fell and William tried to convince his stubborn son that a contract marriage was the right thing to do, there was some commotion over by the hall entry.

There was a fight going on.

They could all hear it. Some kind of brawl that even stopped the conversation between Troy and William. In fact, as Troy looked at the hall entry with some curiosity, a Scotsman suddenly hurled through the door as if he'd been punched or kicked. But the man regained his balance quickly and raced outside again, only to reemerge back into the hall carrying the legs of a trussed-up body. Two other men had the head and torso of the body, but the person wrapped in hemp ropes was struggling against them violently. It took Troy, and everyone else, a moment to realize that Rhoswyn Kerr had been brought to her marriage ceremony in bondage.

Troy's jaw fell open in shock. As he watched, Rhoswyn bent up her knees, kicked out, and rammed the man who was carrying her feet again. The man faltered but he didn't let go this time. He held firm. Behind the men carrying her, in came Keith Kerr, instructing his men not to hurt his daughter.

It was the most astonishing thing Troy had ever seen. He forgot all about his own reluctance as he watched Rhoswyn brought in like a prize. Or a prisoner. In disbelief, he went to stand next to his father as they watched a host of Scots carry in a gagged lady who was wrapped up tightly. She could hardly move, but move she did, and she was still giving them a fight. Troy looked at his father.

"Are you serious?" he demanded. "*This* is to be my wife? Are you mad?"

William had to admit he was rather taken aback by what he saw. If Troy was resistant to this marriage, then the lady was clearly hysterically opposed to it. He was coming to wonder what he'd committed his son to, but he didn't back away from the bargain. A deal was a deal, and Troy could handle himself even in the face of a wild new wife. But he tried to remain calm, if only for Troy's sake.

"Clearly, she is reluctant," he said, looking at Troy's reaction to his understatement. "Lad, if she walked in here happy and eager to marry you, then you would know it was a lie. At least this way, you know what you are dealing with."

Troy's mouth was still hanging open as he looked at the Scots with the lady between them, only he caught a glimpse of James and Patrick, Apollo and Paris. As he turned his head, he could see that they were all trying very hard not to burst out into laughter. Paris in particular; the older knight had a twisted sense of humor so he undoubtedly found a reluctant Scottish bride to be humorous. Anything that irked William and his sons was funny to Paris. That infuriated Troy but, in the same breath, the situation was so unbelievably ridiculous that he, too, fought off the urge to laugh.

He'd never seen anything like it.

"Papa, you cannot be determined that I should go through with this," he said. "Would you really saddle me to a wife who is so violently opposed to this union?"

It was a legitimate question William could no longer deny. His confidence in the matter took a hit when he saw the lady twist so hard that she virtually threw herself from the arms of the men who were carrying her. She hit the hard-packed earth of the hall with a thud and when they tried to pick her back up, she simply squirmed and twisted so they couldn't get a grip on her. He looked at Keith, several feet away.

"So you would marry a wild animal to my son?" he asked, sounding quite unhappy. "I did not make a bargain that my son should marry this... this she-devil."

Keith met William's gaze, unsurprised by the man's reaction. "She is not a wild animal, I assure ye," he said. "She is smart and compassionate when she wants tae be. But she is unhappy that I have made this bargain for her."

"As I am," Troy said. He was finished being silent about the situation. Pushing past his father, he came to stand over Rhoswyn as she lay, bound and gagged, on the ground. When men tried to pick her up again, he shoved them away, one of them so hard that the man ended up on his arse. Troy crouched down next to Rhoswyn and pulled the gag out of her mouth. "I mirror your reluctance, my lady, and it is unfortunate that our fathers have conspired against us as they have. This is not my doing."

With that, he began to untie her, unwinding the bindings that had been all but cutting off her circulation. As the ropes fell away and Rhoswyn sat up, quickly, to pull the bindings free, Troy chased away all of the men that were standing over her, including her father. The Scotsmen didn't want to move so quickly, but a glare from the big knight sent them falling back.

"Get back, all of you," Troy commanded. "Get back before I throw you back."

He had the de Wolfe air of command about him, one that men naturally complied with, English or Scots. In fact, it was a sense of command and control that Rhoswyn, pulling the ropes from her ankles, hadn't heard before. Not even her own father had that same booming presence that all men naturally succumbed to. And that voice…

She'd never heard anything like it.

Like steel wrapped in silk, soft on the surface but hard and powerful beneath. She'd heard it at a distance when he'd been speaking angrily to his father earlier in the day, but the quality of it had been lost on her. Now that he was speaking directly to her, chasing men away from her, the rich timbre was evident. Moreover, his innately chivalric move to free her from her fellow Scotsmen had her attention.

It shouldn't have; she shouldn't have cared in the least. She was ripping the ropes off with every intention of running out of the hall, but something… she didn't know what… was holding her back. She wasn't leaping to her feet as fast as she should have been. In fact, she wasn't moving swiftly at all. She heard the English knight threaten her uncle, who moved to tie up her feet again, and that had her looking at the man like he was the first man she'd ever seen in her entire life.

That voice had her attention.

What was his name again? Her father had told her but she couldn't remember. But she did remember him as the man she'd kneed in the groin and then smashed in the chest with her shield. He was tall, at least a head-and-a-half taller than she was, and he was broader than her by twice. He had shoulders that were impossibly wide.

But it was his face that had her attention – as she'd noted before, he was darker than the pasty-faced men she'd come to know. He had an olive-skinned quality about him, something she'd seen once when a merchant from a land far away had stopped at Sibbald one night on his way south from Edinburgh. That swarthy man had the same darker quality to his skin that de Wolfe's son had, but he hadn't possessed de Wolfe's eyes – they were probably hazel but they looked gold. And he was handsome… so very handsome. She'd noted that from the first, too, and that hadn't changed. He was even more handsome when he was pushing men away from her.

She rather liked it.

That very foolish reaction to him had her dumbfounded. She was in the process of looking at him with a rather edgy expression on her face when he suddenly began pushing everyone far back from her. It wasn't just giving her room to breathe; it was moving them several feet away from her. He pushed those who didn't move fast enough, and suddenly, other English knights were moving in, pushing the Scots out of the way, and abruptly it became a big shoving match that had the older English knights jumping in to break it up before it turned into a brawl.

It was rather chaotic, in fact. Rhoswyn lurched to her feet, rubbing her hands where the ropes had chafed her, watching the man she was supposed to marry chase everyone away from her.

...why in the hell wasn't she running, too?

"Clearly, you did not know what your father had in mind, did you?"

The man she was supposed to marry was suddenly standing in front of her, speaking to her with that delicious voice. A voice that could move mountains. Rhoswyn looked at him, feeling her heart leap strangely.

God, what was wrong with her?

"Nay," she said, staying out of arm's length so he couldn't touch her or grab her.

Troy watched the woman as she moved away from him. She wasn't running, as he had expected, but she was obviously unnerved by him, by the entire situation. To her credit, however, the hysteria seemed to have faded. Now that she wasn't being treated like an animal, she wasn't behaving like one. But he wondered if it was only temporary. He scratched his head, glancing back at his father and the other English who were mostly keeping the Scots at bay. But some were watching him.

An idea struck him.

"Would you be willing to have a private word with me, please?" he asked her. "It is impossible for you to run out of here and not be caught, so if you give me a moment of your time, mayhap we can come to an... an agreement that will not involve wrapping you up in ropes."

Rhoswyn was still rubbing her wrists where her skin was chafed, eyeing him. "What could ye possibly have tae say tae me?"

There was both curiosity and defiance in that question. Troy wasn't sure he could get her to come with him, to a quiet corner, so he simply spoke where they were standing even though there were men within earshot. It was a crowded, chaotic situation at best but, being a rational man most of the time, he knew they had to speak. Something had to be done and he wondered if he was the only one who could do it.

To calm the woman who was to be his wife.

"I have this to say," he said. "My father has made this bargain with your father. You and I, unfortunately, are to be the pawns in their greater game. I do not wish to marry you any more than you wish to marry me, but to refuse would reflect badly on our fathers. My father would be a man who could not hold his word, and your father would be a clan chief who had no control over his own daughter. Do you agree with this so far?"

That voice. Rhoswyn was having difficulty not openly admiring what was music to her ears. Even if he did speak with a Sassenach accent...

"Me pa dinna consult with me," she said. "I have every right tae refuse."

Oh, but she was stubborn, this one, Troy thought. He could see it in her expression as she spoke, in a voice that sounded rich and silky. It was rather beautiful. Even if she did speak with a Scots accent...

"You have no rights at all and you know it," he said, trying not to sound cruel. "Nor do I. Much as your father is your chief, my father is mine. It is the hierarchy of command – my father commands and, ultimately, I do as I am told. So do you. If men did not do as they were told, then there would be chaos. Everyone must take orders from someone. Is that a fair statement?"

Rhoswyn's jaw ticked faintly; she sensed what he was driving at and even though what he said was correct, she wouldn't agree to it. She couldn't. But if she continued to refuse and dispute him, she would sound like an idiot in denial, an animal who did what she pleased, any time she pleased. It was, therefore, with the greatest of hesitation that she nodded her head, ever so slightly.

"Me pa is the clan chief," she agreed.

"And he is in command?"

"Aye."

Troy was surprised she conceded the point. "As my father is in command of the House of de Wolfe," he said. "Let me ask you, my lady – if one of your father's men was to refuse him as you have refused him, what would you do to the man?"

She snorted. "He would be beaten and sent away."

Troy was quick to pounce on that. "Do you want to be beaten and sent away? Because you were close to that only a few moments ago when they brought you in, bound in rope." He watched an expression of doubt ripple across her face and he took a step towards her, lowering his voice. "I do not want to marry you. I do not ever want to marry again. But I have no choice. And you; you do not have any choice, either. All you are doing now is embarrassing your father much as I am embarrassing mine. We are showing little honor in our fathers by denying their wishes. I love my father and I want to show respect to him; I hope you feel the same way about your father. With that said, we may as well let them have their marriage and get it over with."

Rhoswyn eyed him nervously before looking to her father, who was standing about fifteen feet away with William. Both fathers were looking at their children with varied degrees of apprehension. *All you are doing now is embarrassing your father.* It took Rhoswyn a moment to realize that he was correct. But she couldn't help it, so great was her resistance to this marriage. She didn't want to marry a Sassenach; she didn't want to marry anyone. But, as her father had pointed out, if she didn't, then his title and lands would pass to Fergus and his worthless sons. The next chief of Red Keith's clan wouldn't have his blood. Or hers.

God... her father had been right.

Rhoswyn's gaze returned to the English knight; big, handsome... if she had to marry, then she supposed she could do much worse than him. Perhaps he would even teach her the Sassenach warring ways. She forced herself to look on the bright side; perhaps it wouldn't be all bad.

It wasn't as if she had a choice. But in that understanding, she could feel the distinctive spasms of defeat.

She hated it.

"And then what?" she asked. "I marry ye, and then what? What happens then?"

It was a good question. "What do you want to happen?" Troy asked. "Do you want to go home with your father? You know he will make you remain with me. A wife remains with her husband."

Rhoswyn was starting to lose her defiance. She was tired and upset, and the trials of the day were getting to her. She was a strong woman but even she had a limit. The thought of never going home again brought tears to her eyes, tears she angrily blinked away.

"Will… will we remain here?" she whispered tightly.

Troy could see that she was breaking down and he had to admit he was relieved. He sincerely did not want to marry a woman who might possibly put a dirk in his back while he was sleeping. Perhaps she would still try, but he had a feeling that if he could calm her down, and talk to her pleasantly, then maybe they could at least come to some civil coexistence. At this point, that was really their only hope as well as their only choice.

"For now," he said. "Mayhap in time you could even go home and live with your father if you wanted to. I would not wish for you to be unhappy living here or at Kale Water Castle. That is my other holding. My lady… since neither of us has a choice in the matter, then let us get on with this and decide what is best for both of us after the fact. I promise that I will let you do whatever makes you happy so long as whatever it is does not shame me, my father, or your father. Is that agreeable?"

It was perhaps the nicest way to make a truly upsetting situation feel comfortable. Rhoswyn had to admit that she was surprised by the amount of compassion and reason the knight displayed. She had no idea that the Sassenach were capable of such a thing. But beneath all of her resistance and anger, she had to admit there was also a good deal of fear. Truly, she was afraid to be married, afraid of the Sassenach stranger.

Afraid of an unknown future.

But her father had set her on this path and there was nothing she could do. After a moment, she nodded her head, once, but it was enough of a gesture that Troy turned to his father and Keith. He lifted a hand.

"Bring the priest," he boomed. "Do it now before the lady and I change our minds."

Pulled away from the table and his fourth cup of cheap wine, Audric had never been forced to move so fast in his entire life.

CHAPTER EIGHT

S HE WASN'T HUNGRY.

After the hasty mass performed by the priest from Jedburgh, there was much food and drink to be had. It was surprising, considering the English armies had to bring their provisions with them, and that included sides of aged beef that had been carefully packed in straw to keep the temperature even and the meat dry. It was very dry, in fact, so much so that the men had taken to cutting it up and boiling it in a large cauldron they'd found on the grounds of Monteviot. The smells of meat were heavy all over the compound.

But Rhoswyn wasn't hungry for it. She wasn't hungry for anything, nor was she thirsty. Shock had seen to that. She sat next to her new husband at the bigger of the two tables in the hall of Monteviot, watching the English and the Scots feast on the boiled beef. Next to her, Troy – as she'd been reminded of his name by the priest who'd married them – wasn't eating or drinking very much either, and he'd barely spoken to her through the meal. He was more intent on speaking to his Sassenach brothers and cousins, men he'd introduced to Rhoswyn but she'd forgotten their names as soon as he'd told her. The night was disorienting enough without having to remember names that would have no meaning to her.

She just wanted to get this night over with.

Artis and Dunsmore, her cousins, had brought her bedroll and possessions into the hall. They'd been strapped to her big black horse, which had been stabled for the night. Now, the big leather satchel and her neatly-bound bedroll sat next to her feet. On her right, Keith tried to speak to her now and again, but she ignored him. She truly didn't have anything to say to the man. She was torn between being furious with him and not wanting him to leave her. But she knew, after this night, that her life would change and seeing her father would be rare. She missed him already. God, she just wasn't prepared for any of this.

But facts were facts. This was her life to be.

Therefore, Rhoswyn supposed she had no choice but to make the best of it. So much that Troy had said to her rang deep – about not shaming their fathers, about doing what had to be done. He'd spoken to her politely, with that beautiful deep voice, and the truth was that he'd soothed her somewhat. The man possessed some kind of magic to do that.

"My lady?"

It took Rhoswyn a moment to realize that the young knights across the table were trying to capture her attention. There were three of them, big men, but their youthful faces belied their age. The oldest couldn't have seen any more than twenty or twenty-one summers. Two of them were obviously brothers, with black hair and blue eyes, while the third one had a granite-square jaw and dark blond hair. When they saw that they had her attention, the younger black-haired knight smiled.

"My lady, we were wondering," he said. "Where did you learn to fight? You were very skilled in your battle against Troy today."

It was a polite question asked by a young Sassenach who had evidently had too much to drink. They were smiling, their eyes bright, and they seemed rather animated. But Rhoswyn was embarrassed to be the object of their attention and she lowered her gaze, quickly, hoping that if she didn't give them an answer, that they would leave her alone. She didn't realize that Troy had heard the question and now his focus was on the young knights.

"You will address her as Lady de Wolfe," he growled. "And clearly, she learned to fight well enough that she managed to catch me off-guard. But I promise you that had you been in my position, the same thing would have happened. Or worse."

Corbin had been the one asking the questions and he grinned as Troy admitted his shameful defeat. "I am not so sure," he said. "I would not have faltered as you did."

"Is that so? You have a big mouth and an even bigger imagination, de Bocage. She would have run you through before you would even realize what had happened."

Corbin laughed, knowing he was provoking Troy but a little too young to care. "Untrue," he said. "As soon as she revealed herself to me, I would have pushed her back by the face. 'Tis a bold wench who would challenge a man."

He was talking as if Rhoswyn couldn't hear him and his words were a challenge in themselves. Rhoswyn's head came up and her eyes narrowed. She didn't like the arrogant young knight's assertion. She wasn't going to let him get away with it.

"'Tis a fool who believes he can best me," she said, entering the conversation. "Have ye ever fought a woman before?"

Corbin's smile faded as Troy's new wife spoke up. "Never," he said. "I would never fight one."

"How do ye know ye havena? Ye could have fought a very good one and ye just never knew it."

"And you could have been beaten by her," Troy put in for his prideful young friend. "In fact, you have probably been beaten by many women, Corbin. Hell, with the way you fight, my mother could beat you if she had a mind to."

That brought laughter from those around them and Corbin frowned deeply. "No woman can beat me."

Troy looked at Rhoswyn, who looked at him with a rather startled expression. Startled that the man was so close to her, his face now just a few inches from hers. Of course, she'd been sitting next to him all evening but only when he looked at her did she realized just how close he'd been.

Those eyes... she'd been right. They were hazel, but a very pale shade of the color that looked gold in certain light. It was the most beautiful color she'd ever seen. And his lips... he was smirking, but it wasn't at her. It was at the knight across the table. When he spoke, there was some appreciation in his tone.

"This one can," he said.

Before Rhoswyn could reply, he turned away and found his cup of wine. Rhoswyn watched him for a moment, unsure if there was approval in his voice when he'd spoken. She had no way of knowing; she didn't know the man. She'd just met him and she'd just married him. He was her husband, but he was a stranger.

Was it possible that, somehow, the warrior in him was the least bit impressed with her?

"It is impossible for her to best me," the young knight scoffed, disrupting her train of thought. "No offense intended, Lady de Wolfe, but you caught your husband off-guard. He has admitted that. It is the only reason you won. Do you know that Troy de Wolfe can tear men apart with his bare hands in battle? When his anger is roused, you have never in your life seen such a warrior. It was fortunate you caught him when you did. Otherwise, he would have torn you to shreds."

Troy thumped on the table, loud enough to get his attention. "Cease your prattle," he said. "It is over with. Change the subject and speak of something else."

Corbin backed off, but not enough. He put his cup to his lips and drank deeply before speaking.

"If she was my wife, I would put her over my knee," he said, muffled in the cup. "Now that she is your wife, you can punish her for ramming her knee into your..."

Case slapped a hand over his brother's mouth, forcing a smile at Troy. "He has had too much to drink," he said. "I will remove him."

Troy eyed the two brothers. "You had better," he said. "If that young fool rouses my anger, I will rip *his* head from his shoulders.

Remember that."

Case knew that Troy wasn't serious – well, not *entirely* serious – but he pulled his brother from the table nonetheless, yanking him down the bench to where his father was sitting. Troy fought off a grin as he watched Case explain to his father why they had come to that side of the table, biting off a laugh when Michael smacked his youngest son on the side of the head. Corbin yowled.

"Would ye truly rip his head from his shoulders?"

The soft question came from Rhoswyn. Troy turned to look at her, realizing it was the first thing she'd said to him nearly all night. With a twinkle in his eye, he shook his head.

"Nay," he said. "Not really. But it is enough of a threat to move him and his flapping lips away from you. I do apologize if he offended you. He is young and silly, but deep down, I believe he's a good man. He will grow into himself in time."

Rhoswyn watched as down the table, Corbin defended himself from his father's anger. "He reminds me of the young lads that serve me pa," she said. "They're like young colts. Wild, playful, and no fear. They're hard tae tame sometimes."

Troy nodded. He, too, was watching Case and Michael scold Corbin for his behavior. It occurred to him that it might be better to retreat to the marital chamber now that the evening was deepening and the situation in general was calming. Certainly, the lady was much calmer than she had been earlier, which Troy hoped was a good sign for the night to come. He hadn't been a bridegroom in eighteen years, not since he married Helene, and he should have been nervous about it. But he wasn't; he was oddly resigned to it. There was no sense of sexual anticipation, only duty. He had a duty to fulfill.

And so did his new wife.

"Mayhap we should retire for the evening before the situation here gets out of hand again," he said to her. "It has been a tiring day for us both, I am sure."

Rhoswyn's heart began to beat more rapidly, now nervous at what

Troy was suggesting. She wasn't a fool; she knew what a wife's duty was. Her mother had schooled her on it when she had been about eleven years of age, right before Heather Whitton Kerr had passed away from an ailment in her lungs. That had been a terrible time in life to lose one's mother, and Rhoswyn hadn't missed her mother so much as she did at this moment. Wasn't the woman supposed to be here with her, giving her daughter what comfort she could and last-minute advice?

But there was no comfort and no advice. Rhoswyn was alone in all of this and she grabbed her possessions at her feet and abruptly stood up. As Troy said his farewells to his father and the others, Keith realized that his daughter was about to depart. He turned away from his conversation with his brother and grasped her by the arm.

"Are ye leaving, lass?" he asked.

Rhoswyn nodded her head. She was trying very hard not to look at him, afraid she would embarrass herself with an emotional display.

"Aye," she said. "*He* wishes it."

"Ye mean yer husband?"

"Aye."

The hand Keith had on her arm gave her a reassuring squeeze. "'Twill be all right, lass," he murmured. "The Wolfe says that his son is the finest of men. He'll make a fine husband. Be worthy of him. Obey him and be a good wife."

She looked at him, then. "If he is a good husband tae me, then I'll be a good wife tae him."

Keith shook his head. "Yer husband can do as he wishes," he said quietly. "Remember that ye're a Kerr; we hold honor as the most valuable thing there is."

Rhoswyn looked at him, pointedly. "If that is true, then ye should have told me about yer plans tae marry me off. Ye should have been honest, Pa."

Keith wouldn't admit that there was some truth to her words. But he didn't regret what he'd done or how he'd done it. "'Tis over now," he said quietly. "Ye're married tae a de Wolfe now, the most powerful

English family on the border. Ye'll be respected and important now."

That wasn't exactly what Rhoswyn wanted to hear. She was about to leave her father, perhaps forever, and she wanted to hear something sentimental and reassuring. But she knew that was too much to ask. Ever since her mother's death, Keith hadn't been able to speak on his feelings.

Perhaps it was just as well.

"Think of me once in a while, Pa," she said as she turned away, her throat tight with emotion. "Think of the daughter ye gave over tae the English."

"Ye'll thank me for it someday."

Rhoswyn wasn't so sure. All she knew was that she felt she was heading to her doom. As she stood there with her sack and bedroll clutched up against her chest, she realized that Troy was standing next to her, waiting. When she looked at him, uncertainty on her features, he gestured to the hall entry.

"This way, my lady," he said.

He led and she followed, wandering through a maze of inebriated English soldiers, hearing strains of music somewhere as someone strummed a mandolin. It was a smoky hall, filled with dirty men, and the stench was enough to make her eyes water. But she clutched her possessions to her, terrified, as she followed her new husband from the hall.

They exited into the bailey beneath a clear sky and brilliant stars. The storm that had threatened earlier in the day had blown off somewhere, leaving a crisp evening. As soon as Troy hit the dirt of the bailey, he stopped and turned to Rhoswyn. But she came to a halt because he did, looking at him with suspicious eyes. He tried not to smile at the look on her face, as if waiting for him to do all manner of terrible things to her now that they were out of the hall and alone.

"I was waiting so you may walk beside me," he said. "I do not expect my wife to walk behind me."

Hesitantly, Rhoswyn closed the gap, looking the man in the face, wondering if he was really as kind and understanding as he seemed to be. This was the same man she'd beaten in a fight, the same one who had hit her on the side of the head and nearly knocked her senseless. The same man she'd kneed in the groin, as the young English knight had so thoughtfully pointed out. All of those terrible things had happened, but he didn't seem to hold a grudge; at least, on the surface. Who knew what would happen once he got her alone.

She was apprehensive for that moment.

Troy could see the utter anxiety in the woman's expression. He'd seen it all evening, since the priest had married them. She'd been silent and still all night, hardly moving, and he didn't think she'd eaten very much, if at all. Not that he blamed her. Perhaps he was old and hardened, so much so that even a marriage didn't get him too worked up. He had seen nearly forty years; he couldn't imagine that his new wife had seen half of that. She was young, he was old. She was beautiful and he had wrinkles on his face.

It was going to be an interesting evening.

"My brothers have made up our bedchamber," he told her as he led her towards the tower. "I cannot vouch for the comfort of the bed, but I know they did what they could. After the siege, there wasn't much left to work with."

Rhoswyn was walking beside him but she was about five feet away, clutching her possessions to her chest as she looked around the compound. "This is me first time tae Monteviot," she said. "I canna see much tae it."

Troy looked around, too. There was a big stone wall, an oddly large bailey, the tower, outbuildings, and a hall built next to the tower. Most Scottish towers didn't have a hall, but this one did.

"It is not spectacular, but it is strategic," he said after a moment. "But I am sure you already know that."

She nodded. "Me pa said so."

Troy pointed off to the east. "My father's seat of Castle Questing is about twelve miles that way," he said. "My own castle of Kale is five miles to the north, but Monteviot sits close to the English border. It is barely a mile to the south. The *reivers* that had settled here were making great misery for the English villages."

They had reached the darkened tower and it loomed over them. But the stench of smoke and death was strong, and Troy reached out to open the entry door that had been repaired from scraps of wood that they could find. He started to go in but noticed that Rhoswyn wasn't moving. He paused.

"Is something the matter?" he asked.

She was looking up at the tall, bulky tower. "The siege," she said. Then she paused, hesitantly, before continuing. "That smell... me pa said ye were burnin' men."

Troy was honest with her; there was no reason not to be. "It was not by choice," he said. "It was by necessity. The tower was the last holdout; we had control of the bailey, the outbuildings, and the hall, but there were about thirty Scotsmen holed up in the keep. We tried to get them out; we even promised to release them unharmed if they would only leave the tower. They refused so we burned them out."

Rhoswyn understood; she knew battles. She knew how Scotsmen thought. "They would rather die than surrender."

Troy nodded but he didn't reply. She seemed to be rather depressed by the thought so it was better to not comment. He reached out a hand to her.

"May I take your baggage?" he asked.

Rhoswyn shook her head, miffed that he would think her so weak. "I'm capable of carryin' it."

So much for being polite. Troy led her up to the floor above the small solar, the level that had the two undamaged rooms on it. But the smell of smoke was heavier than usual and when Troy opened the chamber door, he could see why; the hearth had malfunctioned and there was a blue layer of smoke in the room. Coughing, he opened the door and went straight to the hearth that was happily blazing away.

"Damnation," he muttered, coughing and kneeling down to tend to the chimney. "Did no one check the chimney when they started this blaze?"

Rhoswyn followed him into the chamber, her eyes burning from the smoke, and quickly set her possessions down against the wall. She noticed there was some kind of oil cloth on the mattress, which was lying on the floor, and she picked up the cloth, waving it briskly and driving the smoke out of the room. She coughed, Troy coughed, as they both struggled with the smoke.

"This was not how I'd hoped the chamber to be," Troy said. "I cannot offer you much comfort, but I'd hoped we'd at least be able to breathe."

It was meant to be a quip, but Rhoswyn missed the humor completely. She continued to fan, moving a good deal of the smoke out of the door. There were two small windows that someone had covered with oiled cloth, and she ripped the cloth free, letting the air from outside suck into the room.

"The smoke will be gone soon enough," she said, though she coughed as she said it. "Considerin' that the rest of the tower smells of smoke, I suppose it willna matter much. There is smoke everywhere."

Troy wasn't oblivious to the fact that she'd jumped right in to help with the smoke situation. She hadn't stood by the door and cowered; this was a woman who was used to action. She'd loosened up through the evening and he thanked God that he wasn't dealing with a wife who needed to be bound hand and foot in order to keep her from hurting others or herself. Moreover, she wasn't trying to run anymore.

He saw that as progress.

"I think the smell of smoke will be here for some time to come," he said, rising from the hearth, which was now properly evacuating the smoke out of a chimney that had been partially blocked. "We shall have to become used to it."

Rhoswyn stopped waving the oiled cloth around because the air was much clearer now. She watched Troy as he went to the door and quietly closed it. Their eyes met when he turned to face her and an awkward silence settled. Troy lifted his eyebrows, thinking he should probably say something that would make them both feel at ease.

"Well," he said, clearing his throat softly as he moved back towards the hearth. "Since we both find ourselves in an unexpected situation this night, mayhap it would be best if we learn something about one another. It might make you feel more comfortable considering we know virtually nothing about each other."

Without the hundreds of English soldiers surrounding her, Rhoswyn was easing up considerably. It was just her and Troy now, and it was natural that she should be curious about him. They were to spend the rest of their lives together, a concept she was having a difficult time with. In truth, she'd never been close to anyone in her life, not even her father, so it was an odd notion. She had no friends, and she had no idea where to even start.

"I dunna know what more I need tae know of ye," she said quietly. "Ye're a de Wolfe. Me pa said that ye're a fine man. What else is there?"

Clearly, she had no concept on what a marriage was like. Troy scratched his chin thoughtfully. "Much more," he said. "More than you know. You should know something of me and I should know something of you."

"Like what?"

"Who taught you how to fight?"

Her chin lifted in a gesture that hinted at defiance. "Me pa."

Troy folded his big arms across his chest, leaning back against the wall. "And how long have you been fighting?"

"All me life."

Troy's eyebrows lifted. "Even when you were a young lass?"

She nodded. "Having no sons, me pa taught me how tae wield a sword and how tae fight. He said it came naturally tae me."

"And you like to fight?"

Rhoswyn had to think about his question; it confused her. "What else is there?"

He shrugged. "I simply meant that most young ladies do not lift swords," he said. "There are many things young women do that do not involve sharp blades or drawing blood."

There was that dry sense of humor again, but Rhoswyn was oblivious to it. Her brow furrowed and Troy could see that she really had no concept of what he was saying.

"But... but this is what I do," she said. "This is *me*."

Troy studied her a moment, wondering what to say next. She didn't seem to be much of a conversationalist, nor did he see much depth to her personality. He hoped she wasn't some dullard; it would be terrible to be saddled to a senseless, foolish woman for the rest of his life, no matter how lovely she was.

"Did your father educate you?" he asked. "What I mean to ask is what more do you know other than fighting?"

She knew what he meant. "Me ma taught me tae sew and sing," she said. "I can read and speak English, Gaelic, and Latin."

That surprised him. "Who taught you that?"

"Me ma. She died when I had seen eleven summers." Now, she was becoming bolder. She didn't want to talk about herself anymore. "Can I ask ye a question?"

He nodded. "Aye."

"Ye told me earlier that ye did not want tae marry again. Does that mean that ye've been married before?"

Troy thought on her question; he had said that, hadn't he? He supposed there was no harm in telling her the truth. She would find out, eventually, given that everyone who knew him knew he'd been married before. Someone would tell her if he didn't.

"Aye," he replied, averting his gaze as he turned to look at the fire. "I was married very young. I had seen twenty-two years and she had seen fifteen years. We had three children together but only one has survived. My wife and two youngest children were killed two years ago."

Rhoswyn found herself inherently sympathetic to that news. "Oh," she said solemnly. "What... what happened?"

"They drowned."

That sounded quite tragic to her. "But ye have one child left?"

He nodded. "My son, Andreas," he said. "He has seen seventeen years and he is fostering at Norwich Castle."

"Ye must be proud of the lad."

"He is my shining star."

Rhoswyn watched him as he spoke, his subdued manner. Even though his answers were without emotion, it was his expression that gave him away. Speaking about his dead wife and children was still upsetting to him even though he tried to cover it up. But oddly enough, his confession somehow made her more sympathetic to him.

It made him more human.

This wasn't a single-dimension Sassenach warrior. This was a man who had suffered great loss but continued to push through it. She wondered if he felt terribly lonely, though. He seemed that way to her.

Then, the guilt began to set in.

This was the same man she'd fought, kneed, hit, and humiliated. Then, she'd refused to marry him so strongly that she had to be carried to him in ropes to their wedding. In her defense, she hadn't cared what the man thought at the time. She still wasn't sure she did, but now she was sliding into that gray area of awkward guilt over her behavior. Something inside urged her to show him she wasn't the wild animal his father had accused her of being.

"Norwich Castle," she said, attempting to continue the conversation. "Is that near London?"

Troy nodded. "It is not too far from it," he said. "About a day's ride."

"Have ye been tae London, then?"

He grinned. "Many times. Have you?"

She shook her head as if she would rather be dead than set foot on the streets of London. "Nay, laddie. Never."

He laughed at the way she said it, the term she called him. *Laddie.* His father called him that on occasion, but no one else had dared refer to him as a lad in a very long time. He rather liked to hear it in her sultry voice, so much so that he didn't mind at all.

"Then we shall go sometime," he said. "Surely you would like to travel out of Scotland and see other places, other people."

She looked at him as if he'd just asked her to go to the moon. "Out of Scotland, ye say?" she asked, astonished. "What would I do out of Scotland?"

"You do not wish to travel?"

She shrugged. "I... I wouldna know how."

Troy's gaze lingered on her a moment. "Did you never go anywhere with your father?"

She shook her head. "Me pa doesna leave Sibbald's. 'Tis our home, ye know."

"I know. But why does he not leave?"

Rhoswyn shrugged. "He just doesna," she said. "I canna recall him leavin' more than just a few times in me life, so comin' tae Monteviot was rare for him. I think he feels anxious when he leaves. He always wants tae go home."

Troy already knew that about Red Keith Kerr; they all knew that the man rarely strayed from home. It could be because he simply loved his home too much to leave it, or it could be because he was afraid when he left home. Troy had seen men who couldn't leave their homes or lift a weapon, anxieties of men who had seen too much battle. It wasn't uncommon. Pushing himself off of the wall, he turned to the fire one last time.

"Well," he said, "if that's the man's choice, so be it. But you may like to travel to London someday. Or we do not have to go to London; we can go to York or Carlisle, or anywhere else you might like to go."

Rhoswyn had never considered anything like that in her life. Leaving her home, her father's lands, had never even occurred to her.

"I say it is enough that I'm here," she said. "I canna think on goin' anywhere else. I've never spent a night away from Sibbald's in me life."

Troy poked at the wood, settling it down into a warm blaze. Her mention of spending the night outside of Sibbald's reminded him of what was to come this night, of what was to be expected. He hoped she had an idea of it, too, because she seemed to have lived a rather sheltered life. He didn't want her going mad with what he was about to tell her.

"Speaking of the night," he said as he stirred the fire, "you understand what it is that married people do on their wedding night, don't you?"

Rhoswyn looked at him sharply, realizing what he was asking, and then feeling her cheeks flame at the mere thought. Did she know? She certainly did. This was the moment she had been dreading.

"Aye," she said. "I know."

"*What* do you know?"

She frowned. "I havena done it before if that's what ye're askin'."

He tried not to smile at her outrage. "That is *not* what I meant," he said. "I simply meant... since I have done this before, if you would like me to explain the situation, I will be happy to."

Rhoswyn had never been so embarrassed in her life. To speak of such personal things with a stranger! But Troy wasn't any stranger; he was her husband. As of tonight, he would be a stranger no longer. But so much about this day had been in upheaval – her entire life was in upheaval, now with a husband who wanted to take her to London and explain the ways of men and women to her. It was almost too much to process and for the first time all evening, her composure was fracturing. Not in the sense that she wanted to run away again, but in the sense that she couldn't comprehend a man who would be so understanding. Not after the day they'd had.

"Why?" she finally hissed, unable to look at him. "Why would ye do this?"

Troy turned from the fire to look at her. "Do what?"

She turned her head away completely. "Be so kind tae me," she said. "Do ye not realize what I did tae ye today?"

"I do."

"Yet ye show no anger?" She did turn around, then, looking him in the eye. "I wanted tae defeat ye and I did. I hit ye and I kicked ye and knocked ye tae the ground!"

"I know."

That wasn't the answer she was looking for. "But, still, ye have been kind tae me," she said. "I dunna understand why ye would do such a thing."

Troy stood up from the fire, scratching his head pensively. Then, he eyed her as he formulated an answer to what was a legitimate question.

"I suppose I did it because you were more upset about the situation than I was," he said. "I am much older than you are, Rhoswyn. I have seen much in life. It is true that I can become angry rather quickly and it is true that you made me angry today with your tactics. But, as my father pointed out, you did not trick me. You simply used the element of surprise. I cannot become angry about that because, in hindsight, it was a smart tactic. As much as I did not like it, you did what you had to do. From one warrior to another, I respect that."

Rhoswyn was looking up at him, listening to that deep, soothing voice. "I did it because I knew I couldna best ye any other way," she said. "Ye're bigger than I am and more powerful. I knew if I dinna strike ye down first, I would never have another chance."

He nodded as he sat down on the edge of the mattress. "I realize that," he said. "You ask why I have been kind to you? Because you were forced into this just as I was, but now that it is done, we must make the best of it. I would like for this union to be a civil one. I do not want to spend the rest of my life fighting with you."

It was the rational way to look at the situation and Rhoswyn realized that she, too, didn't want to spend the rest of her life fighting with him.

"If we must be together, then I would like it tae be civil also," she said.

Troy simply nodded, pleased that she was at least agreeing with him. That gave him hope. With that, the conversation died off and he bent over a leg and began to unfasten a boot.

As Rhoswyn watched, the boot came off and he went to work on the other one, and she began to realize that he was undressing for bed. Or, at least, what was to come in bed. Feeling her nerves all over again, she turned her back on him and looked down at herself; she wasn't one to sleep in her shift. In fact, she'd slept in her clothes since she was a child. It was her mother's influence that made her bathe and brush her hair once in a while but, for that, she wouldn't have cared in the least. And she'd never in her life undressed in front of anyone.

She wore three tunics and the heavy leather tunic on top of that. Her legs were clad in the leather breeches and, like Troy, she wore boots. She glanced over her shoulder to see that he was removing his heavy woolen tunic with the wolf's head on it, so she thought she might as well remove the leather tunic she wore. It was more like an apron and she unfastened the ties, pulling it over her head and tossing it against the wall.

Sitting down on the mattress, she untied her boots, which were nothing like Troy's boots. His were smooth pieces of leather, expertly sewn together and crafted, while her boots were simply pieces of leather attached to a sole that were then held to her leg by a series of ties. Glancing over her shoulder casually to see what state of undress he was in, she could see that he'd taken off his padded tunic, revealing a thin linen tunic beneath. Since he'd removed another piece of clothing, she did too.

Unbeknownst to Troy, every time he would remove something, Rhoswyn would. Vastly uncertain, she didn't want to be dressed any more – or any less – than she was. When he was down to his thin linen tunic and breeches, she was, too. But then he pulled the tunic off and she could see his broadly-muscled back.

He was nude from the waist up.

The mere sight made her heart beat strangely. Illuminated by the firelight, she could see his muscles rippling as he moved. She'd seen the flesh of men before, but not like this. Never like this. It seemed to affect her breathing and her cheeks grew hot. Fearful she was about to embarrass herself greatly, she turned away just as Troy stood up and went to the other side of the bed, pulling back the makeshift coverlet.

"I cannot promise it is comfortable, but it is better than sleeping on the ground," he said. But then he noticed that she was simply nodding, her back turned to him, and he knew why. He remembered a nervous bride eighteen years ago and he had another one now, although under these circumstances, Rhoswyn had every right to be nervous and upset. "My lady, if you are not comfortable doing what must be done tonight, then I will not force you."

Rhoswyn was surprised by the offer but terribly grateful. She turned her head slightly, enough so that Troy could see her fine profile in the firelight.

"I have shamed ye enough today," she said, so nervous that her voice was trembling. "Ye've shown kindness and patience. I would not dishonor ye further by refusin' tae share yer bed."

"No one would know but the two of us. If you do not want to, then we can put it off to a later time when you are more comfortable."

He was giving her the option and it meant a great deal. Was the man so truly kind and patient? She'd never known anyone like him. But she honestly couldn't refuse him what was his right. Everything was so new and uncertain right now but, even so, she'd not lost her sense of duty. She may have hated what the day had brought her, but that didn't mean she was going to be a coward about it. What was it her father had said? *Be worthy of him.*

She was coming to think that she very much wanted to be.

"Yer suggestion is a kind one, but unnecessary," she said. "I willna shirk me duty. But... ye'll have tae tell me what it is ye want me tae do."

Troy realized it was probably difficult for her to say that. He also knew that how he handled this situation would probably affect their entire relationship, forever. He wanted it to be civil, but didn't want any more than that. Aye, she was beautiful and, with time, she would probably make an acceptable wife. But beyond that, he had no hopes or expectations. He'd had love, once, and he didn't expect it or hope for it again. The love he had was for Helene, and that had not gone away these two years yet it had faded into something warm and comforting. When he thought of her, he remembered the feelings he had for her. He didn't particularly want to feel those for anyone else, not even a beautiful Scottish warrior woman who had bested him in a fight.

But that wasn't something Rhoswyn ever need know.

Still, Troy knew how to be kind. His mother had seen to that. The sweet and endearing Lady Jordan made sure all of her sons knew how to treat a woman, and Troy was particularly good at it as evidenced by the way he'd handled the situation with Rhoswyn. When he'd seen her fighting and kicking in the hall, bound in ropes by her own men, he knew that he had to be the one to ease her. It couldn't have come from anyone else. He had to be the more reasonable person at that moment because she was incapable, frightened as she was. So he'd made the effort and now they found themselves in the same bed, on their wedding night.

All was calm and he intended to keep it that way.

"I will not tell you," he said quietly, "but I will show you. Do you trust me?"

Rhoswyn thought on the question. Did she trust him? Strangely enough, she did. The man had proven himself to be kind and honorable so far, inevitably earning what trust she had to give. But given that he was a Sassenach, inherently, she was wary.

But that resistance was fading fast.

"Aye," she said, barely above a whisper. "I do."

"Good," Troy said. "Now... just relax and let me do what needs to be done. Can you do that?"

"Aye."

"And not resist?"

She let out a pent-up breath, as if she'd been forgetting to breathe. "Nay... I'll not."

Reaching out, he touched her on the shoulder, by her neck, and a wild fire ran up and down her spine, causing her breath to come out in a painful gasp. Rhoswyn had never known the touch of any man, so Troy's warm hand against her shoulder sent sparks firing through her body like nothing she'd ever experienced. His other hand came up, touching her other shoulder, and she must have made some kind of noise that suggested she wasn't opposed to his warm, gentle touch because the next thing she realized, his mouth was on the side of her neck.

After that, it all seemed to pass in a blur.

Rhoswyn closed her eyes because the sensations Troy was creating overwhelmed her, swallowed her, and the only way she could fully realize them was to close her eyes and digest the powerful experience. His mouth moved over her neck and onto her back, where he was kissing the flesh. Kisses that caused her body to tremble and her breathing to come in odd pants. As she sat there on the edge of the bed, his big body moved up behind her and his enormous arms went around her, pulling her back onto the bed.

She was on her back now, smelling the stale hay from the mattress as Troy covered them up with a blanket that smelled of horses. It was scratchy and rough, but Rhoswyn wasn't paying attention. Troy was straddling her somehow – she didn't dare open her eyes and look – but she could feel him hovering over her.

And his hands were moving.

Surely, confidently, they were moving. Stroking her arms, moving to her hands and pulling them to his lips. He was kissing her fingers and she could feel his hot breath on her flesh. Then he was nibbling on her hands, her wrists, and he dropped her hands long enough to yank her thin linen undertunic over her head in one swift movement.

He almost yanked her head off with it and Rhoswyn gasped with surprise as she ended up naked from the waist up. Pulled from feelings of warmth and excitement, a flood of embarrassment filled her at her nakedness and she thought to protest but she quickly remembered that she'd promised him that she would not resist. He'd asked her to trust him, so she had little choice. But thoughts of resisting and embarrassment abruptly faded when he came down on top of her and his heated mouth began to suckle on a warm nipple.

Witchcraft!

That was all Rhoswyn could think when he fondled her breasts, suckling between them, and she liked it. Aye, she liked it! Somehow, the man had bewitched her into liking what he was doing to her. Trust took on a whole new meaning as his mouth, his tongue, moved over the flesh of her torso while his fingers now pulled at her hardened nipples, tugging at them, and every time he did it, she would gasp and groan. Her body seemed to be making the sounds all on its own, as if she had no control over what was coming out of her mouth. Something else seemed to have taken hold of her, for things like shame and fear had fled, leaving a quivering and willing shell in their wake.

She had no will of her own.

For certain, Troy seemed to be a man possessed. Along with the kissing and suckling he was doing, she could hear him inhaling deeply, as if sucking in her scent, breathing in her very essence. He was feeding off of it, suckling and biting at her torso, dragging his tongue over her belly. Her breeches were the last frontier, a garment that was laced at her hips to keep them tight, but Troy yanked the ties free and, with one hard pull, drew them all the way down to her ankles.

As he pulled off one of the legs, leaving the other leg still bunched up around her ankle, he shoved his face into the thatch of dark curls between her legs and inhaled deeply. It was intimacy in the most basic way, a man acquainting himself with what belonged to him. It was the scent of his woman.

Then, he went into a frenzy.

Troy's fingers began to probe wet, intimate places. Shocked at the unexpected move, Rhoswyn forgot her promise not to resist and she put her hands on his, trying to pull him away. But Troy wouldn't let her remove his hand; he bent over to kiss her arms, her wrists, before pulling her fingers away to suckle on them. The action forced Rhoswyn back into the realm of warmth and arousal, feeling a strange heat between her legs and having no idea what it was or how to quench it. All she knew was that there was a hunger there now that she'd never had before, and when Troy finally put his manhood against her threshold and thrust slowly but firmly, she began to understand what that hunger was, because he was beginning to feed it.

It was a primal need that took over her instincts. To Troy's surprise, Rhoswyn thrust her hips forward, awkwardly, and he slid into her warm, wet body nearly his entire length. He also quickly realized that she had no maidenhead, probably lost somewhere in the years of riding horses, as sometimes happened with women. But her tight body and grimacing expression told him that she was, indeed, a virgin and he withdrew, coiling his buttocks and driving his full length into her. As Rhoswyn groaned with the unexpected and slightly painful experience, he began to move.

His thrusts were deep and measured, and the pain quickly subsided, leaving that same strange hunger that seemed to grow every time Troy thrust into her. Rhoswyn lay on her back, legs parted and gripping Troy around the neck as he continued to move in her, grinding his pelvis against hers when he was in too deep to go any further. The grinding of the pelvis caused sparks to fly and her body to quiver, and as Rhoswyn was trying to absorb all of the pleasurable and strange new sensations their lovemaking had to offer, the hunger between her legs seemed to roar.

The tremors of that roar rippled through her body as she experienced her first release, bringing a cry to her lips at the exquisite ecstasy of it. Rhoswyn held on to Troy tightly, feeling as if she needed an anchor. Surely if she didn't hold on to something, the effects of that roar would blow her all over the chamber. Gasping, she held on to him as hard as she could, hearing his soft grunt in her ear as he found his release as well.

It was over, but it wasn't over. Troy remained on top of her, still moving in her, still touching her. His lips were on her forehead, kissing her tenderly, and somewhere in the kisses, his soft voice told her to sleep.

Rhoswyn didn't need any prompting; her body was already halfway there, languid and boneless. She couldn't have moved if she'd tried. All cuddled up in Troy's enormous, warm embrace, it was as if nothing else in the world mattered at that moment. She was safe and she was warm, and she was content. She'd never known such satisfaction of the soul in her entire life.

Witchcraft, indeed.

When she awoke the next morning, Troy was gone.

CHAPTER NINE

"A MARRIAGE."

"Aye... a marriage."

The muttered words came from Fergus and Artis, sitting with Dunsmore outside of the hall near a fire they'd built themselves, unwilling and unable to sit inside with a host of Sassenach soldiers while Rhoswyn was married to one of them.

This wasn't the outcome they'd hoped for.

Fergus most of all. He was grossly disappointed by it and grossly insulted that he hadn't been consulted on such a matter. It had been a shocking decision on Keith's part and nobody was very happy about it – *a marital alliance*. Had Keith told him what he'd been planning all along, Fergus would have done his best to talk him out of it. Protested if he had to.

Tie the man down and beat some sense into him if it came down to it.

But there had been no chance for protests because the deed was done. Rhoswyn was married to a de Wolfe son and was even now in the tower with her new husband, doing things that would bring about a de Wolfe heir and a potential claimant to the wealth of Clan Kerr. It was true that because of the laws of *tanistry*, or the Gaelic succession rights, no female or the offspring of a female could inherit the chief's position, meaning that a de Wolfe grandson couldn't become the chief of Red

Keith's clan. But Keith could certainly gift the child, and his daughter, with what fortune he had accumulated. That would split the clan's wealth with a half-Sassenach bastard and no one wanted to do that.

Therefore, those meant to inherit what Keith had were quite displeased with the recent turn of events. But what to do about it was the question.

It was true that Fergus was a man who avoided conflict. It wasn't that he was a truly peaceful man; it was simply that he had a cowardice streak in him, something his brother overlooked. He was family, after all, but that cowardice streak was why Fergus had remained on the hill with Keith's men when Keith and Rhoswyn had gone to confront the English. That was the brutal truth of it. But now Fergus was wishing he hadn't remained behind given the bargain that Keith had struck.

"I canna believe he's done such a thing," Artis said, poking at the flames with a stick. "I never thought the man capable of betrayin' his lands and his people."

"These are *our* lands!" Dunsmore banged his hand against the hard-packed earth. "He's given them tae the English. He'll give it all tae the English!"

Fergus listened to his passionate sons. "He willna give him our lands," he said, his speech slow and weary. "When me brother dies, it will be me who inherits Sibbald's. When I die, it belongs tae Artis. Keith married Rhosie tae the English but that doesna mean all is lost. I'll talk tae him and…"

"No more talk, Pa," Artis interrupted angrily. "Rhoswyn said that Red Keith cared more for the clan than he does for her, but that's not true. He has somethin' else in mind by marryin' her tae the de Wolfe son. I can feel it!"

Fergus sighed faintly. "Ye canna know that."

"He wed Rhosie tae the English and ye knew nothin' about it until it was too late," Artis pointed out hotly. "We know that Red Keith never does anythin' without a plan. And ye heard him today when he told Rhosie that he wished for English grandsons? Ye were there! Grandsons tae come and take over the clan!"

Fergus shook his head. "They have no legal claim."

Artis pointed a finger at him, jabbing it in his face. "Mayhap they dunna, but until Red Keith is put in the ground, his wealth and lands belong tae him. He can do as he pleases. Who is tae say he willna give them over tae his English relations now? We'll lose everythin'!"

Fergus was tired of listening to his sons rage about the implications of their future now that their cousin had married into the House of de Wolfe. He was frustrated enough about it without them stirring the pot. Unwilling to listen to their unsubstantiated speculation, he stood up, stretching his legs. Artis glanced up from the fire when his father stood up.

"We're not finished, Pa," he said. "We have somethin' tae settle."

Fergus shook his head. "We'll not settle it tonight, lads. And I'll not listen tae any more of yer foolish claims."

"Then where are ye goin'?"

Fergus gestured in the general direction of the stables. "Tae piss out all of this foul English wine," he said. "And tae think. I canna think with the two of ye raging as ye are, so I need tae be alone. I need tae think this through."

Dunsmore started to say something but Artis put a hand on his brother's arm, silencing him. Dunsmore looked at him curiously but kept silent as their father wandered away. When Fergus was out of earshot, Artis turned to his brother.

"He willna do anythin' about this," he mumbled. "Ye know that. Our pa is a coward and he willna stand up against his brother. That means *we* must do somethin' about this."

Dunsmore looked at him with some confusion. "Do?" he repeated. "What can we do?"

Artis returned to poking the fire, the wheels of thought churning in his mind. "Rhosie doesna want tae be married tae the English," he said. "Ye saw what we had tae do tae take her tae her own weddin'. Ye saw how she fought it."

"Aye, I saw. But what can we do?"

Artis' gaze lingered on the fire for a moment. "We help her," he said simply. "Mayhap she'll want us tae do away with him."

Dunsmore's eyebrows lifted as he realized what his brother was saying. "Do *away* with him?" he repeated. "Kill him?"

"Aye."

Dunsmore thought that was a very bad idea. "But ye saw the man, Artie. He's a knight. More than that, he's a de Wolfe. Would ye bring the entire House of de Wolfe down on us?"

Artis looked at his brother. "Rhosie bested him," he said. "He canna be so indestructible if she bested him."

Dunsmore still didn't like what his brother was suggesting. He was the weaker of the pair, easily frightened, and his brother's suggestion had him scared. "So what do we do?"

Artis stopped poking at the fire as he seriously considered the question. "We will talk tae Rhosie," he said. "We can come up with a way tae rid her of de Wolfe. If she has no husband, then she'll have no children, and there will be no one Red Keith can give his fortune tae."

It sounded rather simple, but Dunsmore knew there was far more to it than the simplistic way Artis was presenting it. He hated it when his brother schemed like this, but part of him was glad for it. He knew that Red Keith's wealth would stay where it belonged if Artis had anything to say about it.

It wouldn't go to the damnable English.

"We canna talk tae her now," he said, pointing to the tower. "She's with the man she married."

Artis nodded, leaning back against the cold stone wall of the hall. "Not now," he said. "Later. Let us go home with Pa and then we'll come tae visit. By then, surely Rhosie will be a-wantin' us tae help her. The more time she spends with him, the more she'll hate him."

It was an interesting thought, one that, hopefully, would prove true. If Artis and Dunsmore wanted to protect what was theirs, then surely drastic measures had to be taken. But Dunsmore wasn't so sure they should take them against a de Wolfe because it was a potentially devastating situation should de Wolfe seek vengeance on them for a murdered son.

Still… Dunsmore wasn't so sure they had any other choice. If they wanted to protect what was rightfully theirs, then something had to happen.

The de Wolfe son had to be removed.

⁘

"WELL? DID ALL go well last night?"

The question came from William. Troy had just emerged from the tower before dawn to find it full of men ready to depart. In fact, the shouts from the bailey had roused him from his sleep, a sleep so blissful that to pull himself away from it had been difficult. He hadn't experienced that kind of contentment in a very long time.

With Rhoswyn's long, warm body pressed up against him, it had been heavenly, feeling like he was whole again. Losing Helene had taken something from him that, last night, Rhoswyn had unwittingly put back.

And that scared him to death.

Because of that, his father's question startled him. He looked at his father, approaching through the darkness of the early morning, and he resisted the urge to spill out his confusion. It *was* confusion, because last night he'd sworn he didn't have any hopes or expectations of the marriage, but this morning might have seen that opinion change.

"It proceeded without incident," he said, unable to stifle a yawn.

William came to a halt, eyeing his son. "She did not become hysterical again?"

Troy shook his head. "She did not."

William was pleasantly surprised. "Then that is good news," he said. "I will admit that we were worried."

Troy's brow furrowed. "We? Who is 'we'?"

"Me," Paris said as he came up behind William, dressed in full armor at this time of the morning because of the troop movement. "I was worried. God's Bones, Troy, that is no ordinary woman you married. In my daughter, you had a gentle and obedient woman, but the warrior woman you took to your bed... God help you."

Troy looked at his former father-in-law, sensing that all was not well with him. He'd not spoken to him much about the marriage other than right after the bargain his father had made. All four of the older knights had closed in on him, trying to convince him that the marriage to the Kerr heiress was the wise thing to do. But the more Troy thought on it, the more he realized that Paris, throughout the night, hadn't said much of anything about it. His father and Kieran had been doing all of the talking.

That told him that something was amiss.

"It will be fine," William said, looking pointedly at Paris. "Troy is married to the woman and that marriage will create a strong alliance."

Paris still didn't seem apt to discuss it. He simply turned away, calling to Apollo to ensure the troops from Northwood were ready to depart. Both Troy and William watched him go.

"What is it with him, Papa?" Troy asked. "What is wrong?"

William sighed as he returned his attention to his son. "I am not entirely sure, but if I could guess, he does not wish for you to remarry," he said quietly. "He seemed in support of it initially, but as the evening progressed and he ingested too much wine, he started lamenting over Helene's memory."

Troy looked at his father, puzzled. "What about her memory?"

William lifted his big shoulders. "Mayhap he sees it being wiped away with your new wife," he said. "I cannot be for certain that is what he is feeling, but I suspect that might be the case."

"Did he tell you that?"

"Nay, but I have known Paris for most of my life. I know how he thinks."

"And he thinks I am disrespecting Helene's memory by taking another wife?"

William could see that Troy was working himself up. He put his hand on the man's shoulder. "*Nay,*" he said flatly. "He has not said anything to that regard. You know that he would not. But you are Helene's husband and to see you married to another... certainly, Paris must feel torn about it."

Troy stared at his father a moment before charging off, pushing through the crowds of men who were gathering in the pre-dawn. He was following Paris and the man hadn't moved too far away before Troy was behind him, putting a hand on his shoulder and pulling him to a halt. When Paris looked at him, surprised that he had so forcefully pulled him to a stop, Troy got in the man's face.

"Is that what you think?" he hissed. "That my marriage to Rhoswyn is disrespectful to Helene's memory?"

Paris was taken aback. "Who told you that?" he demanded. "I never said such a thing!"

"*Is* that what you think?"

It was evident that Troy wasn't going to back off or back down. There was an intensity in his eyes that only Troy de Wolfe was capable of. He had his father's hazel eyes that, when aroused with anger, took on an almost animalistic gleam to them. Something hard and unnatural. That was what Paris saw now and he hastened to clarify the situation.

"I do not think that," he said honestly. "But it does seem... sad that you now have a wife who is not my daughter. You married her when she was so young, Troy. It has always been you and Helene. And now your father has used you to forge an alliance with Red Keith. I will admit, it did not bother me in the beginning, but I have had time to think on it. It will be strange knowing you are married to another woman and not my daughter."

Troy gazed at the man a moment before dropping his hand from his shoulder. In truth, he could see Paris' point of view. He understood it well.

"Mayhap I am married to her, but she will not take your daughter's place," he said quietly. "She is a wife in name and nothing more. Have no fear. She can never wipe Helene's memory from me, not ever. It is ingrained in me as surely as the stars are ingrained in the heavens. That will never change."

Perhaps that was something that Paris needed to hear at that moment. These were days of change for him as well. It was bad enough losing his daughter but now he felt he was losing her memory as well as her husband took on another wife. But he didn't voice that; it wouldn't do any good.

Patting Troy on the cheek, he turned away from the man and continued on to his troops where Apollo was organizing the party. Troy watched him go as William came up behind him.

"Thank you for telling him that," William said softly. "I think he needed to know that."

Troy turned to his father. "You heard?"

"Aye."

Troy drew in a deep breath, the air full of morning dew and free of the smoke that had been so prevalent the last few days. He looked around the bailey, so full of men, and found himself rather disappointed that he wasn't going with them.

"No one likes what you have done, Papa, least of all me and Uncle Paris," he said after a moment, "but we both understand why you did it. I will make the best of it and so will Uncle Paris. Now, how long do you wish for me to remain at Monteviot? Now that we are allied with Red Keith, there is really no reason for me to remain. I can just as easily put another knight in charge while I return to Kale Water."

He was changing the subject away from the emotional part of the situation and on to the reality of it. William simply went with the shift, unwilling to discuss the marital aspect of it any longer because nothing could change it. Troy and Paris would accept it, as they had to, and that was all he cared about. He'd been in command of his empire for so long, but it was moments like this that made him feel old and worn and tired. He didn't like playing with people's lives but, at times, it was necessary.

Such was the burden of command.

"You mentioned that you were going to send for Brodie and Cassius," he said, moving with the change in focus. "Do you still intend to do that?"

Troy shook his head. "As I said, since we are now allied with Red Keith, I see no reason to overly fortify Monteviot, and that includes pulling my knights from Kale Water. But I might send Brodie here when I return to Kale. I would like to have at least one of my knights in command."

The gates of Monteviot began to swing open; the sounds of grating iron and chains could be heard all across the compound. The troops for Berwick were up near the gate, Patrick's troops, and Troy knew that they would depart first.

"I would bid farewell to Patrick before he leaves," he said. "While I am gone, think of what you would have of me here at Monteviot. Tell me if there is anything you wish for me to accomplish. I am eager to return to Kale Water and do not want to spend too much time here."

William nodded. "You'll spend enough time to see everything properly repaired and the area settled," he said, grabbing on to Troy's arm when the man went to move away. "And you will speak with Keith before you go back to Kale Water. You will at least try to form some kind of bond with the man, Troy. You are his son now and it is important, for the sake of peace and the sake of family, to have a relationship with him."

Troy nodded, distracted. "I will," he said. "Let me see to Patrick and then we shall speak more before you depart. And where is James? I must see to him as well."

William let him go, watching Troy as he headed towards the gates. The land was now starting to turn shades of purples and pinks as the sky above turned colors from the rising sun. As he turned back to the troops from Castle Questing, which were to the rear of the bailey, he caught sight of Audric emerging from the hall.

The priest ate and drank himself into oblivion the night before, so William was surprised to see that the man was up and moving so early. As Troy went off to bid his brothers and friends a good journey, William made his way over to the priest, who seemed to be rubbing his eyes and staggering somewhat. In fact, by the time William reached the man, he had to grab him to steady him. Audric looked up at him, blinking his eyes.

"Och," he said, seeing the rather amused expression on William's face. "It seems that I canna drink Sassenach wine and not feel the effects of it the next day. What do ye make it with? Poison?"

William kept a straight face. "The blood of unpleasant priests."

Audric eyes widened but he saw the flicker of a smile on William's lips so he broke down into a grin. "I always said the English were a wicked lot."

"I cannot disagree with that, but we're no worse than the Scots."

Audric sighed faintly, nodding but realizing that hurt his head, so he quickly stopped. "That be true, in many ways," he said. Then, he spied Troy near the gates, talking with a pair of big English knights. "So yer son survived the night, did he? I had me doubts."

William's gaze moved to Troy also. He was speaking to Patrick and James. But as he watched, Corbin and Case came over to his son, as they were preparing to depart also, and Troy slapped Corbin on the side of the head and the others laughed. Considering how the young knight had harassed Troy's new wife last night, the smack was well deserved. William fought off a grin at the camaraderie – and the irritation – of old friends.

"I had my doubts also," he admitted, returning his focus to the priest. "But he says that everything is well this morning."

"Have ye seen his wife tae ask her the same question?"

"Nay," William said. "But I am sure she will show herself soon enough. Her father is preparing to leave, also."

He was pointing off to the southern end of the hall – the exterior of it – where Red Keith and his men had spent the night, wrapped up in their dirty tunics and sleeping beneath the stars. Audric snorted.

"Could nothin' ye say convince the man tae spend the night in a room full of Sassenach?" he asked.

William shook his head. "Not even when I promised to sleep between him and my men," he said. "There was nothing I could say to convince him otherwise."

"It seems he dunna trust those he's now allied with."

William knew there was some truth to that. "That is what I wish to speak to you about," he said. "I think it is important for you to remain here for a time, at least while my son and his new wife are coming to know each other. Your counsel may be crucial to this marriage being a success. Will you consider it?"

Audric looked at him with some surprise. He hadn't been expecting such a request and was therefore unprepared with a firm answer.

"I dunna know if I can," he said. "I am expected back at Jedburgh."

"I will write to your abbot and ask permission, then. I feel that your presence here is important, Audric. You know the couple; you have seen how they met, how they married. You understand the situation. They may need you."

Audric did, indeed, and it was a volatile one. After a moment, he sighed. "I suppose I could spare some time tae remain," he said. "But send the missive tae the abbot today. I dunna want the man wonderin' where I've gone."

William felt some relief that the priest had agreed to remain behind. "Good," he said. "I will send the missive off before I leave here this morning. Let me attend to it now. Meanwhile, go and tell Keith Kerr that you will be remaining for the sake of his daughter. I am sure he will find some comfort in that."

"Unless he thinks I'm here tae give her or her husband last rites when they tear each other tae pieces."

William grinned. "I am confident that will not happen."

With that, he turned on his heel and headed off into the collection of English men, his destination the provisions wagon from Questing that held all of his possessions, including his writing implements.

Audric watched him go, thinking the man held a strong belief that the unexpected marriage between his son and Keith's daughter would succeed. He could hear it in the man's voice. From what Audric had seen, he wasn't so certain, but he'd been asked to stay and mediate. Or counsel, as de Wolfe had put it. Either way, he was in a position to help this alliance and he didn't take that lightly. He didn't think his superiors would, either. Somehow, he suspected that peace along this entire stretch of border depended on it.

Not surprisingly, Keith was glad to hear of Audric's plans. But he didn't wait for his daughter to show herself, thinking it would be better if he didn't. After her first night as a married woman, he might not like what she had to say, so he and his men left Monteviot as the big contingent from Berwick flooded from the gates.

Keith felt like a coward for leaving his daughter without finding out how she fared with her new husband but, in hindsight, perhaps it was best if he didn't know.

As he'd been saying all along… it wasn't as if he could change things.

Rhoswyn would have to find her own way now.

CHAPTER TEN

FOR SOME REASON, Rhoswyn didn't want to bid her father a farewell. She'd awoken, alone in the makeshift bed and feeling momentarily disappointed that Troy hadn't remained with her. But the moment she sat up, she saw that the fire had been stoked and her clothes, which had been piled up in the corner, were lying on the floor before the fire to warm them before she put them on. That was an incredibly thoughtful gesture and one that brought a rather bashful smile to her lips. Even if Troy had left her sleeping, he'd still thought of her.

Somehow, that meant something.

So, she rose from the bed and pulled her warm clothes on, going to the window of the tower to see the northern part of the bailey and the fact that it was full of men and wagons, men preparing to depart Monteviot. She knew her father was out there, somewhere, but she didn't feel much like seeing him. She knew he would ask her questions about the night, and if the marriage had been consummated, and that wasn't something she wanted to share with anyone, least of all her father. She was still trying to process what had happened last night because, for the first time in her life, she felt like a woman.

She'd never felt that way before.

It was quite a paradox – the woman who had only ever wanted to fight like a man versus the sensual woman that had emerged under

Troy's expert touch. The way he'd touched her, kissed her... was that what it meant to be a woman? To feel warmth and excitement and tenderness? No one had ever told her that aspect of it although, in hindsight, she thought her mother might have tried, but she'd been too young to understand. Certainly, she couldn't have grasped all that had happened last night. All she knew was that she liked, very much, what had happened last night and she was both ashamed to admit it and eager for more.

It made for a very confusing state.

But she didn't want to talk to her father about it. She'd seen the man the previous night and he said all he needed to say to her – or, at least, all she wanted to hear. She didn't want to spoil her memories of last night with her father's questions or last minute advice, and she waited in the chamber as the sun rose until the last of the English troops filtered out of her line of sight. By that time, she could only assume that nearly everyone had left, including her father, so it was then that she put her boots on and made her way down to the entry level of the tower.

But she was hesitant about going outside. She stood in the doorway, peering out into the brisk early morning, and seeing that there were at least a few hundred English soldiers who hadn't left. Some were cleaning up the clutter and debris left behind by the armies while others were repairing part of the stables. She even saw the priest who had performed the wedding mass going into the stables, perhaps to tend his horse. Everyone seemed to have assigned duties so Rhoswyn stepped out into the morning, keeping an eye out for Troy. She found that she very much wanted to see the man, but she was nervous to see him in the same breath. It made for a strange quandary as she headed for the great hall, thinking he might be there. She was nearly to the door when she heard her name being called.

"Rhoswyn!"

Sharply, she turned to see Troy heading towards her, jogging across the bailey from the direction of the stables. He was wearing almost all of the armor she had seen him wearing yesterday when she'd defeated him, but now with the sun glistening off of the steel mail, it glimmered like light reflecting off the water. There was some kind of surreal quality to it and her heart began to thump against her ribcage at the sight of him. Would he be happy to see her, too? Or would he realize what a terrible mistake they'd all made? She held her breath as he came close.

"How did you sleep?" he asked as he came to a halt. "I was up before dawn because my father and his men were moving out, but I did not want to wake you."

That voice. Rhoswyn knew now that it wasn't merely the sight of the man causing her heart to race, but that voice. It affected her like a potion, something that made her feel and react as if she had no control over it.

"I slept well," she said, but the conversation stopped after that and she felt as if she should say something more. "I… I saw the men movin' out earlier. It willna take long for yer father to reach his home?"

Troy shook his head. "Castle Questing is twelve miles from here," he said. "They will be home before supper. Now, my brother, Patrick, will take longer than that. He will not reach home until tomorrow."

Rhoswyn simply nodded. She wasn't very good with small talk, especially to someone she didn't really know. She'd never been very good with the art of conversation in general although, in this case, she wanted to be. She didn't want Troy to think he'd married an idiot.

"I… I remember meetin' yer brothers but I must confess, I dunna remember much about them," she said, grasping for things to say. "Mayhap someday they will return and I will come tae know them better."

Troy thought that sounded rather encouraging; he, too, had feared that he might meet with a wife full of regrets this morning and was pleased to see that, at least on the surface, it wasn't the case. He had to admit that he was rather pleased to see her this morning. It had been a long time since he'd had the opportunity to greet a wife in the morning, although Helene hadn't been much of a morning lover. She was up early, usually grumpy, and that didn't wear off until midday. Funny how he found himself comparing Rhoswyn to Helene, noting one against the other.

With Rhoswyn, he was about to embark on a whole new world.

"Not only will my brothers return to Monteviot, but we shall also go to them," he said belatedly. "I know you said that you have not traveled much, but I should like for you to see where my brothers live and meet their wives. Everyone will want to meet you."

She looked at him, her expression torn between suspicion and apprehension. "Why?"

He laughed softly. "Because you are part of the de Wolfe family now," he said. "My mother calls it the de Wolfe pack, you know. You shall hear it referred to that often."

He said *de Wolfe pack* with a heavy, and perfect, Scottish burr and Rhoswyn's eyes widened. "Yer mother says it that way?"

He noted her surprise. "She's Scot," he said. "Her father, my grandfather, was the chief of Clan Scott. Now, the chief is a close cousin, but my mother is much like you – she is also the daughter of a chief."

Rhoswyn was astonished. "Is it true?" she said. "I dinna know yer mother was Scots. Ye dinna tell me."

Troy shrugged. "We could only speak on so much last night," he said. "You cannot learn everything about me all in one night. As the days go by, we'll learn more of each other, including my mother being Scots. My brother, Patrick, married a Scots, too, as did my Uncle Paris and my Uncle Kieran. We have family ties to the Scots more than most, so my marriage to you really isn't anything shocking in the annals of my family. In truth, it's quite natural."

Oddly enough, Troy didn't seem so much of a Sassenach now that Rhoswyn knew his mother was a Scot, and there were evidently a host of other Scot wives in his family. That thought gave her a great deal of comfort, in fact. She was already warming to him, but that bit of news seemed to warm her even more.

"Then I shall be pleased tae meet yer mother someday," she said.

"But if she's from Clan Scott, they dunna get on well with Clan Kerr. Did ye know that?"

He nodded, a smile playing on his lips. "Hopefully, that will not pertain to you and me," he said. "I know our introduction was brutal, but I hope we get on well, in time."

That soft comment sent her heart beating so fast that she was coming to feel faint. It was flattery, she thought, or at least could have been. It was such a sharp contrast to yesterday and the chaos of the day that she had no idea how to gracefully deal with it. Rhoswyn was accustomed to dealing with men, with battles, with commands and fighting, but introduce flattery into her world and she was at a loss.

Having no knowledge of how to respond to that, she simply looked away, looking across the bailey and saying the first thing that came to mind.

"It seems that everyone is workin'," she said, sounding nervous and hating it. "I can work, too. What would ye have me do?"

Troy could hear the trembling in her tone and he fought off a grin. He made her giddy with kind words and she wasn't accustomed to them; he could tell. He thought it was rather sweet in a way he'd not experienced in a very long time.

"You have a very big job, Lady de Wolfe," he said.

She looked at him as he addressed her by her title for the first time. Of course, she'd heard it last night, from others and from his command to the other knight, but it was the first time Troy had addressed her directly.

Lady de Wolfe.

She rather liked the sound of it.

"I am not afraid," she said firmly. "What would ye have me do?"

Troy's eyes twinkled at her before he turned to point at the tower and the hall. "All of this is your domain," he said. "There is a nooning meal to be planned and then an evening meal. Stores must be inventoried and food must be cooked, and then you must do it all again tomorrow. You are chatelaine now and that is the biggest duty of all."

Rhoswyn stared at him. Then, she looked to the enormous tower, the hall, and she felt a rush of anxiety.

"But…" she said, stammering over her words. "I… I dunna know anythin' of managin' a house. I wouldna know where to begin."

Troy looked at her, seeing that she'd literally gone pale over the past few moments. It was the first time he'd really seen fear in her expression.

"You are being modest," he said. "Surely you know something."

She shook her head, her fear growing. "Nay, I dunna."

"But you said your mother taught you things that ladies should know. Did she not teach you how to manage a house?"

As Troy watched, tears sprang to Rhoswyn's eyes, tears that she very quickly blinked away. "I was never in the kitchens," she said. "Me pa dinna want me tae do woman's work. But… but I can repair the roof of the stable. Would ye let me do that instead?"

Troy wasn't particularly surprised to hear what must have been a difficult confession. She'd been raised as a son; he knew that. He just didn't know how deep that training ran. Now, he could see that it more than likely ran very deep and Rhoswyn was either terribly embarrassed to admit it or afraid to admit it. In either case, she was looking a little shaken, afraid that she couldn't fulfill what he'd asked her to do.

"I do not need you to repair the roof," he said. "I need you to handle the kitchens and the chatelaine duties. You were truly never taught?"

She shook her head, looking miserable. "Nay. I… I am sorry. Are ye sure there's nothin' else I can do?"

Troy felt rather sorry for the woman. Was it really possible that, trained in a man's world, she knew nothing of a woman's place in it? It seemed far-fetched, but perhaps not so outlandish in Rhoswyn's case. He didn't know a lot about kitchens or tending the house and hold, but he'd seen his mother and wife go about their duties. He supposed he could help Rhoswyn figure it out because, for certain, he didn't want her doing things that his men could do.

"Rhoswyn," he said, rather seriously. "I have men to mend roofs and repair walls. I have men to shoe horses and tend the weapons. What I need is a wife who will tend to my house and hold, and make a comfortable home for me. If your father would not let your mother teach you some things, then that was unkind of him. A woman's place is to please her husband and tend his home. You *do* understand that, do you not?"

Rhoswyn looked rather lost with his question. After a moment, she shrugged. "I remember watchin' me ma as she went about her duties," she said. "But I was always with me pa, learnin' from him. And after me ma died, the servants took up her duties. I never learned."

Troy cocked a dark eyebrow. "Then you are about to learn," he said. "That is where I need you most. I believe you are an intelligent woman and you will learn what needs to be learned. Are you at least willing?"

Rhoswyn looked into his face, thinking that if she wasn't willing, then it would disappoint him. Yesterday, she wouldn't have cared, but this morning... she cared. Her father had told her to be worthy of her new husband... but, God's Bones, she wasn't. She knew she wasn't. She only knew how to fight and not how to be a wife. Was she willing to learn? For the first time in her life, she was willing to learn what a woman did. And it wasn't to lift a sword.

She was embarking into new territory.

"Aye," she said after a moment. "I am willin'."

He smiled faintly at her in a gesture that made her knees go weak. "Good," he said. "I do not know very much, but I think I know the basics of it. Come along with me; let us determine what it is you need to do."

Taking a deep breath for courage, Rhoswyn followed.

ᴄʒ

"I SUPPOSE THESE are the kitchens."

Troy said it as if he didn't quite believe it. They were at the rear of the tower, in a small, walled area, but the entire area was torn up. There were farming implements scattered on the ground and two big iron pots laying in the mud. A couple of chickens were scratching about and there was a nanny goat with a kid nibbling on anything they could get their lips on. Troy scratched his head.

"Well," he said thoughtfully, "I suppose the first thing to do is to determine what you have to work with. Pots and that kind of thing. Then, you should probably make sure these animals have feed. The feed, I would guess, is in the barn or around here somewhere. Pen up the chickens and see if they've laid eggs somewhere. You will need those eggs."

Rhoswyn was trying very hard not to feel overwhelmed. She looked around at the utterly neglected area, seeing that the goats looked a little skinny. She'd always had a soft spot for animals so she went to the pair before she even looked to anything else, petting the little kid and running her hands over the nanny's body.

"Poor wee beasties," she said. "They're hungry. I'll go find their feed right away."

Troy didn't stop her; she was already disoriented enough so he didn't want to upset whatever balance she was trying to find. If she thought the goats needed tending first, then he would let her. But he remained in the yard, finding three eggs, while Rhoswyn was off finding something for the goats to eat. It didn't take her long because she pilfered from the horse's feed, the dried grass and grains that Troy had brought with him in his provisions wagons. As Troy found a fourth egg in the ruined yard, Rhoswyn came rushing back with a sack of grain in her arms.

"Here we are," she said as she rushed over to the goats and dropped to her knees, setting the sack to the ground. She tried to rip at the sack but she couldn't break the seams, so Troy pulled out a small dagger and handed it to her. Smiling gratefully, she slit a small hole in the sack and poured the grain onto the ground. "Eat, wee sweetings."

The goats began to munch hungrily and Troy herded the chickens towards the grain so they could eat also. With the animals being fed,

Rhoswyn set the sack of grain against the wall of the tower, since the kitchen yard backed right up to it, and brushed off her hands.

"There," she said, as if feeding the beasts was the most important thing in all of this. "Now, what more would ye have me tae do?"

The fact that she would feed the animals before anything told Troy that Rhoswyn had a softer heart than she let on. A little something more he was learning about her. He put his hands on his narrow hips, looking around the yard.

"As I said, inventory what you have here," he said. "I found four eggs and put them in the hen's pen over there. That looks as if it can use some repairing, too. Mayhap you could fix that so your chickens do not run away or get eaten by hungry men. Once you have cleaned this area up, find me and we shall determine what needs to be done next."

"Next?" she repeated. "How will we even know what tae do next? Although I appreciate yer help, I feel as if one blind man is leadin' another in this matter. Neither one of us knows much about kitchens. Mayhap I should send tae Sibbald's for one of the womenfolk tae come. At least I could learn from her."

Troy scratched his head. "That is a possibility," he said. Then, he cocked his head thoughtfully. "But I have a better idea; I will send for one of my knights and he can bring his wife. I was not going to bring any of my knights here but, in this case, I think I should. His wife can teach you how to run a house and hold, at least the way I am used to things. Would you be willing to learn from her?"

Rhoswyn looked at him dubiously. "An English lass?"

"She could teach you well."

She mulled it over, suspecting it might make him happy if she agreed. She'd married an Englishman so perhaps she'd better learn the English way. Therefore, she nodded reluctantly.

"As ye say," she said. "But... but she willna think me a fool, will she? For not knowin' what I should probably know, I mean."

Troy smiled. "She will be very kind and patient with you, I promise," he said. "Shall I send for her, then?"

"Aye."

"Good."

"When will she come?"

He glanced up at the position of the early morning sun. "If I send a swift rider to Kale Water now, she can be here by sup, more than likely. Kale Water Castle is only ten miles to the north."

It all sounded reasonable to Rhoswyn. She looked around the yard, at the mess around them. It would be a daunting task for anyone. "Ye'd better warn the lass of what she's comin' intae."

There was some dry humor in that statement and Troy grinned. "No warning needed," he said. "English women are not as weak as you seem to think they are. But until she arrives, you can tend to the animals and repair what you can around here. Then we need to discuss what to do about an evening meal. My men will be hungry."

Rhoswyn simply nodded. In truth, she didn't feel so overwhelmed as she had earlier, knowing that help was on the way. If this was to be her lot in life, with a handsome husband she was more than intrigued with, then she was willing to learn. Even from an English woman.

"Then I will do what I can for now," she asked. "When I am finished, where can I find ye? I mean, where will ye go?"

Troy looked at her. Did he hear longing in her voice? Of course not. He'd known the woman less than a day. It was far too soon to hear anything sentimental like that, even though part of him wanted to hear it. But the other part of him was deeply reluctant, convinced that this would be a civil marriage and nothing more. He didn't want to feel anything for Rhoswyn. He refused to. Any feelings he had, as he'd told Paris, were for Helene, still. They always would be.

He was firm in that.

"I am not sure where I will be, but it is not a big complex," he said. "You will easily find me somewhere. Ask one of my men if you cannot locate me; they will know."

Rhoswyn's features tensed with some uncertainty. She looked in the direction of the bailey, seeing the English moving around in the distance.

"They dunna know me," she said. "I am only a Scots tae them."

Troy shook his head. "You are my wife. They know that."

She looked at him, then. "And that alone will cause them to respect me? Nay, laddie. I must earn their respect, I think."

Laddie. She'd said it again. That little term that he rather liked hearing from her lips. "Why do you call me that?" he asked.

"What?"

"Laddie. I'm not a lad, you know."

She gave him a half-grin. "I dunna know," she said. "A habit, I suppose."

He lifted his eyebrows. "You call all men laddie?"

She laughed softly. "Nay, but me pa does," she said. "'Tis a kind term, I suppose. Pa uses it with the men he likes. It's when he doesna call ye laddie that ye should worry."

He could see the humor in her words. He was coming to see that she did have a sense of humor, and he was glad. If she was willing to let it come through, then perhaps she was, indeed, becoming resigned to the situation and the way things were. It was one more step in a series of small steps that she had to take in order to become accustomed to her new life. But she was moving forward, in any case. Troy took a step towards her, leaning down so he was more on her level.

"If ye want tae call me laddie, then I'll answer," he said, mimicking her Scots brogue. "I'll come tae whatever ye wish tae call me."

With that, he winked at her and headed out of the yard, leaving Rhoswyn struggling to catch her breath again. Oh, what that man could do to her!

And the way he walked… he stalked, really. Long, smooth strides. It was a proud sort of walk. She watched him walk out into the bailey and disappear from sight but, still, she stood there like an idiot, thinking of that wink he gave her. There was that flattery again, something she wasn't used to but something she knew she could grow to like. It made her feel special in a way that no one ever had.

Laddie. Perhaps that made him feel special, too. As if they were starting to understand one another.

A grin played on her lips as she turned around and went back to work.

CHAPTER ELEVEN

Kale Water Castle

I T WAS A brisk autumn day as Lady Sable de Moray de Shera sat in front of a warm fire, working on a tiny little tunic. One of the serving women at Kale had just delivered a healthy son and Sable, who was very good with a needle and thread, was finishing up on the warm little garment for the child. She was a thoughtful woman, to friends as well as servants, and well-loved at Kale. She was overwhelmingly loved by her husband, who even after a year of marriage, was as besotted with his wife as he was the day he married her.

With brown eyes, brown hair, and a porcelain face, Sable was exceedingly lovely and possessed graceful manners. Finishing her last stitch, she cut the bits of thread from the garment and held it up, looking at her handiwork. Pleased with it, she considered sewing another one, as she had enough fabric to do so, when the old oak door to the solar pushed open and her husband appeared. Sable smiled at the man as she set the little tunic to her lap.

"Well?" she asked. "What brings you to me? Did you miss me so terribly that you could not stand being parted from me, not even since breaking our fast?"

Cassius de Shera grinned at his wife. A very large man with broad shoulders, dark green eyes, and wavy dark hair, he was a son of the great and powerful House of de Shera. The patriarchs of the family were three brothers who had fought with Simon de Montfort during the tussle for the throne against Henry III. *Lords of Thunder*, they'd been called for their prowess and power in battle, and Cassius was a tribute to that reputation. He was the bastard son of the middle brother, Maximus, but the family had never treated him as if he was any less because he'd been born out of wedlock.

In fact, Cassius was as well-trained and well-loved as the legitimate offspring, hence his presence here in the north. His father had sent him north to train with de Wolfe and learn the ways of the Scots, part of his broader training as a knight, and Cassius was hungry to learn all he could. He'd come to Kale Water right after his marriage to Sable, about a year prior, so they'd spent their entire married life up here in the wilds of the north.

It had been as wonderful as both of them could have ever imagined.

Which made Sable's question something of the truth. Cassius couldn't go for more than an hour without seeing his wife if he could help it, and she felt the same. They were eager lovers, deeply devoted to one another, and he went to her and kissed her on the top of the head as she sat in her cushioned chair.

"Y-You know I cannot stand to be parted from you, in any case," he said. Cassius had been born with a slight catch in his speech, something he'd worked very hard to be rid of. These days, it was barely noticeable. "But I did come with another purpose, believe it or not. A messenger has just come from Troy, bearing great news. The *reivers* have been chased from Monteviot and the tower is now a de Wolfe holding. William has asked Troy to remain for a time to secure it."

Sable was looking at him with some surprise. "So they were successful!"

"Aye. T-They were victorious."

She smiled with relief. "I am very happy to hear that."

Before Cassius could reply, another big body appeared in the solar door and they both looked over to see Brodie de Reyne filling up the portal, his fair face alight.

"Did you hear?" he demanded. "The armies were victorious at Monteviot!"

Cassius nodded patiently. "Aye, we've heard," he said. "I was just telling my wife"

Brodie was grinning broadly. A tall and muscular man, he was from the prestigious de Reyne family, a very large family that had roots in Northumbria and York. He had a vivacious personality, something that ladies took to quite easily, and he had no shortage of female admirers.

With his blond good looks and bright smile, Brodie de Reyne had quite a reputation as a lady's man, something that had worried Cassius until Brodie once said something to Sable that she construed as flirtatious and she'd belted him across the mouth in outrage. After that, Cassius worried no more and Brodie was very careful what he said to Lady de Shera. Any daughter of the great Bose de Moray undoubtedly had her father's fighting skills, so Brodie didn't push Lady de Shera any more than necessary.

In truth, he was afraid of her.

Therefore, when he came into the solar, it was to shake Cassius' hand as if to congratulate them both on Troy's victory, but he made no move to shake Lady de Shera's hand. She might stab him with her needle, anyway.

"I had little doubt theirs would be a great victory," Brodie said. "With so many armies converging on that little tower, the *reivers* never stood a chance."

Cassius nodded. "T-True enough," he said. Then, he held up something he'd been holding in his left hand, a roll of yellowed vellum. "The messenger that came from Monteviot to deliver the news of triumph also brought a missive from Troy. It seems that the de Wolfe victory over the Scots was not the only big event to have taken place."

Brodie's smile faded. "What do you mean?" he asked. "What does the missive say?"

Cassius wriggled his eyebrows, perhaps hinting at the shocking nature of the missive, as he unrolled the vellum and looked at the scribed words. He'd already read them once but he did so again for the benefit of his wife and Brodie.

"I-It would seem that Red Keith Kerr showed up at Monteviot after the battle and demanded de Wolfe's best warrior against his best warrior," he said. "A warrior-against-warrior battle to decide whether or not Keith would demand his outpost returned to him or if de Wolfe would keep it. William evidently pitted Troy against the Kerr warrior."

Brodie's eyebrows lifted. "And?"

Cassius glanced up from the missive. "Troy lost."

Brodie's face went slack with shock. "Impossible," he hissed. "Troy de Wolfe cannot lose. The man is too skilled and too powerful to lose to a Scotsman!"

Cassius held up a hand to ease the man's disbelief. "From what Troy says, all was not as it seemed," he said. "He was asked to fight a Kerr warrior who turned out to be a woman. Troy was so surprised that it gave the woman the upper hand and she was able to force him to submit. At least, that was how Troy tells it."

Brodie's mouth was hanging open. "I do not believe it!"

Cassius' gaze lingered on the vellum for a moment longer before rolling it up and handing it to Brodie. "Believe it," he said. "Red Keith's terms were not the return of Monteviot, however; the terms he set forth were that a man of William's choosing would marry Red Keith's daughter to form an alliance."

Brodie's shock was gaining. "A marriage?" he scowled. "Who was the hapless fool to be forced into that agreement?"

"Troy."

Now, Sable's disbelief joined Brodie's. She leapt out of her chair and snatched the vellum from Brodie's hands. She could read, in fact, and she began to read Troy's handwriting carefully.

"A *wife*!" she gasped as she scanned the words. "I cannot believe it! Now Troy has a *wife*?"

Cassius nodded. "A-Aye, and he needs help with her," he said. "You will note on the missive that he has asked you and me to go to Monteviot. In particular, he asks that you come to help Lady de Wolfe with her new duties. He asks that we come right away."

Sable could read that part. Like Brodie, her mouth popped open in shock but she quickly shut it, looking to her husband with wide eyes.

"We are going to Monteviot, then?" she asked.

Cassius nodded. "Troy has asked it of us," he said. "I-I do not know how long we shall be there, so you had better pack everything you need to be away for a few weeks at least. Brodie, you are in command while I am at Monteviot."

Brodie nodded, taking the missive back from Sable when she finished with it. As he read the missive one more time, Sable was already thinking on what she needed to take and how quickly she could pack.

"I shall have the servants bring my trunks down from the storage room," she said. "I shall bring clothing and personal things, like bedding. But I wonder what more I should bring?"

Cassius shrugged. "Monteviot has undoubtedly seen a serious battle," he said. "T-That means that the outpost itself will be damaged. Even the smallest things, like kitchens and stables, will see damage. I would suggest we bring all we can, expecting to find the place in ruins. I cannot imagine, with the size of de Wolfe's army, that much of the place is still intact."

Sable thought about all of the trunks she had in storage and of all the things she could pack in them. A woman with an innate sense of determination in all things, she nodded firmly and turned on her heel.

"I will go now and begin preparations," she said.

Cassius stopped her before she could get too far away. "How soon do you believe you will be ready?" he asked. "Troy has asked us to come right away, so you cannot take days. You can only take hours."

Sable nodded smartly. "I can have everything packed and ready to go in a few hours," she said confidently. "How long will it take us to reach Monteviot?"

"No more than two or three hours."

Sable thought quickly. "It is not quite the nooning meal yet," she said, thinking aloud. "Give me two hours. I believe I can have everything ready by then. We will need a wagon, however."

"A-Aye, my love."

"And I want to bring Eda and Hazel," she said. "You do not think there are any house servants at Monteviot, do you?"

Cassius shook his head. "Nay," he said. "T-The army would have only brought servants and trades related to the army. I would wager to say there is nothing by way of household servants at that outpost."

"Then I shall bring them," Sable said decisively. "I will need their help."

With that, she blew her husband a kiss and rushed off to complete her task, leaving Cassius and Brodie with the contents of the missive lingering between them. When Sable's footsteps faded away, Brodie looked at Cassius.

"He *had* to marry a Kerr wench?" he hissed. "God's Bones, Cass. That sounds like a nightmare. He could not have done it willingly."

Cassius could only imagine Troy's reluctance at such a thing. Furthermore, he was surprised that the man's father, William, would have suggested it, knowing how Troy was still grieving for his first wife. At least, that was always the impression he got from the man. He honestly couldn't fathom how Troy was handling the situation, but he was soon to find out.

"First he is defeated by a woman in a challenge, and then he has to marry a woman he does not even know," he said. Then, he cocked his head curiously. "G-God's Bones… do you think it is the same woman?"

Brodie was appalled at the mere thought. "I hope not," he said. "If it is… God help the man is all I can say. My grandmother was Scots, you know. Clan Kerr, in fact. She died several years ago but the woman was a spitfire up until the end. As children, we were terrified of her. I think all of the women of Clan Kerr must be fearsome creatures."

Cassius, too, was concerned for Troy and his forced marriage to a Scots woman. "I do not think I have ever heard you mention your grandmother."

Brodie nodded. "Cari was her name," he said. "I remember that she and my grandfather were deeply in love, so I suppose there is some redeeming quality in a Scots woman. But she was terrifying, by God."

Cassius smiled faintly at the real fear Brodie displayed, even after all of this years. "Well," he said, taking the missive back from Brodie. "I-I suppose all we can do is hope for the best and hope that Troy's new bride is not as frightening as your grandmother. But I will admit I am rather concerned with what I will find at Monteviot. Troy is undoubtedly extremely unhappy with this marriage and…"

"And it could make for a miserable situation," Brodie finished for him. "It sounds selfish of me to say this, but better that you're going than me, old man. Best of luck. I fear you will need it."

Cassius simply cocked an eyebrow at the man as he fled the solar, away from Cassius as if fearful the man would rope him into going to Monteviot, too. It sounded like a perfectly ghastly situation at the fallen outpost, one that Cassius and his wife would soon be entering. But Troy had asked for help and they had no choice but to answer the call.

Cassius had to admit that he wasn't looking forward to it.

Any of it.

CHAPTER TWELVE

Monteviot Tower

THE MORE RHOSWYN worked, the more at ease – and the more determined – she became. In lieu of the chaos she was faced with in the kitchen area, it was simply a matter of picking a place to start, and she did.

She started with the animals.

The nanny goat and her kid were her priority at first. They had a little shelter, she could see, but the roof had been ripped off of it, perhaps to make projectiles or even to be used as firewood, so she walked the bailey of Monteviot in a hunt for scraps of wood or rocks to use to repair it. The wood was scattered from the projectiles the *reivers* had made from furniture in the tower, pieces of bed frame or legs of a chair.

On her walk, Rhoswyn came across the priest, and Audric offered to help her. Unused to help of any kind, she wasn't sure how to deter the priest who seemed undeterrable, so she simply kept hunting for wood and other materials while Audric followed her around and picked up pieces on his own.

As they hunted, Rhoswyn paid no attention to the man, but that didn't discourage him. He was determined to help her whether or not she wanted him to. Soon enough, they had quite a bundle of scrap wood and they headed back to the kitchen where Rhoswyn was forced to explain what she was doing. Audric wasn't going anywhere so she could no longer ignore him. He was more than happy to help with her projects and while she fixed the roof on the goat enclosure, Audric worked on the chicken pen, which was also damaged.

Between the two of them, they managed to repair the housing for the animals. Rhoswyn put the goats back into their pen and then she and the priest hunted down all of the chickens, which turned out to be nine more of them, including a cock. They also found more eggs on their hunt, mostly in the buildings behind the kitchen which might have been a buttery or butchery at some point. In all, they collected twenty-one eggs and eleven chickens total, and put the chickens back into their pen while the precious eggs were set aside.

The entire time, Audric kept up a steady stream of conversation while Rhoswyn remained mostly silent. She was wary of the priest from Jedburgh but, more than that, with her conversational skills lacking and not having any friends, she was unaccustomed to being with someone on a friendly basis. Comfortable companionship had no meaning to her. Every time the priest would talk about something, she would look at the man as if greatly annoyed – or greatly confused – by his presence.

But Audric soldiered on. He suspected that the lady was leery of him because of the part he played in her wedding, but it didn't dissuade him. William de Wolfe had asked him to remain and lend counsel to the couple, and that meant earning their trust. Audric had been a priest for ten years but before that, he grew up in the church and was educated by the priests at Jedburgh. An orphan at a young age, the church was the only family he knew and he took his duties very seriously. He knew what it meant for his flock to trust him.

Therefore, he had to earn the woman's trust.

So, he kept up a stream of conversation as they rebuilt the habitats for the animals and collected more eggs, putting them with the four that Troy had found earlier in the day. He continued to follow the lady as she went to the stable to bring hay for the goats and chickens to bed down with, and he stood by and watched her make cozy little homes for the animals. By then, it was after midday and both of them were growing hungry. At some point, they had to think about food and preparing a meal for the evening to come.

As Rhoswyn stood by the goat's pen and looked as if she wasn't sure what to do next, Audric went around the kitchen yard and began to collect the pots that were strewn about to put them all in one place.

"The bread oven looks as if it has survived, my lady," Audric said, pointing to the beehive-shaped structure made entirely of stone. "Mayhap we should build a fire to start the oven?"

Rhoswyn looked at the oven as if it had come from another world. "Why?" she asked. "I canna make bread."

Audric looked around the yard. "Surely there is grain to grind into flour," he said. "Look, there; a sack of grain. We can use that…"

She cut him off. "That is for the animals," she said. "I took it from the English provisions wagon."

Audric went over to it, peering inside. "'Tis barley," he said. "We can make flour out of it and bake bread."

He was forcing Rhoswyn into an embarrassing admission. "I dunna know *how* tae make the bread," she said. "Even if we had everythin' we needed, I've never made bread in me life."

Audric understood now; it wasn't that she couldn't make the bread, it was simply that she had no idea how to do it. In truth, he wasn't surprised – this was the lass who had bested an English knight. He'd seen it. A lass like that had to be trained, for years, and Audric was coming to think that Red Keith had made his daughter a warrior and nothing else. For certain, she seemed very lost in a kitchen. She'd rather take care of the animals and repair their pens than prepare food, and now he found out why.

But Audric was unconcerned.

"Ah, but I have made bread before, many times," he said confidently. "When I was young, one of me duties was in the kitchens at Jedburgh. I can make bread. Would ye have me show ye how?"

Would it be admitting she was helpless if she agreed? Rhoswyn didn't have much choice. He was offering and it was a skill she needed to know. Swallowing her pride, she nodded, once. And it was difficult for her to do that.

"Aye," she said.

Audric beckoned to her. "Then come along," he said. "I will show ye what we need tae do. First, we must build a fire in the bread oven. Can ye do that? If ye do, I'll find what we need tae start the bread."

Starting a fire was something Rhoswyn could, indeed, do and she quickly took to the task. She went out to collect more scattered wood, bringing it back to the kitchen yard while Audric went on the hunt for what he needed to bake the bread. He needed a mortar and pestle, or a grinding stone at the very least, and he went about looking for such things but was unable to find them. When Rhoswyn returned with the wood for the fire, he explained his problem and she was able to improvise two rocks for him to use to grind up the grain.

As Rhoswyn started the fire in the oven, she watched Audric grind the barley for flour and she didn't feel quite so helpless because she'd helped him make the flour in a sense. She'd come up with the rocks for him to use, so she had a vested interested in this process. But she watched him closely as he worked and when the fire in the oven was burning brightly, she went to help him grind up the grain by using another set of stones, wiped off with the hem of her tunic to remove the surface dirt.

It was hard work, but satisfying. Rhoswyn and Audric ground a good deal of the barley grain into a coarse flour, which they piled into a wooden bucket they'd found. It was good for their purposes and into the coarse flour that looked like sand, Audric added two of their precious eggs, a bit of the nanny goat's milk, and enough water to make it a paste.

Bread was in the making.

Rhoswyn was rather thrilled to see how easy it was. Audric sent her on the hunt for salt and she ended up in the bottom level of the tower where there were some food stores. She found baskets of dried, dirty carrots, turnips, dried beans of some kind, and meat that had blue mold on it. In one of the last sacks she checked, she came across the salt she was looking for, as salt was as necessary to men as was the air to breathe. No good Scottish house was without it. She rushed the salt sack out to Audric, who mixed it in with his bread dough. Then, they began to make the flat discs of bread.

It was really very simple and Rhoswyn was eager to do it. She mimicked Audric as the man made flat discs of dough, about the size of man's splayed hand, and laid them on the hot stones of the oven. Once he showed Rhoswyn how to do it, she was making dough discs at an alarming rate, confident in her newfound skill. But Audric called her off of the bread making to go start another fire in the pit in the center of the yard, where it looked as if much of the cooking had been done. The pit was deep and full of charcoal.

While Audric watched the baking bread, removing discs that were finished and replacing them with those that needed to be baked, Rhoswyn started the fire in the pit. At Audric's instruction, she rinsed out both of the big iron pots they'd found, making sure they were free of grit on the interior, and filled both pots up with water from the well. There was one other bucket that they'd located, a smaller one, so it took her some time to do it, but soon there were two pots of water sitting on the pit. Audric had her put all of their eggs into the smaller pot to boil.

In truth, Rhoswyn felt as if she had accomplished a good deal as she watched the pots begin to steam. Soon, they would boil. Looking around the kitchen yard, she noted the fixed animal pens, the bread oven that was working, and the yard in general that had been cleaned of its clutter for the most part. She'd even organized the garden implements and other iron tools she'd come across. Aye, she'd accomplished something today and she felt rather proud of herself.

She wondered if Troy would be proud of her, too.

Oh, but it was a secret and silly wish. That she should look for approval from a Sassenach was foolish, indeed, but she harbored that secret hope. As the smell of baking bread filled the air, she was coming to feel as if taking care of a house and hold wasn't such a difficult job, after all. If the priest knew how to cook, surely he could teach her, too. Surely she could learn to mend clothing or stuff a bed, or any of the other chores that ladies did.

Her confidence in herself was growing.

As Audric continued with the bread, Rhoswyn went back into the bottom level of the tower and brought out the carrots. She pointed them out to Audric, who encouraged her to cook them in the second pot of water that was coming to a boil. She did, dumping several big handfuls into the water before Audric realized she was doing it without washing the carrots of their grime. She'd just dumped quite a few dirty carrots into the water and seemed quite proud of herself, so he was gentle in telling her that she should have washed them first. As he was trying to explain the way of things, Troy entered the yard.

The smell of baking bread had lured him and he entered the yard, looking around with great surprise. He spied Audric, by the bread oven.

"What are you still doing here?" he asked the priest, surprised. "I thought you left with the armies this morning?"

Audric pulled two baked discs out of the oven, tossing them into a basket he had at his feet that was collecting the baked bread, and burning his fingers in the process. He blew at his fingers as he answered.

"Yer father asked me tae remain, my lord," he said. "He thought… that my presence would be best served here for a time."

Troy had no idea what the man meant. "My father asked you to remain? But I do not need a priest."

Audric moved away from the bread oven, brushing at his scorched hands. "Yer father thought I could be of help with… with the lady," he said, lowering his voice so Rhoswyn couldn't hear. Then, he raised it again, loudly. "The lady and I have been bakin' bread and preparin' a meal. She has done very well."

Troy looked at Rhoswyn, who was standing over two steaming iron pots. When their eyes met, she smiled timidly and Troy felt his heart leap, just a little. Flush-faced because of the fire, she was pink-cheeked and radiant. He thought she looked quite beautiful.

"I thought you did not know how to run a kitchen?" he asked her, sweeping his arm at the yard in general. "Now I hear you are baking bread and making a meal?"

Rhoswyn's rosy cheeks flushed even more at what sounded like praise. "The priest has done most of it," she said quickly. "He has been tellin' me what tae do."

Troy smiled at her. "I am sure you are being modest, my lady," he said. "The bread smells wonderful. And what is in the pots?"

Rhoswyn peered down into the simmering water because he was. "Eggs," she said. "We found more eggs and are boilin' them. And I found carrots in the vault – I am boilin' them, also."

Troy could see a film of dirt on the top of the water with the carrots in it. It looked as if she was boiling them in mud but he didn't say anything – he was simply glad she had tried. Not that he had expected less; from what he'd seen, Rhoswyn was industrious. He was glad she was doing what she could, muddy carrots and all.

"I have more provisions in the stables that I shall have brought over here," he told her. "You say you've been in the vault? Is there room for more stores?"

Rhoswyn nodded quickly. "Indeed, there is," she said. "Can I help with the provisions?"

He smiled at her, a sweet gesture because she was so eager to work. He appreciated that quality. "I shall have them brought to you and then you can decide where they go in the vault," he said. "Remain here with the priest and continue with what you were doing. I shall return shortly."

Rhoswyn simply nodded, watching him walk away, before returning her focus to her boiling pots. But as she bent over the carrots, realizing there was a great deal of dirt in the water, she heard Troy's voice again.

That voice...

"Lady de Wolfe."

He was calling to her and her head snapped up, looking at him as he stood by the kitchen gate. "Aye?"

His smile broadened as his gaze lingered on her. "You have tried hard today," he said. "I am pleased."

With a wink, he headed off, leaving Rhoswyn struggling to catch her breath again. Every time he said something kind to her, she had difficulty breathing. What was it with the man that he could make her feel so weak and giddy with a few simple words? It was enough to bring a smile to her lips but when she looked over and saw that the priest was looking at her as well, she wiped the grin off her face and quickly lowered her head.

She didn't want the priest to see anything. Whatever was stirring inside of her for Troy de Wolfe, that was for her and her alone.

She didn't want to share it.

⚃

MORE FOOD WAS brought in by the provisions wagons, which had been kept in the stables. It was more food than Rhoswyn had ever seen in her life.

As Audric continued to bake the discs of bread in the oven that gave off a tremendous amount of heat, Rhoswyn found herself directing several English soldiers, her husband included, as they brought the stores into the ground level of the tower. It was cold and dank down there, smelling of earth, but it was a perfect storage area for preserving food.

Big pieces of salted, dried beef and mutton that had been in the wagons and layered with straw to keep them protected were brought into the vault along with sacks of rye and wheat, beans, peas, onions, and garlic. Big bags of salt were also brought in along with wheels of cheese that had been wrapped up tightly in hemp sacks.

In truth, it was a great deal of food, enough to supplement an army on the move and certainly enough for the fortress, at least for a little while. Certainly, they could address that issue after more of the pressing issues had been solved.

Pressing issues like where to bed down all of the men that had come with Troy. Monteviot just wasn't made for the numbers Troy had brought with him, so as Rhoswyn went back to the kitchens to finish with the coming meal, Troy discussed the situation of bedding down all of his men so they weren't sleeping outside, as they had since their arrival to Monteviot. He wanted everyone under a roof. So once the provisions were all put into the ground floor of the tower, Troy and his senior soldiers headed out into the bailey to decide what was to be done with bedding down an army of this size in a fortress that wasn't designed for so many men.

But he didn't leave before casting Rhoswyn a little smile, something that made her feel warm and giddy all over. Having never had such feelings, she had no idea how to control them or even how to hide them. He smiled and she felt like so much mush, feeling embarrassed and thrilled all at the same time.

Fighting off a grin, Rhoswyn remained in the vault for a little while after he left, moving sacks around, organizing everything. She had a bit of an orderly streak in her and she liked things to be just so. With the foods grouped into meats, grains, and dairy, she had three of the English soldiers help her carry one of the big slabs of beef into the kitchen yard where food was being prepared for the coming meal.

Since the eggs were finished boiling, she used a big wooden spoon to remove all of them and set them aside before retrieving a dirk from her possessions in the tower and using it to cut the slab of beef into chunks. It went into the same water that had been boiling the eggs.

Audric, nearly finished with the bread, came to help her when the last of the bread discs ended up in the big basket. With all of the flour they'd ground, there were a little over a hundred of the bread discs, probably not enough for all of the men that evening, but it would have to do. There were just the two of them to prepare the meal, so the big bread trenchers would have to be shared.

Even though Rhoswyn wasn't an expert at tending a house and hold, even she could see that they needed assistance. They needed kitchen servants and probably servants for the tower and for the hall, and she made a mental note to speak to Troy that evening. Surely he could send for servants from any one of the de Wolfe properties. All she knew was that, even at this early stage, it was too much work for one person.

She needed help.

As Rhoswyn cut the last of the beef and threw it into the water along with a handful of salt at Audric's prompting, she felt rather as if she'd accomplished a great deal on this day, probably more that she'd ever accomplished in her life. In truth, she didn't think she'd ever worked so hard and she had new respect for the chatelaines all over the world because, certainly, their lives weren't entirely simple. Working in the kitchens was hard work, and she hadn't even touched anything that had to do with milking goats or making cheese or butter. She'd accomplished the bare minimum as far as kitchen duties were concerned. She truly had no idea how or where to start on more tasks, but perhaps Audric would.

The thought of the priest who had helped her so much crossed her mind and she looked over to see the man as he carefully stirred the steaming pot of beef to make sure all of the meat was covered with the boiling water. He'd followed her around most of the day, talking to her, instructing her, even as she did her best to ignore him. She was rather glad her attitude hadn't discouraged him because she wouldn't have been able to do any of this without his help.

Truly, he'd been a Godsend. As she stood there and wiped her hands on her tunic, she cleared her throat softly.

"It looks as if the men willna go hungry tonight," she said.

Audric was carefully stirring the pot of beef with a big wooden spoon, then using his fingers to shift pieces of meat around. "Nay," he said. "And it looks as if they have enough in stores for a few days, anyway."

Rhoswyn nodded as an uncomfortable silence settled. "Ye... ye've been a great help," she finally said. "I dunna know what would have happened had ye not lent me yer assistance."

Audric looked up at her; it sounded suspiciously like some form of gratitude, which surprised him. Proud Lady Rhoswyn didn't seem the type to thank anyone, so he was rather touched by it.

"I'm glad tae help," he told her. "I'm glad tae see that ye're tryin' tae please yer new husband."

Rhoswyn's first reaction was one of displeasure at that statement but in the same breath, she realized that the priest was correct. She *was* here to please her husband and she had no function other than that. It was the lot of a wife and she was now among those women who were sworn to please their husbands. Perhaps if she'd married anyone other than Troy, she might have violently opposed the priest's statement. She'd been a strong woman her entire life, not dependent on a man. She didn't *need* a man. But because she'd married Troy... aye, she wanted to please him. He'd told her that he was pleased with her and she liked the feeling his approval gave her.

As if she were worth something.

"'Tis me duty now, I suppose," she said, glancing up at the enormous tower and shielding her eyes from the afternoon sun. "Makin' me husband happy. But I'll admit that yesterday, I never imagined this would be me life today. Married tae a Sassenach? If anyone had told me, I would have called them a bloody liar."

Audric suppressed a grin. "Does it seem so bad, lass?"

She looked at him, wondering if she was brave enough to admit that, so far, it hadn't been bad at all. At least, for her it hadn't. Priests were sworn not to repeat confessions, weren't they? They knew how to keep their mouths shuts, didn't they? Rhoswyn had never in her life had anyone to confide in, about anything, and at times that had made for a lonely existence. But the priest had been helpful all day, so perhaps he wasn't just hanging about to annoy her. Perhaps he was someone she really could talk to.

"Were ye here yesterday when me pa and I arrived?" she asked.

Audric nodded. "I was."

"Did ye see the challenge?"

He knew what she meant. "Ye mean when ye kicked de Wolfe in his man parts?" he asked. When she nodded, a rather horrified expression on her face by his blunt description of what she'd done, he continued. "Aye, I saw it."

Rhoswyn eyed him, half-embarrassed. "I told him I had tae do it," she said. "Had I not tried tae disable him at the first, he would have destroyed me."

Audric shrugged. "Ye did what ye had tae do, lass."

"Do ye think he'll forgive me for it?"

"If what I saw today was any indication, I think he already has."

Rhoswyn was very interested to hear that. "Do ye believe so?"

Audric nodded. "I do," he said. "I had time tae speak with de Wolfe yesterday a little, before ye came. He seems like a reasonable man, for a Sassenach. I think ye could have done much worse for a husband."

Rhoswyn was vastly grateful and vastly relieved to hear the priest's opinion. She looked around the kitchen yard, to the steaming pots, to the pile of boiled eggs, and felt fortified by what she'd been told. If it was true that Troy had forgiven her for their rough introduction, then that was all she could ask for.

"I suppose time will tell," she said, a note of hope in her tone. "Let's show him how the Scots can make a meal, shall we? I'll finish out here if ye'll go intae the hall and make sure it's ready for the food. And make sure there's a fire in the hearth?"

Audric nodded. "Are ye sure ye wouldna like to go do that? I can tend the food."

Rhoswyn shook her head firmly. "Ye've helped so much already and I'm very grateful. But he's me husband… I'll bring his food."

Audric wasn't entirely sure he should leave her alone with the final preparations for the meal, but he didn't dispute her. She wanted to do it herself, so he would do as she asked. Heading out of the kitchen yard and towards the hall, he truly hoped Troy would appreciate all of the trouble his new wife was going through for him. She was trying very hard, and Troy had noticed, but Audric thought he might say a little something more to the knight to let him know just how hard she had worked. For a lass who knew nothing of kitchens or cooking, she'd put in a tremendous effort.

William de Wolfe had asked Audric to remain and help the newly-wed couple, and Audric took that request to heart. Before he headed to the hall, he sought out Troy to tell the man of the great effort his new and inexperienced wife had gone through, just for him. Perhaps it would endear the lass to her new husband, just a little. For certain, for the effort she'd put in, she deserved it.

Whether or not the food was any good.

CHAPTER THIRTEEN

I T WASN'T.

Troy sat at one of the three big tables in the hall of Monteviot, looking at the meal that had been placed before him.

The food wasn't any good.

The beef hadn't been cooked long enough and the carrots were mushy and full of grit. The bread didn't seem too bad, but that was the only thing edible that was put in front of him. Rhoswyn herself had put the trencher of food in front of him and even now, smiled bashfully as he looked up at her. Troy could see just how hopeful she was that he approved of the meal she prepared. God, he just couldn't break her heart.

"You did this all yourself, did you?" he asked.

Rhoswyn shrugged. "The priest helped me," she said. "I dunna even remember the man's name, but he helped me a great deal."

Troy looked down at his food again, a steaming mess of inedible slop. "Audric is his name," he said, scratching his neck as a delaying tactic. He knew he had to eat it but he wasn't eager to get started. "So… you did the cooking yourself, did you?"

He couldn't think of anything else to ask, but Rhoswyn didn't notice. She thought it was more of his flattery. She had another bowl in her hand, something she'd brought into the hall along with Troy's trencher, and she set it on the table in front of him.

"I boiled the eggs meself," she said. "There are not very many, so I thought ye could have yer fill of them before offerin' the rest tae the men."

Troy grabbed at the eggs immediately; he took at least six. They were still in their shells so he had to peel them, which was no great hardship. *Thank God there was something edible at the meal!* He cracked one on the table top and began to peel it.

"Could you bring me some salt for these eggs?" he asked politely.

Rhoswyn nodded eagerly and dashed from the hall. But it was a tactic, really, to get her out of there. Troy waited until she had fled the chamber before standing up with his trencher in hand. There were already a few dozen men in the hall, who hadn't yet been served, and he emitted a piercing whistle between his teeth to get their attention. When they looked at him, expectantly, he held up the trencher.

"Listen, lads," he hissed loudly, as loudly as he could without shouting. "You'll not repeat what I'm about to tell you, do you hear me? You are about to be served inarguably one of the worst meals you will ever know, but if one of you makes a disparaging comment about it, I'll cut your tongue out and heave you over the walls. Lady de Wolfe has tried very hard to make a good meal, so on her effort alone, we shall not be cruel. Eat what you can and give the rest to the dogs. I'm afraid you'll go hungry this night."

The men looked at him with a combination of confusion and apprehension, mumbling to each other.

"What's wrong with it, my lord?" one of the men asked.

Troy tried not to roll his eyes; there were many answers to that simple question. "You will know when you see it," he said. "But not a word, do you hear? Be polite."

He was about to say something more when he could see movement by the hall entry and Audric entered, carrying two big trenchers of food. Quickly, Troy turned his back to the priest and dumped half of the meat and most of the carrots onto the edge of the fire pit. The dogs were hovering and, smelling the meat, raced to wolf it down. Troy then rushed back to his seat at the table just about the time Rhoswyn came back into the hall, carrying a small bowl of salt. Troy smiled pleasantly at her as she returned to the table, handing him the salt.

"Thank you, my lady," he said, resuming cracking and peeling eggs as she hovered over him. "Will you not sit and eat with me?"

Rhoswyn nodded. "I will once yer men have been served," she said. "We have no servants, ye see, and someone has tae serve them, and… well, I was hoping that we might have a few servants at some point soon. It would make me work easier. Do ye think ye can send for some?"

Troy nodded. "Indeed, I will," he said. "I can send to Kale Water or even Questing and have a half-dozen sent over to help you, including a cook. Would… would you like to have a cook?"

A cook! The thought of having a real cook was terribly attractive and Rhoswyn tried not to respond too eagerly to the suggestion. She thought Troy might be disappointed in her willingness to work if she did.

"Aye," she said. "I believe that would be very helpful. I am not a very good cook and yer men need someone who can make them a good meal. I am afraid I can do very little."

Troy muttered a silent prayer – *thank God she is willing to accept a cook!* At least the woman was willing to admit she needed help. That made his life much, much easier because too many days of not eating what she was trying to feed them would leave him with starving men. The Scots could attack and they'd be too weak with hunger to fight them off. Or perhaps that had been Rhoswyn and Keith's plan all along… had he been the suspicious type, he could believe that.

It would have been a brilliant plan.

Starve them all out with bad cooking!

"You have done a remarkable job for someone who has never worked in a kitchen before," he praised her, watching her flush. "Go on, now; finish serving my men so that you may sit and enjoy your meal with me."

Rhoswyn flashed him a grin and was off, seemingly happier than Troy had ever seen her. It was remarkable, really. He watched her as she quit the hall before turning back to the eggs that would undoubtedly be his only food that night. But in doing so, he happened to look at his men who had been served food.

Now, they understood what he'd meant.

The men were looking at their trenchers as if dead puppies were lying all over them, eyebrows lifted and fighting off expressions of disgust. Troy felt guilty that he was the only one with the eggs, but such were the privileges of command. He was going to stuff himself with the eggs and be thankful for them. He had just salted one liberally and shoved it into his mouth as Audric came by his table.

"M'lord," he said, eyeing the room. "I dunna know if ye've noticed, but sup tonight is… is…"

"Inedible," Troy said quietly. "I noticed."

"She wouldna let me help with it after a certain point. I couldna do anythin' for ye."

Troy sighed faintly. "Do you know how to cook?"

"I do. I worked in the kitchens of Jedburgh as a lad."

"Thank God. Is there anything else you can cook while I keep her away from the kitchens? My men need to eat something and I do not wish to upset her when she realizes we cannot eat what she's prepared."

Audric nodded. "I saw the cheese in the vault," he said. "I'll bring that out and I'll make more bread. A couple of yer men are bringin' out a barrel of wine, so the cheese and bread and wine should be enough tae get them through the night."

It was better than nothing at all and Troy nodded. "Very well," he said. "Do what you can. She is trying very hard to help and I do not want her hurt or offended, but we must do something for the sake of my men."

"Agreed, m'lord."

"See to it."

Audric nodded and wandered off as Troy watched some of his men try to eat the gritty carrots, spitting them out back onto the trencher. The dogs were happy as the men fed them the poorly cooked beef but, to the credit of the men, they were doing it under the table so the lady wouldn't see.

Troy had to admit that he was rather pleased to see that his men were following his command and unwilling to upset his new wife. Being that they'd been stationed on the borders for many years, at least most of them, many of them had lost friends and family to the Scots over the years. But it was also true that they served the House of de Wolfe and William's wife, Lady Jordan, was a Scot.

As Troy had pointed out, there were many Scot wives, now including Rhoswyn, so his men were accustomed to treating the wives of their lords, Scots or not, with respect. Troy was pleased to see that Rhoswyn immediately fell into that category.

Troy was on his fourth egg when he heard a commotion from outside in the bailey. He could hear men shouting at each other, enough so that it captured his attention and he swallowed the food in his mouth, rising from the table and heading to the door about the time Rhoswyn was coming in with two more trenchers in hand.

Rhoswyn's attention was on the bailey but she caught sight of her husband as he came to stand next to her.

"I think ye have visitors," she said. "The gates are openin'."

Troy nodded. "Hopefully, my people from Kale Water have arrived," he said. "Remember? I told you I would send for my knight and his wife?"

Rhoswyn looked at him, full of uncertainty now. "They would come so soon?"

He shrugged. "It is not far from here, as I said. It will only take a man at a normal pace a couple of hours at most to arrive here, so I am sure these visitors have come from Kale."

Rhoswyn's attention returned to the riders and wagons that were coming in through the gate. It occurred to her that if there were any visitors at Monteviot, then it was her job, as chatelaine, to make them comfortable. That realization brought on a whole new set of worries.

"Then I… I suppose I must make sure they are welcome," she said. "Where will they sleep? Never ye mind. I'll find a place. And sup! Surely they must be hungry!"

With that, she quickly set the trenchers she was carrying on the nearest table and before Troy could stop her, she was rushing off to bring more bad food for his guests. But she was doing it so eagerly. Slightly mortified at the thought, Troy headed out into the bailey to see who, exactly, had arrived.

The bailey of Monteviot was lit by a dozens of brightly burning torches, staving off the dark Scottish night, as the party from Kale Water Castle entered. As Troy approached the first wagon, he could see Lady Sable de Shera sitting on the bench next to the driver while her husband, Cassius, was at the head of the column astride his big gray rouncey. Cassius caught sight of him and swung his horse around, calling to Troy and bringing the man to a halt.

"My lord!" he called, lifting a gloved hand. "C-Congratulations on your great victory over the Scots!"

Troy wasn't surprised that it was the first thing out of Cassius' mouth, because he knew the man would praise the victory over the *reivers* before even mentioning what else he'd been told, about the surprising marriage to a Kerr lass. Troy stood there, a smile playing on his lips, as Cassius reined his horse close to Troy and dismounted.

"It was not much of a battle, to be truthful," he said as Cassius came close. "We managed to breach the walls easily but the tower was something of a challenge. That was what took the most effort."

Cassius listened with envy; he'd very much wanted to go on the battle march to Monteviot but Troy had forced him to remain behind with Brodie in case there was trouble at Kale or the Lair as a result of the action down at Monteviot.

"What happened?" Cassius asked with great interest. "D-Did the *reivers* refuse to surrender it?"

Troy nodded. Then, he sniffed the air. "Smell it?"

Cassius sniffed, too. He could smell a hint of smoke. "I think so," he said. "D-Did you burn it out?"

Troy glanced up at the big, block-shaped tower. "We burned the roof, which collapsed, but the interior is mostly made of stone, so smoke did most of the damage. However, we did have some burned bodies. It was not a pretty sight."

Cassius looked up at the tower because Troy was. "I w-wish I had been here to see it," he said. "It must have been a glorious sight."

Cassius was young and still looked to battle as glorious and thrilling, something that the older knights had since gotten over. Troy lifted his eyebrows. "It was especially glorious when the Scots poured buckets of piss on Corbin, Case, and Kevin from the top of the tower because those three were verbally harassing them, shouting ridiculous demands. That was the best part of the entire battle."

Cassius' eyes widened. "Say it is not so!"

Troy started to grin at the mere memory of the enraged young English knights, covered in piss. "Believe me, Cass. The three of them deserved it."

He chuckled as Cassius thought on the thoroughly un-glorious mental image. "K-Knowing them as I have come to, I must say that I do not doubt your word, but it must have been quite humiliating for them," he said. Then, he eyed Troy. "Speaking of humiliation – the challenge Red Keith Kerr put upon you…"

Troy knew that subject would come as the focus of the conversation shifted. "It was interesting, to say the least," he said, casual in his reply as if it were nothing to get worked up over. "He proposed a man-on-man battle, the winner of which would relay the terms for Monteviot. Assuming that Keith would ask for his fortress returned, my father pitted me against a warrior of Keith's choice, who happened to be the man's daughter. She was smart about it; she knew she could not best me in a fight, so she used the element of surprise. Damned if she didn't catch me off-guard and, in that brief moment, she won the challenge. It was Keith who dictated that a warrior of my father's choosing should marry his daughter."

Cassius was looking at him with a good deal of chagrin. "Then you did marry the lass who bested you?"

"I did."

Cassius shook his head, unsure what more to say. He didn't want to make Troy feel badly about what had happened, but the truth was that Troy wasn't behaving as if he felt badly at all. In fact, he didn't seem upset in the least. That left Cassius somewhat confused.

"I brought Sable because you said your new wife required help," he said. "Troy, your new wife isn't… belligerent, is she? I do not want Sable exposed to a woman who wants to tear her hair out simply because she is English."

Troy understood the man's fear. "She is not belligerent, but she's not a meek and submissive woman, either," he said. "She is trying very hard to adapt to this marriage, as am I, but the truth is that Red Keith Kerr raised his only child as a warrior. Rhoswyn is a fighter, Cass. She has no idea how to do anything a woman should know how to do, and Sable is the best woman to teach her. Your wife is kind and patient, and I believe Rhoswyn will respond to that."

Cassius was still dubious. From the corner of his eye, he could see Sable being lifted out of the wagon by one of the soldiers, so he went over to collect her. Troy followed, and soon it was the three of them standing next to the wagon as Sable smiled at her husband's liege.

"My lord," she said, bobbing a curtsy because it was protocol even though Troy was a dear friend to both her and Cassius. "Congratulations on your mighty victory."

Troy dipped his head at the woman; he genuinely liked Sable, a very lovely and kind woman. "Thank you, Lady de Shera."

"And your wife? Should I offer congratulations on that, as well?"

Troy broke into a wry smile at the very honest question. "I am not sure if congratulations are in order, but you can wish us well as we both embark on a marriage that was unplanned to say the least," he said. "As I was telling your husband, my wife seems to be trying her best to become accustomed to what has occurred, but she desperately needs your help."

Sable was very serious. "Of course, Troy," she said. "Whatever you need, I am more than willing to help. What is it?"

Troy puffed out his cheeks, lending clue to Sable that she perhaps had a daunting task ahead of her. "Everything," he said. "She needs help with everything. Her father had no sons and raised her as a warrior, so she does not even know where to start as chatelaine. She is genuinely at a loss, although she has been trying very hard today to accomplish something. But I cannot say it was all successful."

Sable thought that sounded ominous. "Oh?" she asked. "Why would you say that?"

Troy sighed heavily, with some embarrassment on behalf of Rhoswyn, because he was about to confess her failings. He felt bad doing so.

"She tried to cook sup," he said, lowering his voice. "Now, keep in mind that she tried very hard, but she has had absolutely no experience with this kind of thing and there are no servants here to help her. She made carrots and boiled beef, but they are inedible to say the least. My men are under instructions to not complain about the food. I do not want her to be upset. But just now, she ran off to prepare some of this terrible food for you, so I wanted to warn you off. I know it is terrible; everyone knows it is terrible. But *she* does not know it is terrible."

Sable looked at him with big eyes, feeling a distinct amount of pity for Troy's new wife. "God's Bones," she finally muttered, looking over Troy's shoulder to the hall beyond, where men were milling about. "Then we shall be gracious with whatever she provides, but I brought two of my own servants and a good deal of food provisions, so mayhap we can set about a preparing a proper meal for the men while not hurting Lady de Wolfe's feelings. I am not sure how we can do it, but we can try."

Troy thought that sounded like an excellent solution. "Do not worry about tonight," he said. "Beginning with the morning meal shall be sufficient. She knows you have come to help her and I am sure she would be more than willing to defer the food preparation to someone who knows more about it, so I would not worry. But thank you for being sensitive to the situation."

Sable simply nodded, looking around the compound as if in search of the mysterious Lady de Wolfe. "And your wife?" she asked. "Where is she?"

He motioned towards the hall. "More than likely in the hall," he said. "Meanwhile, settle your men and bring the provisions wagons over to the tower. There is a chamber there you can use but this entire place has been stripped by the *reivers*, so we really have very little by way of comfort."

Cassius grunted. "I-I thought so," he said, looking to his wife. "I told Sable to bring everything she could."

Sable looped her arm through her husband's elbow as they began to head across the darkened bailey. "I have a great deal packed in the wagons," she confirmed. "Mattresses, linens, coverlets, pillows, stools, pitchers, wash basins, and a variety of other things. I brought everything I could think of but if we are missing anything, we can send to Kale for it. I thought I would decide what was needed first before bringing anything big like bed frames."

They were approaching the hall. "We will need it all," Troy said. "As I said, the tower has been stripped, so there is virtually nothing to use."

Further conversation was cleaved as the open hall door yawned before them. They could feel the heat coming from the chamber, entering the large room that was crowded with men who were trying not to eat the slop they'd been served.

Several of the men greeted Cassius, who was well-liked by the de Wolfe men, but Sable wasn't looking at the soldiers – she was looking at the food on the table in front of them. As they crossed over to the table where Troy had been sitting, Sable paused by one of the trenchers that had been discarded, one that had the bread half-eaten but the meat and carrots still intact. She peered at it closely and even stuck her finger into the carrots to taste them, immediately seeing what Troy was trying to tell her.

They were terrible.

That made her feel even worse for the new Lady de Wolfe. Following her husband and Troy to the table, she allowed Cassius to seat her on the bench before taking a seat next to her. Troy sat on the other side of Cassius, the three of them settling down when a woman blew into the hall with more trenchers in her hand. She headed straight for the table where Troy, Cassius, and Sable were sitting, seemingly very busy and out of breath. Troy stood up as she came near.

"This is my wife, Rhoswyn Whitton Kerr," he said to Cassius and Sable. "Her father is Red Keith Kerr of Sibbald's Hold. Rhoswyn, this is Sir Cassius de Shera and his wife, Lady Sable."

While Rhoswyn smiled timidly, Sable took a good look at the woman, mostly out of shock; she was rather tall for a woman, with skin the color of cream and luscious auburn hair that looked as if it hadn't been brushed properly in weeks. It was rather bushy, hanging all the way down to her hips, and she was dressed in a series of tunics with a pair of leather breeches covering her legs.

But her face… Sable could hardly believe how beautiful the woman was beneath the messy hair and grime on her face. When the woman looked at her with her wide brown eyes, reminiscent of doe's eyes, Sable smiled graciously and stood up.

"I am very happy to meet you," she said. "Troy has told us that it is you who have made this wonderful feast possible."

Rhoswyn found herself looking at a young woman who looked like an angel. Everything about her was so perfect, from the top of her beautiful brown hair to her small hands, clasped primly in front of her. She wore a lovely cloak and beneath it, she could see a hint of a dark green traveling dress. Everything about her looked perfect and ladylike.

And Rhoswyn felt so very, very self-conscious.

"I… I did me best," she said. "Ye must be hungry so I brought ye some food. I will fetch the wine now."

She dashed off again, leaving Sable and Cassius looking to Troy as if uncertain of what they'd just seen. It was Sable who finally gathered her wits and sat down, pulling her husband down beside her.

"She is beautiful, Troy," Sable said. "But she seems so… nervous."

Troy sat down, feeling rather guilty in all of this. "Because she is," he said quietly. "I fear it is too much for her. She has never done this before, so I fear it is overwhelming to her. I suppose I should not have expected so much."

Sable looked at the man; he seemed genuinely remorseful, which surprised her. As if he was sympathetic to the woman he'd been forced to marry. Truthfully, he seemed to have had that attitude from the start – why else would he have sent for someone to assist his new wife? Sable was coming to think that there was more here than met the eye, at least as far as Troy was concerned. Was it possible that he actually had kindly feelings towards the woman who had bested him after only a day?

That wasn't the Troy that Sable had come to know. The commander of Kale Water Castle, the second eldest son of the Wolfe of the Border, was a man who had never come across to her as being particularly compassionate. Fair, aye; the man was fair. Exceedingly fair. But he was also quick to temper and those at Kale lived in fear of rousing that temper. But compassion and gentleness? That was never the impression she'd ever received from Troy de Wolfe, which made her seriously wonder about the woman he'd married.

Perhaps the only compassion the man had ever shown was reserved for his new wife.

"Not to worry," Sable said after a moment, looking at the food on her plate and put off by the sight. "Tomorrow, I shall do what I can to help her. All will be well, Troy. Do not be concerned."

Troy knew he'd made the right decision by bringing Sable here. Already, he felt better about it. But he noticed that Cassius and Sable hadn't yet touched their food and he knew why. Heaving a sigh, he took the bowl on the table that still had several hard boiled eggs in it and put the bowl between them.

"Eat these," he said. "At least you will have something in your belly."

As Sable and Cassius began to peel the eggs, across the hall at the entry, Rhoswyn had taken a pitcher from one of the soldiers who had brought forth the big wine barrel from Troy's provisions. Most soldiers traveled with their own cups so there was no stash of drinking vessels to use. Rhoswyn had to hunt around in the kitchen yard and in the vault of the tower to find something to drink from, and she found a small collection of clay cups in the vault.

They were dusty but she blew at them, cleaning them of surface dirt, and prepared to provide them to her guests. She felt verily proud of herself for having found the cups at all. Topping off the pitcher of wine when she returned to the hall, she was just passing one of the tables when she heard the soldiers speaking on the meal.

"Slop," one man hissed to the other as she passed behind them. "We'd be better eating what the horses are eating than trying to stomach this slop!"

His companion elbowed him. "You heard what de Wolfe said," he muttered. "If anyone complains, he'll throw them over the wall. And he will!"

The first man groaned. "But this isn't fit for a man! The meat is like chewing on leather and the carrots are full of mud!"

His companion hushed him loudly and they both went back to drinking their wine while utterly ignoring the food. Having heard every word, Rhoswyn came to a halt behind them. Then, she looked around the hall to notice that no one else was eating the food she'd prepared but the dogs seemed to be quite well fed. They were moving from table to table, and men were taking their trenchers off the table for the dogs to eat on. As she realized no one was eating, reality dawned.

The food she'd served wasn't fit to eat.

Mortified, Rhoswyn could only think of the fact that she had just served Troy's knight and his lady wife a completely inedible meal that would surely embarrass her husband. And she'd worked so hard today; he'd even told her he was pleased with her. But now, with this terrible meal, surely he was anything but pleased. He was most certainly embarrassed about his inept wife.

Rhoswyn couldn't face him.

Quickly, she spun on her heel and fled the hall, still carrying the cups and pitcher. She didn't want to go to the kitchens because Audric was there, baking more bread, and she didn't want to face the man, either. Certainly, he'd known the food was inedible but he hadn't told her. He'd let her embarrass herself. Well, she didn't want to see him at all. She'd made an utter fool of herself and she didn't want to see anyone.

Verging on tears, Rhoswyn rushed into the tower and ran up the stairs, past the level that contained her bedchamber, and up to the top floor with its half-repaired roof. The English soldiers had been working on fixing the roof but it wasn't finished yet, and the single big chamber was only half-covered. Rhoswyn could look up and see the stars above, with a cold wind whistling in, but that didn't matter. She went over into the corner of the chamber and sat down, setting the wine pitcher and cups beside her. She was just so ashamed. The tears she'd been trying so hard to hold off were coming freely now.

She'd made a mess of everything.

Laying her forehead on her bent-up knees, she let the sobs come.

CB

"I SAW RHOSWYN by the entry but now she's gone," Troy said, standing up to get a better look over the smoke and crowd in the hall. "I wonder where she went?"

Cassius was on his seventh egg and Sable was on her third. When Troy made mention of his vanished wife, they, too, began to look around to see if they spied her somewhere in the smoky room, among the men, delivering more rotten meals.

"Where could she have gone?" Sable asked, bite in her mouth. "Should you go look for her, Troy?"

Troy thought it might be a good idea. Given that Rhoswyn was in a new environment, and not all that stable in it, he thought he might hunt her down just to make sure she hadn't gotten into any trouble. As he moved away from the table, he realized that Sable was following him. When he looked at her curiously, she simply smiled.

"I would like to see this place a little more," she said. "And when you find your new wife, I should like to speak with her. I was hardly able to say a word before she left."

Troy didn't see any harm in that so he let her come with him, but Sable couldn't go anywhere without her husband, so Cassius brought up the rear. The three of them headed out into the dark autumn evening and Troy called to a couple of men within earshot, asking if they'd seen Lady de Wolfe. Both men pointed towards the tower, which Troy took to mean that she'd headed to the kitchen yard again.

It was, therefore, a little confusing, as well as concerning, to find Audric the only person in the kitchen yard. Troy introduced Cassius and Sable to the priest, but the man hadn't seen Rhoswyn, so Troy took a chance and headed into the tower on his search.

She wasn't in the vault where the food stores now were, so he continued up to the first floor small hall, the second floor where there were two sleeping chambers, but still no Rhoswyn. It was purely by chance that he headed up to the third floor even though the roof had collapsed on it, simply to say that he'd searched the entire tower, and he was surprised to hear sniffling when they came up the stairs to the doorway that opened on to that level.

Troy could see Rhoswyn sitting at the far end of the open-roofed chamber, huddled up in the shadows. He could hear her soft sobs. Holding out a hand to Sable and Cassius, silently asking that they remain in place, Troy emerged into the chamber that still smelled heavily of smoke and burned flesh. He was about halfway across the floor when he spoke softly.

"Rhoswyn?" he said quietly. "Are you well?

Rhoswyn's head shot up when she heard his voice. Startled, and embarrassed, she quickly wiped at her face as if to erase all evidence that she'd been weeping but her eyes wouldn't quit leaking. The more she wiped, the more she streaked dirt across her face.

"I... I'm well," she insisted as Troy closed the gap between them and crouched down beside her. She refused to look at him. "I... I was simply weary from the day. It has been a busy day, ye know. And 'tis so noisy in the hall and there are so many men I dunna know, so I came here tae be alone. Just for a moment, ye understand. I wasna shirkin' me duties."

"You were weeping."

"I wasna!"

Troy didn't believe her for a moment. He moved from a crouched position to a sitting one, right next to her, leaning up against the wall of the chamber and effectively boxing her up against the corner. But his expression was full of concern.

"I would not imagine you would ever shirk your duties, no matter how difficult they were or how unfamiliar," he said softly. "Are you sure you weren't weeping? Mayhap because you have been doing something you have never done before? I am still pleased, you know. You worked very hard today."

She snorted, wiping at her running nose and smearing it up her face. "I worked hard at a disaster," she said. "I canna cook meat, I canna bake bread, and 'tis only by a sheer miracle that the men in the hall are able tae eat anythin' at all. The meat is like leather and the carrots are cooked in mud!"

The tears were coming again. The more she talked, the more embarrassed she became. Troy had to fight off a smile; he felt so terribly sorry for her but it wasn't in a critical sense. It was in the sense that she was a proud woman and she tried something that she'd failed at. He could see that Rhoswyn was much like he was; he didn't like failure, either.

"'Tis only your first time doing such things," he said. "You cannot expect to be perfect the very first time, with no one to really help you. I am sure you will do much better tomorrow."

Rhoswyn shook her head vehemently. "I am *not* goin' tae do this again tomorrow," she insisted, sniffling. "The priest says he can cook. Let him! I've shamed ye enough with what I've done tonight."

She was starting to sob angrily and Troy reached out, putting a hand on her back in a comforting gesture.

"Is that what has you upset?" he asked. "You feel as if you have shamed me? Lady, you have pleased me greatly with your attempts to learn. You tried something you had never done before and even if it did not come to fruition the first time, the fact remains that you tried. To refuse to try, or to quit, would have been to shame me. But I do not think you are a quitter."

His words brought Rhoswyn a great deal of comfort. Wiping at her cheeks, she eyed him. "Not usually," she said. "But I'd be a fool tae think yer men could take two nights of cookin' like this. They'll rebel and then where will ye be? With no army and a wife who canna cook! Ye'll be the laughin' stock!"

Troy burst into soft laughter. He liked the way she said it; quickly and self-depreciating. Rhoswyn scowled at him for a moment, as if insulted by his laughter, before breaking into a grin that she tried very hard to stave off. His hand, still on her back, moved to her shoulder and pulled her against him as he kissed her temple, a gesture that had Rhoswyn's cheeks flaming deeply.

"Well," he sighed. "At least you can hold a sword. If I have no army, then it will be you I send into battle. Surely there would be no fiercer warrior in all the north."

Rhoswyn was coming to feel the slightest bit better. Troy was comforting and kind, exactly as he had been nearly the entire time she'd known him. He wasn't angry that she'd destroyed the evening meal, nor was he shamed. In her estimation, that was an extremely patient man. She was coming to appreciate him more by the moment.

"Are ye sure ye're not ashamed of me?" she asked.

He shook his head. "Absolutely not. As I said, to shame me would have been not to have tried at all."

Her tears were fading now, comforted by a husband who seemed to know the right thing to say. As she opened her mouth to respond, she caught movement out of the corner of her eye and caught sight of Sable as she came into the chamber. Rhoswyn stiffened, embarrassed at what Sable might have heard, but Sable smiled gently at her as she approached.

"I am sorry to intrude, Lady de Wolfe," she said, "but I wanted to thank you for inviting me here to Monteviot. I enjoyed the bread and the cooked eggs you made. And I also wanted to thank you for pulling me out of Kale Water Castle. I am hoping you can use me here, to help you with your duties. I have grown so bored at Kale that coming to Monteviot is a lovely change."

Troy smiled faintly at Sable, a smile of thanks, before turning to look at Rhoswyn, his arm still around her shoulder. "Do you hear that?" he said. "Lady Sable is at your service. If you want her to show you how to cook a meal or sew a garment, then she can do that. You can learn a great deal from her."

Rhoswyn looked at him, coming to understand that these English weren't here to shame her. They were here to help her. She'd never had such help in her life, not from anyone, so it was a foreign concept. But she knew that, much as they were being kind to her, she must be kind in return. In truth, she was very grateful for their offer.

"I am thankful ye came when ye did," she said to Sable. "Ye can save the English from one more night of me cookin'."

Sable grinned. "I am very happy to help, my lady," she said. "In fact, if you'd like, I can start helping tonight. Will you allow me?"

Rhoswyn was very interested in what she meant. "How?"

There was so much Sable could show her tonight, from preparing rooms for her visitors to preparing for the morning meal. So very much that she was happy to take charge of. Sable moved closer, holding out a hand. It was the hand of friendship, the hand of help. Rhoswyn looked at it dubiously, then looking to Troy for reassurance. He nodded his encouragement and she hesitantly reached out to take it. Sable pulled Rhoswyn to her feet but didn't let go of her hand, looking her straight in the eye as she spoke.

"I'll show you," she said quietly. "Worry no more, Lady de Wolfe. Help has arrived."

CHAPTER FOURTEEN

THERE WAS SOMETHING about the scent of Rhoswyn that fed Troy's lust in a way he'd never before known.

Womanly, musky. Something that filled his nostrils and went right through to his brain. She had long limbs and a long torso, and an hour before dawn, he'd managed to pull her clothing off, roll her onto her back, and cover her with his body. His mouth was all over her flesh, feeding on her breasts, as he wedged himself between her legs and thrust into her warm and tender folds. She gasped a bit and he knew it was because she was still sore from the previous night, unaccustomed to a man's intrusion into her body.

But that was going to change.

Perhaps it was because Troy hadn't been with a woman since Helene's death. Or perhaps it was because something about Rhoswyn really did arouse him. Whatever the case, he thrust into her mercilessly until he found his release, but he didn't relinquish her after that. He simply remained on top of her, holding her, his body still embedded in hers, kissing and touching her until he could feel himself grow hard again. Then he made love to her a second time, climaxing so hard that he bit his lip with the sheer force of it. And then he kissed her, deeply, his tongue tasting the honeyed recesses of her mouth as he moved in and out of her until his manhood was flaccid. He could feel what he'd put into her, making her very slick, and he wondered about the magnificent sons he would have from the woman.

Considering the mother, they would be the most powerful sons the Marches had yet to see.

Two days of knowing Rhoswyn had brought him to some conclusions. As he lay in the pre-dawn darkness, listening to the fire as it popped and crackled, burning low in the hearth, Troy knew that there was something about her that wildly aroused him, as if he couldn't control himself. The smell of her, the feel of her – all of it created a combination he couldn't seem to resist. Another conclusion was that for all of the lust he was feeling for her, that was *all* he wanted to feel for her. He couldn't let his hunger for her cross the line into emotion. To do so would be to diminish the love he had for Helene. Gone or not, she was still the wife of his heart.

He wanted to keep it that way.

But, God… he had a feeling it was going to be difficult. As he lay there and listened to the birds, coming alive as a hint of dawn approached the horizon, Rhoswyn was laying on her side and he was right up against her, their warm flesh touching. His arms were around her, his right arm slung over her and his right hand by her left breast. He had his hand around it, feeling the warmth and softness in his palm. He kept thinking about their first full day together, and how hard she had tried to please him. And, God's Bones, she was humorous when she wanted to be. When she smiled, she had slightly protruding eyeteeth on an otherwise brilliant set of teeth, but he found her smile very charming.

Just like the rest of her.

There was a soft knock at the chamber door, rousing him from his thoughts. Before he could move, Rhoswyn was leaping to her feet, grabbing at the tunics that were cast on the ground. She also grabbed for a dagger, all of this as Troy sat up in bed, watching her rush to the door with the blade in her hand ready to kill whoever was on the opposite side of the door.

"Who is it?" she demanded.

The voice was muffled on the other side of the panel. "It is Sable, my lady," she said. "It is time to go to work."

Standing naked at the door, Rhoswyn turned to look at Troy with a rather apprehensive look on her face. "I… I must dress," she called back as Troy tossed the woolen coverlet off and went for his clothing. "I'll be out in a moment!"

Troy could see that Rhoswyn was trying desperately to dress and not expose herself to him, so he turned his back on her as he went for his breeches and tunic. He found them quickly, sliding them on his muscular body and stoking the fire as Rhoswyn pulled on her leather breeches and the layers of tunics she usually wore. Troy glanced over his shoulder at her as she pulled on her boots, tying up the leather straps. In a flash, she was throwing open the chamber door.

Sable was standing on the landing, looking properly groomed and radiant in a dark blue wool traveling gown, one that was made for the rigors of travel or work. Rhoswyn came barreling out of the chamber, smelling of smoke and sex, in that order. Sable had been married long enough to know what a man's musk smelled like. It didn't seem to vary much. She smiled pleasantly at Rhoswyn but looking at the woman, her heart ached for her. She was an utter mess. Her beautiful hair was in a rat's nest and smelling as if she'd just rolled in a man's bed and probably a few pig pens, too.

Sable knew she couldn't let the woman walk around like that, not if she was to be a proper wife to a very important border lord. She further knew that if the de Wolfe women got a look at her – Troy's mother, for example – there would be hell to pay. She put her hands up to prevent Rhoswyn from rushing down the steps and on to the duties that await them.

"Good morn, Lady de Wolfe," she said. "Will you wait here a moment? I must speak with your husband."

Rhoswyn nodded, looking at Sable curiously as the woman entered the chamber where Troy was. She continued to watch as Sable whispered something to Troy, something that made him look at Rhoswyn as if considering what Sable was telling him. She suspected that whatever it was, it was clearly about her, because Troy finally nodded before both he and Sable turned to approach her as she stood in the doorway. Troy cleared his throat softly, perhaps a bit nervously, as he began to speak.

"My lady," he said. "Lady Sable has pointed out something to me that we must address. Now, I realize that you have spent your life being trained as a warrior and living among men. For that reason, you have picked up the unfortunate habits of men."

Rhoswyn cocked her head curiously. "Habits?" she repeated. "What habits?"

Troy wasn't quite sure how to tactfully tell her that she looked like an unwashed animal, so Sable spoke kindly.

"Lady de Wolfe, you have married into a great family," she said. "When you became his wife, your situation changed. There are things that are expected of you now, like being a chatelaine. I am here to help you learn how to execute your duties flawlessly, but there is much more to being Lady de Wolfe than merely being an efficient chatelaine. It means that you will dress and behave like a lady because, in doing so, you honor your husband greatly."

Rhoswyn had an idea that Sable was speaking of her appearance and she looked down at herself, slovenly-looking, and began to feel some embarrassment.

"I dunna have anythin' else tae wear," she said. "These are me clothes. I have always worn them."

Sable could see that Rhoswyn was feeling self-conscious and she reached out to gently touch the woman's arm. "You needn't worry at all," she said reassuringly. "I will show you what you need to know and we can purchase fabric to make you fine clothing. Would you like that?"

Rhoswyn didn't know what to say; dressing and behaving like a lady was perhaps even more frightening than learning to be a chatelaine. But gazing into Troy's handsome face made her reconsider. He was smiling faintly at her and she was seized with the desire to please the man. It seemed that all she wanted to do was please him. Certainly, he deserved a wife he could be proud of, in every way. When he nodded encouragingly, her hesitation broke down completely.

"Aye," she said, looking to Sable. "I would."

Sable smiled brightly as she turned to Troy. "My lord, will you mind helping me?" she asked. When he nodded, she continued eagerly. "My servants are already in the kitchen yard, preparing for the morning meal, but they also started a very large pot of water to boil. I need that hot water and some kind of tub to wash in. Is there one here?"

Troy was thoughtful as he looked at Rhoswyn to see if she knew of something like that. "I have not seen anything that can be used as a tub, but I believe I did see an iron pot that was big enough for a man to climb into," he said. "It is near the kitchen yard, near the outbuildings."

"Ah," Sable said. "Pots of that size are usually for stripping bones. It probably would not be very clean, at least for our purposes. Do you have a barrel we could use? An old wine barrel, mayhap?"

Troy held up a finger. "I think I know," he said. "There is something like that in the stable, used to hold feed for the animals. Where would you like me to bring it?"

Sable already had Rhoswyn by the arm, pulling her to the only other door on that level, beyond which was the room she and Cassius had slept in that night.

"Here!" Sable said. "Bring it in here with the hot water. And hurry!"

Troy would never forget the expression of apprehension on Rhoswyn's face as Sable dragged her into her bedchamber. But it was good for her to be a little apprehensive of what was to come, as it would make her more docile to Sable's intentions. As Sable's whispered words had been made clear to him – *your wife is in need of a good scrubbing* – he had been forced to agree. In truth, Rhoswyn's dirt hadn't bothered him, for it wasn't something he particularly noticed, but to have the woman cleaned up... he could only imagine how beautiful she would be. It was all part of learning how to be a proper wife.

With a grin, he quickly went about the assigned tasks as Lady de

Shera had asked. There was a sense of purpose in the air this morning and Troy was eager to see the end result.

As Troy went off to do Sable's bidding, Rhoswyn found herself pulled into the chamber her guests had slept in the night before. After Troy and Sable had found her weeping on the top floor, they had immediately put her to work helping bring Sable's things up to the borrowed bedchamber, and that included things Rhoswyn had never seen before – beautiful trunks, fine mattress shells all rolled up and waiting to be stuffed with fresh straw or feathers, smaller capcases that contained mysterious potions. They even smelled good, lined with lavender and herbs.

Moving Sable and Cassius into the chamber also involved stuffing one of the mattresses that Sable had brought with some of the straw that had been stored in the barn. It wasn't very fresh, but it was dry, and Rhoswyn helped Sable stuff the mattress while the men moved in the last of the trunks from the provisions wagon. Soon enough, it was like a chamber of wonders, filled with more possessions than Rhoswyn had ever seen.

This morning, the chamber was still stuffed full of things that someone had carefully organized. But Rhoswyn didn't have time to inspect anything because Sable put her in the corner and told her to remain, and she did. She stood there while Sable began to open trunks and pull forth items – clothing, combs, and other things that Rhoswyn couldn't really identify. She had no idea what was going on but she knew that it all had something to do with her and the clothing she was wearing.

Truly, it was pathetic, her clothing. Compared to what Sable was wearing, a proper lady's garments, she looked terrible. But they were all garments from her father – or what she'd happened to come by in her years of living at Sibbald's. In fact, the leather tunic she wore had belonged to her grandfather. There was absolutely nothing she owned that had been made for her except the leather breeches. The tanner at Sibbald's had made those for her a few years ago when her legs grew long and the breeches she had no longer fit. Of course, she knew what fine ladies wore, never more obvious now with Sable around. They wore lovely surcoats and shifts. But Rhoswyn didn't have any of that.

A situation that was soon to change.

Troy arrived carrying a very big copper pot or bucket up from the stables; it was difficult to tell what it was because it was badly dented and the interior of it was black with oxidation, but he'd had his stable hands rinse it out and try to at least clean it up before he brought it up to the ladies. Sable inspected it closely and it seemed as if the oxidation didn't rub off, or come off, so she deemed it safe for her purposes. Sending Troy and his men for the hot water, she lined the pot with two large pieces of a sheer linen fabric and set out a variety of phials and combs as she was waiting for the water.

Still, Rhoswyn said nothing because she had no idea what was coming. When Troy and his men returned, it was with buckets and smaller pots of hot water, and Sable directed them to pour it into the lined copper tub. Steaming water splashed in and Sable put drops of oil into the water that filled the chamber with the smell of lavender. On the floor beside the pot, she seemed very busy preparing potions and other things, and that went on until the pot was about half-full, and Troy and his men left the chamber and shut the door. Then, Sable turned to her.

Or turned *on* her. The demands began to come forth.

"Off with your clothing, my lady," she said. "Into the tub with you."

Rhoswyn's eyebrows lifted in surprise. "Get... get *intae* it?"

Sable nodded briskly and went to her, reaching out for her. "Allow me to assist you."

She didn't really give Rhoswyn a choice. She began untying the leather ties that held together the leather apron and, from that point on, Rhoswyn could only stand there like a dullard as Sable virtually stripped her. When they came down to only her breeches and a thin tunic left, Rhoswyn balked, feeling very self-conscious, but Sable gently coaxed the remaining clothing from her by holding up a large piece of drying material, made from a combination of wool and even rare cotton, woven together so it would wick the water off the skin.

But Rhoswyn wasn't concerned with drying her skin. She was concerned with shielding her nakedness, which Sable thoughtfully did with the drying linen. But she was concerned about the pot of steaming water that was meant for her. She might as well have been looking at the deepest loch in all of Scotland for all of the fear she was feeling.

"But…" she stammered as Sable tried to direct her into the pot. "But what will ye have me do?"

Sable pointed to the pot. "Sit in it, please."

Rhoswyn was beside herself. "*Sit* in it?"

Sable nodded patiently. "Sit in it and I shall bathe you."

Rhoswyn hesitated. "I dunna like water," she insisted. "I canna swim. I dunna want tae sit in it!"

Sable remained patient. "It will not hurt you, I promise," she said. "And you will not drown. You've not drown in a bath in all these years and that will not change today."

Rhoswyn stared at the steaming pot. "I havena… that is, I dunna take a bath. I have a cloth and bucket I use sometimes, but I never… *swim* in it."

Sable was rather shocked to learn that Rhoswyn had never before taken a bath but, given the dirt on the woman, she wasn't particularly surprised. She thought it was time for a little brutal honesty with a woman who probably had no real idea of the situation she was in and what was expected of her.

Sometimes a little forthrightness was needed.

"You are not expected to swim in it," she said. "You will sit in it and I will wash the dirt from you. My lady, please do not think I am trying to be cruel, but it is time for total truth. Do you believe we should be truthful with each other?"

Rhoswyn eyed her warily. "Aye."

"Do you believe that friends are concerned for one another? Because I very much wish to be your friend."

Rhoswyn shrugged. "I dunna have any friends."

Sable smiled. "Then I am honored to be your first," she said. "Please know that, as your friend, everything I do is for your own good. I would never do anything to harm you or to shame you. You must believe that. Now, from one friend to another, the way you are at this moment is a disgrace to your husband. You smell like a barnyard and you look like you have not combed your hair in years. That does not honor your husband, my lady. It makes men feel a great deal of pity for him."

Rhoswyn was torn between defiance and the realization that Sable was correct; she *was* rather dirty. And smelly. She looked down at herself, seeing the stains on her tunic, knowing her hair was a mess, and she began to feel very awkward and embarrassed.

"No one has ever said such things," she defended herself weakly. "Me pa... he looks the same as I do."

"And you want to look like a smelly man for the rest of your life?" Sable countered. Then, she shook her head firmly. "Nay, you shall not. Now, remove the remainder of your clothing and get into that tub or I shall have to do it for you. I may appear small and weak, but I can give you a fight if that is what you are looking for. I will clean this dirt off of you or die trying."

It seemed like a rather passionate declaration simply for a bath, but Rhoswyn believed her. These English women had different ways when it came to dress and cleanliness, or so she'd heard, and she had no doubt that Lady Sable saw Rhoswyn as a great challenge. The woman probably wouldn't hesitate to club her and drag her into the water. Because she didn't want to be clubbed, and she didn't want to fight against a woman who had only been helpful since the moment they met, Rhoswyn begrudgingly removed her leather breeches, her tunic, and then jumped into the water, splashing it over the sides.

Fighting off a grin, Sable went to work. The first thing she did was take the two bone combs she'd set out and began to comb through Rhoswyn's considerable mane, which was matted and dirty. It was a shame, too, because it was such a lovely color, and the texture was thick. As Sable combed, Rhoswyn grunted in pain until Sable stopped and handed the woman a lumpy bar of white soap with flecks of lavender buds in it.

"Here," she said. "Begin washing yourself while I work on your hair."

She resumed combing and Rhoswyn resumed grunting but, in between groans of pain, Rhoswyn lifted the soap to her nostrils and inhaled the lovely lavender fragrance. She rubbed the bar between her hands in the water and it turned into cream against her flesh. It also washed away the dirt; she could see it. After that, she began to rub the bar with vigor against her skin, washing off the years of accumulated dirt. But every so often, a tug on her head would bring a yelp from her lips.

"Och!" she said as Sable combed out a particularly bad knot. "Ye'll pull the hair right from me head!"

Sable didn't ease up. She continued to use the big comb to detangle and the finer comb to smooth through the hair.

"I am sorry," she said, although she wasn't. "Your hair is very matted."

Rhoswyn was rubbing the bar up and down her arm. "It gets that way."

"You should comb it every day so it does not get that way."

"I dunna have a comb."

Sable tugged on a big mat, causing Rhoswyn to flinch. "That will change."

Rhoswyn's head jerked back as Sable broke through the tangle. "I have a feelin' much will change now."

There wasn't any self-pity in her words, simply a statement of fact, but it made Sable think. Rhoswyn seemed to come from a very different world than she knew. She was curious about it, and about her.

"Tell me of your life at Sibbald's," she said, genuinely interested. "Do you have brothers? Sisters?"

Rhoswyn shook her head as she scrubbed the grime on her left wrist. "Nay," she said. "Just me pa. Me ma died when I was young, and I never had any brothers or sisters."

Sable finished with the last of the big mats. "I have two sisters," she said. "Douglass and Lizbeth."

"Are they married, too?"

"Douglass is," she said. "She married a great knight. My husband's uncle, in fact. But Lizbeth is younger than I am and not yet pledged."

"Pledged," Rhoswyn muttered. "That was somethin' me pa never spoke much of."

"Why not?"

Rhoswyn rinsed her arm off in the water. "Who would marry me?" she asked flatly. "I can fight better than most men. No one wants a wife who can best him."

Finished pulling out the tangles, Sable began to comb the hair out with the fine-toothed comb. "Have you always known how to fight?" she asked. "I must say, I have never heard of a woman being trained for such things, but it would be a useful skill to have, I suppose."

Rhoswyn assumed she was only being kind about it. More and more, she was coming to realize that her father had not raised her as he should have. "Useful tae a man," she clarified. "But it seems that the English are less impressed with my skills. I canna use a sword tae cook a meal or stuff a mattress."

Sable set the comb down and reached for a big wooden vessel on the ground. "That is true, but if we were to be attacked right now, you would know what to do, wouldn't you?"

Rhoswyn started to reply but Sable took the big wooden vessel, filled it with water, and poured it over Rhoswyn's head. Rhoswyn shrieked when water poured into her mouth, sputtering as Sable poured several loads of water over her head to thoroughly wet her hair. After that, the conversation died as Sable began to scrub Rhoswyn within an inch of her life.

She took the soap Rhoswyn had been using on her body and rubbed it all over her hair, digging her fingers into the scalp and scrubbing. Rhoswyn ended up having to hold on to the edges of the tub because she was being buffeted around so, enduring the scrubbing and scraping and then more rinsing, followed by another rinse through her hair with something that smelled like vinegar.

It was an experience Rhoswyn would never forget, but it was also an experienced she ended up rather enjoying. It was lovely soaking in hot water and having someone scratch her scalp. She had no idea what she'd been missing and when it came time to get out, she did so reluctantly. The water was cooling, but the room was cooler, and she quickly wrapped up in Sable's amazing drying cloth, sitting on a small stool in front of the fire as Sable went to work combing out her wet hair.

"And how was your bath, my lady?" Sable asked, grinning at Rhoswyn's relaxed posture. "Did you enjoy it?"

Rhoswyn sighed, warm and clean and feeling wonderful. "I would do it again, very soon," she said. "I must ask me husband if he will allow me tae purchase soap."

Sable combed out the long, wet tresses. "Do you not have any?"

Rhoswyn yawned. "I'm sure ye guessed that I dunna," she said, turning somewhat to look at Sable. "I have nothin', m'lady, except the clothin' ye saw me wearin'. I dunna own a comb and I dunna have any of the wonderful things that ye have. It's not that me pa denied me; I suppose I dinna know tae ask for them."

Sable had suspected as much. "Well," she said briskly, "I shall speak with Troy. There must be a nearby village where you can purchase some things that you will need, as the lady of the house. And I will help you sew dresses, if you will allow."

Rhoswyn shrugged. "I dunna know how tae sew," she said. Then, she sobered somewhat. Showing gratitude was difficult for her. "Ye... ye've been very kind tae me, Lady Sable. I never knew any English until a few days ago, and the English I've met have been very kind."

Sable grinned. "Did you expect otherwise?"

Rhoswyn couldn't see the woman, as she was facing away from her, but she could hear the humor in her voice. Having never had a friend, it was easy for her to let her guard down with Sable's kindness. It was rather nice having another lady to talk to.

"All I've ever seen of the English are their men," she said. "I've never been this close to an English woman before, so I dunna know what tae expect."

Sable continued combing and Rhoswyn's hair was starting to dry by the warmth of the fire, the lovely gold and red shades becoming evident.

"I have known plenty of Scots women," she said. "Troy's mother is Scots, in fact. She is very kind. I have, therefore, had experience with many kind Scots women."

Rhoswyn could sense there was a sisterhood there, a mysterious thing that she was part of now and didn't even know it. *The de Wolfe women.* That sisterhood of women married to the most powerful knights on the border, now including her. Desperate to understand, to become what would honor her husband, forced her to turn around and look at Sable.

"Will ye teach me all ye know?" she begged softly. "I feel so… foolish. I never expected tae marry and I certainly never expected tae marry a Sassenach knight, so there is so much I dunna know. Tell me tae do it and I shall. I shall do whatever ye tell me I should because I dunna want tae shame me husband. He's been so… so kind and patient, too."

Sable smiled into the woman's face, sensing that there was more than simply wanting to please her husband behind her request. There was softness in her eyes as she spoke, suggesting to Sable that Troy may have already made a conquest of his new wife. Much as Sable had been astonished at Troy's manner towards Rhoswyn, she was astonished at Rhoswyn's behavior towards Troy. Was it possible that the two of them had already found attraction and even affection with one another? Truly, it was something to marvel.

"I will teach you all that I can, I promise," Sable assured her. "The first thing you should learn is that it is important to groom yourself for your husband. No man wants to live with a slovenly woman, so you will brush your hair every day and you will wash at least your hands and face. You can wash your entire body once a week, but no less. I will tell Troy that he must buy you soaps and oils so you can keep your skin from cracking and also so that you may smell pleasant. Men like women who smell pleasant."

Rhoswyn was digesting everything eagerly. "They do?"

Sable nodded firmly. "They do," she said. Then, she turned Rhoswyn around on the stool so that the woman was facing the fire again. She gathered the woman's damp hair in her hands and began to plait it into a thick braid. "And your clothing; you must not wear your tunics or breeches any longer. It is unseemly for a woman to do so and Troy would appreciate a wife who did not dress as a man. I think I have two dresses that will fit you, as you are taller than I am and the hem of the skirts are longer, but I will tell Troy that he must go to town this very day to purchase fabric for you. You must have your own clothing."

These were vital lessons that Rhoswyn had missed and she knew it. She was most eager to go along with it all, for Troy's sake. She could feel Sable tugging at her hair before finally wrapping it at the base of her neck and using big iron pins to secure it into a bun. Standing back, Sable surveyed her handiwork.

"Perfect," she declared. "Your hair must be combed and secured daily. Do you wish for me to show you how?"

Rhoswyn nodded. "I... I do."

Sable smiled. "I will show you tonight when you let your hair out," she said. Then, she spun around to the trunks that were lined up against the wall. "For now, we must find you something to wear."

Still wrapped in the big drying linen, Rhoswyn stood up and went to peer over Sable's shoulder as the woman dug through three big trunks against the wall. She would pull forth something, look at it, and either cast it aside or put it in a neat pile on the floor. Rhoswyn continued to watch curiously as Sable finally set aside two long cotes, laying them out on her mattress to get a look at them.

One cote was a shade of dark green, long of sleeve and with a square neckline, while the other one was a pale shade, a faded red. It was very lovely. Both of the garments were made of wool and when Sable was finished inspecting them, she pulled the drying cloth off of Rhoswyn and went to work.

A shift went on first, soft as a butterfly's wing, followed by the green cote. It was all one piece – sleeves, bodice, and skirt, and it was secured by a series of stays up the back. Sable closed up the stays and handed Rhoswyn a pair of leather slippers for her feet. When Rhoswyn looked at them curiously, not really knowing what they were, Sable showed her the slippers on her own feet so Rhoswyn knew what to do. She slipped them right on. They were a little tight, but they fit, and she marveled at her feet.

"So simple?" she asked in awe. "I always wear me boots, but these shoes are so simple!"

Sable smiled as Rhoswyn's focus was on her feet. "They will be durable, at least until you can have a tanner make you a pair of your own," she said. Then, she stood back to admire her handiwork. She had to admit that Rhoswyn was one of the more beautiful women she'd ever seen – auburn hair, pale skin, slender torso. She suspected that Troy would be very pleased. "You will be able to work easily in this. How do you feel?"

Rhoswyn looked at the gown, warm and comfortable, and put her hands up to gingerly touch her pinned hair. "I... I dunna know," she said. Then, she grinned. "I suppose I feel like a lady."

Sable laughed softly. "You look like one, too," she said. "I have a feeling your husband will be very pleased."

The mere thought made Rhoswyn's belly quiver. "Will we show him, then?"

Sable reached out and took her hand. "Of course we will," she said. "You clean up very nicely. Now, promise me something."

"Anythin', if I can."

"No more tunics and leather breeches."

Rhoswyn struggled not to giggle. "Nay, no more. I promise."

"And wash the dirt from your face and hands daily."

"I promise."

"And comb your hair!"

It was a command and Rhoswyn started to laugh. "If I must."

"You must! If you do not, I will chase you down and do it for you!"

She was grinning as she said it and Rhoswyn continued laughing as they headed to the door. "With the trouble ye've gone to today, I wouldna dare disappoint ye, m'lady."

Sable opened the door, but her focus was on Rhoswyn. "We are friends now," she said. "You will call me Sable."

It was difficult to describe how Rhoswyn felt at that moment. From a woman who had grown up having no one to talk to, and no friends to speak of, to now having a friend all her very own, and a pushy little English lass at that. But it didn't matter; Rhoswyn felt as if someone cared for her, for the first time in her life. She felt as if she mattered.

"And ye'll call me Rhoswyn," she said softly.

"I would be happy to."

Sable squeezed Rhoswyn's hand and led her out of the chamber, down to the hall where Troy was lingering with Cassius, Audric, and a few other men.

Rhoswyn would never forget the look on Troy's face when he saw her. Surely the faces of all of the angels in heaven had never shone so happily.

CHAPTER FIFTEEN

Jedburgh

T ROY COULDN'T SEEM to keep his eyes off of her.

They were nearing the outskirts of Jedburgh on a bright autumn morning, having left Monteviot not two hours earlier at the command of Sable who instructed Troy to take his wife to town and buy the woman things she needed. Sable got no argument from Troy, who was more than delighted to take the beautiful creature he'd married into town to buy her things. He wanted to buy her things.

But he wanted to stare at her more. He couldn't seem to *stop* staring at her.

Rhoswyn rode next to him on her big black horse, astride in her borrowed dress because she had no experience in riding sidesaddle as women did. Because of that, Sable allowed her to put her leather breeches back on but they were concealed beneath the big skirt of the cote so no one could see them. Riding her excited horse on this glorious morning, Rhoswyn couldn't remember ever having been so happy.

For certain, she was coming to realize there was much to be happy for.

A husband who seemed very attentive and a newfound friend who had made her feel like a true lady. Aye, there was a good deal to be happy for amongst these Sassenach and as the Troy, Rhoswyn, Audric, and twenty English soldiers approached the outskirts of Jedburgh,

Rhoswyn kept glancing at her husband only to find him looking at her. She would flush and grin coyly, looking away from him, which made the man chuckle. She could hear him.

"So, my lady," Troy finally said as they crossed over into the city limits. "According to Lady Sable, you may spend my money freely as long as it is on fabric for clothing and any number of things that a proper lady needs. I asked her to come with us but she felt that her presence was better served at Monteviot. Personally, I think she wanted us to be alone."

Rhoswyn turned to look behind them, at the soldiers and the priest that were following them to town. "We are *not* alone, laddie," she said. "We've an entire contingent of men followin' us."

Troy turned to glance at his men. He was dressed in full battle regalia, looking the same as he did the day Rhoswyn kicked him in the groin and smashed him in the face with her shield. But she looked markedly different from that day; groomed, smelling sweet, and dressed in a garment that fit her rather snuggly considering she was taller and heavier than little Sable, Rhoswyn had never felt so light of heart. They were here in Jedburgh to buy her whatever she wished, and she was giddy with excitement. But she was even more giddy to be with Troy.

"Do not pay attention to my men," he told her. "Pretend they do not exist. Pretend it is only you and me and my fat purse."

Rhoswyn laughed softly as she looked around the town as they entered. Since they were on the outskirts, it was residential buildings surrounding them, lining the street with stone houses and thatched rooves, and then little alleyways where children were playing. She could hear them calling to each other, running up and down the muddy alleys with dogs chasing after them.

They passed by residents who were dumping chamber pots into the street or hanging clothing up to dry, residents who looked at them with suspicion as they passed into town. One old woman gave Rhoswyn a rather hostile expression and Rhoswyn glared back.

"I canna remember when I last came tae Jedburgh," Rhoswyn said as the nasty old woman passed from her sight. "Me pa dinna like tae leave Sibbald's, although he did send his men intae town for the cattle market."

Jedburgh was a big cattle town, with one of the largest cattle markets on the borders. Troy turned to the priest. "The cattle market is to the north of town, is it not?" he asked.

Audric spurred his little palfrey forward, putting himself between Troy and Rhoswyn. "Aye," he said, pointing up the avenue. "It is at the edge of town, every sixth day except durin' the winter time. But if ye're lookin' for merchants, then they'll be near the square. All of the merchants gather there to sell their wares."

Troy was straining to catch a glimpse of the merchant district up ahead. It was nearing noon and the streets were very busy as people went about their business. The road they were on had come up from the south, but it was a main road that went straight into the middle of the city. By traveling upon it, they had bypassed the castle, which was to the south and staffed by men from the Earl of Carlisle. It was an English-manned castle, given over to the English for the time being in one of the many times it had changed hands between the English and the Scots.

Troy knew the garrison commander, a man by the name of Allerley, and he'd had limited contact with him because the de Wolfe lands ran to the south. He knew he didn't like the man because he was a pompous ass who made the decisions and sat in his castle while his men did all of the work. Therefore, he had no intention of paying the man his respects for entering his city, although that would have been good manners. Troy simply wanted to get in, accomplish his business, and get out. As they headed into the middle of the village, Troy turned to the men behind him.

"Hartrigge, Lanton," he said to the two soldiers in front of the others. "Find a place for the men to settle somewhere around here where I can easily find them if necessary. Then, I want you two to head to the north where the cattle market is and see if there is anything to purchase right now. They may have some that have come in early for the next sale. If they do, find out how many and the price. Come find me after that. We will need cattle for the men at Monteviot, so we may as well look into it while we are here."

The soldiers nodded smartly and moved swiftly to do his bidding. Meanwhile, Troy began hunting for a livery and he found one at the edge of the village center, just off the main road. He could see the corral. Knowing that was their destination, he took his wife and Audric over to the livery and paid the livery keep handsomely to feed and water the animals.

Dismounting his steed, he moved to help Rhoswyn off of her bulky horse but she dismounted quite ably, her skirts flipping up and showing her leather breeches underneath as she did. She didn't even notice about the skirts, unused to them as she was, so Troy flipped them back down as he came close. Rhoswyn, realizing what had happened, looked at him with some chagrin.

"Och," she said, smoothing her skirts down. "I dinna think."

A smile played on his lips as he looked at her. "I know."

She sighed sharply. "Can ye even stand yerself, having tae mother me every second?" she said. "I'm a driggle-draggle!"

He tried not to laugh. "Not for long," he said. "You are well on your way to being a proper lady. I have every confidence that you will learn quickly."

She pursed her lips wryly. "If I can manage to keep me skirts down."

He did laugh, then, and took her by the elbow. "That is why you have me here, to remind you," he said as he pulled her out of the livery. "Do you think I want men seeing what belongs only to me? Absolutely not. What is under that skirt is for my eyes only."

Rhoswyn's cheeks flushed a shade of pink; she knew what he meant. That her body was reserved only for him and, so far, he'd taken advantage of that. But she had to admit that she'd quickly come to like it.

Crave it, even.

As they walked together out onto the road, even now, she could feel his body beside hers and her body was immediately drawn to him, tingling with the anticipation of his touch even though they were in a public place. Everything about him made her tingle.

But it wouldn't do to talk about things like that, especially with the priest around, so she shifted the focus away from what lay beneath her skirts.

"Lady Sable said that we must find a merchant with all manner of goods such as fabric, soaps, and oils," she said. "She says tae find a merchant who has Spanish soap."

Troy's brow furrowed. "*Spanish* soap?"

Rhoswyn nodded confidently. "I am sure the merchant will know what I mean," she said. Then, she turned to Audric, who was trailing along behind them. "This is yer town, Audric. Do ye know where we can find a merchant who has Spanish soap?"

Audric wandered up beside them as they walked, noting that Rhoswyn had looped her hand through Troy's elbow, so naturally it was as if she'd always been doing it. They looked quite comfortable together.

"Ye mean castile soap," he said. "I've heard of such things. We have a rich parishioner who is fond tae confess her love of spendin' money. She buys sweet almonds from the holy land and soap from Spain. The woman buys things she doesna even need!"

Both Troy and Rhoswyn looked at him in surprise. "You are not supposed to speak of confessionals," Troy said, amused. "God would frown upon such things."

Audric cocked an eyebrow. "I dinna tell ye the name of the woman, so God has no cause tae be cross with me," he said, watching Troy grin. "I know who ye need tae visit – a merchant at the end of the square who has goods from all over. Ye can smell his shop as ye come close because he has many mysterious potions and perfumes."

Rhoswyn was very interested. "Truly?" she asked, looking out to the square as they started to head north, through the bustle of people. "Where is he?"

Audric pointed in a general northerly direction. "Over there," he said. "Look for the busiest shop and ye'll find him."

Troy couldn't help but notice that Rhoswyn was pulling on him as she walked. He had to walk faster to keep up with her. She was singularly focused on finding the merchant shop that Audric had described and, to be certain, they could soon smell exotic and mysterious scents upon the wind. Like the lure of sirens, pulling shoppers to their financial doom, the scents grew stronger as they approached what seemed to be a very popular stall. People were moving in and out of it with their shopping baskets in-hand.

Surprisingly, Rhoswyn wasn't intimidated by the sight of shopping women even though she'd never visited such a stall in her life. This was a first. But her morning spent with Sable had made her more comfortable – and curious – about the things that made ladies' skin so soft or smell good, and she was eager to look at all of the wondrous items.

Troy took her up to the threshold of the shop but he would go no further, as he explained, because it wasn't a fitting place for men. It was strictly for women. Rhoswyn was preparing to go it alone but Troy emitted a sharp whistle between his teeth and called over the merchant who owned the shop, standing just inside the door and speaking with another customer. As the man approached, irritated that he'd been whistled at by the big knight, Troy spoke with authority.

"I am Troy de Wolfe," he said. "My father is William de Wolfe and unless you are an imbecile, you have heard of my family. This lovely creature is my wife and she is in need of anything and everything a well-dressed lady needs. You will personally escort her through your stall and make sure she has all that is required. You will be handsomely paid for your efforts."

The name de Wolfe meant something on the borders. The merchant's eyes widened at the mention of the name and, suddenly, he wasn't so irritated. In fact, he nodded eagerly and turned to Rhoswyn.

"Of course, Lady de Wolfe," he said; he spoke with a decidedly northern English accent. "Come inside. What do you wish to see first?"

Rhoswyn had no idea what she should shop for first, but rather than appear uncertain by his question, she thought back to what Sable had told her. *Fabric. Soaps. Oils.*

"I would see fabrics, soaps, and oils," she said firmly. "I want Spanish soap."

The merchant seemed perplexed by her answer, but quickly, he figured out what she meant. "Ah!" he said. "Soap from Castile! Aye, I have it!"

With that, he took her by the elbow to guide her into the stall, but Rhoswyn didn't take kindly to the man putting a polite hand on her so she pulled her elbow free. That didn't seem to deter the man, who was chatting up a storm as he told her of all of the wonderful products he had in his stall, and he grasped her again by the elbow.

As Troy watched, Rhoswyn pulled her elbow free of the man no less than three times as they headed into the shop. He grinned at her reluctance to be treated like a proper woman and helped by a man, in any fashion. She was too independent for that. Out of the corner of his eye, he caught Audric looking at him.

"She has much to learn," he explained quietly, turning to survey the village center now that Rhoswyn had passed out of his line of sight. "She has no idea how to behave as a lady."

Audric could see Rhoswyn deep in the shop now, moving through the piles of merchandise with the chatty merchant. "I believe Red Keith did the lass a great disservice raisin' her as he did," he muttered. "Mayhap he simply dinna think on how it would affect her as a grown woman. The man wanted a son and he made her intae one, but now the lass must struggle with the consequences."

As the priest spoke, Troy suddenly spotted a host of English soldiers entering from the south side of the village. He recognized the colors right away – the brown and yellow of Deauxville Mount. The barons of "The Mount", as it was called, was the family of de Troiu, a family that used to be allies with the de Wolfes many years ago but an incident between William de Wolfe and a leading member of the de Troiu family had ended that alliance.

William would never discuss the exact circumstances of the separation. But one night when Paris had too much to drink, he told Troy that Daniel de Troiu, then the head of the family those years ago, had tried to steal Troy's mother away. It had evidently culminated in a nasty battle and since then, the name de Troiu was not permitted to be spoken anywhere in the halls of Castle Questing, Northwood Castle, or any other de Wolfe ally or property. That left Deauxville Mount as an outcast in the north, allying with questionable local barons. The once-proud family had dwindled in both wealth and prestige, and now was considered the dregs of the border.

In truth, de Wolfe and de Troiu had become hated and bitter enemies over the years, so not only was Troy surprised to see de Troiu soldiers, he was uncomfortable seeing them as well. There weren't very many of them – perhaps ten that he could see – but he knew his twenty-man contingent was nearby and he didn't want them getting into a scuffle with the de Troiu men. He hoped his soldiers had better sense than to engage them. Audric, seeing that Troy appeared rather on edge as he gazed out over the village center, turned to see what had the man so uneasy.

"What is it, m'laird?" he asked.

Troy's gaze was still on the de Troiu men as they filtered into the town, but rather than upset the priest with his concerns, he simply shook his head.

"Nothing," he replied. "There are a great many people in town today, including soldiers. I was simply noticing the soldiers."

Audric was too short to see what Troy, with his height, could see. He simply returned his attention to the stall, where the merchant had brought forth a big basket that now had a pile of goods in it for Rhoswyn. And the pile was growing. As he watched the lady examine a piece of cloth the merchant had given her, his thoughts turned to his very reason for being here and the day Troy and Rhoswyn had met. Strangely, it seemed like years ago.

"I told ye that yer father asked me tae stay tae help ye and the lady in the beginnings of yer marriage," he said. "But I must say that I've seen nothin' that needs me help. She has calmed down admirably and ye've been very patient with her."

Troy didn't take his eyes off the distant de Troiu soldiers who were starting to head in his direction. "There is nothing more I can do," he said. "She did not want this marriage, nor did I, but blaming her for it would not solve anything. Moreover... when handled properly, she can be quite pleasant. She is a hard worker and unafraid to do something she is not familiar with, like trying to become a lady or cook a meal. At least she is willing to try. That shows strength of character."

Audric looked at him as he spoke, thinking that the man sounded very much like he was infatuated with the woman or, at the very least, appreciative of her. He had suspected it since yesterday, but today saw that opinion grow.

"No de Wolfe wife would be any less," Audric said. "Surely this is the lass ye've been waitin' for all yer life – strong, intelligent, and devoted."

Troy shook his head. "Nay," he replied. "I've not been waiting for her all my life. You see, I was married once before but she died two years ago. She was a woman I had known all my life. I never expected that I would live to an old age without her."

Audric hadn't known that Troy had been married before, a marriage that evidently ended on tragedy. Frankly, he was shocked, now scrambling to find the right words to convey his sympathies.

"I dinna know," he said quietly. "I am sorry for yer loss."

Troy thought on Helene but as he did, thoughts of Rhoswyn swept over him. Thoughts of her were stronger than thoughts of a wife who had died, someone he'd loved very much. But now, all he could think of was Rhoswyn and her fine body, an instant lust and desire that made his heart race. Helene had never had that effect on him, not ever, but the more he tried to remember his love for Helene, the more thoughts of Rhoswyn overwhelmed him.

God, what was happening to him?

"It was a difficult time," he said to Audric, trying to distract himself from the fact that, in his mind, Rhoswyn was overwhelming Helene. "She drowned, and my two youngest children with her. I have an older son but he was fostering at the time. In fact, I have not seen him in a year. He favors his mother, you see, so seeing him reminds me of her. Sometimes it is difficult to look at him and not feel the loss. He inherited none of my Saracen darkness and all of his mother's pale English beauty."

Audric thought on the boy as his father described him. "Saracen?" he repeated. "But yer father is English."

Troy smiled weakly. "His grandmother was Saracen," he said. "She was a dark and sultry beauty, so I am told, and I favor her and her heathen roots. I am sure you have noticed that I am darker than most Englishmen."

Audric had. He remembered thinking how dark Troy appeared when he'd first met the man. "That explains a good deal," he said. "But those in the Holy Land, where yer great-grandmother was from, are cunnin' fighters and bold warriors, so I've heard. Surely that spirit is within ye, also."

Troy nodded, thinking on his Saracen blood, but only briefly. He was still stuck on thoughts of Helene and Rhoswyn, still wrestling with the fact that he couldn't seem to remember his strong feelings for Helene at this moment. He loved her, didn't he? He'd told Paris that he would only and always love her, but after a few days of being married to a woman he never wanted to marry in the first place, it was as if he didn't know his mind any longer. Something had changed.

He didn't want it to change.

"Mayhap," he said belatedly, distracted with his other thoughts. "I would like to think I have something of my father in me and not mostly heathen tribes."

"Ye have the blood of de Wolfe *and* the Saracens in ye – ye have the blood of legends."

Troy looked at the priest, who had made the statement softly and matter-of-factly. *Ye have the blood of legends.* Perhaps it was true; he did have the blood of legends in him. In any case, he was becoming uncomfortable and edgy with thoughts of Helene and Rhoswyn on one hand and the approach of de Troiu's men on the other.

Since he was without his soldiers at the ready, he didn't particularly want to be seen by enemy soldiers, especially with his wife around. He didn't want her caught up in anything, should something get started. With that in mind, he turned for the stall.

"I will see how Rhoswyn is coming along," he said. "You will remain here. I shan't be long."

Audric watched him duck his head down in order to enter the low-ceilinged stall. "I thought ye said it wasna a fit place for a man?"

Troy snorted. "It is not," he said. "But I have a feeling she might let the merchant talk her into buying everything in the stall and I am not sure I have that much money with me."

Leaving the priest grinning, Troy headed into the dark, smelly stall that was stuffed to the ceiling with merchandise. As big as he was, he was trying very hard not to knock anything aside. He passed a table that had dozens of glass phials on them, or fragile alabaster and he made sure not to brush against it.

In the rear of the stall, he caught sight of Rhoswyn's auburn head with the merchant next to her as they inspected piles of fabrics. Troy could already see that there were neatly folded stacks of fabric in the big basket that the merchant had brought out to carry her goods, but she was closely inspecting an orange silk that glistened in the weak light. In fact, the orange reflected some of the highlights of her hair color. When she saw Troy approaching, she quickly set the silk down.

"I… I was lookin' at it because it was so lovely," she said, sounding as if he'd caught her at something she shouldn't be doing. She pointed to the basket. "Everythin' I've selected is very durable. The merchant says so."

Troy craned his neck, trying to catch another glimpse of the orange silk. "What about the orange fabric?" he asked. "Do you not want that, too?"

Rhoswyn turned to look at it again, hesitantly, as the merchant spoke up. "It is very fine silk, my lord," he said. "But it comes at a dear price."

"How much is it?"

The merchant picked up the fabric in question and held it up. "It is wild silk all the way from Rome," he said. "This is enough to make a lovely garment for the lady."

"*How* much?"

"I would accept an offer of six pieces of silver for it."

"Sold. Put it in the basket."

Rhoswyn's mouth popped open in surprise as the merchant gleefully rolled up the silk so it wouldn't crease. "But…"

Troy waved her off. "You will need a beautiful dress to wear for the times when we have privileged guests," he said. Then, he looked at the merchant. "Show her any other fine fabric you have."

Rhoswyn was beside herself. As the merchant called to his wife and the two of them began hunting in the rear of the stall for the expensive material, Rhoswyn went to Troy and hissed at him.

"Six pieces of silver?" she said through her teeth. "Are ye mad, laddie? That money would feed Sibbald's for a month!"

He grinned at her. "Shut your mouth, woman. I told you I wanted you well-dressed."

Her eyes widened, both in humor and in outrage. "Ye'll regret sayin' that tae me. I dunna take such words from any man."

He grabbed her, whipping her into his arms and planting a delicious kiss on her sweet lips. That lust he felt for her compelled him to kiss her again, listening to her gasp as he pulled away.

"You'll take it from me and you'll like it," he breathed. "Do you understand?"

Rhoswyn swallowed, struggling to catch her breath as she was pressed up against him. "Aye."

"Aye *who*?"

A flicker of a smile crossed her lips. "Aye, laddie."

That wasn't the answer he was looking for but he couldn't remain stern enough to tell her so. She was toying with him; he could see it in her eyes and it inflamed his desire for her like nothing else.

"Cheeky wench," he hissed. Releasing her, he turned her around so that she was facing the merchant again and slapped her lightly on the rump. "Buy something else beautiful. That is a command."

Rhoswyn didn't argue with him; she simply turned and grinned at him, feeling such warmth and attraction to the man. Any man who would give her commands and slap her on the arse was someone to be appreciated, she thought. No one had ever dared do it. But Troy had.

And she loved it.

"As ye wish, m'laird," she said. "I'll spend yer money and more besides."

"Now, I did not say *that*."

She giggled. "'Tis too late," she said, moving towards the merchant and his wife as they came at her with their arms laden with beautiful material. "I shall select the most costly piece they have."

Troy simply shook his head at her, grinning, watching her as she went over to the merchants and began rifling through their products. He saw her looking at something glittery and blue, holding it up to the light, and he couldn't take his eyes from the expression on her face. She looked so… happy. She *was* happy, and so was he.

In fact, it took Troy a moment to realize that he hadn't been this wildly happy in years. Sheer, unadulterated joy that made him want to take Rhoswyn in his arms and kiss her until she fainted, which for her would probably never happen. She was tough and she was strong, and he loved that about her.

But he loved it when she submitted to him, too. Just a little.

Is this what it meant to be happy again? Was that why he could only think distantly of Helene, as if she were a warm memory and nothing more? Rhoswyn scorched him like the fires of hell, a blaze in his belly that was only quenched when he took her to his bed and had his way with her long, strong body.

God help him, he never knew it could be like this again, this strength of happiness again. He married a woman who kicked him in the groin and hit him in the face when they'd first met. Instead of letting that set the tone for the marriage, he'd had to be more under-standing and more forgiving than he'd ever been in his life, but it took him a moment to realize that those two qualities were something Helene had always tried to impress upon him. *Be forgiving*, she used to say. *A gracious man is a great man.* But he'd ignored that advice until now.

Was it Helene's influence that had made him a better man for Rhoswyn?

He wondered.

Lost in thought, he turned for the front of the stall, mulling over the recent events in his life that had brought him to this moment. He was just coming out of the stall and catching a view of Audric before he abruptly caught sight of four de Troiu soldiers who were right at the mouth of the stall. In fact, he'd nearly run into them.

Now, he was exactly where he didn't want to be.

As part of the de Wolfe empire, Troy always wore very specific armor – a mail coat that went to his knees, a black de Wolfe tunic over that, and then a breast plate, of the latest military protection at that time, that essentially covered his chest. There was newer technology in armor being developed all of the time and William made sure that he and his sons were on the cutting edge of it. But the breast plate had something to identify Troy as being part of the House of de Wolfe, and that was a stylized engraving of a wolf's head on the upper left portion of the breast plate. It was a badge. Even if one didn't recognize him or his colors, most men of the north recognized the wolf's head.

The de Troiu soldiers were no different.

They recognized the wolf's head immediately, before they even saw Troy's face, and the four of them pulled into a suspicious group, scrutinizing Troy as a powerful and important knight from the House of de Wolfe. As soon as they started doing that, Troy turned to Audric.

"Quickly," he hissed. "Find my soldiers. Send them to me *now*."

Startled, and the slightest bit frightened, Audric scattered away, completely ignored by the de Troiu soldiers. Troy tried to move away, too, but as he knew, the soldiers were on to him. Old rivalries came out.

"De Wolfe," one man snarled. Then, he spit on the ground. "*That* is what I think of de Wolfe."

Troy didn't reply; he simply stared at them. They were mere soldiers and he wasn't going to get into a verbal debate with them. They were beneath him.

"Be on your way," he said evenly. "I have no personal quarrel with you but that will change if you do not move on."

The man didn't like being challenged. "And who are you?" he demanded. When one of his colleagues tugged on him and pointed out that he was a knight, the man brushed him off. "So you're a knight; who is to care? You're alone, knight. Where is your army?"

Troy cocked an eyebrow. "I do not think you wish to find that out. It will not go well for you."

The soldier's colleague was increasingly trying to pull him away while the other two soldiers were simply standing there, watching. One big mouth was doing the talking for all four of them.

"Is that a threat?" the soldier said. "You high and mighty de Wolfes like to give orders to the rest of us, but I won't listen to you. Whatever you defend, knight, has been stolen from others. Old William de Wolfe is a thief and if you serve him, you are a fool!"

Troy still didn't rise to the challenge, although one more taunt and his temper would be unleashed. He could feel it beginning to rise. "Be on your way," he said again. "I have no time for you rabble."

Now, three of the soldiers were tugging on the fourth, who seemed to want to get into a fight. But the fourth soldier wouldn't move; he was an older man, perhaps even as old as William, and there was much hatred in his heart for de Wolfe. Troy could see that simply by looking at him.

"And that whore of a wife that old William has," he hissed. "Do you know her? She has taunted many a man on the border with her wicked ways. If that offends you, then do not be angry with me. I'm just the messenger to deliver such news. But surely you have heard it from others."

Now, they were speaking of Troy's mother and his hackles went up. They could taunt him and even taunt his father, but the moment the soldier brought Jordan into the conversation, Troy found himself rising to the situation. He put his hand on the hilt of his broadsword, sheathed against his left leg.

"I would not say another word if I were you, vermin," he growled. "You are a dead man already, only you do not know it yet."

Because the knight put his hand on his sword, the three companions instantly drew their weapons, terrified they were about to enter into a losing battle. But Troy couldn't see the fear on their faces; he was staring down the man who had just insulted his mother. Before he could tell them for the last time to move on, a figure suddenly appeared between him and the four soldiers.

"Are ye stupid, all of ye?" It was Rhoswyn and she was flashing a rather large dirk in her right hand, shiny-new and clearly something she'd picked up in the merchant shop. "Are ye so full of English ignorance that ye seek tae take on a knight who can dispatch all of ye without effort? If ye want tae save yer own lives, then get out of here. Get out of here before ye rouse his anger!"

She was spitting mad, flashing the dirk in their faces. The men were backing away because a woman who was clearly mad was threatening them. All but the antagonist of the group; he had backed off but he didn't move away completely. His venom turned to Rhoswyn.

"And what's this?" he demanded. "Another de Wolfe whore? Do they have women fighting for them now? 'Tis a man without ballocks that lets a woman do his fighting for him."

Rhoswyn's eyes narrowed. "Spoken by a man who doesna understand the depths of his own worthlessness."

The three de Troiu soldiers looked at her in shock. It was an excellent insult and more than one of them looked as if he was verging on a grin. Before Troy could pull Rhoswyn out of the way, their aggressive comrade snarled at her.

"That's not what your mother said to me when I bedded her last night, lass."

Rhoswyn didn't hesitate even though she could feel Troy grab her arm. "Aye, yer mother," she said. "I know the wench well. She's such a filthy chit that when she takes a hot bath, she makes her own gravy."

The three soldiers burst out laughing at the surprising insult as their aggressive comrade's features registered pure outrage. This was no longer a game where he held the upper hand. In fact, the Scots wench had cut him down to size. Him *and* his mother. He immediately drew his sword.

"You'll pay for that, lass," he growled.

Rhoswyn had the dirk and she didn't wait for the man to charge her. Yanking her arm from Troy's grip, she went right after him, kicking him in the groin much as she had attacked her husband on that first day. When the soldier doubled over from the blow, she rammed the dirk into the back of the man's neck.

He was dead before he hit the ground.

After that, it was bedlam. With Rhoswyn out of control, Troy unsheathed his sword, charging at other three soldiers simply to protect her, but only one held his ground to engage. The other two ran off, screaming for their colleagues, and suddenly the entire village center erupted in a mass of screaming people running for their lives. De Troiu men were rushing towards the merchant's stall while most of the de Wolfe men came rushing over as well, pulled from where they'd been waiting out their lord.

The de Wolfe soldiers saw the de Troiu men and the fight ensued.

Swords clashed all around the central square of the town where the well was, and the women who had been washing their clothes fled in terror. After Troy dispatched his opponent, leaving the man bleeding out on the dirt, his priority was Rhoswyn.

She had started this mess and although he knew she was capable in a fight, he didn't know how capable she was until he saw her fighting with a de Troiu soldier who was nearly twice her size. He was a big man but she didn't let that stop her. As Troy watched, she ducked under the man's swipe, fell to her knees, and rammed her dirk into his foot. It went all the way through his shoe, through muscle and bone, and into the dirt on the other side.

As the man screamed and doubled-over, Rhoswyn withdrew the dirk from his foot and shoved it into his throat. He, too, fell to the ground, mortally wounded by a crazed Scotswoman.

Troy could hardly believe his eyes. Rhoswyn was good; nay, more than good – she was a smart fighter. But she was in the middle of a battle with men who were wearing protection and all she had on was a woolen cote. No matter how competent in battle she was, that cote wouldn't protect her from a blade and Troy knew he had to get her out of there. More than that, he simply didn't want her to fight. He knew she was trained for it, but he didn't care. He didn't want his wife fighting. He was terrified she was going to be gored while he watched.

Pushing through the crowd of men, he came to his wife as she was setting her sights on another English soldier. He grabbed her by the arm before she could get away and dragged her over to the edge of the fighting, back in the direction of the merchant's stall. The entire time, Rhoswyn struggled against him, finally pulling away from him and turning to him angrily.

"What did ye do that?" she demanded. "There are more men out there tae fight!"

Troy thrust a finger into her face. "Not for you," he said angrily. "Go back into the merchant's stall and wait for me."

Rhoswyn couldn't understand his anger or his words. "I willna," she said heatedly. "Those men must be punished!"

Troy was so furious that he was beginning to sweat. When he spoke, it was through clenched teeth.

"Listen to me and listen well," he growled. "When I married you, you became my wife. My wife does not fight my battles. My wife also listens to my wishes and she obeys them. Right now, you are not doing either of those things. You *will* obey me. Now, get into that merchant stall and wait for me. Is this in any way unclear?"

Rhoswyn was truly at a loss. She'd been raised a warrior; it was her natural instinct to fight. And now Troy was telling her not to do what came naturally to her. *Is this in any way unclear?*

It was *all* unclear.

"But... but I can help ye," she insisted. "Why will ye not let me help ye?"

He snapped. "I do not want your help. In fact, I did not need you to defend me. Do you have any idea how foolish you made me look in front of those soldiers?"

Rhoswyn was stricken. "Is that all ye care about?" she asked. "That I made ye look foolish? Those soldiers were goin' tae kill ye! I couldna stand by and watch that happen!"

Troy's anger deepened. "If you believe that, then you have little faith in my abilities as a knight," he said. "You made us both look like fools, Rhoswyn. You do not seem to understand that I am perfectly capable of settling my own affairs. I do not need another warrior; I need a wife."

She cooled dramatically. "I am tryin' tae be that. But when can a wife not defend the husband she adores?"

Troy's head snapped to her, his expression one of shock as well as anger. *The husband she adores?* Nay, he wasn't going to believe that. He *couldn't* believe that. Now she was lying to him.

...but, God... what if she wasn't?

"What you did has nothing to do with adoration," he said, his voice hoarse with rage. He simply couldn't believe she had feelings for him.

Adoration, she called it. He couldn't believe it because, if it was true, then it would make it easier to admit that he might be feeling something for her, as well. *It can't be true!* "Furthermore, I do not need your defending, not now and not ever. And I do not need you lying to me about your reasons for your actions. If you cannot be what I need you to be, then mayhap I do not need you at all."

With that, he turned on his heel and charged out into the fray, dropping men and fighting off the de Troiu soldiers who were beginning to break up and flee. He had to run because he couldn't look at her any longer, fearful that the conversation would become more and more heated, perhaps more and more emotional. He just couldn't do that to Helene. He couldn't disrespect her memory because, deep down, he wanted to admit that there was something there for Rhoswyn. He *was* feeling something.

But she would never know it.

As Troy used battle to distract himself from the turmoil in his heart, Rhoswyn simply stood there, feeling as if Troy had just taken that big broadsword he used and shoved it right into her guts. She felt as if she'd been cut to shreds by his anger, by the fact that she'd made him feel like a fool.

By his words, he couldn't have done more damage to her if he'd tried.

I do not need you lying to me about your reasons.

Those were the only words she could hear, cutting into her brain, searing their particular brand of pain into her fragile heart. It wasn't a lie, any of it. She *did* adore him; she knew that now. When she'd seen him facing off against four heavily-armed soldiers, visions of his bloodied body flashed through her mind. It would kill her to see him injured, or worse. That was how she knew, at that moment, that she adored him. All of the warmth and attraction she felt for the man had turned into something else, something deeper.

But Troy didn't understand that. And if he did, he'd rejected it. He didn't understand that all she'd wanted to do was to help the man she adored. To him, she'd shamed him. All of the bad meals and slovenly dressing couldn't embarrass the man, but one thing did – her attempts to fight for him. Finally, she'd done that which she'd feared.

He was ashamed of her.

If he didn't need her, then she would leave. She *had* to leave. Gutted, and devastated, Rhoswyn dropped the dagger in the mud and made a dash for the livery where her horse was tethered. She was running blindly, so very shattered by Troy's words.

Taking her big horse from the livery corral, Rhoswyn tore off through a secondary road south that would take her out of the village and to the countryside beyond. Sibbald's Hold was only an hour or so away; she knew she could make it by nightfall.

At that moment, she only had one thing on her mind – going home and forgetting about the three days of her life when she'd been her happiest. For her, it had only been fleeting and the life to be, the one she'd had a taste of, was only something now to be revisited in her dreams. Troy's words had made it clear that the dream was ended.

Mayhap I do not need you at all.

For certain, the dream was over.

CHAPTER SIXTEEN

I T HAD BEEN less than an hour after the start of the skirmish Rhoswyn had instigated, an hour that had Troy stewing in his anger with his wife. He'd killed at least three de Troiu soldiers and wounded a few more before they fled in a panic.

Meanwhile, three of his own soldiers had been wounded so he'd helped one of the sergeants tend to the wounded, one man with a fairly serious gash to his forearm. The merchant who had accumulated such a pile of goods for Rhoswyn was also the one who supplied fine silk thread to sew the wound up. Troy took care of it, as he was a good battlefield medic. He sewed up the man's arm and purchased the goods for Rhoswyn.

In truth, it had taken Troy all that time to calm down. He'd been so bloody confused about Rhoswyn that he'd literally had to put her out of his mind while he mopped up the fight she'd started.

The husband she adores.

Those words kept flashing through his mind, as much as he tried to ignore them. He had himself convinced that she'd only said it to soften his anger against her. She'd lied to him about why she'd entered the fight when the truth was that, perhaps, she really couldn't help herself. She'd been raised a warrior and the scent of a battle in the air brought all good warriors in for the feeding frenzy. She'd tried to tell him that it was because she wanted to defend him.

He just couldn't believe her.

He didn't *want* to.

It was all very puzzling, in truth. As he paid for the merchandise and thanked the shaken merchant for supplying the goods for Rhoswyn, he noticed that his wife hadn't gone back into the merchant's stall as he'd told her to do. He assumed she was somewhere between the merchant's stall and the livery, more than likely sulking after the tongue-lashing he'd given her. In truth, it was a painful conversation for him to remember. He regretted some of the things he'd said to her because he'd said them in anger, but he didn't regret all of it. There were lines that needed to be established in this marriage so it was good to establish them early.

Still... some things, he should not have said. As he came out of the merchant's stall, pondering the things he'd said to Rhoswyn, he found Audric standing on the roadside.

"You were not hurt in that skirmish, were you?" Troy asked him.

The priest shook his head. "Nay, m'laird," he said. "I stayed well away from the fight. Who *were* those men?"

Troy glanced out to the village center, which had been torn up a bit in the fight. Only now were villagers returning to repair the minimal damage.

"Enemies of my father," he said. "I saw them enter the town when we were standing here, waiting for my wife in the shop, but I'd hoped not to confront them. In fact, I'd hoped to leave this village without a battle but it seems that was not to be. Speaking of battles, where is Rhoswyn?"

Audric shrugged. "I have not seen her since the fight started. But I will admit – I hid across the road, over in the field. A battle is no place for me."

Troy looked at the little man, a half-grin on his lips. "Then you did not see Rhoswyn challenge them?"

Audric shook his head, appearing somewhat concerned. "Did she, now?"

"She most certainly did."

Audric sighed. "I canna say that I am surprised, given that the lass knows warrin'."

Troy's smile faded and his jaw began to tick faintly. "It is *all* she knows," he said. "I suppose I cannot expect miracles after only three days, but I was hoping she would have the sense not to try and fight again."

"*Again?*" Audric repeated. "'Tis goin' tae take more than three days tae break the woman of what her father has done tae her. Ye've been patient so far; ye must continue tae be patient."

Troy sighed heavily. "I am afraid that I was not very patient with her this time," he said. "She said that she was defending the husband that she… oh, it does not matter. I believe she said it simply to make an excuse for entering the fray."

Audric was watching him closely; the man seemed greatly troubled over the situation. "She said that she was defendin' her husband? It isna unusual for a wife tae defend her husband, m'laird. With Lady de Wolfe, however, I have a feelin' she'll not back down from any fight that involves ye."

Troy didn't like the sound of that. "I am afraid of that, to be truthful. She is going to get killed if she keeps that up and I do not want to bury another wife. It would be… difficult."

Audric sensed that there was something more on his mind. "Aye, it would be difficult," he said. "Ye're concerned for her, then?"

"Of course I am concerned for her."

"Is that why ye became angry with her? Out of concern?"

Troy was becoming increasingly agitated. "I became angry with her because she inserted herself where she did not belong," he said. "I am perfectly cable of handling a volatile situation and I certainly do not need the help of a woman. She made me look like a weak fool, and then for her to justify it by saying she did it because I am her husband and she adores me… that was a cheap trick, a lowly attempt to play on my sympathies."

Now, the situation was starting to make some sense. The woman had displayed some sentiment and de Wolfe was having trouble accepting that. He was careful in his reply.

"Since the moment ye and the lady married, ye've been inseparable," he said. "At least, it seems that way. I have seen ye two together a great deal. I thought ye were gettin' on splendidly."

Troy kicked at the ground, agitated. "We are," he said. "At least, we were. Oh, hell, I do not know anymore. I thought we were getting along well enough, certainly well enough considering our first meeting."

Audric studied the man, his irritation. "And ye feel as if she has somehow betrayed that? As if it was all a lie?"

Troy stopped kicking the ground. He was having difficulty looking at the priest. "She tried to tell me that the reason she challenged those soldiers was because she adored me and she did not want to see me injured," he said. "'Tis just like a woman to say something like that, to play on my sympathies."

"What if I told ye it was the truth?"

Troy did look at him, then. "It could not possibly be the truth."

"Why not?"

He scowled. "Because we have known each other three days!"

Audric smiled faintly. "I've seen the way the lass looks at ye," he said quietly. "When she told ye that she adored ye, I dunna believe she was lyin'. I believe she does."

Troy just stared at him and, as Audric watched, something odd rippled through his expression. Was it disbelief? Was it joy? It was difficult to tell.

"How can that be in so short a time?" Troy asked quietly.

Audric shrugged. "Look at the life the lass had before she met ye," he said. "Not much of one, if ye ask me. Raised by a father who wanted a son, never knowin' someone to be kind and patient with her. Ye gave her all of that, m'laird. Ye endeared yerself tae her. Of course she adores ye. And a woman like that... with such strength and fight in her... she probably adores ye with everythin' she has."

Troy's gaze lingered on the priest a moment before looking away. He was starting to think that he'd been overly cruel to Rhoswyn when she confessed her feelings. But she had terrified him, for so many reasons. Was it true? Did she really mean what she'd said?"

Confusion reigned.

"I do not want her adoration," he finally muttered. "I cannot have it."

"Why not?"

"Because I swore I would never love anyone other than my wife, Helene. My heart belongs to her and it always will."

Audric could see the conflict in the man and he felt rather sorry for him. In a gesture of pity, he put his hand on Troy's forearm.

"Helene has no more need for yer heart," he said softly. "She's with Our Lord and in heaven. She has all the love she needs. Do ye really think she'd be so selfish as tae expect ye tae never love another? Wouldna she want ye tae be happy again?"

Troy thought heavily on Helene; whereas her sister, Athena, Scott's wife, had been a bold personality, passionate in everything she did, Helene was the quiet and passive type. A generous woman with a heart of gold. Troy knew the answer to Audric's question – of course she would have wanted him to be happy again. She would have wanted him to love again.

It was his own guilt that was holding him back.

"I do not know anything anymore," Troy said, shifting the basket of goods he was holding and setting out for the livery. "I do not know what I want to feel, for anyone."

Audric didn't say anything more about it. It was clear that Troy was in a great deal of turmoil and, sometimes, a man had to sort such things out for himself. As Troy headed off to the livery to find his wife, Audric followed. He followed because William had asked him to keep peace between his son and his new wife, and Audric suspected this might be one of those times. He was determined to do what he could.

But Rhoswyn wasn't in the stable when they got there, and neither was her horse. Realizing she had fled, Troy knew it was to either one of two places – either she'd gone back to Monteviot, which he highly doubted, or she'd run home to her father, home to Sibbald's Hold where no one would become angry at her for starting a fight or for defending a man with all her heart. In truth, Troy had no doubt she'd gone back to Red Keith.

His nasty words had sent her right back to her father.

It was with a heavy heart that he realized what he'd done. He further realized what he had to do – he had to get her back. He had to apologize for his angry words, but beyond that, he wasn't sure what more he wanted to say. Could he tell her that he adored her, too? Probably not. He wasn't sure he could form the words, terrified that they were true words. All of it, true. But he knew he had to bring her back, no matter what. She was his wife and he wanted her by his side, where she belonged.

Troy sent his men back to Monteviot while he headed for Sibbald's Hold, less than an hour's ride to the east. He'd never been to Red Keith's stronghold but he knew the general direction, and a confirmation from Audric told him that he would be heading down the right road.

Although he'd told Audric to return to Monteviot with his men, somehow, no one seemed to be obeying him today. Audric followed him and Troy was halfway to Sibbald's Hold when he finally realized the priest was trailing him. The man did a rotten job trying to stay out of sight. Therefore, Troy came to a halt and waited for the man to catch up to him, and, sheepishly, Audric did.

Beneath the setting sun across a gloriously green landscape, Troy and Audric headed to Sibbald's Hold together to try and salvage what they could of Troy's marriage.

Troy knew he'd been wrong. But whether or not he could tell Rhoswyn was the key.

03

SHE WOULDN'T TALK to him.

Keith knew something terrible had happened when his daughter had come charging into the bailey of Sibbald's Hold. In truth, he'd been expecting her much sooner and he'd been expecting to defend himself against a very angry young woman, furious that he'd married her off to a Sassenach. But the young woman that returned to Sibbald's Hold didn't seem angry; she seemed devastated. She'd dismounted her horse, run into the tower, and run to her chamber and slammed the door. No amount of coaxing from Keith or Fergus or even Artis or Dunsmore could get her to talk to them.

She sat in her chamber and wept.

They could all hear her.

It was a situation filled with mystery, not the least of which was how she'd been dressed; in a lovely cote and her hair had been washed and styled. She looked like a true lady, something none of them had ever seen before. That astonished them almost more than her abrupt return.

As the afternoon turned into early evening, Keith sat on the steps outside of her chamber and listened to his daughter weep. Eventually, the weeping faded and there was only silence.

Dark, uncomfortable silence.

"Rhosie, lass?" Keith called to her on more than one occasion. "What can I do for ye? Why did ye come home?"

No answer.

There was no answer for a solid hour after her return. The weeping had ceased, that was true, but that made Keith uncomfortable. Rhoswyn wasn't the silent type. He could only hope she didn't have a dagger in the chamber with her and had slit her wrists in her hysteria. Not that she was the dramatic sort, but stranger things had happened. She'd spent three days away from her family and her home, and there was no telling what had gone on. Finally, nearly two hours after she'd returned home, he knocked softly on the chamber door and called to her again.

"Rhosie, please," he begged softly. "What has happened? Why are ye returned?"

Still no answer. Frustrated, and concerned, Keith was about to turn away when the door suddenly jerked open. He froze, waiting for Rhoswyn to come forth, but she didn't. Timidly, he peered into the room only to find her over by one of several small windows that brought ventilation and light into the rather dark tower of Sibbald's. The window faced west and she watched the sunset as colors of gold and pink danced on the stone walls. Hesitantly, Keith entered the chamber.

"Are ye all right, lass?" he asked, genuinely concerned. "What happened?"

Rhoswyn didn't say anything for a moment; she had only recently regained her composure and wanted to keep it. She didn't like to cry or suffer emotional outbursts, but that was exactly what she had done. She didn't want to do it again.

"He says he doesna need me," she said. "If he doesna need me, then I am home tae stay."

Keith's brows drew together. "And that was what drove ye home in tears?" he asked, incredulous. "Surely there is more tae it than that, lass. Did he beat ye?"

"Nay. And if he did, ye know I would beat him in return."

Keith nodded. "That's the daughter I raised," he said proudly. "Was he cruel tae ye, then?"

Rhoswyn shook her head. "Nay."

Keith scratched his head, confused. "If he dinna beat ye and he wasna cruel tae ye, then why did ye come home in tears? Surely it was somethin' terrible."

Rhoswyn sighed heavily. She didn't want to share her deepest feelings with her father. But at the moment, she was emotionally battered. She'd just received the biggest disappointment of her life. It had felt so good to have someone to talk to, like Lady Sable or Troy or even the priest. She and her father didn't have that kind of relationship but she found herself wanting to tell him everything.

She simply couldn't hold it back.

"The marriage ye asked of de Wolfe was the best thing ye could have done for me," she said, turning away from the window to look at him. "I canna describe how it was, Pa. All I can tell ye is that the past three days at Monteviot have been the best days of me life. They were kind tae me and Troy... me husband... he is the most wonderful man in the world."

Keith was shocked to hear it. Truly, the man was at a loss. "He *is*?" he asked, astonished. "Then why are ye home, lass?"

The question was too difficult for Rhoswyn to answer. She began to tear up so she looked away from him, her gaze finding the sunset landscape beyond the window once again.

"Because I canna be what he wants me tae be," she said, her throat tight with emotion. "He wants a wife, not a warrior, and I canna be a wife only. 'Tis in me blood tae fight. Ye taught me that. But he doesna like it when I do. He finds it shameful and... and I canna shame the man."

Keith was slowly walking in her direction as she spoke, coming to stand on the other side of the window, his focus on her face as she watched the sun set. He wasn't a particularly sensitive man, but he could sense a great deal of turmoil from his daughter. She was the strongest woman he had ever known. And now, he sensed that somehow, somewhere, the English had broken her. He didn't like to see it.

"Ye are shameful tae no man," he said, his anger turning towards Troy. "Did he tell ye that?"

Rhoswyn quickly wiped at tears that were threatening to fall. "He told me that I made a fool of him."

"How did ye do such a thing?"

She hesitated. "Because we went tae Jedburgh and while we were there, wicked soldiers confronted him," she said. "I went tae help him and he told me I shamed him."

"*How* did ye help him, lass?"

"I defended him," she said. Then, she turned to him angrily. "I put meself between me husband and the men who would hurt him. I couldna stand by and watch him become injured or killed, Pa. I had tae help him so I did. I adore the man and I dinna want tae see him hurt!"

By the time she was finished, she was weeping again and Keith stood by, stunned, as he watched his daughter break down. But in that nearly-shouted explanation, he saw a good deal of the situation and it was far more than he'd expected. His daughter had tried to fight men off from her husband who, as a knight and a competent warrior, didn't take kindly to his wife trying to fight off his enemies. But more than that, she said something very key to the entire situation – *I adore the man*. Shockingly, Rhoswyn had feelings for the Sassenach she was forced to marry.

Aye, Keith was seeing a good deal clearly.

"Oh," he said, trying to digest what he'd been told. "I see. Ye love the man, do ye?"

Rhoswyn wiped at her face, tears dripping off her chin. "I dunna know!" she said. "I… I suppose I do. Aye, I *do*. But he is ashamed of me and I am never goin' back tae him, do ye hear? Ye canna make me and if ye try, I'll… I'll run off and ye'll never see me again!"

Keith held up his hands in a soothing manner. "No one is makin' ye go back tae him," he said calmly. "If ye want tae stay her and think on things, ye can."

Rhoswyn stormed away from the window and over to the hearth, which was cold and full of soot. She began angrily throwing pieces of peat into the gaping, black hole.

"I have already thought on things," she said. "He doesna want a wife who shames him and I willna go back tae him. It is finished."

Keith shook his head as he watched her start a fire. "It is *not* finished, lass," he said. "He's yer husband. Ye canna simply walk away from him."

"I can!" she insisted. "Now, go away, Pa. Leave me be."

Keith was inclined to remain but thought better of it. She was agitated enough and his presence probably wouldn't calm her. Perhaps after a night's sleep, she might feel differently in the morning. But if she didn't, Keith was going to take a trip to Monteviot and find out just how ashamed Troy de Wolfe was of his wife. If he was too ashamed, then Keith would have some harsh words for him. How a man could make a woman fall in love with him only after a few days and then profess to be ashamed of that woman was beyond his grasp.

"As ye wish," he said, moving for the chamber door. "I'll leave ye be. Shall I send ye sup?"

"Nay."

"A drink, mayhap?"

"Nay."

Keith reached the door and paused, his gaze lingering on his daughter. "Does he know ye've come here?"

She shook her head. "Nay," she said. "I took me horse and left. I dinna tell him."

"Surely he'll figure it out," he said. "What do I tell him when he comes for ye?"

Rhoswyn looked at him, angrily. "He willna come for me," she said. "He told me he dinna need me. But if he comes… *if* he comes, tell him I willna go back with him. I willna live with a man who is ashamed of me."

With that, she turned away, her soft weeping to continue. It angered Keith because he'd raised his daughter to be strong, to know that tears were a sign of weakness. Perhaps the marriage to de Wolfe had made her weak somehow, even in the short amount of time they'd been together. He hated that she seemed weak.

That wasn't his daughter.

He was starting to regret his demand of a de Wolfe marriage; perhaps this was all his fault. He'd wanted an alliance too badly to think of the effect it would have on his child. He'd expected many things of that marriage, but Rhoswyn falling in love with her husband hadn't been among them. It would have been much better had she not. Aye, he regretted his decision immensely now.

Come the morrow, he'd travel to Jedburgh to speak to the priests about an annulment.

Perhaps that would be best, after all.

CHAPTER SEVENTEEN

"**W**HAT HAS HE done tae her?"

It was a soft question from Dunsmore to Artis as the brothers sat in the lord's hall of Sibbald's. It was dark but for the fire in the hearth, casting long shadows on the walls as the sun was nearly down outside. It was a lightless, haunting room as the brothers gathered around the single long feasting table.

"He must have beaten the woman senseless," Artis rumbled. He had a cup of liquor in his hand, the biting and strong liquor that a local beer wife made from mashed barley and rye. It could get a man drunk quickly and Artis was very fond of it. "Why else would Rhosie come runnin' back tae Sibbald's? She's been beaten beyond reason."

Dunsmore was furious to hear that. They'd all been listening to Rhoswyn's weeping and Keith's soft pleas since the woman returned almost two hours earlier, an event that had upset the whole of Sibbald's Hold. Rhoswyn Kerr was the strongest woman any of them knew and for her to run from the English, it was a certainty that something terrible had happened.

Something had to be done about it.

"Remember when she married him?" Dunsmore asked. "Remember how we said we had tae help her? For the sake of all of us, we had tae rid her of her Sassenach husband? Do ye recall?"

Artis waved at his brother irritably. "I remember," he said. "I'm not a dullard, ye know. I remember exactly what we said."

"Well?"

"*Well* – we'll have tae talk tae Rhosie when she gets hold of herself and ask her what she wants tae do," he said. "Mayhap she wants tae kill the man herself. If she does, then we'll help her."

"And if she doesna?"

"Then we'll do it anyway. Our plans havena changed, Dunnie. If we want tae keep what we have, then the Sassenach has tae be eliminated. He represents those Sassenach grandsons for Keith that will take away our fortune."

Dunsmore nodded, already hating those grandsons that hadn't even yet been born. "'Twill be a pleasure," he growled. "Any man who would…"

Footsteps stopped their conversation. They could hear them echoing in the stone stairwell, the one that led to the upper chambers of the tower where Rhoswyn was. Keith had been up there with her ever since her return, so Artis and Dunsmore assumed it was their Uncle Keith.

They were right.

Keith grunted with exhaustion as he came into the hall, heading for the table where his nephews were sitting, perhaps waiting for news of Rhoswyn. At least, that was what Keith assumed. The entire fortress was presumably waiting for word about Rhoswyn and her unexpected return. Keith made his way across the darkened room and sat heavily on the bench next to Artis.

"Pour me some of yer liquid fire, Artie," he said, referring to Artis' favorite drink. As his nephew poured, Keith ran his hand through his dirty hair in a weary gesture. "I dunna know what tae say about yer cousin, lads. She returned home, but not for the reasons I thought she would."

Artis handed his uncle the drink. "Why did she come?"

Keith took a drink of the alcohol, smacking his lips because it was so strong. "It seems that she dinna mind being married tae the Sassenach," he said. "According tae her, he was patient and kind for the most part, but he canna stomach her need tae fight, which is as natural tae her as breathin'. They had a quarrel and he told her he dinna need her, so she's come home. Only he doesna know she's come home, so I suspect he'll come for her soon enough. A man simply doesna let his wife run home."

Artis' eyes were glittering with the force of that news; he didn't dare look at his brother. Was it really possible that Rhoswyn's husband would end up here?

"Then… then ye believe the Sassenach will come tae Sibbald's tae claim her?" he asked.

Keith took another long drink of the strong alcohol. "Aye," he said. "She ran off and dinna tell the man. If he's smart, and I'm assumin' he is, then he'll know where she's gone. He'll come for her."

And come right tae his death. Artis was beside himself with glee at the realization. He was coming to think that Rhoswyn's return home was a most fortuitous event, better than they could have dreamed of.

"When?" Artis couldn't help himself from asking.

Keith shrugged. "Soon, I would think. He'll need tae claim what belongs tae him and, being a de Wolfe, I doubt he'll wait."

Artis hadn't heard such good news in a very long time. Truly, it was the perfect situation – they wouldn't have to go to the Sassenach; *he* would come to *them*. They would help Rhoswyn do away with the man who had not only made her miserable, but who represented a shake-up in their clan that would disturb them all.

God's Bones, it was a God-given situation and it was difficult for Artis not to show his glee. To cover the smile that threatened, he downed a big gulp of his drink.

"How does Rhosie feel about it?" he asked casually. "I mean, does she want him tae come? If the man sent her back to Sibbald's in tears, I canna imagine she's very happy with the thought of him comin' for her."

Keith didn't sense anything in his nephews other than sympathy for Rhoswyn's plight. He couldn't have known that every piece of information he gave them was being used towards the planned destruction of the de Wolfe son. He knew his nephews to be rash and, at times, foolish, but scheming wasn't something they usually did. Had he only known that, in this case, they were fearful for their future and what they believed belonged to them, he might have handled them differently.

But he didn't know. They were family, after all. And family didn't scheme against family. But to them, Troy de Wolfe wasn't family.

He was the enemy.

"She says she's not goin' back with him," Keith said, draining the last of the fire water from the cup. "She may change her mind come the morrow but, for now... she canna live with a man who is ashamed of what she is. And mayhap that's me fault."

Artis cocked his head curiously. "Why would ye say that?"

Keith inhaled slowly, deeply. It was a weary and sad gesture. "Because I turned her intae a warrior and not a fine lady, as her mother wanted," he said. "Mayhap... mayhap her mother was right all along."

Artis put a hand on Keith's shoulder. "Ye canna blame yerself," he said. "Ye did what ye had tae do. Ye made Rhosie a good fighter."

"But what about makin' her a good wife?" Keith looked at his nephew. Already, he could feel that strong drink pulsing through his veins, magnifying his emotions. "I dinna prepare her for her role in life and now she is sufferin'. 'Tis my fault, all of it."

Artis patted the man in a feigned show of comfort. He didn't understand his uncle's sadness because, to him, a fine warrior was better than a fine wife any day.

"Dunna worry, Uncle Keith," he said. "All will work out the way it should. Rhosie should never have married the Sassenach tae begin with. She should have remained here, with us. She should have remained with the people who accept her for what she is."

Keith was quickly growing sad and miserable, realizing that the way he raised his daughter did not do her any justice. The de Wolfe son should have been presented with a wife; instead, he'd married a warrior. That never bothered Keith until this very moment because it occurred to him how ill-prepared Rhoswyn had been going into the marriage. He didn't know why that had never occurred to him before.

He'd been a selfish man and an even worse father.

"She said that she was happy with him," he muttered, rising from the table. "She was happy with him but the man was shamed by her warrior instincts. I'm not sure that's something she can ever overcome. 'Tis part of her."

It seemed to Artis and Dunsmore that he wasn't looking for an answer to that particular dilemma. He was muttering as he left the table and crossed the floor, heading out to deal with his problems on his own. Only when the man quit the hall did Artis turn to his brother.

"Ye heard him?" he hissed. "De Wolfe is comin' here!"

Dunsmore nodded eagerly. "When he does, we'll be a-waitin' for him. Right intae our very own trap!"

Artis poured himself more alcohol and poured his brother some as well. Collecting his cup, he lifted it to his brother as if to toast their good fortune.

"Tae family," he said quietly.

Dunmore lifted his cup in return. "Tae what belongs tae us."

Never were truer words spoken.

☙

THE SUN WAS down by the time Sibbald's Hold came into view.

It sat in a small valley amidst rolling green hills, surrounded by smaller farms that dotted the land. There were sheep everywhere; between the three-quarter moon and the remnants of the setting sun, Troy could see the little white dots on the darkening hills. He could smell them, too. Surrounding Sibbald's enclosure was a large herd, managed by several men and dogs, and he'd had to identify himself before they'd let him pass. Even then, they men followed him all the way to the walled enclosure.

The enclosure was bathed in a moonlit glow, with spots of golden light coming from the windows of the tower itself. Sibbald's tower was comprised of a large L-Plan tower, three stories in height. L-Plan towers were usually those that were originally built as a single tower but somewhere over the years, were expanded with a wing that literally made the tower in the shape of the letter "L".

Troy had seen a few of these L-Plan towers over Scotland through the years, as the Scots seemed to be fond of adding those additional wings to expand the footprint of the structure and maximize space in the smaller fortresses. But the thick, impenetrable L-Plan tower was nearly the only thing Sibbald's Hold had – it was in an enclosure with walls that weren't very tall and, in fact, Troy could look over the top of the walls and see the enclosure within. The place was overrun with dogs, with an entire pack coming out to sniff him and his horse, who didn't take kindly to the canines.

Dogs yelped as the horse kicked out and swung its big head, chasing the dogs away. But the moment they entered the bailey, they only went a few steps before coming to a halt because the bailey was so small. The tower was directly in front of them. There was a stable to the east, small outbuildings to the north, and then the massive tower stretched above them.

Troy couldn't help but notice that the men who had followed them from outside the walls were now standing behind him. He could feel their suspicion in the darkness. Unwilling to take a silent stance now that he'd arrived, he turned to the men gathered behind him.

"My name is Troy de Wolfe," he said. "I am Rhoswyn Kerr's husband. I am assuming she is here and I have come for her. Bring me Keith Kerr."

There was some hissing and shuffling going on. Men were pushing each other in the darkness until someone finally broke off from the pack and ran into the tower. When that happened, Troy dismounted his horse, as did Audric, and the two of them stood in tense silence as they wait for Keith to make an appearance. There was a great deal of tension and unease filling the air around them, for a myriad of reasons.

"Do ye truly believe she's come here, m'laird?" Audric muttered, leaning in Troy's direction. "Those men did not tell ye if she is."

Troy was looking up to the big tower. Lights were filtering out from the tiny windows, telling him that there were people, and life, inside.

"Mayhap they do not know," he said. "It is possible that she simply slipped in, but if she hasn't come here, then we must enlist Keith to help search for her. Either way, this was the best place for me to come under the circumstances."

Audric shrugged in agreement, but the truth was that he was uncomfortable with the gang of men behind them. He was Scots, and a priest to boot, but Troy was English and a knight. He was a direct threat. He knew Troy must have been uncomfortable, too, but to the man's credit, he seemed perfectly at ease, even when the Scots began to hiss insults at him.

"Cù Beurla," one of the men behind Troy snarled.

Having a mother who was Scottish, Troy had grown up having Gaelic spoken to him on occasion. He knew the language, so when one of Keith's men called him an English dog, he was well aware of it. And he barked back.

"Bi faiceallach cò thu a chanas tu ri cù Sassenach," he said, loud enough for them to hear. "Tha an cù seo na mhadadh-allaidh agus tha e a 'ruith ann am pasganan."

Be careful who you call an English dog. This dog is a wolf and he runs in packs. It was a calm statement of fact and an even calmer threat. After that, they didn't hear any more disparaging comments directed at Troy. He didn't even turn around to see the expressions of surprise on the faces of the men behind him when they realized he could understand him. Next to him, he heard the priest hiss.

"Do ye know the *Gàidhlig*, then?" Audric asked with some awe. "Ye speak flawlessly."

The corner of Troy's mouth twitched. "I told you that my mother is Scottish," he said. "She taught us the language when we were quite young. It has come in handy here on the borders."

Audric's gaze lingered on the man. "Ye are a man of many talents, de Wolfe," he said. "I think I am comin' tae like ye, just a little."

Troy's grin broke through as he turned to the man. "Just a little? I should think I would be your favorite person in the world by now."

Audric snorted but he was prevented from replying as men began to come out of the tower. Several men Troy didn't recognize until Keith suddenly came into the moonlight. Then, he could see the man clearly. He didn't even give him a chance to speak before he was walking towards him.

"Is she here?" he demanded.

Keith's expression suggested he wasn't at all surprised to see Troy. Having just left his nephews in the hall, he'd been standing in the foyer of the tower, mulling over his bad choices with his daughter, when one of his men had come to tell him that Troy de Wolfe had arrived. Oddly enough, he'd felt a surge of satisfaction with the news that Troy had arrived. But satisfaction for what? That he'd been right? That the English was as predictable as he thought he was? But satisfaction also mingled with doubt – so the man had come for Rhoswyn. It was his right, as her husband.

But did he want to send him away? Keith truly couldn't decide.

"Why would ye think that?" he finally asked.

Troy wasn't in the mood for an evasive old man. "Because she has run away from me, presumably to return home. Is she, or is she not, here? Because if she is not, then I will not waste my time talking to you. I must go look for her."

Keith paused, still debating on how to reply. Truthfully, there was only one thing he could say to the man who seemed rather frantic. He relented.

"She is here," he said.

That brought about a good deal of relief on Troy's part; Keith could see it. "Is she unharmed?"

"She is."

Keith didn't seem willing to give out any more information, but Troy had expected more of a response. The man seemed very resistant to Troy and his purpose. With that in mind, Troy handed the reins of his horse over to Audric as he moved closer to Keith.

"Well?" he said. "Where is she? I must speak with her."

Keith looked at the man; he could see the strain on his face, even in the moonlight. Concern, he thought. Or was it fear? Did the man simply want his property returned to him and nothing more? A little tipsy from Artis' liquid fire alcohol, Keith was in his own world of concern. A mistake he'd made had cost his daughter a great deal and, in truth, he had something to say to de Wolfe about it before he headed to Jedburgh to seek an annulment from the man who was ashamed of his daughter's warrior instincts. As of this moment, that was still his intention – an annulment. But he wanted to let de Wolfe know *why*. What he'd done hadn't been fair to either his daughter or his daughter's husband. He should have known that marrying a warrior to a warrior would not have been a good match.

Crooking a finger, Keith pulled Troy away from the gathering of men that had formed behind him. He pulled him across the darkened yard, over towards a big Yew tree that stood nearly in the center of the compound. The heavy branches stood out against the night sky, black outlines of limbs. When they were beneath the tree and away from prying ears, Keith turned to Troy.

"She came home this afternoon and has only now stopped weepin'," Keith said, somewhat critically. "She said ye dunna need her any more. She says ye're ashamed of her for her fightin' instincts. Ye knew she was a warrior when ye married her, de Wolfe. Why should her warrior instincts shame ye?"

Troy sighed heavily. So his sharp words had hurt her, enough to send her home to her father in tears. He felt like an ogre, a vicious beast with a sharp tongue and the anger to unleash it. But he could see that Keith was vastly displeased about the situation so he hastened to relay his point of view. Rights or no rights, he had a feeling he would have to go through Keith to get to his wife at this point. Like a good father, Keith was intent on protecting his daughter.

"I am not ashamed of her warrior instincts," he said evenly. "But she has to learn to control them. She has to understand when it is appropriate to give in to those instincts and when not to. Did she tell you what happened?"

Keith nodded, folding his arms across his chest in a rather unfriendly gesture. "She did."

Troy didn't think he was any closer to seeing Rhoswyn at this point so he hastened to tell Keith the whole story. "We were in Jedburgh," he said. "There were some enemies of my father in town and when they confronted me, your daughter suddenly put herself between me and four armed men. She had no armor, no protection, and simply a small dagger she was threatening them with. She could have easily been killed but she did not seem to understand that. And the truth is that I never told her that she had shamed me; I told her that she made a fool of me trying to fight armed men who were challenging me, *not* her. It was not her fight but she stepped into it without thought to the consequences."

Keith had to admit that it sounded a good deal like his daughter. She was aggressive, always wanting to be right up front in a battle. She rarely listened to her father's commands so he could only imagine that she didn't think she needed to listen to her husband's. Perhaps de Wolfe had been given a good reason to scold her.

"Then why did she tell me that ye said ye dinna need her?" he asked.

Troy let out a grunt of exasperation, of regret. "I told her I needed a wife, not a warrior," he said. "I told her that if she could not be what I needed her to be, then mayhap I did not need her at all. In truth, I was so frustrated and angry at that point that I said something I should not have said. I did not mean it. But that woman is as stubborn as I am and my anger got the better me."

Keith knew, very well, what it was like to be overwhelmed with frustration where Rhoswyn was concerned. Aye, he knew that well, indeed. He could feel himself relenting from thoughts of an annulment because hearing the story from Troy, it sounded like it was just a misunderstanding, something his daughter might have instigated. Certainly, Troy wasn't acting like a husband who didn't need, or appreciate, his wife.

"Then ye do need her?" he asked. "Or, at the very least, ye want her returned?"

Troy nodded firmly. "I do," he said. "My lord, I know that our marriage was… unexpected. But in spite of that, it has not been unpleasant. Your daughter is a woman of good character, of strength, and of determination. You should have seen her the day after our wedding, trying to learn how to run a household and cook a meal. She tried so very hard and I was deeply impressed with her efforts. She knew absolutely nothing about the undertaking, but she did her best. We were in Jedburgh today because I was purchasing fabric for new clothing for her and perfumes and soaps, everything that a lady needs. We were getting along fine until the enemy soldiers confronted me and she felt the need to intervene. I hurt her feelings and, for that, I am deeply sorry. But she will never know unless I can tell her. Now… will you *please* let me see her?"

He spoke eloquently and with conviction. Keith believed him without question and the idea of annulment was gone. Clearly, this was a man who appreciated Rhoswyn. What had she said? That she'd been happy as Troy's wife? Keith could see now that the feeling seemed to be mutual. But there was something else his daughter had told him; he wondered of Troy was even aware.

"I dunna believe she would have been so upset with all of this had she not developed feelings for ye," he said quietly. "She loves ye, laddie. Did ye know that?"

Troy just stared at him. That seemed to bring all of his impassioned pleas to a halt. He didn't say anything for a moment but Keith saw him swallow, hard, in the moonlight.

"I do not know how that is possible after having only known me for a few days," he finally said. "Mayhap she only believes it is love because…"

Keith cut him off. "Rhosie never says anythin' she doesna mean. If she says she loves ye, then she does."

Troy didn't know what to say about all of that. There was such turmoil in his heart that it was difficult to speak at all.

"Will you *please* let me speak with her?" he begged softly. "Keith, I must. Do you not see that?"

He called the man by his Christian name. Somehow, in this situation, it seemed appropriate, and Keith didn't mind. All he could see was a man in front of him who was earnest and repentant, a man who seemed to truly want to make amends for harsh words. He hadn't said that he'd loved Rhoswyn in return, or even that he had feelings for her, but his expression told Keith that there was emotion in the man. He felt something for Rhoswyn even if he couldn't voice it.

Even though Rhoswyn had said she did not wish to see him, Keith had a feeling she would change her mind come the morrow. If she truly loved the man as she said she did, then she would come to see reason, eventually.

Better give her the night to do it.

"She is deeply upset," Keith said after a moment. "I fear if ye speak tae her tonight, it will do more harm than good. She said she dinna want tae see ye, so ye need tae let her sleep on it. Rhosie can get herself worked up and then she is beyond reason, so give her the night. I'll let ye speak with her on the morrow."

She dinna want tae see ye. That wasn't the answer that Troy was looking for but he had to respect it. The last thing he wanted to do was upset Rhoswyn more.

"As you wish," he said, sounding depressed. "Will you at least tell her I am here, even if she does not want to see me?"

"I will tell her."

There was nothing promised beyond that and Troy understood. He'd never felt quite so despondent. "May I at least find shelter in your stable for the night?" he asked. "I do not wish to leave the grounds in case she will see me."

Keith nodded, pointing in the direction of the stable. "There is a sod house behind the stable that me men sometimes use," he said. "Ye can sleep there tonight. Hopefully, tomorrow will bring a brighter day for us all."

Troy simply nodded, watching the man as he turned and headed back into the tower. Once Keith disappeared from view, there wasn't much he could do except retreat to his borrowed shelter and wait out the night. There was no way he was leaving without speaking to Rhoswyn. Without telling her how sorry he was and how he didn't mean it when he said he didn't need her.

He needed her more than words could express.

If that meant he loved her, then perhaps he could no longer deny it.

CHAPTER EIGHTEEN

HE CAUGHT A flash of blond hair, brushing by him.

It was a sunny and bright day, with the green hills of Northern England surrounding him. Troy was standing in a field of some kind with a stream rushing through it. He could see the water bubbling and hear laughter all around him. Another flash of blond hair ran past him and he turned to see a figure he knew, very well.

Helene was dressed in a white gown, all flowing and long. Her blond hair was unbound, falling in soft waves to her buttocks, and she looked as she did when she had been a very young woman, right before they had married. She was tiny, and curvy, unlike the rest of her family who had been tall and slender. Helene didn't follow that mold, but Troy thought she was the prettiest de Norville daughter of the bunch. That was why he'd married her.

She was smiling at him. God, she looked so young. He hadn't seen her that young in years. When he extended a hand for her, she passed through his fingers, like water. He couldn't get a grip on her. He couldn't touch her but he could most definitely see her. It made the pain of losing her return in a harsh, painful wave.

"You're here," he said, elated. "Why are you here?"

Helene smiled at him. But around them, the landscape shifted from bright and sunny to dark and stormy. Clouds formed. It began to rain.

"You must go, Troy," she said. "There is nothing for you now."

He was puzzled. "You are here. I am staying."

Helene shook her head, her blue eyes as bright as he had remembered them. "You cannot," she insisted in the soft way she used to do such things. "You must go on."

Troy was still puzzled. He reached out to touch her but as he did, she morphed into something that wasn't Helene. His hands passed through a mist and when the mist finally took shape again, he found himself looking at Rhoswyn.

"'Tis me," she said.

Troy was greatly confused, greatly torn. "Why... why are you here?"

Rhoswyn, too, was nebulous. He couldn't seem to touch her. As he reached for her, she backed away. "Helene is gone," she said. "Ye must come tae me."

Troy couldn't seem to speak. As the rain began to fall, no one got wet, but the stream and the land around him grew wild with water. Rhoswyn faded away into the mist again, turning back into Helene.

"You must go on, Troy," Helene said softly, her smile gentle.

Tears came to Troy's eyes. "I do not think I can."

Helene nodded as she came towards him, the rain pounding all around her as she remained dry and serene. "You must open your heart."

Tears spilled down his cheeks. "But I do not want to leave you."

She was so real looking that he swore he could have touched her. "You will never leave me," she said. "And I will never leave you. I wish joy for you now. Be joyful. And you must go on."

With that, she faded from view and the storm continued to pound. She was gone, just like that, and Troy stood there weeping.

A crash of thunder startled Troy awake. It was nearing morning as a storm broke over the land, and the sound of rainfall pelted the small window of the sod house where he and Audric had been sleeping. It took Troy a moment to realize that he'd been dreaming.

A dream!

Sitting up, he wiped at his face, realizing that there were, indeed, tears on his cheeks. He wiped them off, feeling exhausted and emotional. *Damnation!* The dream seemed so bold, so vivid, as if he had truly been speaking with Helene. God, he could almost touch her. And her eyes! He remembered those eyes, so alive and warm. He had missed those eyes.

But then came Rhoswyn.

Ye must come tae me.

That's what she'd said in his dream. And Helene – what had she told him? That he must go on? How was it even possible he should dream such a thing? Troy wasn't a man to believe in divine intervention. In fact, he'd stopped believing in God when Helene and the twins had drowned. He remembered telling his father that if there was a God, surely he wouldn't have let such a thing happen. Since then, Troy was convinced that God was a myth and nothing more. He was a tale for children, made up to force them to behave. Those children grew into adults who still believed in that tale. But Troy didn't; not any longer.

But his dream may have just changed that opinion.

Helene had told him what he'd needed to hear. He'd been in such horrific turmoil over his feelings for her, and for Rhoswyn, that something had to give. Was it possible that God had allowed Helene to enter his dreams, knowing how devastated he'd been these past two years, to tell him what he must do? He could hardly believe it. God had ignored him up until now.

Perhaps God chose this moment to speak.

On the floor at his feet, Audric let out a rattling snore, undisturbed by the rain and thunder outside. Troy stared at the man, thinking of his history with him. Audric had come to Monteviot to bury the Scots dead and ended up remaining at William's request. Audric had been following Troy around and he really had never understood why until this moment. Was it possible that Audric had been sent by God to look out for him, to help him understand what his new course in life was to be?

Audric had said that William had asked him to stay, but Troy wasn't so sure anymore. Perhaps Audric was a direct conduit from God, straight to Troy. And tonight of all nights, fed him the dream that was necessary for him to choose the right course in life.

Literally, like a bolt from heaven, Troy knew what he had to do. He had to face Rhoswyn and confess his feelings as she had confessed hers. Helene had told him as much.

Be joyful. And you must go on.

That was exactly what she had said. It was as if she'd given him permission not to live in the past, not to linger over a love that was now only a memory. It was a love that Troy had been sworn to, a love that had caused him great guilt when he realized he was feeling something for Rhoswyn. Now, Helene had taken away that guilt.

It was time for him to move on.

Dressed in his tunic and breeches for sleep, Troy pulled on his boots and charged out into the rain.

☙

RHOSWYN COULD HEAR the rain, too. Mostly, she liked thunderstorms because there was a certain peace with them, she'd found. She loved to listen to the rain and to the rumbling of the clouds but, at the moment, she found no peace with what she was hearing. All she could think of was Troy, here on the grounds of Sibbald's, having come to bring her back.

Keith had told her everything last night. He'd told her of his conversation with Troy and he'd seemed to be on the man's side. Keith had even lectured her about interfering in the man's business, which is how the entire situation got started. Rhoswyn was angry with her father for siding with Troy even though, deep down, she knew there was some truth to what he'd said. But in her defense, she had truly felt that Troy was in danger and she felt it her duty to protect him.

But the man didn't need protecting. Even she knew that.

But she had been fearful for him; so very fearful. That had prompted her to act. But in hindsight, she supposed she knew that he didn't need her help. Troy was a powerful knight and he had been fighting battles for a very long time. But she was accustomed to fighting, to being in the front of a fight, and it was her instinct to defend Troy when she saw those nasty soldiers harassing him.

It was difficult to admit that, perhaps, she'd been wrong.

But she was only willing to consider her misstep because Troy had come so quickly. He hadn't been too far behind her in coming to Sibbald's and according to her father, he seemed genuinely concerned and genuinely remorseful. He'd asked to see her immediately but Keith had told him to wait the night. It was probably good advice, for both of them. That way, emotions would have calmed before they spoke. All she wanted to hear was that he did need her, and all she wanted to say to him was that she was sorry she'd shamed him. She hadn't meant to, but she had. A night of little sleep, of Troy heavy on her mind, and she knew what she had to say to him.

"Rhoswyn!"

A very loud voice wafted in from outside, carried upon the cold breeze and muffled by the rain. At first. Rhoswyn thought she might have dreamed it. She sat up in bed, her ear cocked as the thunder rolled and the rain fell. Then, she heard it again.

"*Rhoswyn!*"

Startled, she leaped to her feet and ran to the tiny window. Her window faced west, away from the sunset, so all she could see was a gray landscape and rain. She couldn't see who was calling her name because of the angle of the window, but she knew it was Troy. His deep, booming voice... that voice she'd fallen so heavily for... aye, she'd know that voice anywhere.

It was the voice of the man she loved.

"Rhoswyn, it is Troy!" he said again, his full voice reaching above the sound of the rain and filling her ears. "I know you are in there and I hope you can hear me because I have much to say to you. If you do not come down to the bailey, then I shall shout it for all to hear!"

God, she was so happy to hear his voice but, in the same breath, feelings of hurt and frustration crept into her heart. Feelings from yesterday, when he had so badly damaged her with his harsh words.

Mayhap I do not need you at all.

Those words were still ringing in her head. Even though the man had come to Sibbald's to tell her that, perhaps, he'd been lying when he'd said them. He'd been angry with her and said something he didn't mean. But how did she really know he didn't mean it? She didn't honestly know the man. At least, she didn't know him as deeply as she should have. They'd only been married these four days now. How can one come to know someone so deeply, so fully, in so short a time?

How could she have fallen in love with him and hardly have known him?

She had no idea how to answer that question, but she did know one thing – his voice was close; very close. *He* was close, and the anticipation was more than she could bear. Rhoswyn had a feeling he was just out of her sight because he sounded very near. He was more than likely standing in front of the entry, the vestibule area, and her window was just to the right of it. She wouldn't go running to him like a weakling but she certainly wanted to hear what he had to say.

Above the rain and the thunder, she yelled from her window.

"What is it ye want, Troy de Wolfe?" she shouted from the window. "Ye made yerself clear that ye dunna need me. Why did ye come?"

After everything Keith had told her last night, Rhoswyn knew why he had come – or, at least, her father's version of why he had come. But she wanted to hear it for herself. Soon enough, Troy moved into her line of sight.

As the rain poured and the thunder rolled, he moved up beneath her window, looking up at her as water spattered on his face. His dark hair was plastered back against his skull and those golden eyes were blinking rapidly as the rain hit them. But the expression on his face was something Rhoswyn had never seen before, like a man who had seen the face of God and had lived to tell the tale. So much in his expression was wide open, beseeching.

Vulnerable.

"I came to tell you that I am sorry," Troy said. He was still shouting, but not nearly so loudly as he had been. "I said cruel things to you and I should not have. My only defense is that you frightened me."

"I thought I shamed ye?"

He blew the rain out of his mouth. "You did," he said. "You put yourself into a situation that was not your business, as if I was not man enough to handle it myself."

She flamed. "I told ye why I did it! I did it tae help ye!"

He put up a hand. "You did not let me finish," he said evenly. "By putting yourself into that situation, you put yourself in harm's way. Those men were armed and you had a little knife you thought to fend them off with. While admirable, it was foolish. Do you know why I became angry? Because I was terrified that those men were going to run you through and there would have been nothing I could have done to save you."

Rhoswyn stared at him as he stood down there, being beaten by the elements. As she stood there, she felt someone coming up behind her and she turned to see that Keith had made an appearance. He'd heard the shouting, too, and he'd come to see what was transpiring.

But Rhoswyn held him off from showing himself to Troy, fearful that Troy wouldn't say everything he wanted or even needed to say if he knew Keith was there. It would be much better if he thought he was only talking to Rhoswyn.

Still… he was shouting their business for all to hear. But Rhoswyn wanted to think this was just between them. Troy had come to get her back… she wanted him to try.

"I can take care of meself," she said after a moment. "Ye dunna need tae worry about savin' me."

Troy wiped the water from his eyes. "You are my wife," he said. "I will always worry about saving you, whether or not you like it. And when I said I needed a wife and not a warrior… I meant it, Rhoswyn. I have thousands of warriors at my disposal, but only one wife. It is a very big role you fill in my life and although I know you were raised to fight, I do not need you to do it. I do not *want* you to. And I am not trying to be cruel by telling you that, merely honest. I want my wife to work beside me, to laugh with me, to tend to my home and to my children, if we are so blessed. But fighting… I will be honest and tell you that it is a man's work. In our home, I want it to remain that way."

Rhoswyn listened to a man who seemed very repentant about what he'd said to her, but also very honest in what he was telling her. She sensed a fragility from him that she'd never sensed before. Yet, what he was telling her was truthful – fighting *was* man's work. Still, it was the only thing she'd ever known. But she very badly wanted to be the wife he wanted her to be.

"I know it is a man's work," she said, feeling some vulnerability of her own. "I… I'm just not prepared for bein' a wife. I tried; ye know I tried. But one moment in town when I thought ye were in danger dashed all of the tryin' I'd been doin'. Mayhap I was simply lyin' to meself about it, thinkin' I could become a lady."

Troy could hear defeat in her voice, defeat he knew he'd put there. He didn't like to hear it, not from the strongest woman he'd ever known.

"I do not want you to be discouraged by what I've told you," he said. "I simply want you to find your place in the world. In *my* world. I have seen you work over the past few days and I told you I was pleased. *More* than pleased. I do not want to go back to Monteviot without you, sweetheart. Please do not make me leave alone."

Sweetheart. Rhoswyn nearly swooned as he called her a pet name, a term of endearment. Nothing had ever sounded so wonderful to her ears. She looked to her father as if, suddenly, she believed everything he'd told her. Troy *had* been genuinely remorseful with what had happened. It made her heart swell with hope that, perhaps someday, he might even feel something for her. She knew she loved him; she didn't expect such things from him, not now. What she felt was her own private paradise. But someday... perhaps there would be love between them.

She could only hope.

"Ye are?" She returned her attention to Troy. "Pleased, I mean."

"I am."

"What about not needin' me?"

Troy sighed heavily. "I was angry when I said it," he said. "I should not have said it. Forgive me, Rhoswyn. But do you understand why I was so angry with you? You know I've already lost one wife. I could not stand to lose you, too."

All of the hurt and anger drained out of her at that moment. It must have been very difficult for him to admit such a thing. Of course she wanted to forgive him; not wanting to see him, telling her father she never wanted to speak with Troy again, was her anger speaking, too. She understood what it was to be angry and say things one didn't mean because she was guilty of it, too.

"Ye'll not lose me," she said. "And I'll go back to Monteviot with ye. But if ye're ever in danger and I get the urge tae fight again..."

He put up his hands. "If I need your help, I will ask," he said. "But *only* if I ask. Is it a bargain?"

She fought off a grin, thinking that it sounded like a most reasonable deal. "'Tis a bargain."

A smile spread across Troy's lips. "And, Rhoswyn?"

"Aye?"

"I am glad you adore me because I... I adore you, also."

Her features went slack with the impact of his words and all she wanted to do was go to the man and throw her arms around him. Every harsh word, every sorrowful feeling melted away until all she could hear were those words ringing in her head –

I adore you, also.

They were the most wonderful words she'd ever heard.

But the warm and tender moment was cut short when something went sailing past Troy's head. He'd been looking up at Rhoswyn and caught the movement out of the corner of his eye. He ducked, but not quickly enough. Something clipped him on the forehead and he went down as two bodies suddenly rushed him, coming from the direction of the tower. Troy was suddenly was under attack and Keith ran from the chamber, cursing a blue streak, with Rhoswyn right on his heels.

It wasn't strange how quickly she forgot her bargain with him. *If I need your help, I'll ask.* He didn't ask, but she was going to help him, anyway.

At that moment, the instinct to protect him was stronger than that promise.

CHAPTER NINETEEN

THEY'D BEEN WAITING.

Artis and Dunsmore had been up before dawn, knowing that Troy was on the grounds, preparing to carry out their plan against the man.

As far as they knew, Rhoswyn still hated her Sassenach husband and nothing had changed to that regard. They hadn't yet spoken with Rhoswyn about it, but that didn't matter. It became less about helping Rhoswyn do away with her husband and more about Artis and Dunsmore and their original fear – the fear of Keith giving away his fortune to his half-Sassenach grandsons. In their minds, that was all it was about.

And they needed to take care of the problem.

So, they were up at dawn, arming themselves for their attack on the English knight. They had listened to the conversation between Keith and Troy the night before, tipped off by a servant that Troy had arrived and Keith was speaking with the man. They'd hovered in the entry of the tower, listening and watching, hearing some of the conversation between Keith and Troy, but not all of it. Troy had come to make amends with Rhoswyn and that was the last thing Artis and Dunsmore wanted.

They had to move.

Armed before sunrise with a halberd and a short sword, assuming it would be easy between the two of them to dispose of de Wolfe, they crept from the bedchamber they shared in the tower just as a storm let loose overhead. Thunder and rain pounded the old tower as they slipped down the dark stairwell, past Rhoswyn's chamber with the door closed, wondering if she was awake yet. They had to get to her husband before she relented and had contact with him. But by the time they hit the entry to the keep, they could hear the shouting going on.

The Sassenach had other plans.

Standing in the doorway as the rain beat down, they could see Troy as he stood beneath Rhoswyn's window. The man was without his armor and weapons, calling up to Rhoswyn. They could hear their cousin, too, as she responded. At first, it seemed as if they were arguing, something more about Rhoswyn trying to fight men she shouldn't have been fighting and inserting herself into her husband's business.

Artis and Dunsmore were pleased to hear the initial tone of the conversation, one of anger and hurt. In fact, it gave them confidence for what they were about to do. But very quickly, the tone of the conversation turned into something else. Troy was apologizing and, like a fool, Rhoswyn was falling for it.

So much for her not going back to her husband.

As the conversation progressed, Artis knew that he and his brother would have to act quickly. They would have to end this situation once and for all, before the Sassenach armed himself and before Rhoswyn agreed to return to him. Once that happened, their task would be considerably more difficult, and they were great opportunists. It had to be now or never.

They had to move.

Artis had the halberd, which was, in truth, a big ax with a very big blade. It was versatile and quite deadly. As Troy gazed up at Rhoswyn, clearly occupied by the woman, Artis hurled the weapon at Troy's head. Over the rain and thunder, somehow, the English knight heard it coming – or saw a flash of the blade – because he suddenly dropped to the ground, but not fast enough. The weapon clipped him as he fell to the ground, sending the ax hurtling off in another direction as it ricocheted. As Artis ran to collect his weapon, Dunsmore ran to attack their victim.

Troy was dazed but he wasn't senseless. The handle of the halberd had hit him in the forehead but he lay there for a moment, listening very carefully to what was coming next. He was under attack, and without his broadsword or his armor. So the best thing he could do was wait and listen to see what the enemy was going to do next. Lying on the ground was also the best way for him to make the smallest target. Therefore, he lay there, waiting, and in little time, he heard footsteps running in his direction.

He was ready.

The footfalls came very close and he quickly rolled into them, intending to trip his attacker, which he did quite ably. He rolled right into the man's feet and tripped him up. He heard the man grunt as he fell over him, right into the mud. When he did, Troy leaped to his feet and pounced. Ripping the short sword from the man's grip, he cut his enemy's throat before he ever saw his face.

In truth, he didn't care who the man was. All he knew was that the man was trying to kill him. Therefore, Dunsmore Kerr died with his face in the mud and blood pouring out of a gash in his neck that ran from one ear to the other, defeated by the Sassenach he had thought would make an easy kill.

Not so easy, after all.

But Troy didn't know who the man was and he surely didn't care. He didn't recognize him as Rhoswyn's cousin. He had a weapon now and as he turned, he saw Artis running in his direction with the halberd held high. It was a mistake; Troy went down to one knee and undercut Artis, slicing the man through the midsection, literally. When Artis didn't fall fast enough, Troy stood up, dropped the sword, and used his hands to snap Artis' neck. He, too, then fell to the mud next to his brother, his head twisted all the way around so that even though he'd fallen on his chest, his face was pointing up at the angry sky.

Two men dead in less than a minute.

Troy picked up the short sword and collected the halberd where it fell, feeling the rush of battle. He wasn't surprised by the attack, to be honest, considering the reception he'd received when he'd arrived. But now he was sure there were more to come. Surely there weren't only two men trying to kill him; surely the whole damnable clan was out for his blood. He lifted his weapons and bellowed to the entire complex.

"Are there more of you?" he shouted. "Come now and let me take a piece of you!"

His shouts reverberated off the stone and some of Keith's men, who had risen at dawn to go about their chores, emerged from their sleeping areas. There were outbuildings as well as stables, and since space was at a premium, men slept anywhere they could. Now, they were emerging to see two dead bodies on the ground and an enraged English knight. Even for the Scots, it was a shocking sight.

An enraged Troy with weapons in his hands was the first thing Rhoswyn saw as she came flying out of the tower alongside her father. Troy was posturing for battle and blood pouring down the left side of his face, while two dead bodies lay at his feet. As she approached, she could see that the dead men were her cousins. But, much like Troy, she had no idea if there were more.

As enraged as Troy was, Rhoswyn was even more enraged. She couldn't believe that her clansmen would attack her husband, unprovoked. In truth, she wasn't even upset to see that her cousins had been killed; they had attacked Troy and he had every right to defend himself.

"Who else will move against me husband?" she shouted at the men who were emerging into the yard to see what the commotion was about. "If ye want him, ye'll have tae come through me first! Who will be the bravest?"

As Troy and Rhoswyn were positioned for a fight, Keith's reaction was markedly different. He was reeling with disbelief as he stood over Artis, looking at the destruction Troy had unleashed on the man. He was sickened at the sight; sickened for his brother and for a legacy that had been so instantly and brutally ended. As he stood there looking at Artis, and then Dunsmore, all he could do was shake his head.

He simply didn't understand.

"What did they do?" he asked the painful question. "Why... *why* did they do this?"

Rhoswyn heard the question. She whirled to her father, her eyes flashing. "Because they hated him," she hissed. "Look what they did tae him; they tried tae kill him! We all saw it!"

More men were emerging to see what had happened, including Audric. He'd been sleeping like a rock when shouting had awakened him. By the time he emerged from the sod house, it was to see Troy fending off two Scotsmen who were woefully underclassed against Troy's knightly training. His first instinct had been to rush in and help Troy, also, and he'd even picked up a pitchfork that had been leaning against the stable wall. But Audric wasn't a fool – as he'd told Troy in Jedburgh, he was better off being far away from a battle. He wouldn't have been any good, but he would have tried, pitchfork and all. Thankfully, it seemed he wasn't needed.

Still, a mood of shock and confusion was filling the air as everyone was trying to figure out what had really happened. Troy couldn't let his guard down and Rhoswyn wouldn't, and as they stood there, waiting for something more to come charging out at Troy, they all heard a groan coming from the direction of the tower.

It was Fergus. The man emerged into the muddy, rainy morning, his gaze on his dead sons. He groaned again when he realized that it was both sons on the ground, bleeding into the mud. He staggered over to Artis as Keith simply stood there, unable to help his brother. Fergus fell to his knees beside his oldest son, grabbing at the man, trying to pull him to his feet.

"Nay, nay," he moaned. "What has happened? Who did this?"

Before Troy could answer, Rhoswyn did. "They tried tae kill me husband," she said angrily. "Pa and I saw it. They threw an ax at his head and tried tae kill him. They're dead because my husband had tae defend himself against them!"

Fergus stopped trying to pull at his son. He could see, clearly, that the man was dead, but the words spouted by Rhoswyn had him reeling. The man could hardly catch his breath.

"My God," he gasped. "I can hardly believe… I canna believe they would do such a thing."

Keith looked at his brother. "They did," he said, sighing heavily. "They tried tae kill the man and he has the right tae defend himself. But why would they do it, Fergus? They never made mention of their hatred towards him. I never heard them mention a word about it."

Fergus' hands flew to his head as if in agony. "They did it because… they must have done it because they were afraid."

Keith frowned. "Afraid of what?"

Fergus was sliding deeper and deeper into anguish. "Afraid of this marriage ye made without consultin' the rest of us," he said. "We discussed it on the day ye forced yer daughter intae this marriage and me sons were unhappy about it, but I never thought they'd act against him. I never thought…"

He trailed off and Keith's brow furrowed, confused by what his brother was telling him. "Act *against* him?" he repeated. "What do ye mean?"

"I mean that ye should have consulted with all of us before ye married Rhosie to a Sassenach!"

Keith's brow furrowed. "Twas not yer decision tae make."

Now, Fergus was moving swiftly from shock to anger. "It 'twas!" he cried. "When ye married her tae an outlander, ye threatened everythin' we have! Me lads had a right tae fight for it!"

Keith's confusion was growing. "They have a right tae nothin'," he hissed. "Everythin' at Sibbald's is mine tae do with as I please. They are not me sons – they have no right tae anythin' unless I say they do!"

Fergus stood up, weaving unsteadily as he faced off against his brother. "Only by birth are ye our father's heir," he said, his voice quaking with emotion. "Ye have no sons, only a lass ye tried tae make intae a son. But she's *not* a son. Dunna ye even know that? Because of her, everythin' ye had would go tae me upon yer death, and from me it would go tae me sons. Sibbald and her fortune belongs tae us and they wanted tae protect it from the Sassenach who dinna deserve any of it!"

"*I* say who deserves it!"

"Me sons are dead because of ye!"

With that, Fergus suddenly lifted his hand and it was too late that Keith realized his brother had a dirk. All good Scotsmen had dirks, as part of what they wore on a daily basis. It was an unusual man who did not arm himself, even at home. But instead of lunging at Keith, in his madness, Fergus lunged in Rhoswyn's direction.

It was an unexpected move, but Rhoswyn was fast and alert. She saw the flash of the blade and stumbled backwards to remove herself from his range, but as he brought his arm down, Troy intercepted him and grabbed him by the wrist.

Now, the fight was between Troy and Fergus.

The man had gone after Rhoswyn and Troy wouldn't stand for any man attacking his wife. Surely, he should have killed him. But in his last flash of sanity before reaching out to snap the man's neck, he saw the bodies of Fergus' sons and, in that moment, he realized that one more death would be a waste. Fergus was mad with grief and Troy understood what it was to be mad over the death of a loved one. He understood it all too well. Therefore, in an uncharacteristic display of mercy, he simply disarmed Fergus and shoved him to the ground.

There had been enough killing already.

Keith ran to his brother to see to him, putting his hands on Fergus as the man burst into sobs. It was a horrific moment for all concerned and Troy took the dirk in his hand and tossed it, so far that it sailed to the far end of the bailey and even over the wall.

"Too many have died this morning already," Troy said. "One more death will not help this situation. I killed in self-defense once, but I will not kill an old man who is out of his head with grief."

Keith, on his knees next to his grieving brother, simply nodded his head. "For yer compassion, I thank ye," he muttered.

Troy's gaze lingered on the two brothers a moment. It seemed that they had their own troubles to settle between them. And in seeing Keith and Fergus, somehow Troy was reminded about his own brother, Scott, whom he'd not seen since Athena and Helene's deaths. Much as he hoped to see his brother again and resolved any issues they may have had between them, he couldn't deprive Keith and Fergus of the same. It was a bond of brotherhood he understood very well. But even stronger than his understanding of brotherhood was his understanding of the love of a good woman. He'd known that once, too, and it had been the strongest thing in the universe.

He turned to Rhoswyn.

She was standing a few feet behind him, her sad gaze moving from her father and her uncle to her husband. The expression on her face was something between hope and sorrow, appreciation and adoration. There were so many things mixed up on her lovely face and Troy pointed a finger at her.

"I told you that I could not stand to lose another wife," he said firmly. Then, he lowered his hand and softened his stance. "Nor could I stand to see a brother lose a brother. Rhoswyn, I am coming to think that God has had a hand in bringing you into my life. I had a dream… mayhap someday I will tell you about all of it, but suffice it to say that I was told that I must move on. You were in the dream and you told me that I must come to you. I am here if you want me and for the rest of my life, I shall belong to you and only you. And I will adore you until the day I die."

Rhoswyn went to him, standing so close to him that she was brushing against him, her chest to his chest, rain-wet clothing against rain-wet clothing. All of the poets in all the world could not have described the beauty and power of that moment. He was the Sassenach husband she never expected to have, but the man she could not live without. The future was theirs for the taking. Reaching up, she timidly touched his face.

"And ye have me heart, me faith, and me loyalty until the moment I take me last breath," she said softly. "I canna promise that I will always be perfect, laddie, but I will always try tae be what ye need me tae be, for now and for always."

Troy smiled, pulling her into his arms as the rain stopped falling and the sun began to peek out from behind the clouds. It was the promise of a new day, a new life, and a new love for them both. And somewhere in those bright rays of sunshine, Troy thought he saw a shadow with long blond hair, running amidst the brilliant green hills. He thought he heard laughter, too – Helene's laughter with the joy that Troy was finally moving on with someone who was most worthy of him.

It was time.

Be joyful. And you must move on.

He had.

EPILOGUE

Year of Our Lord 1273
March
Castle Questing

I T WASN'T AS if she was hiding, because she wasn't.

She'd had a specific purpose in mind when she'd left the feast in the great hall of Castle Questing and had gone on a hunt for the chapel.

It wasn't as if meeting dozens and dozens of family members had petrified her and chased her right out of the hall, although some might see it that way. She'd met her husband's brothers, Patrick and James, in a more congenial atmosphere this time, because the first time she'd met them had been in the midst of her unexpected marriage mass. This time around, there was much more friendliness and warmth between all parties. She'd even received a hug from them both, something that had made her feel most wanted and welcome.

Nay, it wasn't as if that gang of Sassenach family members had chased her away because she found them all rather pleasant. Troy's sisters, Evelyn and Kathryn, had been extremely welcoming, as had Brighton, Patrick's wife, who was also Scots. She'd met the wives and husbands and children, everyone related to Troy and who were now related to her, and she'd honestly never seen such a big family in her entire life. Coming from a relatively small clan, to suddenly acquire such a big family was quite overwhelming.

But the one person that had been missing from the feast had been Troy's twin brother, Scott. Troy had told her what had happened to him – how he'd fled after the death of his wife and refused to have anything to do with the family – and it was something that Troy had been deeply hurt by. They were all deeply hurt by it, so when the de Wolfe family spoke of Scott, it was in whispers of sympathy and hope. They were such a tightly-knit family and it was obvious that even missing one of their own was deeply troubling.

Even so, it was clear there was one person who held the family together, like the stitches on a giant quilt of many patches. Lady Jordan de Wolfe, Troy's mother, was a Scotswoman to the bone and when she was first introduced to Rhoswyn, she spoke to her in Gaelic for a solid hour before switching to a language everyone could all fully understand. An ageless beauty, Jordan was the heart and soul of the entire family. Rhoswyn could see that immediately, and she felt comforted and welcome by Jordan from the start. Having missed her mother these many years, Rhoswyn was deeply pleased that Troy's mother was so kind and gracious. She liked her immediately.

In fact, Jordan sat with her during the entire feast, explaining family relations to her – for example, who Kieran and Jemma Hage were – as well as giving her a taste of her own background and how she and William had met. It was a fascinating story, in truth. As for the extended familial relations, Rhoswyn was told that Kieran was called "uncle" by Troy, but he really wasn't. He was a cousin, to be exact, because he'd married Jordan's cousin, Jemma, a fiery Scotswoman who even had Rhoswyn a bit intimidated.

Jemma was sweet and humorous, but she ruled with an iron fist and was a no-nonsense kind of woman that had Rhoswyn's stamp of approval. She thought she might even like Jemma more than Jordan, because Jemma was much more like Rhoswyn's personality. She understood her. And as the evening progressed, she felt more and more at home with Troy's vast family, a true blending of English and Scots.

They really weren't so bad.

But there was something Rhoswyn had been meaning to do before she and Troy had even arrived at Castle Questing for the great feast, something she'd wanted to do for quite some time. This was the first time since their marriage that they had visited Castle Questing, and as the evening deepened and Troy stood with his brothers, laughing and drinking, Rhoswyn put her plan into action. It started with asking Jordan for directions to the privy.

Under the guise of going to relieve herself, Rhoswyn slipped from the hall and went on the hunt for Questing's chapel. But it wasn't a simple task, by any means. Audric, who was still with them at Monteviot after all these months, and who literally traveled with them everywhere, tried to follow her from the hall because he'd become as protective over her as her husband was, something that drove Rhoswyn into angry fits. For a woman who was quite capable of protecting herself, to have men want to protect her was insulting at the very least.

As if she needed them!

But it wasn't only Audric who clung to her like a shadow. Cassius and Sable had come to Castle Questing as well, having become regular visitors to Monteviot. Since Cassius and Sable had no family this far north, Troy was always happy to bring them home to Questing, where Cassius enjoyed his time with the de Wolfe brothers and Sable found great companionship with the woman.

And this time was no different; while Cassius had spent his time with Troy and the other de Wolfe brothers, Sable had remained steadfast at Rhoswyn's side. They were best friends now, so they were together quite regularly. But when Rhoswyn left the hall to attend the privy, it was not only Audric that she had to evade, but sweet Sable as well. Both were well-meaning, but Rhoswyn wanted to be alone for what she had in mind.

She didn't need an escort.

Therefore, she felt rather cruel to have ditched her friends in her quest for the chapel, which wasn't hard to find. It was a long, slender structure built at the far end of the castle complex and the three long, slender lancet windows inlaid with precious colored glass with scenes from the crucifixion told Rhoswyn that it was, indeed, the chapel.

Beneath the bright sliver moon, she quickly made her way to the building.

Once inside, it was cold and dark but for several prayer candles burning up at the altar. It gave the chapel a rather eerie glow, with phantom shadows dancing on the wall. Other than the colored glass in the windows, the interior was rather plain with a dirt floor and carved wooden altar. Timidly, Rhoswyn made her way into the chapel because she was specifically looking for something.

Or someone.

Her heart was pounding with anticipation, and perhaps a little fear, as she moved. Behind the altar was the burial vault for the de Wolfes as well as for the family that had built Castle Questing, the House of Dudforth. In fact, nearly half of that long, slender chapel was dedicated to the burial vault. Picking up one of the prayer candles from the altar for a little light, Rhoswyn could see that there were several tombs and monuments as she entered the dark, spooky area.

But she was looking for one in particular.

Some of the graves were sunk into the ground, with stones announcing who lay beneath, but there were at least six above-ground vaults, three without any effigies, which was usual in these cases, but the other three above-ground vaults did, indeed, have effigies on them. On the right side of the chamber towards the rear, she could see an above-ground vault made from stone that had what looked like a newer effigy on it of a woman.

When she stood alongside the vault and lifted the candle for a better look, she could see that it was the effigy of a woman holding two young children at her side. At the woman's feet was a wolf, and on the wolf were inscribed words. Rhoswyn held the candle down low so she could make them out.

Lady Helene, beloved wife of Troy

Arista – Acacia

They are simply sleeping

This was who she'd been looking for.

She'd come to pay Lady Helene a visit.

But it was an emotional moment. Tears came to Rhoswyn's eyes as she held the candle high again to look at the stone effigies, which hadn't been painted yet. It was customary to paint the stone or wood effigies to look more lifelike, but these effigies remained unpainted. They were gray and somber looking. Moving to the head of the vault, Rhoswyn found herself looking down at the face of a woman, fine in beauty, who, indeed, appeared as if she were only sleeping with her two young daughters beside her. Rhoswyn sniffled, wiping away the tears that had formed.

"I… I dunna have much time, but I… I wanted tae speak tae ye," she whispered. "Ye dunna know me, but me name is Rhoswyn. I married Troy. M'lady… I dunna even know where tae start, but I think ye helped yer husband a while back. He told me ye appeared tae him in a dream and told him that he needed tae move forward. M'lady, if ye did that, then ye have me thanks. He needed tae hear it from ye. I dunna know if he could have done so without it."

The only response was the whistle of the night wind outside, singing softly as it blew along the big stone walls. Rhoswyn stood there for a few moments, gazing at the face of the woman Troy had loved before. Instead of jealousy or any sense of competition, all she felt was warmth. Gratitude and warmth. Timidly, she reached out, touching the woman's cheek.

"I know he loved ye deeply," she whispered. "I believe that, deep down, he still does. But he loves me now, too, and I love him. I love him so very much. If… if ye were worried about that, then I can assure ye that he is most loved. I will do me best tae take as good a care of him as ye did when ye were alive. I thought ye should know."

More sounds of the wind, blowing gently against the building. Rhoswyn's hand moved from the effigy's face down to the left hand, which was placed over the figure's belly. The right arm held the two girls. Rhoswyn put her fingers over the stone hand for a moment, warm flesh against the cold rock.

"I... I may come back tae speak tae ye from time tae time," she said. "Wherever ye are, I know ye still love Troy and I will want ye tae know how he is. I want ye tae be at peace knowin' he's well cared for." She removed her hand from the effigy and stood back, putting that same hand on her gently swollen midsection. "We are expectin' our first child this summer, in fact. Troy told me that when ye were expectin', ye spent yer time being sick. I've not been sick, thankfully, but I eat everythin' I can get me hands on. Troy tells me that it means our child will be the greatest son England has ever seen because he'll be a strong lad."

She was grinning as she spoke. But the smile soon faded as she gazed at the effigy's face one last time. She'd said what she'd wanted to say and time was growing short; she knew that Troy, who kept a close eye on her, would come looking for her if she didn't return soon and she didn't want him to find her here. This was a moment between her and Helene, and no one else.

She wanted to make it count.

"Sleep well, lassie," she said softly. "With yer bairns, sleep well. I... I just wanted tae meet ye and tell ye... thank ye. If not for ye, I wouldna know such happiness. I owe ye everythin'. And I *will* do ye proud."

The tears were back and she struggled against them, wiping at them. She kissed her fingers and placed those fingers on Helene's stone cheek before turning away, feeling as if she'd just accomplished something that was needed for the sake of her soul. She'd been wanting to speak with Helene since her marriage to Troy and now she'd finally had the opportunity.

So much had happened in the past six months of marriage, so much joy and discovery, and she knew she owed it all to Helene in a sense. Whether or not she'd really appeared to Troy in a dream, or whether or not it was Troy's overactive imagination, could be debated. But with a little faith, Rhoswyn was willing to believe that Helene had made her presence known.

And Rhoswyn had been determined to thank her.

Turning away from the tomb, she had her head down as she headed out of the burial vault. Just as she neared the altar, she heard a noise and she looked up, seeing Troy and his mother standing there. Lady Jordan was weeping softly and even Troy had tears in his eyes. By the looks on their faces, Rhoswyn knew they had heard most, if not all, of what she'd said and she felt rather apprehensive about it.

She'd been found.

"I dinna know ye were here," she said to them. "Why did ye not say somethin'?"

Troy sniffled, wiping at his eyes. "Because that would have been interrupting something unerringly beautiful," he said, leaving his mother to go to her. "We were just coming out of the hall to look for you when we saw you come into the chapel. Please do not think we were eavesdropping; we simply did not want to interrupt you."

Rhoswyn shook her head. "I dinna think ye were eavesdroppin'," she said. "Are ye angry?"

He shook his head, putting his arm around her shoulders and kissing her forehead. "Never," he murmured. "The depth of your compassion and honor continues to amaze me, Lady de Wolfe. For what you said to Helene... you have my undying gratitude. I know it would have made Helene very happy."

Rhoswyn was relieved that he wasn't angry with her for slipping away from the feast or, worse, invading Helene's sanctuary. But she still wanted to explain herself.

"I felt as if I needed tae show me respect tae her," she said. "In a sense, I'm followin' in her footsteps. I know she meant a lot tae this family, so I felt it was right tae honor her."

"I'd expect nothin' less from ye, lass," Jordan said, reaching out and taking hold of Rhoswyn's hand. "And ye mean a lot tae this family, too.

I know Helene is proud of ye. Now, come with me. 'Tis cold in here and we must take good care of ye and the babe."

Rhoswyn allowed herself to be dragged along by Jordan, who was being very motherly and sweet with her. She cast a look at Troy as she walked away, suggesting that she was quite happy with Jordan's attentions. It had been a long time since she'd known the warmth of a mother.

Troy moved to follow the pair but something held him back. He found himself turning towards the tomb of his first wife and two youngest daughters, going to stand next to the stone vault and gazing down upon the trio. Normally, moments like this would have been deeply painful for him. But since his marriage to Rhoswyn, since he'd been able to do so much healing, now all he felt was bittersweet memories of what had been. But he did bend over to kiss Helene's effigy on the cheek, softly.

"You would like her," he whispered. "She is honest and loving, much as you were, but unlike you, there are times when she scares the hell out of me. Give that woman a sword and she can do some damage. Remind me to tell you more the next time I see you."

With a chuckle, he winked at the effigy and headed out of the vault, following the path of his wife and mother as they headed back to the great hall where the de Bocage brothers, Case and Corbin, who had come all the way to Castle Questing with their father from Northwood Castle, were trying to engage some of the older knights in an arm wrestling competition and being summarily beaten by Kieran, the strongest man in the realm. Troy could hear the shouting and laughing even as he quit the chapel.

All was well in the world again, with family and friends, and as he crossed the bailey, he imagined that somewhere, in the bright sunshine and rolling hills of a heaven that wasn't far off, Helene was smiling and laughing, too. She was happy and at peace, and so was he. When his very large son finally made his way into the world four months later, both Troy and Rhoswyn took the baby to visit Helene when he was old

enough to travel, but they also brought a very special guest with them –
Troy's eldest son, Andreas.

Returned from fostering at his father's request, Andreas was a gentle boy who immediately took to his new stepmother, and she to him.
The journey to Castle Questing to visit Helene's grave was part of the
familial bonding and healing for them all. Perhaps some would have
thought that morbid to introduce their new baby to the long-dead wife,
but neither Troy nor Rhoswyn thought so in the least.

After all, it was to Helene that they owed their very happiness, and
it was with great joy that Troy introduced Gareth de Wolfe to Helene
and the girls. Andreas was right by his father's side when he did so. *Be
joyful*, Helene had told him, and he was.

Wildly so.

The darkest de Wolfe was dark no more.

CB THE END 80

Children of Troy and Rhoswyn

Gareth

Corey

Reed

Tavin

Tristan

Elsbeth

Madeleine

De Wolfe Pack Series:

The Wolfe

Serpent

Scorpion

The Lion of the North

Walls of Babylon

Dark Destroyer

Nighthawk

Warwolfe

ShadowWolfe

DarkWolfe

ABOUT KATHRYN LE VEQUE

Medieval Just Got Real.

KATHRYN LE VEQUE is a USA TODAY Bestselling author, an Amazon All-Star author, and a #1 bestselling, award-winning, multi-published author in Medieval Historical Romance and Historical Fiction. She has been featured in the NEW YORK TIMES and on USA TODAY's HEA blog. In March 2015, Kathryn was the featured cover story for the March issue of InD'Tale Magazine, the premier Indie author magazine. She was also a quadruple nominee (a record!) for the prestigious RONE awards for 2015.

Kathryn's Medieval Romance novels have been called 'detailed', 'highly romantic', and 'character-rich'. She crafts great adventures of love, battles, passion, and romance in the High Middle Ages. More than that, she writes for both women AND men – an unusual crossover for a romance author – and Kathryn has many male readers who enjoy her stories because of the male perspective, the action, and the adventure.

On October 29, 2015, Amazon launched Kathryn's Kindle Worlds Fan Fiction site WORLD OF DE WOLFE PACK. Please visit Kindle Worlds for Kathryn Le Veque's World of de Wolfe Pack and find many action-packed adventures written by some of the top authors in their genre using Kathryn's characters from the de Wolfe Pack series. As Kindle World's FIRST Historical Romance fan fiction world, Kathryn Le Veque's World of de Wolfe Pack will contain all of the great storytelling you have come to expect.

Kathryn loves to hear from her readers. Please find Kathryn on Facebook at Kathryn Le Veque, Author, or join her on Twitter @kathrynleveque, and don't forget to visit her website and sign up for her blog at www.kathrynleveque.com.

Bonus Chapters from ShadowWolfe,
Book 4 in the de Wolfe Pack Series
(Hero is Scott de Wolfe, twin brother of Troy de Wolfe)

ॐ

CHAPTER TWO

Four months later

THEY STOOD IN a great cluster on the rise of a gentle, green hill, the sun behind them setting low in the red sky. Their black silhouettes were strong against the muted dusk, men clad in armor and seated on magnificent warhorses. Somewhere, a night bird sang softly upon the damp evening breeze, giving the twilight a gentle feel though the warriors on the hill told of a different story. There was a strained anticipation this night, as thick as the summer humidity, as the knights gazed upon the fertile valley below.

"You are quite sure they know of our arrival?" one knight mumbled. He sounded confused. "They do not look prepared in the least."

The question was directed at a knight lodged slightly forward from the rest. He sat atop his great chestnut charger, his gaze perhaps more focused than the others. "Indeed, they are quite aware." He was a big knight, with blue eyes and skin that had been pocked by eruptions in his youth. Even though there was a gentleness to his manner, and a soft voice that was low and deep, he was not the sort of man one would care to tangle with. He, perhaps more than any of them, could be quite formidable when aroused. "Fear not, my brave comrades. I sent word ahead myself. Castle Canaan is, indeed, expecting us."

"But you recall what du Rennic's knights said, Stewart," another knight said to him; the knight was a long-limbed man with luscious auburn hair concealed beneath his helm. "They threatened our lives if they ever saw us again and I, for one, do not feel like entering the enemy's den this night."

Sir Stewart Longbow shook his blonde head patiently. "They were merely expressing their anguish at du Rennic's passing, Milo. You know as well as I that the threats were empty. Moreover, they have no choice. Our liege has been ordered to assume control of Castle Canaan and that is exactly what we shall do." He sighed faintly, perhaps with a measure of trepidation. "Castle Canaan is without her illustrious lord. She is vulnerable in every aspect. To have her without du Rennic at the helm is to leave the entire Fawcett Vale vulnerable because Canaan controls the road from Carlisle to Kendal. She is far too valuable to leave alone and well they know it."

Sir Milo Auclair scratched his dirty hair beneath the helm. He wasn't going to argue with Stewart, for the man was supremely wise and calm in matters as complex as this one threatened to become. But all of the knights were understandably wary. Since Nathaniel du Rennic's death back in December, the lord's men had made no bones about their grief and fury. And this evening, in what should have been a simple matter of being welcomed into an ally's stronghold, threatened to start up another war altogether.

They were being kept outside, waiting like beggars.

The knights of Scott de Wolfe's stable were lost to their own thoughts, anticipating the battle to come. They wouldn't turn away and they wouldn't be kept waiting. Frankly, they didn't like the idea of a fight simply to gain entry. Stewart started to say something to them, words of encouragement or reproach perhaps, but his attention was diverted by a vision in his periphery. The knights, sensing his distraction, turned their full focus to the sound and sight of pounding hooves.

There wasn't one man there who did not feel a distinct twinge of pride and, perhaps, consternation. A shadow, outlined by the setting sun, came down from a higher rise where it had been perched among a cluster of oak trees. The charger itself was larger than anything known to man; a Belgian steed of such enormous strength and temper that the beast had not one bit in its mouth, but two for maximum control. Its hooves alone were the size of a man's head as they pounded the sweet English earth. Silver in color, its mane and tail had been shortened to bristly nubs to make it less vulnerable to attack in the heat of battle. And each man would swear, when the horse looked at them, that there was blood in its eye.

It was a horse bred to kill.

But the horse was nothing in comparison to the master astride it. A man this size would have to have a massive horse in order to support both his mass and weight in full armor. A sword as long as a woman was tall hung down his left leg, the hilt set with semi-precious stones, and the hand that rested upon it was the size of a small boulder. Effortlessly, he rode the Belgian stallion, the menacing horse as gentle as a kitten under its master's guidance, for everything about the man reeked of intimidation and power. Wickedly, his armor gleamed red in the setting sun as he approached the assemblage of knights and the men. They focused on him as if they were eager and adoring children, awaiting his words.

"I see no welcoming party from Castle Canaan, Stewart," the massive knight rumbled. His voice was so low that his words came out a growl. "Is it possible that they did not receive your missive?"

Stewart did not seem intimidated by the man in the least. He was quite calm when he spoke. "Possible, my lord, but doubtful. They are simply being obstinate, I fear."

Scott de Wolfe's helmed head turned in the direction of the enormous castle, surrounded by a moat fed by a stream that was, in truth, a small lake. It would be no small feat to breach her. Castle Canaan was a magnificent fortress built to withstand a siege and de Wolfe did not relish the thought of having to burn it to the ground should du Rennic's men prove difficult. He was only here on the king's orders, after all. It wasn't as if he had a choice in this, either. A massive mailed hand came up and raised the three-point visor as if to gain a better, unobstructed view.

"The drawbridge in the southern gatehouse is down but the portcullis is in place," he observed. "What of the northern gatehouse?"

"It is sealed tightly, my lord. The bridge is not down."

"Then this is a paradox, wouldn't you say?"

He was addressing Stewart, as was usual. Although his men greatly respected him, it was not a habit for him to address them personally. All communications usually came through Longbow. It has always been thus, very formal and with strict protocol.

"They are inviting us, yet not inviting us," Stewart responded. "We may cross their bridge, but we may not enter the castle."

Scott's hazel eyes were deep and intense. They had a way of shielding his true thoughts, a talent that worked well in his profession. But his granite-jawed face was anything but unreadable; he always looked hard no matter what he was feeling and had ever since that dark day two years ago when he'd lost half of his family to tragedy. The de Wolfe before the loss was a completely different man from the de Wolfe after it. These days, he was a dark, cold, and unfeeling man. Still, he was not insensitive to the grief of du Rennic's men but he wouldn't let them turn his army away.

He'd come with a purpose.

Scott lowered his visor. His men, watching every move their liege made, also lowered any visors that were raised and prepared to move forward. They always mimicked his movements, out of fear or out of obedience it was difficult to determine; de Wolfe never gave an order twice and, sometimes, he never even gave the initial order. He somehow expected his men to read his mind, which they had fortunately become quite adept at doing. He was a man who led by actions far more than by words.

"Then we shall accept their invitation to cross their drawbridge," he growled. "Tell the men to prepare for a skirmish should du Rennic's men attempt anything stupid. Only the knights will mount the bridge.

Tell the bulk of the army to encircle the shores of the moat and position the archers. They shall await my orders. If Canaan does not open her gates, then I will let the arrows fly."

Stewart nodded, motioning for Milo to give the word to the army. When Milo thundered off, Stewart turned to de Wolfe and engaged him in a tactical conversation and the three remaining knights, who had thus far remained silent, turned to one other. Huddled in a small group behind the more powerful players, they were the junior members of de Wolfe's knight corps.

"You know du Rennic's men, Jean," the knight on the left said to the knight in the middle. "You have fought closely with a few of them, have you not? Do you really believe they will resist?"

Sir Jean-Pierre du Bois shook his head sadly, his dark brown eyes focused on the distant gray-stoned fortress. He was young and from a good Norman family that was old friends of the House of de Wolfe. "'Tis hard to say," he said. "They are good men and extremely loyal to him. His death affected them tremendously."

The man to his right snorted rudely, a big, burly knight with unruly dark hair that tended to remind one of a nest for birds. "They would be fools," Sir Stanley Moncrief rumbled. "De Wolfe will tear the fortress down around their ears and leave their carcasses for the birds."

The first knight who had spoken felt the back of his neck tingle. It always tingled when there was a fight in the air and Sir Raymond Montgomery didn't like the sensation one bit.

"They cannot blame de Wolfe for du Rennic's death," he said. "They're fighting men; they know better than anyone of the perils of battle."

Moncrief shook his head again. He scratched his torso, chasing the fleas in his woolen undergarments even deeper into his skin. "But du Rennic did not die in battle," he mumbled what they already knew. "He was assassinated."

Jean-Pierre nodded sadly. "And they believe de Wolfe is responsible."

"He is *not* responsible," Moncrief insisted. "There was nothing he could do about it."

Jean Pierre nodded his head again in agreement as he noticed that Scott and Stewart had concluded their conversation and Auclair was returning to the group. The army was preparing to mobilize and there was a sense of determination in the air, the kind of conviction that was always present before a battle.

"Nay, he is not responsible," he said quietly, gathering his reins. "But they know that the arrow du Rennic took was meant for de Wolfe himself. In a sense, that makes him responsible more than most."

"Du Rennic happened to be in the wrong place at the wrong time," Stanley hissed, lowering his voice as Milo came near. "De Wolfe had nothing to do with that."

The conversation died as the army moved forward. The sun continued to set, casting the landscape of Cumbria into a cluster of shadows and torches and a fortress preparing for a siege.

CB

"CHRIST, HERE HE comes. Now what?"

It was an expectant question. Five men stood in the dark tunnel leading from the portcullis to the bailey, a thick-walled corridor carved into the massive walls of Castle Canaan. Smoke was heavy in the air, the result of sooty torches burning in the passage. Soldiers stood about, waiting for orders, as a legion of troops filled the ramparts above. The smell of a battle was in the air as de Wolfe's army approached from the west.

The knight who asked the question faced the four men surrounding him, all of the men dressed to the hilt in armor and weapons. Their faces were lined with fatigue, their battle-hardened expressions piercing. It was obvious that a decision had to be made, but none seemed willing to make it.

"Well?" the knight demanded again. "What are we going to do? Do we stand against de Wolfe or do we let him in?"

A tall, muscular knight with well-coifed dark hair crossed his thick arms. Sir Kristoph Barclay was older than his comrades, moderately intelligent, and soft spoken. But he was a true follower rather than a leader. He didn't want the responsibility of making a bad decision.

"It's your choice, Jeremy," he said. "As our lady's brother, I would say it falls upon you and your father to make the decision. And we will abide by any choice you make."

Sir Jeremy Huntley glanced at the man by his side. Sir Gordon Huntley was an older version of his son, somewhat folded by age but nonetheless possessing the same indomitable strength and will. The two men gazed at each other with the same-colored eyes, a deep blue, and it was not difficult to read their thoughts. Jeremy, a strikingly handsome man with thick dark hair and enormously wide shoulders, cocked an eyebrow at his father.

"Well?" he asked. "What do you say, Da?"

Gordon was a wise man. He could outfight or outfox any man alive, even in his advanced years, and was greatly respected for his abilities. So great were his engineering skills that he had built the catapults and the special, double-strung crossbows used by the army of Castle Canaan and copied by nearly half of the troops in Northern England. Which was why Jeremy, as hot-tempered as he could be, was unwilling to make an arbitrary decision without his father's approval. The man was supremely intelligent.

Gordon scratched his white beard, then his crotch as he fumbled for a reply. "You are all well aware of my opinion on this," he mumbled. "I've never made any secret of it."

Jeremy glanced sidelong at the others. "We know, Da. But the time has come for decisions."

Gordon shook his head. "We made quite a few threats against de Wolfe."

The knights nodded and grumbled, but there was no clear reply. Gordon continued. "Scott de Wolfe is a great warrior from a fine family. He is the son of William de Wolfe, for Christ's sake. If Nathaniel knew how we had shown such disrespect to de Wolfe after his death, he would not be at all pleased."

A young knight with tightly-curled blonde hair tried to present a brave front. "Lord Nathaniel took the arrow meant for de Wolfe," he very nearly shouted. "Had we..."

"Had we shown ourselves as honorable knights, we would not be in this predicament now," Gordon shot back, cutting off the young man's tirade. He gestured with an upraised hand. "Do you realize the embarrassment we have shown ourselves by denouncing de Wolfe and then showing him such inhospitable behavior at his arrival? The man is our liege. More than that, he is part of the House of de Wolfe and a favorite of the king. We cannot fight him. We cannot deny him his right to claim Castle Canaan."

Jeremy scratched his head, a half-ashamed gesture, and held up his hand to the curly-haired knight so the lad could not argue. "Enough, George. My father is right. We've all known this from the beginning." He grunted and shook his head. "We have all acted stupidly. Even so, our anger is not appeased."

Sir George de Vahn kicked dejectedly at the ground but said nothing. Beside him, Sir Adam de Ferrar's brown eyes focused on his mistress' brother and father.

"We said quite a few things in anger, Jeremy, there's no doubt," Adam said. "De Wolfe has not forgotten. Whether we welcome him with open arms or put up a fight, I suspect our fate will be the same."

"What do you mean?" Jeremy asked.

"I mean that he is angry with us no matter what we do." Adam was well-spoken for his youthful years; he looked like an impish little boy but spoke like a man. "If we open wide to him, he could very well pour in here with his men and punish us all for our harsh words and insolent behavior. Should we resist, he'll punish us anyway."

Gordon shook his head. "Foolish, young Adam. De Wolfe is not unfair. But we must apologize for our conduct. We were angry and we spoke inappropriately."

"So we simply turn Castle Canaan over to him?"

"We've no choice."

"I wish that arrow had hit him."

They all heard George's grumble. Jeremy, unable to disagree, simply looked away. The pain of Nathaniel's death was still so fresh that he had not the strength to refute or scold the knight. Adam and Kristoph glanced at Gordon, waiting for his reaction.

The old man could feel the attention. He gave himself a moment of pause before replying.

"George de Vahn, I knew Nathaniel better and longer than anyone. The man was my friend. Our alliance was only strengthened when he married my daughter. If anyone should be incensed by all of this, it should be me." He reached out, half-grabbing, half-slugging the young knight's shoulder. "But I will tell you now: behave yourself. Keep your opinions to yourself. De Wolfe will crush you like a bug if you show any resistance and well you know it. Instead, display to our liege some of the integrity and graciousness Nathaniel tried to impart into your thick skull. For him, we owe at least that much."

It was as close to an encouraging speech as Gordon could come. He wasn't much for pretty words. The others listened carefully, knowing he was correct. They had shown little honor since Nathaniel's death with their threats and anger. It wasn't as if de Wolfe had killed Nathaniel himself, but he might as well have.

"So we let him in," Kristoph said quietly.

"Aye," Gordon murmured. "Pray the man is in a forgiving mood."

"What of Avrielle?"

Jeremy's question was soft but to the point. They all felt a stab of trepidation at the inquiry, gazing warily at Gordon. Every time they saw Lady du Rennic wandering about like a mute, disconsolate waif, their anger mounted tenfold. Perhaps they would have come to terms with their grief by now if she hadn't been a constant reminder of their dreadful loss. Even more than their anger towards de Wolfe or their grief for Nathaniel was their tremendous concern for their mistress' mental state.

"We shall take turns with her," Gordon said, exhaustion in his voice. "'Tis best if she is watched."

"He'll think she's mad," Jeremy hissed, raking his hands through his thick hair. "He'll throw her the vault and lose the key."

Gordon ignored his son. "She's not mad," he said firmly, though unsure if he believed it. "She's simply dealing with the loss of her husband in her own fashion. She'll recover, as will we all. Now, take your posts and prepare for de Wolfe's arrival."

The knights reluctantly disbursed in anticipation of Baron Bretherdale's arrival as Gordon continued into the bailey. When he was sure no one was watching, Gordon lifted his eyes beseechingly to the heavens.

"Please, God," he prayed softly. "Please do not let her show her madness to de Wolfe."

Behind him, he could hear the portcullis cranking up, the thick, old ropes grating against their tracks. Someone was shouting and the army crowding the bailey began to form ranks. Gordon should have been there to receive Baron Bretherdale and not leave the duty to a group of disgruntled knights but he found, at the moment, that he had more important things on his mind.

Like finding his daughter and preparing her for the worst.

∝

"WHERE IS LADY du Rennic?"

Scott's question went unanswered for the moment. Frankly, he wasn't astonished by the hostility he was meeting with. The tension, as he had suspected, was palpable, but the blatant animosity was not only unnecessary but foolhardy.

A line of knights stood between him and the keep of Castle Canaan, men he had fought alongside countless times. Men that Nathaniel du Rennic had been extremely proud of, and for good reason; they were excellent, obedient knights. Now, these same men who he had once trusted his life to stood glaring at him as if he were the Devil incarnate. Scott couldn't decide whether to become angry or laugh. He thought, considering his normally decisive nature, that he was exhibiting extreme patience by not quashing them on the spot. But there was a very good chance his grace would not last into the next hour at this rate.

"Lady du Rennic is heavy with child, my lord," Gordon finally replied. He had appointed himself the spokesman of the group; he wouldn't allow any of the others to speak. "She begs forgiveness for not greeting her liege personally."

Scott's intense eyes focused on the old man. His gaze could be so piercing at times it seemed like he was looking straight through a man's soul. Gordon felt the harshness of the stare, as if shards of glass were pricking into his brain.

"You did not answer my question," Scott rumbled. "*Where* is she?"

"Inside the keep, my lord," Gordon said steadily.

"I would speak to her."

He would swear until the day he died that the knights of Castle Canaan puffed up at that very moment as if preparing to defend their mistress against something of unspeakable horror. Gordon struggled not to appear nervous or defensive himself. Lady du Rennic, after all, was his daughter and it was his duty, more than any of the others, to protect her. He remained restrained and calm.

"If I may, my lord, suggest that now would not be a good time," the old man said. He didn't like this whole damned situation, torn between hostilities and emotions he would rather have done without. "She is not feeling well and I fear your presence might affect her physical and mental state."

Scott didn't like to be refused. He stared at the old man as he debated whether or not to enforce his demand. He didn't want to use force, but most certainly he would if he had to, and he would only reason so far. After that, he would let his sword do the talking.

"I am her liege," he said simply. "I would speak with the wife of

Nathaniel, a noble and loyal servant."

Gordon nodded patiently, putting a hand on his son's arm as the man huffed and trembled with the rage in his heart. "I understand your position, my lord," he said patiently. "But you must understand that Lady du Rennic has been through quite a bit over the past few months. She grieves terribly for her husband. Her mental state is weak at the moment and I fear that your presence will only remind her of her loss. It was for you, after all, that Nathaniel sacrificed himself. I would suggest it would be better to wait to speak with her. You may, indeed, carry on business with me and my son in her stead."

For the first time, Scott looked at Jeremy and was met with an outrageously challenging glare. The man was an extremely powerful knight who had fought well for Scott in the past. He was cunning and skilled, and passionate about his loyalties. But at this moment, Jeremy's bright blue eyes blazed with bitterness. Scott realized, as he continued to gaze at the man, that he would have to gain control of Jeremy in order to control the troops of Castle Canaan. Even more than the old man, if Jeremy Huntley decided to fight, the army would willingly follow. He was the kindling to a fire that threatened to explode at any moment.

"Huntley," he rumbled after a moment. "You are a wise, intelligent man."

Jeremy was cold. "As you have always known me to be, my lord."

Scott crossed his arms, limbs the size of tree branches. "Then tell me what you think of me."

It was a wide open, leading question. While the knights of Castle Canaan seemed to falter, unsure of the answer they expected, Jeremy remained steely. Gordon prayed that his son would reply with respect, but perhaps not total honesty. A little white lie at this moment could preserve their lives; an offering of truth could destroy them. He hoped Jeremy could differentiate between the two.

"You are my liege and Baron Bretherdale," Jeremy finally said. Gordon thought he spoke through clenched teeth. "King Henry gifted you with lands in east Cumbria and Castle Canaan is your subject.

What more should I think of you?"

It was a careful answer and Scott appreciated the delicate balance it evoked. Huntley was certainly walking a fine line and they were all aware of the fact. But Scott intended to push him off that line one way or another. "Do you respect me?"

"Aye, my lord."

"Do you believe me to be powerful, just and fair?"

Jeremy hesitated slightly. "Aye, my lord."

"Then why do you rebel against me?"

Jeremy blinked slowly, pondering. He was not intimidated by de Wolfe, for they had known each other for many years because they had both served the king in several operations for the crown. The fact that Scott was twice his strength didn't matter in the least, nor did the fact that Scott had a frightening reputation for pulling enemies apart with his bare hands. There was no one in the entire world who could best Scott de Wolfe in hand-to-hand combat, of which Jeremy had no intention of entering into. He'd seen de Wolfe in battle too many times to entertain any thoughts of engaging him and coming out in one piece. It was only purely out of respect for de Wolfe's higher rank that he carefully sought his answer, and not the fact that Scott could smash him like an ant if provoked.

"Do you wish me to be frank, my lord?"

"Please."

If he wanted it, then Jeremy would give him what he asked for. Nodding his head, he broke from his harsh, crossed-arm stance and rubbed at his stubbled chin. "Very well," he said. "Then I shall expect frankness from you as well and shall begin with this question; why have you come here?"

Scott cocked a well-arched brow. "I am clearly not here to answer your petulant questions."

"Indeed not, my lord, but certain things must be established. I must ask again; why have you come to Castle Canaan?"

On Scott's left, Stanley Moncrief growled low in his throat. "Insolent bastard," he said. "You've no right to question your liege, Huntley. Answer the damned question!"

Castle Canaan's knights surged forward. George and Adam flared, half-encouraged by Kristoph who himself was too wise to enter into a melee. Were there to be fighting, he would let the younger men take the first blows, leaving the easier ones for himself.

Gordon, however, threw out an arm to stop his knights from their aggression while also keeping an eye on Jeremy. His son had a temper that could explode with as little as a misdirected expression. His unpredictability was legendary. When Jeremy had been a young squire fostering at Okehampton Castle, his peers and masters alike had referred to him as Sparky, the lad who ignited into a full-blown rage with the slightest spark. And with his size and strength, an uncontrollable temper was not such a good thing.

To make the situation more volatile, de Wolfe's junior knights flared, huffing and grunting and throwing insults. Moncrief lashed out a bear-sized hand and smacked George on the helm. Jean-Pierre pulled the burly knight back and into the arms of Raymond Montgomery who, unfortunately, had a temper of his own thanks to his Scottish heritage. He and Moncrief told Adam and George in no small detail what they would do to them should a sword fight ensue.

Scott would not bother himself with men who could not control their emotions. Knights were cursing and growling, surging like the tides, but he would allow Longbow and Auclair to deal with the unruly bunch. In the midst of it all, he continued to gaze at Jeremy, remaining focused on the original question.

"I've come to protect my lands," he replied evenly. "Why would you oppose me?"

Because Scott was calm, Jeremy found it very easy to maintain his own control even though the knights were verging on a tantrum. "I do not oppose your need to protect your holdings," he said. "I oppose your need to take possession of Castle Canaan."

Scott cocked an eyebrow. "Who said I was here to take possession? I am here because Castle Canaan is strategic." His emotionless façade flickered and his eyes narrowed curiously. "Did you truly think I was here to take Castle Canaan away from you?"

Jeremy nodded slowly. "She is a fine fortress, my lord. Her liege is deceased. What am I to think when you bring an army and demand entrance? Of course you should want to take her."

Scott could see where this was leading, realizing that the grief of du Rennic's passing wasn't the only thing occupying their minds. They obviously feared for their autonomy in light of an absent liege and he was prudent with his answer.

"You are to think that Castle Canaan is mayhap the most valuable property in all of Cumbria," he said. "These lands you sit upon are particularly vulnerable as well as valuable; and they are *my* lands. I occupy Castle Canaan to protect the road between Carlisle and points north to Kendal and, subsequently, the heart of Cumbria. Moreover, you have neighbors who have been thirsting for this property, to secure it for those who oppose the king, and if I am here with my army, they will not dare move against it. I do not do this to confiscate du Rennic's property or threaten your independence, but to secure stability. Don't you know me better than that, Huntley?"

It was apparent he did not. Or perhaps he did. In any case, Jeremy's arrogance seemed to deflate. After a moment, he sighed heavily and scratched his head. "We thought you had come…"

Scott cut him off. "I know what you thought. And you were wrong."

"I've been wrong before, my lord."

Scott didn't say anything more. He found he was more irritated than he had been before. Apparently, these men who had fought for him knew very little about him and Scott prided himself on his just reputation. Their distrust was like a slap in the face. Turning away from Jeremy, he growled to Stewart.

"Bring in my troops," he said. "Station my guards alongside Castle Canaan guards. Double the number along the perimeter and send out scouts to make sure this vale is clear of any potential threats. Although we are not expecting a problem, neighboring warlords know the Canaan is vulnerable with Nathaniel's death and I would ensure they know that I am occupying it. I want that message to be loud and clear. By sundown, I would have this fortress heavily fortified and my intelligence fed."

Stewart nodded, issuing orders to the knights loyal to de Wolfe and ignoring the knights of Castle Canaan. As the de Wolfe troops began crossing the drawbridge, bringing about their catapults and weapons decorated in the de Wolfe colors of black and silver, the five knights of Castle Canaan drew it all in with a measure of bewilderment. Whether or not de Wolfe had any intention of occupying Castle Canaan, for all intents and purposes, they were, indeed, subservient to Baron Bretherdale.

"He said he wasn't here to take over," Kristoph mumbled, almost to himself. "But look at him; his men are taking charge. They are bringing in their weapons and their troops!"

Jeremy merely cocked an eyebrow at the activity taking place. He didn't know what else to say for, in truth, he was a bit confused himself. He still didn't want de Wolfe here, but he supposed for all of their resistance and slander they had been dealt with extremely fairly. He should consider it fortunate that de Wolfe, for once, was in a forgiving mood. Turning on his heel, he headed for the bailey.

"Keep an eye on them, Barclay," he told Kristoph. "Report to me after you have a grasp of their movements."

Kristoph nodded silently. George and Adam made themselves scarce, moving to the ramparts to evaluate the movements of the incoming army and secretly wondering what the days of de Wolfe's occupation would bring. From the events in the bailey, it would apparently not be a temporary or peaceful thing.

ShadowWolfe is available now in eBook and print!

50641329R00172

Made in the USA
Middletown, DE
02 November 2017